BEYOND THE CRUSHING WAVES

LILLY MIRREN

black lab press

Epub ISBN: 978-1-922650-01-6

Paperback ISBN: 978-1-922650-03-0

Hardback ISBN: 978-1-922650-02-3

Large print ISBN: 978-1-922650-04-7

Version 1.0

Published by Black Lab Press 2021

Cover design by Carpe Librum.

First published worldwide by Black Lab Press in 2021.

Brisbane, Australia.

www.blacklabpress.com

For my children, who carry my heart with them wherever they go.

❧   I   ❧

Dreams forge brimming hope,
Beyond the crushing waves;
Coastal fiery sunsets,
And rain-drenched, sweeping plains

— *AUSTRALIA,* BY BRONWEN
WHITLEY 2021

PROLOGUE

1909 OXFORD, ENGLAND

KINGSLEY FAIRBRIDGE

The folded sheet of paper floated to the ground, caught on the breeze, resisted its descent a moment, then fluttered to the left and veered off the footpath, landing in a mud puddle. The shiver that rippled the water's surface indicated the presence of a dozen or more tadpoles and Kingsley Fairbridge grimaced as he bent to retrieve the sodden paper. He shook the water from the pamphlet, regarded it with a sigh of despair, then continued on his way. His footsteps echoed down the narrow street as he rounded the corner and climbed a steady slope.

It wasn't far now. Soon he'd be standing in front of the Oxford Colonial Club, addressing them on an issue he regarded as one of the most pressing to face the modern world. His stomach tightened and nausea gripped him, but he shook it off and scurried forward, sweat beading on his pale brow. What should happen if he forgot his purpose — if the words he'd rehearsed so many times slipped from his conscious mind? He'd pulled more than a few strings to gain this audi-

3

ence. If he mishandled the situation or flubbed his speech, there was no way he'd be invited to stand before such company again — certainly not based on his own credentials.

His father and great-grandfather were well respected enough to get him access to England's elite for an afternoon, but what happened next would be entirely dependent upon him and his ability to communicate the vision he'd had several years earlier for how to expand the empire while at the same time improving the lives of countless English subjects. As he saw it, there were two problems facing the modern empire, and one single solution that might very well address them both.

If only he could inspire the men he was about to face, his entire life would change. Not to mention the countless others who would benefit from the insight he'd spent years honing in preparation for this moment.

Fairbridge dodged around a woman scolding a child in a perambulator. The feather on her hat fluttered in the frigid wind over a scarf that wrapped around her chin. Her ample rear blocked the entire footpath. With a stern glance in her direction, he stepped off the path and around her, nostrils flaring as his newly polished black boots squelched in the sucking mud. Just what he needed. He'd spent the morning shining the boots, brushing off his best suit and running over his notes so that he would make the best possible impression. Now his shoes would be soiled, and he'd sweated through his suit.

He turned onto High Street, his heart rate accelerating at the sight of the crowd: men and women navigating their way between shops and restaurants; ladies peering beneath fanciful hats into windows; and horses with heads bowed and necks bent smartly, drawing carriages at a clipped pace down the centre of the street. His top hat shifted as he climbed the few stairs that led to the Japanese restaurant. With a collection of folders and several dozen pamphlets in a briefcase clutched to his chest, he used his free gloved hand to adjust his hat. The sweat had seeped through his shirt now and was well on its way to dampening his entire torso. He could only hope it wouldn't be obvious to the members of the club how nervous he was.

"Good afternoon, sir," greeted the doorman before nodding and opening the timber door.

He muttered a response, swallowed hard and headed inside. The sombre lighting gave him pause for a moment, but his eyes soon adjusted, and he took in the sight of the restaurant with a sweeping, if somewhat impatient, glance. This couldn't be the place. Surely he hadn't misunderstood the address written to him by the club's secretary. A wave of panic gripped his chest. He startled when a man in a dinner suit, with a high collar in place of a tie, addressed him.

"Can I help you at all, sir?"

"Ah yes, thank you. I'm looking for the Colonial Club, if you please."

"Right this way, sir. Follow me."

Fairbridge swallowed again, then dutifully followed the man in the suit. They bypassed the restaurant, skirting down one side of it, then stepped through a set of doors and into a large, enclosed room. It was decorated in shades of red and black. There were rows of seats placed one before the other throughout the entirety of the room, and all facing in the same direction — pointed at a solid lectern.

The man stepped to one side, linking his hands behind his back. "Here you are, sir."

Fairbridge gave him a nod, then walked further into the room. Men in black suits lingered around a bar at the back of the room while waiters slipped elegantly between them with white-gloved hands offering silver platters of canapés.

Dark timber panelling lent the room a sturdy tone; a chandelier overhead sparkled and glimmered, sending dappled light across black-clothed shoulders, broad and narrow alike.

"You must be Fairbridge," suggested a voice at his shoulder.

Fairbridge faced the voice with a forced smile. "Yes, indeed I am."

"I'm Handley Smythe, the club secretary. It's a pleasure to meet you." Handley held out a paw, his round, freckled face shining with a grin.

Fairbridge shook his hand, returning the smile as a feeling of relief washed over him. "The pleasure's all mine, I assure you. I was beginning to think I was in the wrong place."

"No, you're most definitely in the right place. We're really looking forward to hearing what you have to say. The entire place is buzzing with it, let me tell you. Your reputation, or at least your father's and great-grandfather's, precedes you. We're most anxious to hear your perspective."

Fairbridge dabbed at the beading sweat on his forehead with a handkerchief and followed the fellow through the club to the other end of the room, where a chair awaited him.

Smythe clapped his hands together and shouted to the group. "Listen up, gentlemen. We have a guest with us today. I'd like to introduce to you Kingsley Fairbridge. He comes to us from Rhodesia by way of Oxford University, where he studies as a Rhodes scholar. Please join me in welcoming him to our humble club."

The group ceased their conversations and turned to face Fairbridge, applauding lightly. Cigar smoke drifted towards the ceiling and gave the room a cloistered feel.

With some degree of murmuring and a scraping of chair legs on the timber floor, each man in the room took a seat except Fairbridge, who rummaged in his briefcase for a moment, then pulled out a small stack of pamphlets. He scanned them a moment, reading the title over in his mind for the hundredth time: "Two Problems and a Solution". Then, he handed the pamphlets to the nearest fellow, who took one and passed on the rest of the stack.

A glass of water stood on the lectern by his right hand. He took a sip and cleared his throat, then blotted his forehead again. No need to review his notes — he'd done it so many times, he knew them by heart. With fifty pairs of eyes aimed his way, he began to speak.

"I propose to establish a society in England for the furtherance of emigration from the ranks of young children, of the orphan and waif class, to the colonies.

"I propose, therefore, to take out children at the age of eight to ten, before they have acquired the vices of *professional pauperism,* and before their physiques have become lowered by the adverse conditions of poverty, and give them ten to twelve years of thorough agricultural education at a school of agriculture."

There was a smattering of applause throughout the room. Men

removed cigars from their mouths and leaned together to exchange remarks amongst themselves. Fairbridge straightened his back and continued, growing in confidence.

"Imperial unity is not a phrase or an artificial thing. Great Britain and Greater Britain are and must be one. The Empire has two problems that require a solution. The colonies are in need of good English stock to help realise the potential of the mammoth unused farmlands, while England itself struggles to find purpose for the growing number of destitute children within its borders."

There were murmurs of agreement, along with several distinct head nods. Fairbridge had found his audience. He smiled to himself, his voice rising a little higher. "Now there are in England over sixty thousand *dependent* children – orphans or homeless — who are being brought up in institutions, who will be put into small jobs at the age of twelve or fourteen, jobs for which they become too old at eighteen. They have no parents, and no one standing in any such relation to them. What have they before them that can be called a future?"

He paused as a silence descended on the room. The men from the Colonial Club considered his words through their puffs of smoke and over the rim of squat crystal glasses. He revelled in the seriousness of the moment. This was his chance to make a mark on the world that would allow him to be introduced in future by his own name and not his great-grandfather's or his father's. His voice trembled as he continued.

"Here and now, let us found a society to take as many as we can of these children overseas, to train them in our own colonies for colonial farm life. We want schools of agriculture in every part of the Empire where good land is lying empty for lack of men. This will not be charity — it will be imperial investment. There will be no pauper strain attached to our farm-schools; every child will be worth far more than the price of his training to the colony he will eventually help to build."

❧ I ❧

CURRENT DAY

MIA

I'm having one of those days where it feels as though my tummy might explode. Maybe *explode* isn't the right word, and *tummy* certainly isn't the technical term. *Uterus* would be more specific, although I don't think of it that way, since to me a uterus is something dark and cozy, hidden deep inside my body and housing an adorable cherub who's yawning and stretching before rolling back over to fall asleep. Instead, my entire abdomen feels as though something horrid is stretching it taut from the inside out — working its way slowly to the surface like a wombat on the hunt for carrots. The wombat kicks fiercely against my bladder, bringing a grimace to my face as I do my best to ignore his repeated taps.

I'm enormous, so even though the picture of a wombat rolling through the dusk, snuffling after its next meal, seems appropriate for the baby. *I* could better be described as a gigantic seal or walrus. I should be beached on top of a piece of floating ice way out in the middle of the vast ocean. In fact, I like that idea. Ice would be welcome right about now — I can see myself lazing around on top of a frozen white shelf. Though it'd have to be a big one to hold me.

The Brisbane summer heat is more than I can take. I've lived here for years, but I still can't get past the humidity. There's a cloying relentlessness in the sun as it bakes the top of my head during the few moments I'm traveling between the car and the house. I can't escape it —it's already left a trail of sweat down the centre of my spine, and my maternity jeans are soaked through.

Why am I wearing jeans in forty-degree weather? Because when I last went clothes shopping, my stomach only protruded slightly over the waistband of my pre-pregnancy jeans, and I couldn't stand the look of the maternity shorts on my chubby little legs. They hadn't been chubby before the strip turned pink, but the only way I'd managed to stave off constant nausea in my first trimester was to fill my stomach with a constant stream of snack foods.

Of course, it'd been a chilly spring day when I'd chosen the jeans, and I'd thought more about fashion than the weather. I'd had a plan to lose the weight from the first trimester by switching to a whole-foods diet. It'd be better for me and for the baby. I'd been determined, certain I could do it. I'd imagined myself in my third trimester as a cute, sprightly woman with nothing but a bump up front as I jogged my way through the final weeks of pregnancy. Just like the celebrities you see splashed across the fronts of magazines piled on wire stands in grocery shops at every checkout, with headings like: *Didn't gain a pound, Bounce back after pregnancy,* and *Show off your bump!*

Instead, I'm waddling up the footpath to Gammy's house with one hand pressed to my twinge-y lower back and the afterburn of my first daily bout of indigestion still haunting the back of my throat.

I knock at the door, then peer through the glass window beside it. The old Queenslander where Gammy lives is in dire need of a new coat of paint. One more thing to add to my list of to-dos before the baby comes. Although I'm running out of time as the list grows daily. Ben says I don't have to do everything before the baby gets here—I'll still be able to do some things after.

My entire life these days is divided into those two categories: before the baby and after the baby. It's my own little version of *anno domini*, but it seems more final. Like I shouldn't plan for anything after the baby comes. The date looms unknown on the horizon, as though enshrouded in a mist and there's a burgeoning urgency to do everything now, before it's too late. To clean my house, purchase everything the baby could possibly need for its first six months of life, to find those last few pieces of furniture I've been procrastinating over, to get my hair done, to paint Gammy's house, to have coffee or lunch with every one of my friends, to go away with Ben for one last jaunt, and make sure everything is added to my list so I can check each item off one by one.

There's no sign of Gammy, so I huff back down the half-dozen steps to the grassy yard and waddle around the side of the house, past the garage that Gramps added on in the nineteen seventies. It's the same colour as the house, and you'd never know he added it later. He was always good with his hands, could build anything he wanted even if he wasn't trained to do it.

With another glance at the garage, I frown as I hear the soft strains of jazz music drifting from the open kitchen window along with the faint aroma of something burnt. I shuffle past Gammy's prized rose bushes, their red and pink blooms filling the air with a pungency that's heady and sweet and brings a hint of a smile to my heat-reddened and sweat-streaked face. The roses drown out the burned smell and I hope I've only imagined it was there in the first place, tainting the air with an all-too-familiar reminder that maybe Gammy won't be staying in her home as long as we'd hoped.

"Gammy!" I call as I round the house and head up the back steps. There are more of them here than out the front. The laundry is tucked beneath the steps, and I can see Gammy isn't in there, although there's a small basket of laundry balanced on the edge of her washing tub, the clothes damp and twisted, ready to be hung on the Hills Hoist clothesline that fills up a good third of the backyard.

She's in the kitchen, bent over the table reading, her half-moon glasses perched on the end of her nose, grey hair a mess of layers and half-curls as though she's just run her fingers through it. A newspaper is splayed out on the kitchen table in front of her on top of a plastic tablecloth dotted with bright yellow daisies.

She glances up at me as I push through the screen door, and it bangs shut behind me. "Hi, Gammy."

"Well, Mia, my dear, what are you doing here?" She stands and hobbles towards me. Her left hip always gives her trouble after she's been sitting.

"I thought I'd check in and see how you're doing."

"I'm fine, just reading the paper. Then I thought I'd do some gardening before it gets too hot."

"That ship has sailed," I sigh. "It's going to go over forty today, I think."

Gammy arches an eyebrow. "Well, I don't mind the heat."

"But I don't want you to get heat stroke," I object.

She reaches for my hand and squeezes it, her blue eyes twinkling. She isn't one for shows of affection, but I can tell she's happy to see me. Her cockney accent is stronger than usual when she offers me a cup of tea. I accept and sit at the table to wait, watching as she fossicks through the dishwasher for clean cups.

"Never mind about me. I've been out in worse heat than this, and worked harder in it too. Everyone's so concerned about things like heat and working hard these days. In my day, we just did what had to be done, no matter the weather."

I nod, pushing back a grin. Gammy's always talking about the way things used to be. Although, her past is still something of a mystery to me. I know she's from England, but other than that, I don't know much, and I haven't really thought about it until now. With the baby coming, suddenly there's a growing desire inside me to understand where I came from, to know all the family stories, so I can tell them to my little one when the time comes.

Why haven't I asked more questions?

"I thought you were raised in England, Gams. It doesn't get so hot there, does it?"

Gammy glanced at me over the boiling jug. "No, not in England it doesn't. And yes, I was raised there, in the East End of London. Until we moved here. But that was a long time ago. I've lost most of my accent, you know."

I stifle a chuckle. No one would ever accuse Gammy of having lost her accent.

She hands me a cup of tea. It's steaming hot, and there's only a dash of skim milk to cool it. Gammy likes her tea to scald the inside of her mouth. At least, that's what I always cry about when I burn my tongue on her brew. She laughs at that and tells me to toughen up. It's something Dad likes to point to, one of the many scarring comments that moulded his childhood. He and Gammy don't get along. He says she didn't give him the love he needed as a child; she tells him she wasn't about to coddle him, and he had it too easy. Neither one of them will give the other any ground. And that's where I come in — the peacemaker. I want everyone to get along. I love my family. I wish they'd all love each other as much as I do them. But I can't make them. I know because I've tried.

"Thanks, Gammy," I say as I blow on the tea, sending a cloud of steam towards her lined face.

I push a strand of red hair behind my ear and lean towards the tea, cupping it with both hands even though I'm already stiflingly hot. Tea is one of the things Gammy and I share in common — we both love it, even in the middle of summer. It's one of the ways she breaks up her day— it's her excuse for quality time and conversation. That's something I learned early on with Gammy. When she was younger, she was always moving — cleaning, cooking, ironing, gardening, shopping. The only way I could get her to sit still and talk to me was by sharing a pot of tea together at the kitchen table. It's our pause button in a busy world.

"So, when did you move to Australia? I can't quite remember," I say, studying her expression.

She sighs. "Let's see. I must've been about nine..."

"Nine?" This is news to me. I thought she'd been an adult. If not, where are the rest of her family? The only one I know is Auntie Char, who lives in New Zealand. She's not really my aunt, but my great-aunt, and Gammy's sister. She's glamorous and educated, and she never had children of her own so whenever I see her, she spoils me in ways that got my attention as a kid. I remember the Easter egg full of Smarties and the glossy books with pages of exotic animals she gave me one year. We didn't see her often, even when she lived in Brisbane, because I was always traveling with Mum and Dad. But I cherished the times we had together. Still, what about the rest of Gammy's family?

"Maybe I'm wrong. You know, I get things a bit mixed up sometimes." Gammy takes a sip of tea and stares out through the back screen door at the yard beyond. Sunshine streams through the screen, leaving a blinding rectangle of light on the brown and white linoleum.

I'm about to ask another question when she stands and leaves the room, shuffling again on her bum hip.

I frown. "Gammy?"

When I follow, I find her folding towels in the front room. Once upon a time it'd been Dad's bedroom, and before that, an enclosed porch. The heat bakes the room like a Dutch oven on a bed of coals.

"Everything okay?" I ask, leaning against the door frame and folding my arms across my bump.

Gammy grins. "Of course."

"How is Gramps?"

"He's fine. He says they're spying on him."

"Who's spying on him?" I quirk an eyebrow.

"The nurses." Gammy chuckles. "I told him not to worry—they're only flirting. It seemed to calm him down a little."

I hate hearing about Gramps' struggles with dementia. He isn't the sharp but kind old man I remember from my childhood any longer. In fact, sometimes he doesn't recognise me when I visit the aged care home where he lives. He and Gammy had been married for almost sixty years, and only in the past year have they ever been apart. It's hard on them, but I don't know what else to do with him. It's too dangerous for Gramps to live at home, and too hard on Gammy to care for him. They fought me over the idea of him leaving home to live in a care facility for months, until one day Gramps went wandering and they found him at midnight ten kilometres from home, disoriented and dehydrated. That was when Gammy finally relented, and Gramps moved out of the house the following week.

"Is Ben excited about the baby?" Gammy asks, setting a neatly folded blue towel on top of a pile of white ones.

I shrug. "I think so. It's hard to say. He's working so much at the moment. I feel as though I barely see him."

"Are you still working?"

I shake my head. "No, I finished up a couple of weeks ago. I told you..."

She smiles. "Oh yes, that's right. Sorry, love. It's getting close now, isn't it? I can't wait to meet the little bub."

"I know, and it seems like I still have so many things left to do. I'm constantly rushing about cleaning, cooking, folding, sorting, and buying more things than I really need."

"You're nesting," replies Gammy with a knowing nod.

"I don't know —maybe I am. I'm anxious about everything. And it doesn't help that Dad is so against me leaving my job. He's making me even more stressed."

"What do you mean?" Gammy stops folding, her eyes narrow.

I sigh. "He doesn't think I should quit my job. Says it's unrealistic and irrational for me to stay home with the baby long term. Six weeks is all I need, he says."

Gammy shakes her head, but doesn't say anything. She continues folding towels.

"He says I trained for so many years to be a doctor, and it's silly for me to give that up and stay home. That I'm wasting my education."

Gammy grunts. "Is that what you think?"

I groan, pressing my hands to my abdomen, feeling the tightness of the skin, the warmth, the slight movement within. He's been growing inside of me for almost nine whole months and I'm in love with him already, even though we've never met. It's hard for me to imagine bringing him into the world, then heading back to work again so soon. I want to be there for every first—his first smile, his first laugh, his first steps, his first word. "No, I want to be home with the baby. Mum and Dad always put their careers ahead of everything, and I spent my entire childhood being cared for by nannies, or in boarding schools away from them. I don't want that kind of life for my children. Besides, that's why I chose to be a GP instead of a surgeon like Ben. I wanted flexibility for when I decide to go back to work. I don't want my job to be everything to me. Family's more important. But of course, Dad can't understand that."

Gammy reaches out a hand towards me, beckoning me closer. She takes my hand in hers and squeezes it. Her eyes glimmer with unshed tears. "You listen to your heart, love. I'm proud of the woman you've become. We weren't wise to this kind of stuff back in my day, with all your self-help books and podcasts and so on you've got these days. We didn't have all this information about pregnancy, babies, and parenting —we just did the best we could. But you're gonna be a good mum —I can see that already. You're selfless; you always have been. You're the sweetest granddaughter I could've asked for."

She never says anything bad about Dad, but I can tell when she's unhappy with him by the way her lips pinch together. She and Dad are about as different as two people can be without trying. But she loves him, the way any mother loves her son. So, she keeps her opinions to herself —most of the time anyway.

When she releases my hand, I glance down at the small writing desk that's squashed into the space beside the bed where Gammy is folding towels. There are scraps of paper and newspaper clippings scattered over its surface. Things I haven't seen before. I take a step closer and study them, reaching out to finger the edges of one of the clippings. It's old and has been carefully cut out of a newspaper. I can see the date at the top of the page. It's from June, 1954. There's a photograph of a group of about a dozen skinny kids with knobbly knees standing in a field, in line. They're wearing shorts, shirts, and scruffy jumpers with holes in them. Their hair is cut haphazardly, as though they've done it themselves without a mirror. They look cold. Their skin is pale, although the entire photograph is black and white, so it's hard to tell if they're paler than they should be. They're on a farm. Some are bending over, some standing straight. A few have dented metal buckets at their feet.

I pick it up, holding it closer. There's something familiar about two of the faces — the closest boy and girl. "What's this, Gam?"

Gammy glances at me, then studies the clipping in my hand. "Oh, it's nothing. I liked the look of it, something about the smiles on the children's faces. Are you staying for lunch, love?"

"Um, no, I can't. I thought we might visit Gramps and then I've got to go. I've got a million things to do today."

"Oh, it's a shame you can't stay, but I'm glad you want to see your grandfather. I was hoping you'd drive me over there this morning."

"Come on, let's go before it gets too late. He's better in the morning, and I don't know when I'll see him next since the baby could come any day now."

We haven't settled on a name yet. Ben wants to give him an English name, like Brody, to go with his surname of Sato. But I like Akio, which is Japanese for bright and is Ben's middle name. In the end, I have a feeling we'll use both. Brody Akio Sato has a nice ring to it, and Brody is Dad's middle name, so there'd be another family connection, which feels comforting in a way.

I've never been a traditionalist, but as my due date approaches, I'm finding pleasure in little traditions and rituals that give a sense of structure and connection to the generations that've come before me. I'm thinking of putting together a family tree, since I know so little about my ancestors, where they're from, what they did, and what they've overcome. I know virtually nothing about Ben's family either, but he seems not to have the same sense of curiosity as me. Although, mine is brand new and perhaps it's the hormones driving me more than anything else.

I carefully fold the clipping and push it into the purse hanging over my shoulder by a single thin leather strap. I know when Gammy is being stubborn — she lifts her chin and gets a vacant look in her eyes — and when she does that, there's nothing I can say that'll convince her to change her mind and tell me about this photograph. So, I'm going to take it to Gramps. He never turns me down.

The drive to the nursing home is a quick one. Only ten minutes. Although I never call it a nursing home in front of Gramps or Gammy. It's an assisted living facility. They hate nursing homes and I can't really blame them. But what else are we supposed to do when neither Gammy nor I can lift Gramps into or out of the shower anymore and we can't keep track of him every single moment of the day? Not to mention how belligerent he can get when we try to make him take his medication in the evenings when he's sundowning.

I walk in through the automatic glass doors with Gammy's hand in mine. Her fingers are swollen at the knuckles; blue veins stand out on the backs of her hands where the skin is translucent. I love the feel of her hand in mine. It's like traveling back in time to when I was five and she walked me to my first day of school, with Mum scurrying along ahead of us in her stilettos and emerald business suit telling us to hurry or we'd miss the bell.

Gramps sits in the corner in his favourite recliner, his gaze fixed on the flat-screen television set attached to the opposite wall. A game of cricket plays out across the screen, the volume set to nuclear. Gammy kisses his cheek, turns down the volume and fusses over him. His face lights up at the sight of her, and he reaches for her hands to hold them still a moment while he looks her over, smiling. It brings a tear to my eye. I'm so much more emotional these days. I don't know if it's only the pregnancy. Or perhaps it's because I'm bringing a baby into a family that's so splintered. Whatever it is, it has me pondering what kind of life he'll live and who he'll love.

Ben's parents live in Japan and speak only a few words of English. They'll video call us when the baby comes, but I don't know when they'll visit or how often. Then there's my parents, the jet-setters who barely come home and when they do it's more of a fly-in, fly-out scenario, during the short space of which there's usually some kind of blow-up with Gammy and Gramps over something ridiculous. The last time, it was about Gramps' medication. Dad said the nurse should be in charge, and I argued we could trust Gammy to dish out his meds on a daily basis. All that to say, my family has its issues, and I don't know how my little boy will be able to count on them when all is said and done.

"Mia, come over here, love," says Gramps, holding out a hand in my direction.

I hurry to his side and take his hand, kissing the back of it as I get the lump of emotion in my throat under control. I clear it with a cough. "How are you today, Gramps? Feeling better?"

Confusion washes over his features, his thick, bushy white eyebrows knitting together.

"Last time I was here, you had a bit of a cold," I explain.

He nods. "Oh yes, much better, thank you."

I can't tell if he remembers the illness or if he's covering for his lack of clarity. He does that a lot. Either way, it's good to see he recognises me and Gammy, which he still does most mornings.

We chat about the weather, his latest aches and pains, the activities they've been offering in the rec room. Gramps asks me about the baby, and I tell him the due date is next week, so we'll be greeting the baby soon.

"I don't know how much I'll be able to visit for a little while, just until I get the hang of being a new mum."

He smiles, nods. "Oh yes, of course. Don't you worry about me, love. I'll still be here waiting when you're ready to visit. I can't wait to meet the little scamp."

Gammy is filling the kettle in Gramps' tiny kitchenette. She's ready for her next cup of tea. Her life has become a repetitive procession of tea and biscuits.

"Shall we have a cuppa, then?" is her favourite expression.

While she's occupied, I pull the photograph from the newspaper clipping out of my purse, press it flat with the palm of my hand and hold it up for Gramps to see. He peers at it, adjusts his glasses, and lurches a little closer.

"What's this?"

I glance back at Gammy, my cheeks warming. I don't like going behind her back, but I want to get to the bottom of this. Why was the clipping on her writing desk? Why won't she tell me about it?

"It's a photo I found on Gammy's writing desk. Do you recognise it?"

He shakes his head. "No, I don't think so. Hold on, maybe..."

Gammy marches over, frowns and Gramps glances up at her. She shakes her head imperceptibly, but I see it, and it sends a cold shiver over my neck.

What was that?

"No, I'm not sure, love. But maybe you could turn up the cricket. The poms are losing, and I don't want to miss that."

I sniff. "You *are* a pom, Gramps."

He smiles. "Maybe once, but not for the last sixty years. Besides, those whiny sods sold me down the river, or more like, across the ocean..." He grimaces, leaning back in his recliner as I pump up the volume.

His words raise more questions than answers, but I can see he's not going to divulge anything more, especially with Gammy hovering close by. She sets a cup of tea on the table beside his chair with a couple of shortbread biscuits. I wave her off. I'm not ready for another cup myself, although I nibble on a shortbread. It helps stave off a brief bout of nausea. I sit at the small kitchen table and we chat over the top of the blaring television set. Then I pull the photo into my lap and study it quietly while Gammy and Gramps talk about the state of the nation and how everything is going to the dogs faster than you can say Jack Robinson.

There's a caption below the photograph that I hadn't noticed before.

It says: *Children pick peas at Fairbridge Farm in Molong, New South Wales.*

That's it, nothing more, no names or any other identifying descriptions. Although, the face of one little boy and the girl standing next to him make my breath catch in my throat again. I've seen them before. The thought crossed my mind the first time I looked at the photograph, but now I'm certain. If it's Gammy and Gramps, why don't they just say so? And if it is them, I wouldn't know it because I've never seen photographs of them as children, and this photograph is grainy and a little out of focus. Still, the feeling lingers. And the look Gammy shot Gramps when I pulled the clipping out of my purse made my heart beat a little faster. They're hiding something. Or maybe I'm imagining things, since I can't comprehend what my little, old, sweet grandparents could possibly want to hide from me. But I can't shake the thought, and I know I won't be able to let this one go.

$\maltese$ 2 $\maltese$

OCTOBER 1953

MARY

Gloom crawled across the East End of London. The moist exhale of a remnant fog hung over the rubble, creeping around the ends of the nearby tenement building. Bricks, some whole, most in pieces, lay strewn across the ground. A few had been piled here and there by industrious scamps looking for something to do or somewhere to play. One half of a wall climbed suddenly out of the rubble and turned a corner, marking where the edge of the building had once stood.

A light drizzle tickled the end of her nose, and Mary Roberts sneezed.

"All right, then. No need to cheat, you," cried her sister Charlotte, a frown creasing her pale seven-year-old features.

"Not cheating, Lottie, you daft girl. It's the rain making me sneeze."

Lottie raised her makeshift sword high over her head and brought it down as hard as her thin arms would allow, the stick glancing off Mary's own sword as she stumbled backwards over a pile of bricks.

She held up her stick to block another parry, then scuttled backwards, crouched low to the ground. "You're never gonna win, Blackbeard!"

Lottie set the end of her stick on the ground and wiped her nose with the back of one tattered sleeve. "Oi, I don't know why I've got to be Blackbeard every time. I want to be the hero, saving the day. It's not fair. You always make me play the baddie."

Dirt streaked Lottie's face. Her blue eyes glistened with unshed tears. Her nose was red and her lips a faint shade of purple.

Mary sighed, set down her own stick and wrapped an arm around her sister's shoulders. "You can be the hero next time. Come on, let's get you inside. It's cold out here, and you without a coat."

They sidled around the edge of the bomb crater in the middle of their jousting stage and, arm in arm, trotted towards the tenement building. A trio of boys, three brothers, squatted around something on the ground up against the brick wall. The way forward lay around them. The only other route involved leaping across a large puddle that Mary was certain Lottie wouldn't manage and would end up with wet, muddy feet and no change of socks to warm her feet with.

She waited a few moments, impatience nipping at her heels. She caught a movement out of the corner of her eye — a rat nosed through the wreckage, searching for scraps.

Hunger clenched her stomach. She pursed her lips, tapping a foot as she studied the boys, hoping one of them might move out of their way. Then all of a sudden, she pushed past them with a loud "excuse me". Lottie followed close behind, doing her best to balance in a line and shimmy by the children. She lost her footing and leaned a hand on one of the boys to steady herself. Mary glanced back and saw the look of horror on her sister's face as she realised what she'd done.

Jimmy Myer was twelve years old, a dim boy who was as mean as a cornered badger. Lottie knew better than to mess around with one of the Myer boys. But it was too late to reprimand her now.

Jimmy jumped to his feet, his face blooming a dark shade of red as he turned on them.

"What do ya think you're doing? Did I say you could sidle past me like the two stray cats you are?"

Behind him, his brothers laughed uproariously. One of them mimicked the wail of a cat. The other laughed even louder.

Lottie faced him, her mouth ajar, her small hand trembling in Mary's.

Jimmy took a step towards her, pumping one fist into the palm of the other hand. "I guess you need some schooling."

Anger swept up Mary's spine and burned in her cheeks. She grabbed Lottie by the arms and pushed in front of her.

The movement caught Jimmy off guard for a moment. His eyes narrowed.

"I can teach you both a lesson just as well as one of you," he threatened, pushing the sleeves of his too-small coat up both arms one at a time. "Two little girls. I'm gonna enjoy watching you cry."

Mary recognised in him the same savage look she'd seen on the faces of the dogs that scuttled and scowled their way around the community, lurking in dark corners and coming out to fight when they were boxed in. And like those feral creatures, it'd take more than her usual sweet words to get out of this one.

Her eyes narrowed as adrenaline coursed through her veins. "I'd just as soon teach you!"

One fist lurched out and popped him in the nose.

He howled in surprise and clutched at his bloody nose, stumbling away from them.

"Come on," said Mary, reaching for Lottie's hand.

She dragged her sister after her, running around the scattered bricks and dodging craters filled with muddy water. Rain misted against her face, blinking wet on her eyelashes. Her nose was so cold, it barely registered any sensation at all. She looked over her shoulder and saw the boys hadn't followed. In fact, they seemed to be embroiled in some kind of scuffle amongst themselves, so she slowed her pace, puffing small clouds of white into the frigid air.

Mary looked up as they drew close to their home, her gaze taking in the sagging roof, the reaching black mould that'd climbed the brick face of the unit around the front door coated in a thin layer of peeling blue paint. She pushed the door open then traipsed up the steps to the second level. No welcoming rush of warmth greeted her when she stepped through an ajar door into their flat. Either they'd run out of coal for the fire, or the open front door had robbed the place of its heat while they played.

"Mam!" she called.

There was no response.

Lottie skipped inside, slumped onto the top of a milk crate, and wrapped her arms around herself, pulling her threadbare brown jumper tight around her tiny frame. Mary pushed the door closed and locked it.

"Cold in here too," Lottie complained with another dash of her hand at her running nose.

"I'll get the fire going."

The cramped living room was furnished with overturned wooden orange boxes, milk crates and a single worn-out armchair which was reserved for their mother. She spent the evenings when she was indoors with them sitting in the chair, sipping whisky, and darning or knitting. She loved to knit and did it whenever she was able to rustle up some yarn, needles clicking and flashing. Those were the good nights. The times they shared together as a family. But they were becoming rarer with each month that passed. In fact, Mary could hardly remember the last time they'd all spent the evening together by the fire. These days, they barely had enough coal to last.

The fire in the stove lay cold and black behind the rusted door on its little squeaky hinges. Remnants of coal dusted the space and Mary leaned down to brush it to the side. She set down the crushed ball of old newspaper and went to work to set up a steeple of kindling.

"We'll fetch more kindling tomorrow," she muttered beneath her breath. Kindling was her job. Hers and Lottie's. Mam wasn't often home, so didn't much care whether or not there was a fire in the grate —at least that was what she'd yell whenever they asked her about it.

She bought the coal when she could afford it, but anything else was up to the girls.

Lottie curled up on the floor to watch Mary work. She tucked her legs beneath her skirts, one toe poking through a hole in her shoe and a matching one in her stocking.

"One day, I'm going to live in a warm place," said Lottie, with another attempt to wipe her nose. "Warm and dry."

"And we'll eat oranges every day," added Mary, with a smiling glance at her sister.

"Yes, and plump sausages too."

"With potatoes and gravy." Mary licked her lips, imagining the burst of flavour hitting her tongue, the crisp brown skin of the sausage and the salty gravy covering a mound of creamy mash. She'd eaten the meal once when she was four years old and they'd visited her grandparents in the north. They'd lived in a house all their own, with a yard and everything. She often thought about running away to see if she could find them again, although she didn't recall where exactly they lived and hadn't seen them since.

"That sounds lovely," replied Lottie, her eyes shining with the reflection of light from the fire as it rose through the open door of the stove before her.

Mary sighed and reached out a hand to stroke Lottie's cheek, pushing a strand of oily hair behind her sister's ear. "I'll get it for you someday. I promise, I will."

۞

"WHAT ARE YOU LAZY GIRLS DOING? YOU'LL BURN THE BLOOMIN' house down, you will."

The slap of her mother's hand stung Mary's face before the shouting registered in her addled mind. She leapt to her feet, dazed and sleepy. The fire had warmed one side of her body. The other side was cold from where she'd lain on the hard floor.

Her mother shook Lottie awake before striding to stoke the fire. "Where's tea? Anyone would think I haven't taught you little scamps anyfink useful at all."

"Sorry, Mam. I must've gone off to sleep," said Mary, rubbing at the place on her cheek where her mother's cuff still stung.

"You'll be sorry if you don't get to it now. I'm hungry as a wolf, am

I. Been workin' all day, fingers to the bone, and this is what I come home to. You shiftless lot, laying about as though you're Lady Muck. Get a move on, or it's a floggin' for the both of you."

It was dark in the unit, apart from the light from the fire that danced on the stained walls. It was spooky at night. Mary hated the dark, but not as much as Lottie did. So, she pretended to be brave for her sister's sake and told her there was nothing to fear in the night. But she didn't really believe her own words.

There was plenty to fear, as far as she was concerned. Rats that might eat your face, stray cats who'd come in after the rats and stayed to scare the living daylights out of her if she got up in the night for a glass of water. There was Mam, who came home drunk more often than not, and whose predilection for the thin piece of cane she hung behind the bedroom door was always stronger when she'd spent the night nursing a bottle in her hands. It stung Mary's legs where it landed in rapid succession, and if Mam went for Lottie, Mary would push in, leaning over her sister to take the blows herself as her sister sobbed in her arms. But her heroics only made Mam madder than a hornet, so Mary's legs fairly bled with the slashes of the cane then.

The worst nights of all were when Mam's gentleman friends came to call and spent the night in Mam's cot. They'd invariably be in as bad a state or worse than she was. They'd leer at the girls through whiskey-soaked eyes and tell jokes Mary didn't quite understand that made Mam laugh until her face was red. Those were the nights when Mary let Lottie sleep against the wall in their shared bed so she could keep watch on the door.

The first thing to do was turn on the single electric bulb to light the living room. But when she flicked the switch, it stayed dull, without even a shimmer of light. She reached for another switch, the one over the kitchen sink, but it didn't light either.

The shilling under the stairs must've run out. They'd need to add another to the meter if they wanted the electricity back on. But with the mood she was in, Mary knew better than to bother Mam about it tonight. There was nought to be done. She'd have to make tea in the dark or by the light of a candle, if there were any to be found.

After searching high and low, Mary found a stub of a candle left in the cupboard over the sink. She lit it and set it on the small kitchen table, careful to slip a piece of cardboard under one table leg to keep it from wobbling and displacing the candle. Then she sliced three pieces of stale bread and chunks of cheese that were wrapped in waxed paper and stowed in the tiny cubby beneath the bench. She wished there was some fresh milk for Lottie to drink. Her sister was skinny and had a pale, gaunt look about her that worried Mary. Instead, she brewed a pot of tea and used the leaves from the morning's pot to give the hot water a little weak flavour. There was some sugar left in the canister, so she added a spoonful to each mug of tea before setting them on the table.

There was also the cough that wracked her sister's frail frame and hadn't left since a bout of flu last winter that'd scared Mary to death. It was the blue tinge to Lottie's face that'd brought a flash of under-standing — if Lottie died, Mary would be all alone in the world. There was no one else who cared, no one else to hold her hand or snuggle up against her on the coldest nights. She couldn't let that happen. So, she'd spent every waking moment nursing her sister back to health or scouring the streets for an opportunity to steal a piece of fruit or a day-old loaf of bread from the local bakery.

Finally, Lottie had recovered, but the wet, hacking cough remained. It worried Mary every time she heard it. She was determined to do something, to find her sister something nourishing to eat, to get her a second pair of wool socks or a thick coat. Anything to keep her safe for one more day.

"Tea's ready!" she called.

She set three plates on the kitchen table surrounding the candle that flickered and fluttered in the small breeze that crept through the cracks in the plaster walls.

They sat down together, Lottie beside Mary who sat across from Mam. Mam ate slowly in between gulping swallows of whiskey from a battered tin cup. The girls ate in silence. The bread stuck in Mary's throat. It was dry and difficult to chew. She filled her mouth with tea in an attempt to soften the doughy mouthful, then swallowed. The tea was weak, but sweet, and brought a rush of hunger pangs as soon as it landed in her empty stomach.

Mam's face seemed haunted in the faltering light from the candle's thin flame. Her cheeks were hollow, her eyes like dark sockets. She clutched her knitted shawl around her shoulders, covering a tear in her collar where a reddened scab showed through. Mary was curious about what had happened but didn't dare ask — there were few things she had the courage to question Mam about. She'd learned the hard way that any question Mam didn't like resulted in a cuff to the cheek or a blow to the head. Sometimes the question jumped from her mouth before she realised it, and still surprised by her own brazen confidence, she failed to duck when Mam's palm connected with her cheek.

"I lost my job today," Mam said suddenly.

Mary's heart fell. No job meant no more money for bread or cheese, no more coins for under the staircase. No chance of a new coat for Lottie. Not to mention Mam's temper was infinitely worse whenever she was out of work. But Mary knew better than to say a word about any of her fears. Fears were things you kept to yourself like rag dolls made from the scraps of clothes that no longer fit — she lined them up deep in her soul and dressed them in remnants, hovering over them with wary eyes, but never talking about them out loud.

Lottie exchanged a worried look with Mary, eyes wide and doleful, like the eyes of a frightened fawn. Mary wanted to hold her close and tell her everything would be all right. But Mam hated it when she did that, so instead she offered Lottie a wobbly smile.

"I was feeling poorly, sorry for myself and angry. Because who is that scoundrel Frank to fire me for doing nothing more than taking a break when my knees felt poorly in the bad weather? Nothing but a smarmy old tosser who likes to make out he's the big man. But I ran into some ladies today. They was goin' around the Bethnal Green, talking to people about an opportunity. So, I thought, I'm in want of an opportunity, me and my girls. I'm going to listen to what they have to say. They've got a chance for us, a chance at a better life."

"What is it, Mam?" asked Lottie.

Mam smiled at Lottie, cupped her cheek with one hand, her eyes glittering in the dim light. "They're comin' by the house tomorrow to talk to us about it. Be sure to wash up and comb your hair —there's my girls. Tomorrow, everything will be better. You mark my words."

Mary's stomach tightened into a knot. She didn't like the sound of it — whatever the opportunity was, it scared her when Mam's spoke that way. But maybe this time would be different. After all, things couldn't get much worse. Anything would be better than staying every day in the unit with Mam, unable to face the winter without new coats or shoes, and with nothing in their stomachs but a gulp of sugar-water or whatever she could steal from the shop on the corner. One day she'd be caught, and then what would happen to Lottie?

"Yes, Mam," she replied.

Lottie added her agreement.

"Now run along off to bed. You don't deserve a good night's sleep after the lazy way you've spent the afternoon. I can see you didn't do a bit of cleaning while I was gone. But I've got a friend coming to see me —Stan's his name—and I want you out of the way. He's a good man and might change things for us if I get my way. But if he sees the two of you, it'll ruin my chances, so go on now and stay out of sight. If I see either of you again tonight, you'll be wishing you'd stayed abed."

Mary hurried Lottie up the narrow staircase, ushering her past the broken step and the side of the staircase that hung crooked and tripped her up whenever she forgot to dodge around it. They each rubbed a finger over their teeth. Mary'd seen some of the children in the terrace houses a few streets over talking about their new tooth-brushes and showing them off to their friends, so she figured they could just as well use their fingers to do the same job. Then, after their evening ablutions were done, they climbed into the small bed they shared in the same room as Mam's cot. The room was separated with an old sheet hung from the ceiling with pegs and a piece of string.

"You get in first," Mary said. "Since Mam's got a visitor coming tonight."

"I don't know why that means I've got to be squashed up against the cold wall," muttered Lottie, climbing beneath the threadbare blanket and curling up with her hands fisted beneath her chin.

"Because I said so, that's why," snapped Mary. She had no desire to ruin the last vestiges of her baby sister's innocence before it was needed.

Lottie's eyebrows lowered and her bottom lip protruded. "Don't nick the blanket. I'm chilled through as it is."

"I won't." Mary climbed in beside her sister, back-to-back, lifting her knees high to keep as much warmth in her body as she could.

"I wanna sleep by the fire," whined Lottie.

"Hush," replied Mary, then rolled over and wove her arms around her little sister, pulling her close. She stroked the hair back from Lottie's forehead and kissed her tear-damp cheek. "One day, we're going to get away from all of this," she said. "And I'll feed you cream buns and hot tea that's as black as night. You'll have brand-new clothes that no one has ever worn. And I'll comb all the tangles out of your hair and braid it up over your head like a princess."

"What else?" urged Lottie before shoving a thumb into her mouth and sucking it.

"We'll ride bikes in the sunshine and only stop to pull fruit from the trees to eat until we're too sick and fat to eat more. Then we'll swim in the ocean and float on the waves to shore."

"I don't know about waves. They sound scary to me, like they might crush me into sand."

"Not these waves," countered Mary, still stroking Lottie's hair. "They're gentle, soft waves. Warm and will carry you easy."

Lottie sighed. "I wish I could visit the beach."

"It's like paradise."

Lottie propped herself up on one elbow. "How would you know? You've never been."

Mary smiled. "I saw a picture once, in a book at Grandma and Grandpa's. You were too young to remember, but it was beautiful. The waves were blue and green, and they look so peaceful and happy."

Lottie lowered herself onto the bed once again and shoved her thumb back into its place.

Mary continued. "We'll be happy there, in that paradise. Just you and me, full to the brim with good food and warm as two loaves of bread pulled fresh from the oven."

Downstairs, the front door slammed shut and a murmur of voices climbed the stairs. Mam's laughter tinkled like bells, high-pitched and ringing out in the stillness of the night. Lottie scowled and shrunk lower beneath the blanket with her eyes squeezed shut. Mary's eyes closed too, but she turned back to face the wall, her body taut, waiting.

She would sleep, but not soundly. As she lay there, she imagined those waves and how they might look as they curled to shore under the brilliant sun. She imagined how it might be to touch them, what they might sound like, and pondered over whether she'd be too afraid to wade beyond the edge when she saw them. She didn't know how she'd do it, but she knew, deep down to the soles of her feet, that she would. One day, she'd take Lottie and the two of them would leave this all behind. They'd never come back, and they'd live close by those blue-green waves happily for the rest of their days.

❦ 3 ❧

OCTOBER 1953

HARRY

Rows and rows of white-sheeted beds, black metal frames rising in arches above thin mattresses, filled the long rectangular room. Harry Evans tugged and patted the sheets on his bed until there wasn't a wrinkle left, then stood straight, hands at his sides, feet together, chin high.

Each bed had a boy assigned who stood as straight and tall as he could manage, some reaching higher than others. The youngest wobbled and almost fell, but caught himself in time before Mr Smythe saw his lapse.

Harry let his gaze wander, drifting to one of the windows, the one closest to him in the red brick wall that enclosed one side of the room. Outside, the last of the orange leaves on an old oak fluttered in the breeze, threatening to pull loose at any moment and wave its way to the leaf-scattered ground below. Rain drizzled against the windowpane and the grey overcast sky hung low over the sodden earth. He inhaled a slow breath as a shiver ran through him. Winter was the worst time of year at the Barnardo's Children's Home in Barkingside, Essex. He sensed it coming on the whisper of the frigid air that nipped at his ears and tickled his knees behind the holes in his wool pants.

"March downstairs, if you please," called Mr Smythe, or *Commandant Smythe* as the older boys called him behind his back. They joked he'd come directly to the orphanage from Hitler's army after the war, but Harry knew it couldn't be true from the man's broad cockney accent and tendency to shout the national anthem, singing 'God Save the Queen' with his eyes fairly watering as strands of hair flapped across his face with every energetic lurch in time to the music.

He followed the boy in front of him down the rows of beds, then through the door and down the wide staircase to the school rooms below. Every boy was dressed in the same uniform: a black suit, buttoned up to his chin; long black pants; and scuffed black shoes. English lesson came first, and he was eager to get started. It was raining outside, so he couldn't play anyway, and besides that, he couldn't get enough of the books the teacher had handed out earlier in the term. The English teacher, Mr Wilson, had kind eyes and had found a way to gather enough books so that every boy in the class had one to read. They could read them, he'd said, then pass them on to the next boy. That way, everyone would have something to read for the rest of the year.

It was the first time in his eleven years of life that he'd managed to read more than a few words together. And although the going was hard, he sounded out each syllable one by one and before he knew it, he'd fallen into a story of pirates, a shipwreck, cannibals, and mutineers written by a Mr Daniel Defoe that made his hair stand on end and kept him up well after bedtime reading by the light of the moon whenever there was one, until Mr Smythe marched upstairs for rounds.

He found his seat at one of the many desks lined up in the room and pulled the book from beneath his armpit, setting it on the desk in front of him to stare at its cover.

"Harry, psst!"

Davey Miller grinned over the top of an open book at Harry. He winked and nudged something forwards on his desk with a tip of one finger. Harry's eyes narrowed. It was a slingshot. They'd been finding whatever scraps they could around the Home and fashioning them into slingshots. Some things worked better than others. He'd come to appreciate the simple efficiency of a supple leather strap attached to the fork of a sturdy stick, but leather was hard to come by. So, more often than not, his slings involved a scrap of fabric torn from an old shirt.

Fabric slings didn't work as well when aiming a rock or pebble at an object, but the boys made do with what they had. Their enjoyment in the sport remained untainted, and the two of them had become obsessive in their search for the ultimate slingshot materials. They spent hours every day scouring the courtyard and the gardens behind the Home looking for the perfect forked stick. And whatever time they could spare inside the spacious old structure scouring bedrooms, the library, the laundry when they could manage it, and even the kitchen if the cook stepped out for a smoke, in their quest for the perfect scrap of fabric, leather or string. A sturdy elastic band was considered the ultimate find, but so far, Harry hadn't managed to come across one since the last one broke.

Something hard slapped into Harry's cheek. Startled, he lifted a hand to where the skin still stung. A giggle turned his head, and he found himself staring directly into Jamie White's brown eyes. They were almost black, really. At least, in Harry's mind they were. They were narrow and slitted, and his mouth pulled into a liberal, gaping grin as he laughed. His brown curls bounced with the movement. Seated directly behind Harry, he flicked something, and it landed on Harry's nose. A spit wad.

Harry's nostrils flared. "Stop it, Jamie."

"Oh, stop it, Jamie," the boy mocked him, rocking his head from side to side. "Stop it."

Harry spun in his seat to face forward even as another spit wad slammed into the back of his head. He grabbed for it, wresting it from where it'd gotten lodged in his hair and threw it back in Jamie's direction. Jamie caught his hand and slammed it down on the desktop, holding it there.

He leaned forward and glowered at Harry. "Got something to say, Harry?"

Harry shook his head, mute as the entire classroom quieted. He hated that he never knew what to say when Jamie came after him this way. It was as if his brain shut down and he couldn't manage to string even two words together to defend himself. Everyone was watching. Every boy in the room had his eyes trained on the two of them, waiting to see what might happen. Hoping for a fight. It was one of the few things that the boys of the Barnardo's Children's Home looked forward to — a rare serving of bread-and-butter pudding for dessert, and the excitement of a bout of fisticuffs.

Harry's hand smarted beneath Jamie's fist. He pulled at it, but Jamie wouldn't release him. He was a big boy, fourteen years old, and muscular. When they stood side by side, Harry came only to his shoulder. His face was pocked with red pimples, and there was a wide gap between his stained front teeth. He scowled.

"Whatcha gonna do? You ugly orphan pillock. Where's your mam, huh? Doesn't want you, does she? No one does. You're here because you're all alone."

Harry's eyes stung, a lump wedged in his throat. He wouldn't cry, couldn't cry in front of Jamie. He'd never live it down.

"You're here too," he whispered.

Jamie's eyes narrowed. Then he threw back his head and laughed. "I know I'm not wanted. Doesn't bother me one bit. But you're still living the lie, innit? You're nothing but a bastard. You think she's coming back for you when we all know the truth. She's finished with you."

He released Harry's hand, and Harry pulled it close to his chest. He flexed it once, then he pounced. Fists flailing, he pounded on the larger boy with every ounce of strength he had. Buoyed on by his anger, he didn't notice the tears trickling down his cheeks while hatred burned in his heart.

Within moments, Jamie had turned the tables and had Harry on the floor beneath him. His hard, sharp fists found their mark on Harry's nose, his cheekbones, then his stomach. The wind was sucked from Harry's lungs, and he curled into a ball in an attempt to protect his abdomen from Jamie's rage even as he worked to suck air into his lungs. Around them, boys gathered and silently cheered. They didn't want to draw the attention of the masters, but they revelled in the fight, eyes gleaming.

Still Harry's tears fell.

It wasn't because of the beating. After years living at the Home, he was accustomed to the pain. The masters beat him whenever they had the chance. The older boys gave him a walloping on a regular basis as well. He'd hardened his heart to it all. But the reminder that he was a bastard child with parents who didn't love or want him always sent him flying into a rage. It was like a knife had been plunged into his heart and was being turned slowly to inflict the worst kind of damage. It was a pain he couldn't ignore. Jamie knew it and was merciless. He loved to throw in Harry's face that his parents visited and wrote to him, that they had a plan to get him back. Unlike Harry, whose mother rarely came and that Harry wasn't certain who is father was. He held onto the idea that Mother loved him. But the fear was there in the back of his mind, hovering like a crow over carrion. Why didn't she come? Why did she leave him there?

One of the boys whistled to let them know a master was on his way. If they were caught, the two boys would be beaten by the master, and possibly some of their audience as well. The cane if they were lucky. The master's fists if they weren't. The boys in the classroom scattered, finding their seats at the small timber desks. Jamie jumped away from Harry, smoothing his hair back into place with a grin. He wiped the blood from the side of his mouth with the back of his hand, eyes fixed on Harry's face.

Harry stood slowly, sucking hard to draw breath. He found his seat, his head spinning as he lowered himself into it. He used his shirt to wipe the blood from his nose and lips, then raised his head to face the front as the master, Mr Wilson, walked into the room. His eyes watered, but he blinked the tears away and drew in a deep breath, finally filling his lungs with the cold air that often made him cough in the middle of the night when his single blanket wasn't enough to keep him warm.

"Good morning, class. Let's run through our spelling words, then we'll read the next chapter of *Robinson Crusoe*. I know you're dying to hear what happens next. How does that sound?"

Jamie didn't dare lodge spit balls at him when the teacher was standing up front. Although Mr Wilson was the kindest of the masters, he was still strict about disruptions and misbehaviour. But Harry knew it was only a matter of time until the torment started up again. He didn't know what he'd done to provoke Jamie's ire, but the boy had taken to tormenting him from the first day that Mam had dropped him at the Home's gates with a promise to return when she could. She strode away, ignoring his cries, head bent against the driving rain as it wet his cheeks and mingled with his tears. He'd been three then. So long ago now. He couldn't imagine another life. But his old life came back to him in his dreams and grew a longing that built to an ache in his chest that lasted for days afterwards.

Harry's mind wandered as the teacher wrote lines of spelling words on the board. He opened the desk, stowing his book carefully, and pulled a slate and slate pencil out to work on the spelling assignment. But his thoughts strayed to Mam and when he would see her next. The image of her face in his mind's eye wavered and faded. It'd been months since he'd seen her last. She'd waved at him through the fence and he'd run to greet her. Held her hand between the tall steel fence posts. They were cold and chafed. She looked thinner than he'd remembered, and a few strands of grey streaked her dark, almost black, waves that'd been pulled back into a bun at the nape of her neck. Her deep blue eyes held onto his gaze, and he'd fought back the urge to throw himself over the fence and into her arms.

"When will you take me home?" he'd asked, heart hammering against his rib cage.

"Soon," she'd promised. "When I get a good job, I can finally find us a place to live. The room I'm renting isn't fit for a child. You'll be better here until then."

"No, it's not better here," he'd complained. "Please, Mother. Take me with you."

"I can't, little one." She'd cupped his cheek, her fingers rough. "Be a good lad, won't you?"

Then she was gone, with a swirl of navy coat around her thin stockinged legs. Her shoes clacked on the cobblestone, and she hurried away. He'd stood there for an age, still feeling the rough of her hand on his cheek, the way she'd squeezed his arm, remembering the kiss she'd planted on his forehead. His throat fairly ached with the tears that wanted to fall but wouldn't. He was eleven and too big to cry. But he couldn't walk away, not until the feeling passed.

And now, all these months later, he could barely remember how she'd looked — the curve of her jaw, the black eyelashes that rimmed her blue eyes, the pale skin that pulled tight over high cheekbones. He let his eyes drift shut for a moment, hoping her face would come to him like a photograph against the blackness of his eyelids, but there was nothing more than a swirl of navy and black and a sadness he couldn't shake.

At the end of the class, Mr Wilson called all the boys to attention.

"I'd like to make an announcement that for some of you may be life changing. We will welcome some visitors tomorrow. They're coming to talk to you about an adventure, not unlike Robinson Crusoe's. A chance for you to make a better life for yourselves. I can't say anything more about it yet, but please do come to class tomorrow with an open mind. I will see you all then."

Harry stood to his feet, packing away the slate and pencil into the desk. He tucked his book beneath his arm.

"Harry, come here please," said Mr Wilson, combing fingers through his thin red hair. He was mostly bald on top, but he combed long strands of hair over the bald patch to hide it. His spectacles hung on the tip of his nose, and he looked down at Harry through them as the boy made his way to the front of the class.

"Yes, Mr Wilson?"

Mr Wilson half-sat on the edge of the desk, a smile on his thin lips. "Are you enjoying the book?"

"Yes, sir. It's wonderful."

"Good, I'm glad to hear it. Keep up with your reading and you'll go far in life, Harry."

Harry dipped his head. He knew it wasn't true. Boys from his neighbourhood didn't go further than the local bottling factory or flour mill. If he was lucky, he'd get a job working in one of them for forty years. If he was unlucky, he'd end up collecting and selling rags on a street corner to make ends meet.

It was how life was for the people he knew, and for him as well whenever he managed to escape the confining walls of the Home and make his own way in the world. His cheeks warmed as shame washed over him.

"You're a smart boy," continued Mr Wilson. "Don't give up on yourself."

"Yes, sir," he mumbled.

"These visitors tomorrow— give them a chance. Listen to what they have to say. It's an opportunity that might be just the thing you're looking for, my boy."

Harry raised his head, his gaze finding Mr Wilson's clear blue eyes. "Me?"

"Yes, you."

"But I've gotta stay here and wait for Mam. She could be back any day now as soon as she lands a job. She told me so. I don't want to stray too far in case I miss her. Even for an adventure."

Mr Wilson's features clouded and his brow furrowed. "I understand, Harry. But before you make any decisions, Mr Holston has asked to see you in his office after class."

Harry's heart leapt into his throat. Mr Holston was the headmaster at the Home. He never asked a boy to his office for good news. Usually, whatever he had to say was accompanied with several licks of the cane to the hearer's bare rear end.

He swallowed hard. "Yes, sir."

Mr Wilson reached into his desk and pulled out a plump red apple. He rested it on his palm and pushed his hand out to Harry. "Would you like an apple?"

Harry's stomach clenched with hunger at the sight of the fruit. He took it and pushed it deep into his pants pocket. "Ta, sir."

THE HEADMASTER'S OFFICE WAS DARK AND CLOSETED. THE BOYS were all afraid of Mr Holston. He'd as soon use a calm, kind tone to address a boy as he would to whip him. His face would shift with his mood — at once open and jovial, the next moment dark and cruel. The boys never knew which face they'd get. He was a tall man, broad-shouldered with narrow brown eyes that couldn't seem to settle on one boy for long, always moving, shifting, blinking.

Harry drew a deep breath, his heart pounding with his book beneath his arm. He raised one fist and knocked on the door. It barely made a sound. His knuckles were cold, and the hard timber sent a whisper of pain through his bruised hand. There was no response, so he tried again, this time rapping louder.

"Enter!" called Mr Holston in a brusque tone.

Harry bit down on his lower lip, pulled the heavy door open, and stepped through into the office. His eyes took a moment to adjust to the dim lighting — he scanned the room, taking in the shelves of dusty leather-bound books, the table with a blue and white china wash bowl and jug, the sturdy dark-timber desk that looked as though it had sat in its place for a hundred years without moving.

Mr Holston held a pen in one hand poised above a stack of papers. "Ah, Harry, you're here."

Harry swallowed. "Mr Wilson sent me."

Mr Holston set his pen on the desk and stood to his feet, coming around the desk to rest a hand on Harry's shoulder. Harry's pulse thudded in his throat as his mind raced to understand what he was doing in Mr Holston's office — had he broken something, crossed someone, or said the wrong thing and didn't remember it?

"Take a seat, lad." Mr Holston's tone was cordial. Warm, even, if Harry calmed his anxiety long enough to think about it.

He relaxed a little and sat in the proffered high-backed chair. Mr Holston leaned on the desk with one leg hitched to sit on the edge closest to Harry.

"Mr Wilson tells me you've been doing well in class."

"Yes, sir. I think I have."

"That's good to hear. You know, one of the things we look for in you boys is a mindset that might lift you out of the misery of your parents' world. I think perhaps you have that."

Harry wasn't sure what he should say in response. He was accustomed to the men who ran the Home talking about his family, friends and neighbours from back home as though they were criminals, vagrants, and less than worthless. It was a constant refrain. Everything they did in the Home was an attempt to help children like Harry out of the swamp of their birth. But Harry couldn't reconcile that with the fact that he longed to be back there with Mother.

He'd swap the Home for his real home in a heartbeat. Even though Mother had dropped him at the gates all those years ago, he spent every day looking forward to the time when they could be together again. They'd tried once, a few years earlier. She'd come for him unexpectedly. The headmaster had objected, but in the end couldn't do anything to stand in her way. Excitement, joy, and a wellspring of emotion had flooded over him as he'd walked away from the tall, imposing building with his small hand squeezed tight into hers. But within a few months, she'd lost her job, they'd been evicted from their flat, and she'd bundled him up and dragged him, kicking and screaming, back to the Home to try again.

Mr Holston waited, but Harry remained mute. He cleared his throat.

"Well, the reason I raise the subject is that there's a chance for you to change direction."

"Mr Wilson said we were to have visitors tomorrow," he piped up.

Mr Holston smiled, his moustache twitching. "Yes, quite."

"But I told him, if it means going away somewhere, I can't do it. You see, I'm waiting for Mother..."

Mr Holston drew a slow breath. "I wanted to talk to you about your mother, Harry."

Perhaps this was the moment he'd been waiting for. She was coming for him. He should pack his bag, be ready to leave.

"I'm afraid she recently came down with pneumonia."

"Is she okay?" He forgot his policy of saying as little as possible to the headmaster. If Mother was sick, he should go to her. She needed him.

Mr Holston's face took on a hangdog expression. He linked his fingers together in front of his belt. "Unfortunately not. She fell quite ill very quickly, it seems. Didn't have a strong enough constitution to deal with the disease and fight it off. She died last week. I'm sorry to be the one to have to break the news to you, lad. But she won't be coming back for you, and you should learn to shoulder that burden now since you must. It's time to face a future of your own making, my boy."

Harry's breath caught in his throat. He stood to his feet slowly, the world spinning around him. Books seemed larger, then faded into the distance. He wobbled, reached for the wall, and set his hand against it to steady himself.

"Mother's dead?"

"I'm afraid so, lad." Mr Holston hovered. "Are you well? Can I get you some water, Harry?"

Harry shuffled towards the door. "I'll be all right, Mr Holston. Thank you, sir."

It couldn't be true. He didn't want to believe it. Mother was gone? All this time he'd been waiting for her, holding out hope they'd be a family again, and now she wouldn't come. He had nothing to hold onto any longer. No one to call his own. He'd never met his father. Mother hadn't told him who the man was, no matter how he'd begged her. She'd simply said he wasn't worth the mention. It'd always been him and Mother. They were a team. There was no one else. No aunts, uncles, cousins, or grandparents. Just Harry and Mother — and when they were together, the world was right and good and pure. When they were apart, everything seemed bleak. Even a bowl of blackberry pudding soured in his mouth when he missed her.

He made his way up the staircase, avoiding the rooms where chattering boys were congregated doing their chores or washing up for supper. He couldn't face anyone, not yet. They'd know from his countenance something was wrong—he couldn't hide it. And they'd ask until he told them. This was something he didn't want to share with anyone. It was too painful, too raw. It was his burden to carry alone and all he wanted was to curl into a ball in some dark, shadowy place and let it burn within him.

The clatter of boots in the hallway made him duck beside a small timber closet. He pried open the door and slipped inside. Two dozen threadbare coats brushed against his cheeks as he pushed his way into the closet and then settled on the timber floor, legs crossed. He plucked the book from beneath his arm, found the apple in his pocket, and settled back against the hard slats to read. He longed to let his mind wander, to travel to a distant tropical island, so he could forget the pain of knowing.

After a while he heard boys clamour down the stairs for supper. Then back up again. His stomach growled with hunger, but he had no intention of leaving his hideaway for a bowl of gruel or a thin soup with stale bread on the side. His back ached and he'd lost feeling in his feet from the confinement of the tight space, but still he didn't move. He read, letting himself be drawn into the battles, the conflict, the drama of survival.

When a few of the boys huddled close to the closet, he shifted in place, annoyed by the interruption that'd pulled him from the pages of the book. It'd be bedtime soon and he'd have to emerge or the ward boy would know it and report him missing. He peered out through the closet's keyhole and saw three small boys sharing an orange. Oranges were hard to come by in the Home. He wondered where they'd found it, and the sight of it made his mouth water.

Davey was there with the group, peering over the balustrade to make sure no one stumbled upon them and their bounty while the others ate their share. Then he took the piece offered to him and shoved it into his mouth, his cheeks bulging.

The sound of footsteps on the staircase came hard and fast. The boys seemed to melt against the closet, unable to find anywhere to run to at such short notice, and with mouths packed full of orange slices.

"What have you got there?" asked the handyman, Bill Swan, his voice rasping as he puffed his way up the final steps.

No one could answer. Their cheeks bulged but they didn't chew, no doubt in an attempt to hide the evidence.

Davey swallowed, red-faced. "Getting ready for bed, sir."

Bill glowered at him with gnarled hands pressed to his thin hips. His eyes were like pieces of coal and his cap slanted forward over them, throwing shadows on his face that set his haggard features to stone. "Getting ready for bed, is ya? Likely story. I see you eating. Hand it over before I call the headmaster."

Two of the boys shuffled in place. Davey crossed his arms over his chest. "We can't."

"Why not?"

"It's gone," he replied.

Bill scowled. "You cheeky little so-and-so. Come on — it's a hiding for you, lad." He grabbed Davey's arm and pulled him hard towards the stairs.

Harry's heart thudded in his chest. He couldn't stand by and let Bill take Davey. He'd seen what Bill's hidings did to little boys many times over the years. They always came back and collapsed on their beds exhausted, with tears wetting their pillows in silence for hours after lights out. Bill didn't know when to stop, is what they told him after. His hidings were legendary.

Harry pushed through the closet doors with a grunt, shoving the book down the back of his pants as he did. "It was me. I took the orange. I found it in the kitchen and shared it around. They didn't know where I got it."

The other boys gasped. Davey's face was pale, his eyes blinking as Bill shoved him aside and lunged for Harry.

"Fine, if that's how you want it. Come with me, you little scoundrel."

Harry stumbled after him, glancing over his shoulder to see Davey shaking his head in disbelief. Harry's stomach clenched with fear. He knew what was coming, but there was no backing out of it now. He lifted his chin and wrenched his arm free of Bill's grasp. Bill spun to face him, spittle wetting the corners of his mouth as he raised a hand to take aim. But Harry simply stepped forward to walk behind him, his head high. Bill blinked, then led the way downstairs to the basement where he kept his tools and supplies with Harry on his heels.

4

MIA

I'm a walrus. A whale. What's bigger than a whale? A whale shark. Maybe, I'm not sure, and I don't have the energy to reach for my phone to search random questions like *what's bigger than a whale?* Besides that, I'm sure it's me — my photograph will show up beside the first search result as being the only creature on this wide green earth that's bigger than a whale.

I can't sit up. I'm lying on my back on the couch, and if I try to sit, I simply flounder in place like a prone turtle, legs flailing. This is ridiculous. Only a few months ago, I had abs. I had nice, strong, flat abdominal muscles and I could sit up whenever I liked with very little effort. Now, no dice.

Why do I live in Brisbane? It's far too hot here. I wasn't thinking clearly when I decided to set up my life in this subtropical oven. And buying a Queenslander home, which is all timber slats and high ceilings, with no insulation, was also a terrible idea, since now there's not even a whisper of breeze. All the windows are open, allowing flies to roam freely through the house, and I'm wallowing on a leather couch baking in my own sweat because my husband and I wanted to be *green* and didn't install air-conditioning.

I flop about a little longer, finally adjusting my position so I'm lying on my side now, which takes some of the pressure off my bladder.

"Honey, I'm home!" Ben does this cute little entrance every night when he gets home ever since I finished work for maternity leave. He likes to tease me that I'm barefoot and pregnant and that we're the perfect family from one of those old-fashioned television shows. He teases me about it only because he knows that I've secretly always wanted to be in one of those families — you know the type, where the mother stays home and bakes biscuits and pikelets for her children, listens to them talk all about their day, and helps them with their homework while Dad's out working for a living. Then they all come together to eat dinner around the table every night and tell jokes, laugh, and then kiss each other goodnight. The kids wander off to bed while Mum and Dad cuddle and kiss in the kitchen and bicker over who will wash the dirty dishes and who will dry.

The reason I spent my childhood longing to jump into the television screen and join a cute, clichéd, happy family was because that was the furthest thing from what I had.

Don't get me wrong—Mum and Dad did the best they knew how to do. I know they loved me and they love me still. Only, they aren't the best at showing it. And quality time is definitely not their default love language. The constant stream of nannies who cared for me spent much more quality time by my side and helping me through the never-ending stream of homework my private schools piled on my shoulders than either of my parents ever did. They were far too busy — Dad with his work as a consul-general for the Australian Department of Foreign Affairs and Trade, and Mum with her charitable events and active social life.

Ben walks into the living room, bends low to kiss my forehead then disappears into the kitchen. His hair is mussed and there are tired shadows around his eyes. He's had a long day. I can tell by the slump of his shoulders how work has treated him, but he won't talk about it unless I draw it out of him. He has a habit of keeping it all to himself, which I try to tell him isn't healthy. But it's just how he is, and I love every bit of him anyway. Seeing him brings a warmth to my heart even after two years of marriage and four years together. That tingling feeling of excitement in my gut is still there. I can't believe I get to spend my life with him.

"Long day?" I call in the direction of the kitchen.

He grunts in response, then reappears with two tall glasses of iced tea filled with cubes of ice. He sets them on the coffee table beside me, then takes my hands to help me sit up. Finally. I moan with the relief of it.

"Thank you. I've been lying there without the energy to get up for about half an hour since I woke from my nap."

He chuckles, sits opposite me on the edge of the coffee table and hands me my glass of iced tea.

"Glad I could rescue you."

"You're my hero," I croon, fluttering my eyelashes at him. I wonder for a moment if he still thinks I'm cute, or if he sees a whale fluttering its eyelashes and it hits me right in the gut. I push the feeling aside, blaming hormones, and offer him a smile.

"How was work?"

His black hair stands spiked on end and his dark brown eyes crinkle at the edges as he forces a smile. "Fine."

I take his hand with one of mine and squeeze it. "Honey..."

His smile evaporates. "I lost a patient in emergency surgery. But I don't want to talk about it. Okay?"

"Okay," I reply.

"How was your day?"

I take a sip of tea, then sigh. "I thought I'd get so much done on maternity leave. I mean, I've had every single day for the past six weeks, but it's frustrating how little I've achieved."

He drains half of his glass, then sets it on the table. "Sweetie, you can't put so much pressure on yourself. Your only job right now is to take care of yourself and little Peanut."

We call the baby *Peanut* because that's what he looked like in the first ultrasound — a tiny little peanut that moved and had a heartbeat.

"I know... anyway, I cooked a casserole for dinner and made an extra one to take to Gammy's. I thought I'd run it over there while you have a shower. Then I can be back in time to eat together."

"Sounds good to me. There's a game on tonight, so I'm happy to stay in and relax."

"I think staying home's about all I can manage at the moment anyway. I'm asleep by eight o'clock."

"Right in time for the game to start," he adds with a wink.

I laugh. "You and your Friday night football. I can't believe you care —you're from Japan."

He shrugs, his eyes twinkling. "I'll be a citizen soon. I've got to fit the part, and I take my preparation very seriously."

He kisses me, then leans back on the couch with a sigh. He's tired —I can hear it in his voice.

"Well, fine. You can ditch me, your loving wife, for a football game tonight. I suppose I will get over it. You're lucky you're so good-looking."

He chuckles and downs the rest of his tea.

He takes my empty glass and his back to the kitchen, and I heave myself to my feet to follow him.

"Didn't you have a doctor's appointment today?" he asks, putting the glasses into the dishwasher.

"Yes, I went to see her this morning." I inhale a slow breath. "She says they'll have to induce if the baby doesn't come soon."

"What's going on?" he asks, facing me and leaning against the bench. He pulls me close, but my enormous belly separates us, keeping me at a distance instead of in that special place beneath his chin where I love to rest.

"It's the gestational diabetes. They don't want to let him go past my due date."

He shrugs. "Okay. Well, keep me updated." He sounds like a doctor for a moment instead of my husband and a soon-to-be father. But I'm used to it. If Ben's anxious, he flips into doctor mode to manage his emotions. Maybe I do it too. I'm not an anaesthetist like he is—I'm a GP—but I have my own version of doctor voice, just like he does.

I kiss him on the lips, relishing his softness and wishing I could linger. "I've got to go, but I'll be back soon."

I take the casserole dish from where it's cooling on the stovetop and wrap it in a towel to carry to the car. On the way down the hall, I pause at the nursery — the room where the baby will live once he's had a few months in the bassinet by my bed. It's painted a soft blue. There's a white cot in one corner, a matching white change table, and adorable animal stickers along one wall. There's a lump growing in my throat as I imagine us there, me changing his nappy, him cooing and laughing over the sight of the stickers by the change table. It's a picture of domestic bliss, one I've pined for most of my life. I'm finally on my way to having the family I've always dreamed of.

When I waddle past the home office, I spy my medical bag beside my desk, and it prompts a flash of guilt.

I should be working. I'm wasting my talents.

The thought is swift and ethereal. But it's not mine. It's Dad's voice that's drifting through my mind. He's in there, inside my head, pushing me on, spurring me forwards. Always pressuring me to be the best I can be and not to give it all up to be a mum. He'd say the word *mum* with a hint of derision. Which is bizarre because I know how much he loves and respects my own mother. But for some reason, he doesn't want that life for me. He's told me as much. I've assured him I don't have any intention of spending my days sipping wine at the golf club or organising charitable galas, but he won't listen. Says I should be working. Should be working. Should be working.

Why?

That's what I ask him, but he doesn't have an answer for that. Only that I shouldn't waste the gifts I've been given. Given by who? That's the next question on my lips. And he can't answer that one either because he doesn't believe in God the way I do. So, he can't explain who's given me these gifts that somehow aren't being used unless I'm working.

It's a tangled web of strange beliefs he's built up around his life, as though his worth is only found in what he manages to achieve. But that's not how I feel. At least most of the time, it's not. Unless his voice in my head is particularly loud that day. But the rest of the time, I know what I want out of life — family and love. I care about my career, and it'll still be there when I'm ready to return to it. But it doesn't define me.

I want my own family, I also want Dad to mend the rift between him, Gammy and Gramps. I don't know what caused this division that stands like a sentinel between them — silent and cold. He complains about them, about his childhood, but honestly, I can't imagine they could've been so bad, since they're the best grandparents a girl could ask for. Maybe he's exaggerating, or maybe there's more to the story than I've been told.

I drive to Gammy's, a twinge of pain in one side, then a pummelling from Peanut against my bladder. The bathroom will be my first stop when I get there. I'm grimacing as I pull into the drive and the car bumps over the curb up her driveway. I park behind her old Holden Commodore station wagon with the rust stain on its rear bumper. And when I climb out, I'm already sweating again even though my car is cool.

I carry the casserole down the side of the house and through the back door, which she never locks. It opens into the kitchen, which is where I need to be and where she always sits at this time of day. She's not there, sitting as usual at the kitchen table. I slide the casserole dish into the fridge and waddle off to look for her with a quick stop at the toilet. She's in her bedroom. I see Gammy's feet first — they're jutting out horizontally from behind the bed, and that's what sends the shock to my heart that makes me inhale a gulp of breath.

"Gammy!"

With a rush, I'm kneeling by her side. She's conscious and smiles up at me with a wobbly grin that's lopsided and brings me giddy relief. There are tears on her cheeks, and her eyes glisten with them.

"I'm okay, love. It's my ankle, I don't think I can stand."

Her hand goes to my shoulder and I lift and swivel her the best that I can until she's sitting upright beside the bed. I don't think I can carry her weight to get her up onto the bed, and as though reading my mind, she says,

"I don't want you to lift me. You could hurt yourself, love."

"I'm calling the ambulance," I say, struggling to my feet.

"Don't bother them. I'm sure it's only a sprain. I'll be right as rain in a few minutes."

"No, Gammy — I want to get you checked out. You're living here alone, so I can't risk you falling again on a sore ankle."

She admits I'm right with an arch of her eyebrow and a dip of her head. So, I call triple zero and tell them the back door is unlocked. Then I call Ben, and his phone goes right to voicemail. Either he's in the shower or he's fallen asleep in front of football again. After that, we wait. I sit on the bed above her and stroke her hair with my hand while she leans back against it, eyes drifting shut.

"What happened?" I ask.

She swallows. "I walked into the room and the edge of the rug must've been wrinkled or something. I tripped over it and fell. When I tried to get up, my ankle hurt so much, I couldn't manage it. I'm glad you came when you did. Who knows how long I might've lain there."

The truth of her words is like a knife to my gut. She's right. This is something I've dreaded ever since Gramps moved into the assisted living facility. How will I know if something happens to Gammy? There's no one to watch her and she refused to leave her house and live in *that place* with Gramps. So, I visit her whenever I can, but it's not every day, and the idea that she might've spent the night on the floor in pain, all alone, is hard for me to swallow.

She raises a hand to my face, presses it to my cheek, but it's fisted around something, and she doesn't open it. I reach for her hand, my brow furrowing with curiosity.

"What have you got there, Gammy?"

The photo falls free of her grasp. The one with the skinny, cold-looking children that I returned to her after I showed it to Gramps. The one she didn't know anything about when I asked her. Tears pool in the corners of her eyes when I flatten it and hold it up for her to see.

"Why are you holding this? Who are these people, Gammy?"

The tears spill down her weathered cheeks, turning her eyes red around the edges and making her sniffle.

"Char," she whispers as she extracts a tissue from her sleeve and wipes her nose with it.

"You want to talk to Auntie Char?" I ask. Charlotte is her younger sister, and my great aunt. I haven't seen her for at least a year, although I know she and Gammy are close. They speak on the phone every day, and whenever she hears Charlotte's voice, her whole face lights up like a ray of sunlight slanting through grey clouds after rain.

"Char," she says again as she begins to sob.

My phone is in my pocket, so I pull it out and dial Auntie Char. She answers on the second ring.

"My darling, Mia, how are you?" she answers in a cheerful tone with a resonant voice that draws people to her. "You're in luck. I don't usually hear this thing ringing, but I was playing solitaire on it when you called. Isn't that serendipitous?"

"Hi, Auntie Char. It's good to hear your voice. I'm afraid Gammy's had a fall and hurt her ankle."

"Oh dear, is it bad?" she asks.

I shake my head, even though she can't see me. "I don't think so. But we're waiting for the ambulance just the same. She's asking for you and seems pretty upset."

Charlotte sighs. "I'm jumping on the next plane. You tell her, I'll be there as soon as I can."

"Thank you," I reply, a lump growing in my throat. I don't have siblings, but I've always wished I could've had a sister like Charlotte. She never had a family of her own, so we're her family — that's what she's always told us. It's as if I have two grandmothers on the same side. They look so much alike, but everything else about them as different as can be.

I hand the phone to Gammy to talk, and they exchange a few words before Gammy hands back the phone, crying harder now. I tuck the phone away and lean down to wrap my arms around her, even with my awkward tummy in the way.

When I pull back, I cup her cheek and ask, "What's wrong, Gammy? Is it hurting, or do you miss Charlotte?"

She lets her eyes drift shut and tears continue to push their way from her blinkered eyes.

Now I'm crying too. I can't help it. I don't think I've ever seen Gammy cry before in my life and the sight has me ruined. I inhale a loud sob, then my throat closes over as I do my best to hold the tears in.

When she looks at me, her eyes are glazed as though she doesn't really see me. "I killed a man once."

Her words push the air from my lungs. I gape and stare at her. Did I hear her right? She said the words quietly, a whisper. Maybe I misheard. It couldn't be that.

"What?" I ask.

She breathes in and out, slowly and steadily, her tears quieting now. "I killed him. Only Gramps and Charlotte know about it —I've never told a living soul other than them in all these years. But I can't keep it to myself any longer. It's tortured me, what I've done. I need to get it off my chest." Then she exhales and leans back against the bed to stare up at the ceiling.

I don't know what to say, what to do. So, I rest my hand on her shoulder and sit in silence, reaching for words that might make sense in this moment.

Suddenly, there's a siren in the street. The ambulance pulls into the driveway. I hear the paramedics coming around the side of the house. I release Gammy's hand and stand to my feet, take one more look at her upturned face, and hurry to meet them.

※ 5 ※

OCTOBER 1953

MARY

T he frigid air clung around Mary's nose and mouth through the tattered scarf, wet and burning against her chafed skin. She sniffled and let her nose drip into the scarf, where the dampness grew. With quick steps, she scampered along the street towards home, her bare hand clenched around the extra sweets rations she'd earned by helping old Mrs Whatsamy down the block with her shopping. She'd carried the bags from the grocers to the old woman's unit, up three flights of stairs, and then held out her hand for the ration coupons with a grin on her face.

It wasn't often she got extra rations, but she did what she could to find work around the neighbourhood. Mrs Whatsamy —Mary couldn't recall her name exactly, something with a difficult pronunciation that made her tongue twist into a knot when she tried it — made her and Lottie stay for tea. She spoke with a thick accent and offered them a slice of soft, sweet cake with layers of what tasted like cream and honey.

Mary had never eaten anything as delicious in her life before. Except maybe the toffee her grandmother had let her suck on that one time they'd visited all those years earlier. The remnants of the cake still sang in her mouth, taste buds dancing to the sweetness she wished would never leave.

"What was that we ate?" asked Lottie, jogging along beside her, puffing as she worked to keep up with Mary's pace.

"I don't know, but I'm gonna go by Mrs Whatsamy's place every day to see if she needs anything. Maybe we can get another slice and some more ration coupons."

Lottie nodded her agreement, her blonde curls bouncing.

Mary scowled at her sister. "Where's your warm cap? Mam's gonna be furious with me if you get sick again."

Lottie coughed, covered her mouth with her hand, then wiped her reddened nose with the back of her hand. "It's at home, I think. I don't know. I couldn't find it."

"You mean, you didn't really look." Mary shook her head in frustration. It was one of the things that sent a tingle of anger up her spine the way that Lottie never looked properly for anything. She did a half look, then declared she couldn't find it. Of course, as soon as Mary searched, she'd spot it in no time.

"I did, truly I did."

"Never mind. We've got bigger things to fret over. We didn't find anything for supper but these ration coupons for sweeties. Mam's going to whale on us for sure."

Lottie fell silent, chewing on her lower lip.

Mary focused her mind on what she had to do. It was teatime, and Mam would be home, waiting on them to make the tea. She still had a few hours until she had to find something for supper. Mam hated to eat bread for both tea and supper. But it was all they'd had for days since Mam got the sack. Perhaps she could find something nice with the ration coupons before then.

She took hold of Lottie's cold hand in hers, doing her best to warm her sister's thin fingers by curling her own around them and squeezing tight as she marched down the street. She pulled Lottie into Maynards, then slowed her pace as she approached the counter. She swallowed hard at the look on the man's face who stood behind the counter, watching her through a pair of round spectacles.

"Can I help you?" he asked.

Mary held up the ration coupons. "I'd like to 'ave some sweets, please."

He peered down his nose at the coupons and took them from her with a sigh. Then he smiled, his eyes warming as he took in the sight of them. "You can pick what you like, love. They're not rationing sugar no more. Didn't you hear the announcement last month? Sugar rations are over. Times is changin'. Grand, ain't it?"

Mary scanned the store. Shelves lined the walls filled with rows and rows of glass jars. Each jar held a different colourful sweet. Her mouth watered and her stomach clenched at the sight of liquorice-flavoured wood chews, hard-boiled lollies with twirls of pink and blue, black taffy rolled in paper wrappers, colourful necklaces made of round, hard sweets, multi-coloured love hearts with writing on them, liquorice of all sorts, sherbet fountains and Mary's favourite, butterscotch gums. Well, she didn't know if they were her favourite since she hadn't tried most of the other lollies there, but she'd had a butterscotch. Old Mrs Whatsamy had given her one for the time she helped light the oven when the lighter was playing up. She'd spent the entire morning sucking gently on it, hoping it would never end, the light buttery flavour making her entire mouth quiver in delight.

"I want a gobstopper," piped up Lottie beside her, breaking into her reverie.

Mary inhaled a slow breath. "How much for a gobstopper?" she asked.

"A farthing apiece," the man replied, leaning one elbow on the counter. "Or you could 'ave four for a penny. But I can't add anything more to your mam's slate. She hasn't paid for what she owes for at least six months now. So, you'll have to pay upfront today, girls."

If they couldn't charge the sweeties, it didn't matter if they were a pound or a penny, since Mary and Lottie didn't have a single coin between them. She'd counted on being able to run up the charges on their slate, but now they'd have to go home empty-handed.

"I guess Mrs Whatsamy didn't know about the ration coupons," she muttered to Lottie. "And Mam hasn't paid up in a while."

Lottie wiped her nose again with the back of her hand. "Does this mean no gobstopper?"

Mary sighed, gazing longingly at a jar of raspberry drops sitting on the edge of the counter before spinning on her heel. "Let's go."

Lottie teetered after her as Mary rushed through the open doorway. "But I'm hungry," she whined.

Mary's eyes narrowed. "Too bad, I guess. We don't have a penny or even a farthing. Let's get home before Mam loses patience waiting for us."

She scurried along the street, past the cinema and over the curb to cross in front of a tram whose bell rang as if in protest. They leapt up onto the footpath on the other side of the street. Two women ambled past, smoking cigarettes and pushing prams with red-cheeked babies tucked all around with blankets and knit caps. Another woman, perched straight-backed on a bicycle, puttered by with a black leather bag strapped to the back of the bike and a scarf tied over her hair.

The sisters passed a fruit stand, and Mary resisted the urge to reach out and grab two apples from a towering pile of them until she'd checked over her shoulder. The shopkeeper watched her closely, a folded newspaper in his hands as he lounged on a wooden stool, a cigarette dangling between thin lips. She shrugged to herself, eying the apples one last time before continuing on her way.

Three children whooshed past them on scooters, wheels clacking on the cracks in the pavement. One had a stick of liquorice protruding from his mouth. His plump cheeks sucked hard to hold it in place, both hands clenching tight to the handlebars as he rode.

"I don't wanna go home," cried Lottie and she dug in her heels, putting a quick stop to Mary's headlong pace.

Mary faced her, heart pounding. "Lottie, don't cause trouble. You know we've got to get home. We're late for tea as it is. Mam will take it out on me."

"But I hate it there," replied Lottie, yanking her hand free and folding her arms over her chest. There was no warm glow in her cheeks. Her eyes looked dull, and her thin frame seemed more fragile than ever.

Mary wished with all her might that she could do something, anything, to change their lives. If only they could run away to the country. She imagined they'd find all kinds of wonderful things to eat, warm grass to lay on, trees to climb and horses to pet. They could sit against the trunk of those trees and take enormous bites out of apples so red and shiny, she'd be able to see her own reflection in their skin. Then Lottie would get as plump as the apples themselves, and the colour would return to her cheeks. They'd be happy in the country. Maybe they should try for it, or they could hitch a ride to their grand-parents'. She didn't recall where they lived, but surely it couldn't be too hard to find if she could only get a bit of information out of Mam. Perhaps that night, when Mam was halfway through the whiskey, before she got too sloshed, she'd ask about Grandmother and Grandfather.

She pulled Lottie into her arms and hugged her tight. "Don't worry, I'll think of something to get us out of here soon. I hate it just as much as you do." She couldn't tell her sister that she was afraid. That she didn't know where they'd go or how they'd live if they ran. It was bad where they were, but she knew the streets, recognised the faces around her, had figured out how to survive in that place. If they went some-where new, how could she take care of the two of them?

When they reached home, they stopped short at the door and listened. No sound from inside gave away what kind of mood they'd find Mam in. They slipped off their shoes inside the door and tiptoed into the dank living room. Mam hadn't opened the curtains over the single narrow window, so the room was cast in shadows. She sat on an orange crate, not in her chair. That was the first thing Mary noticed because Mam hated the orange crates. Said they left welts in the backs of her legs.

The next thing she noticed was two women, one seated in Mam's chair, the other standing behind Mam. Both held chipped tea mugs aloft, with pinkies raised. They wore posh clothing— the one who was seated wore a charcoal pencil skirt and blue blouse. One long, plump leg was crossed over the other. The lady behind Mam wore a red frock with white polka dots all over it. The frock puffed out into a round skirt that fell just below the woman's knees. She studied Mary through a pair of large, round glasses.

"There you are," said Mam, rising to her feet and brushing her hands down the front of her skirt as though to remove any creases. Her cheeks were pink, and she used the voice reserved for guests that sent a chill down Mary's spine.

"Sorry, Mam. We lost track of time."

Mary braced herself, keeping Lottie hidden behind her as she did her best to read Mam's mood. She sighed inwardly when Mam offered her the tight smile that meant they should be on their best manners since they had visitors.

"Never mind all of that. Here are some ladies for you to meet. Come, come..." Mam beckoned Mary and Lottie closer.

Mary shuffled forwards, bringing Lottie with her. Lottie peeked from behind her sister, and Mam reached out to pull her to stand side by side with Mary.

"They're both sturdy and healthy, as you can see," said Mam.

Mary's thoughts spun. Whatever Mam was up to, she didn't like it. She felt as though she was a prized lamb being led out to show before it was taken to the slaughter.

She crossed her arms over her chest. "So, what's this then?"

"Watch your mouth," hissed Mam, her eyes flashing for a single moment before the smile pushed onto her face again. "These ladies are here to talk to us about an opportunity. I told you about them, you recall?"

The lady who was standing set down her teacup on the sink and faced both girls with a slight bend to her back, as though to get down on their level. Her eyes sparkled. "Hello, girls. My name is Miss Margaret Tanner, and I'm an honorary secretary of the Fairbridge Society. Have you heard of it?"

Mary glanced at Lottie, who returned her look with wondering eyes.

Mary shook her head. "No, Miss."

Margaret straightened. "Well, the Fairbridge Society was set up to help children, such as yourselves, find a better life."

A better life? It was as though the woman had read her thoughts. It was all she wanted for herself and for Lottie. But how could it be?

"Oh?" was all she said in reply. She wasn't ready to give too much away, to be too eager. All her life, she'd learned the lesson that if she didn't want anyone to take advantage, she should keep as much of herself to herself as she could manage.

"That's right," chimed in the second woman after a sip of tea. "We offer families like yours the chance start afresh in a new environment."

Mam nodded along with the women, her eyes glowing. "What do you think, my loves? Should we try for a new life?"

"What kind of new life? Where?" asked Mary, letting her hands fall to her sides.

"In Australia. Have you heard of it?"

"No," replied Lottie, her brow furrowed. "Is it near the ocean?"

Mary felt very grown up. She'd heard of Australia, but Lottie was too small to know about such things. Still, the only thing she understood about it was that it was far away and there were kangaroos. She'd always wanted to see a kangaroo, but the idea of traveling so far left a sick feeling in the pit of her stomach.

"It is," replied the second woman, red lips pulling into a polite smile. "You'll travel on a luxury boat, free of charge. And when you get there, you'll have free accommodation, clothing, and all the food you need. You'll live at a Fairbridge Farm School, with horses, sheep, and cattle, where you'll attend classes, learn new skills, and play with the other children who live there."

"You want us to go all the way to Australia?" asked Mary.

"We're offering you a ticket to travel to Australia and start a new life. You'll be riding ponies to school in the sunshine, picking oranges every day, and visiting the beach whenever you'd like."

Lottie's eyes brightened. "Oranges and ponies? Oh, and I love the beach."

"You've never been to the beach," retorted Mary with a roll of her eyes.

Lottie pouted. "But I *know* I'd love it."

Miss Tanner rested a hand on Mary's shoulder. "You could get a good education, learn to read and write, and make something of your life. For children, such as yourselves, with no father to provide for you, and no marriage to legitimise you, this is your best option for having a full and successful life."

She squirmed as the woman's words washed over her. It wasn't the first time someone had brought up the lack of a father in their family. She heard the words often enough, having been called a bastard by the other children in the neighbourhood for as long as she could remember. But hearing it come from those red, glossy lips put an ache in her chest.

Still, the idea of a new life fell like seeds into Mary's mind, sifting and drifting down into her thoughts until they came to a rest. Her eyebrows pulled low as she considered the prospect. They could move to a new country and get away from this place once and for all. There was nothing tying her to their home, no one she cared about besides Lottie and Mam. No one she'd miss.

"Is it warm there?"

Miss Tanner giggled, a light tinkling sound that stirred Mary's heart. "It's so hot, you'll want to take a dip in a pool every day."

"A pool?" exclaimed Lottie. "Oh, boy!"

Mary liked the idea of hot weather. It'd been so long since she'd been truly warm, she'd do anything to be warm.

"I like hot weather," she mused.

"That's good to hear. I'm glad you're interested."

"What about you, Mam?" Mary sought her mother's gaze. "Do you like the idea?"

Mam's face flushed red. "I think it's grand. I can't give you girls that kind of life. It sounds a bit like a fairytale to me."

"You like hot weather too," added Lottie, giggling.

"I do, love. You're right about that."

"But do you want us all to go?" pressed Mary. There was something about the way Mam's cheeks pulled tight and the glassiness of her eyes that made Mary feel a little adrift deep inside.

"Well, I was talking to the ladies here, and they said that what folks usually do is send their kiddies first, then follow after, like."

"It's called the One Parent Scheme," added Miss Tanner with a nod. "Your mother will travel to Australia after you, and you'll be reunited when she arrives."

Mary's eyes narrowed. "So, you wouldn't come with us?"

"'Course I would. Just not right away. I could get things sorted here while you make your way over on the boat and get started on your new lives. Then, I'll meet you. Isn't that right?" She faced the women, who both dipped their heads in agreement.

"That's right," agreed Miss Tanner.

That changed things. Mary's stomach did a flip — she thought she might be sick. But she couldn't tell whether it was excitement, fear, or both. Her heart pumped hard, sending the blood rushing through her body, setting all her nerve ends tingling.

"Oh," replied Lottie, her hand sliding into Mary's. "There's a boat?"

"Yes, a big one," replied Miss Tanner.

"What do you say?" asked Mam, her gaze finding Mary's and fixing there.

"I don't know," replied Mary. "But you'll meet us there?"

"I'll meet you there, I promise."

❧

WHEN THE VISITORS LEFT, THE HOUSE WAS EERILY QUIET. MARY SET about boiling the kettle. She and Lottie had missed tea entirely, and now they had to face Mam's inevitable wrath over having found nothing for supper. She'd thought there was plenty of time and she bit down on her lower lip, misery pooling in her gut.

"I'm hungry," moaned Lottie beside her.

She glared at her sister. "Hush. Mam will hear you and then I'll get what for."

Lottie moaned again, but quieter this time, as she danced from one foot to the other.

"What's wrong with you lot?" asked Mam, coming downstairs. Her voice was chipper, but Mary knew it wouldn't last.

"I'm sorry, Mam, but we didn't find anything for supper. I helped Old Mrs Whatsamy with her grocery bags, and she gave me sweeties ration coupons as payment, but they wouldn't accept them at Maynards — said sugar rationing is finished." She wouldn't mention anything about the fact that they couldn't charge there, it would only set Mam off.

Mam pressed her hands to her hips and studied Mary through narrowed eyes. "That old codger did you wrong. I'll have a word with her about ripping off..."

"Don't, Mam, please," begged Mary. "I'm sure she didn't realise."

Mam puffed air through her nostrils. "Don't know about that. Anyway, it don't matter none now. You two are headin' down under. Your life is about to change for the better. Ain't that the truth."

Mary exchanged a glance with Lottie. "I guess."

"And to celebrate our good fortune, I bought us three whole eggs, plus some day-old bread. So, we're having fried egg sandwiches for supper."

Lottie grinned, exposing the gap where her two front teeth had fallen out over the past weeks. "I love fried egg sandwiches!"

"Don't we all. Now step aside, love. I'm gonna make them myself, a special treat for the two of you before you go."

When they sat down to eat, the entire room was filled with the delicious scent of eggs, butter, and toasting bread. Mary thought her stomach might turn inside out if she didn't get food into it soon, and Lottie's eyes seemed to bulge out of her narrow face at the sight of the sandwich on her plate.

Yellow yolk leaked warm and treacly over the side of the thick slices of white bread. Mary licked her lips and pretended to listen while Mam said the prayer. Then she lifted the meal to her mouth and took a bite. The flavour of the egg exploded on her tongue and butter dripped down her chin and she let her eyes drift shut to savour the moment.

Mam took a bite, then spoke around her mouthful. "I know you're worried about the trip, but it's for the best. I don't know when I'll find more work, and the two of you are as skinny as young rabbits. Besides, Stan says things'll be easier for all of us this way."

Mary's stomach dropped. "Stan?"

Mam blinked. "He thinks it's for the best. Says I can move in with him, get a job, and save some money—for the trip, you know. So we can follow you there."

"You're moving in with Stan?" asked Mary as a lump filled her throat.

"Of course I am. I don't wanna live in this hellhole alone, not without the two of you to keep me company. Stan says we can be a family. Things are lookin' up for the lot of us. You'll see."

Mary swallowed a mouthful of egg and bread, but it seemed to stick in her throat. The flavour lost its appeal, and the yolk congealed on her tongue. Mam wanted them out of the way so she could start her life again with Stan. Mary wasn't surprised— it was Mam's way to think only of herself. But the pain of it still stabbed her in the gut like a knife.

She reached under the table to squeeze Lottie's hand. Her sister seemed unaware of the conversation they were having and instead was focused on licking a trail of sticky yolk from her plate.

"That's fine, Mam. We'll get right on that boat then, and we'll be ready and waiting for you when you come." Mam wasn't coming. She knew that. Her heart hardened a little more, as it did every time Mam broke it, and she raised her chin setting her thoughts on the adventure ahead. Mam was lying, but she was right about one thing — this was a chance for Mary and Lottie to have a new life. Even if it was without Mam, even if they'd be entirely on their own with no one to look after them, she didn't care. She could take care of Lottie as she'd been doing her whole life. And there'd be ponies, sunshine, oranges every day, and the big blue ocean for them to swim in whenever they liked.

❦ 6 ❧

OCTOBER 1953

HARRY

With a grimace, Harry rolled onto his back. His legs were still raw from the beating he'd received at Bill's hand. But the pain of it was nothing in comparison to the ache in his heart. He stared at the ceiling overhead, blinking the sleep from his eyes as the realisation dawned once again. His mother was gone, and he was all alone in the world. She was never coming back to fetch him, would never wrap him up in her arms and make everything all right. A sob welled in his throat and he pushed it down, glancing around at the other stirring boys to make sure none were looking.

He wasn't ready to share his news with anyone, not even Davey. It was too new, too raw. Besides, if Jamie saw tears in Harry's eyes, he'd use it as an excuse to go on the attack, and that was the last thing Harry needed. All he wanted to do was dig a hole, crawl into it, and disappear. But there was no chance of that. He had to go down for breakfast or he'd be in trouble all over again.

In the dining hall, Harry found a seat beside Davey and set his bowl of porridge and plate of toast on the table next to his friend. One of the older boys said grace, and the entire group dug into their porridge as one. Harry was always hungry in the mornings, more than at any other time of day. His stomach was like an empty cavern waiting to be filled. The porridge wasn't quite hot and didn't have nearly enough brown sugar in it for his taste, but it suffused the hole within and warmed him after the frigid rush down the stairs.

"You okay?" asked Davey around a mouthful of toast slathered with butter and marmalade.

Harry shrugged, but didn't respond.

Davey stopped chewing to study him, one eyebrow arched. "What's wrong?"

Even the question brought tears to Harry's eyes. He stared at his bowl, unable to say anything for fear of bursting into tears. He was far too big to be crying, especially in front of the entire group of boys. He'd never live it down.

Davey seemed to sense his struggle and inhaled a sharp breath. "We'll talk about it later."

Harry dipped his head and returned to eating.

"Did you hear anything more about the mystery meeting we're having this morning after breakfast?" asked Davey.

"What meeting?"

"You know, the one Mr Wilson was talking about. They're doing it after breakfast."

Harry swallowed. "Who told you?"

Davey rolled his eyes. "Jamie."

"Then I'll believe it when I see it. I forgot about the whole thing."

"Well, I didn't. If they're offering a way out of this place, I've already decided that I'm gonna take it. You?"

So much had happened since Mr Wilson's class, Harry hadn't considered what he'd do. But it made no difference to him now. Stay or go, he didn't care. What should it matter what became of him now?

"If you go, I'll go," he replied.

Davey grinned. "Glad to hear it."

AFTER THEY'D FINISHED EATING, HARRY NURSED A LARGE CERAMIC mug of hot, milky tea between both hands, thawing the tingling cold from his palms. Davey nudged Harry with one elbow and dipped his head in the direction of the dining hall doorway. Bill, the handyman, slunk through the doorway, shoulders hunched in his threadbare grey coat. With a mop in one hand and a bucket in the other, he scurried across the hall to the other side and slipped out the far door.

Davey's nostrils flared. "One day I'm gonna get that tosser."

Harry didn't reply, simply stared at the place where the handyman had disappeared. His legs were still bruised from the lashing he'd received, but the pain was welcome now. It reminded him that he was still alive and gave him something else to focus his mind on other than the fact that his mother was gone. He'd always assumed his father had died on a muddy field in France at the end of a Nazi rifle since so many other fathers had, and no one would tell him differently. It was better than believing his father was out there somewhere but didn't care to know him. And now Mother had left him behind with no one to love who would ever love him back.

Mr Holston banged the crook of his timber cane on the end of the table, silencing the dozens of conversations and the happy laughter of one hundred boys. "Listen up, boys!"

Two women walked to the end of the long timber dining table and stood waiting. They were dressed like the ladies Harry had seen in London when he'd visited Kensington with his mother. She was a seamstress and landed a job for a woman there. These women reminded him of his mother's client — well dressed, with peaches and cream complexions, tasteful makeup, and shining hair pulled back in waves from rosy faces.

The boys put down their spoons and mugs of tea and turned their heads to listen as one of the women cleared her throat to speak. She wore a blue frock with a thin black belt tied around her plump waist. Her eyes sparkled, and the red on her lips glistened under the fluorescent lighting.

"Good morning, boys," she said. "It's lovely to be here with you this morning. My name is Miss Margaret Tanner, and I'm here to talk to you about possibilities."

She went on to tell them about a spectacular adventure that was available to as many of them as would like to take it. They'd travel by boat to a foreign land where they could learn farming skills, attend school, ride ponies, bathe under the warm rays of never-ending sunshine, and eat as much good food as their tummies could hold. She showed them brochures, which the boys passed around, their voices a dull murmur as they exclaimed over the sight of the sturdy, smiling children in glossy photographs.

The pain in his heart still weighed Harry down so that he could barely hold up his head. Still, the idea of embarking on an adventure, not unlike Robinson Crusoe did in the tattered pages of the book hidden beneath his pillow upstairs, sparked a curiosity in him. He'd always longed to live in the country, away from the Home with its loveless droughty halls. A tiny flicker of nervous excitement twinged in his gut and Harry exchanged a look with Davey, who grinned from ear to ear.

CURRENT DAY

MIA

Gammy needs a glass of lemon, lime, and bitters. Not Sprite, not lemonade, but lemon, lime, and bitters. No substitute and no off-brand attempts at meeting the mark. So, I'm on the hunt, waddling as fast as my swollen feet will allow through the hospital hallways.

And she killed a man.

The thought lingers in my mind as I scour the floor for a vending machine or a tea and coffee station.

She killed a man and even though two days have passed, I still haven't found out anything more about it. I'm a chicken, of course. This is well documented. I hate confrontation or making people upset. And as much as I love Gammy, she's a little bit scary at times. Not in a dangerous kind of way, but still. Her steely-eyed gaze can make the strongest person squirm. I've seen it happen plenty of times.

Besides that, I'm not sure I really want to know. If it was a confession, it could change everything I believe about my grandmother, my family, and my life. She could go to prison if she starts confessing all over the place. And what if it's just the beginning? What if my sweet little grandmother is a serial offender? That's not information I want. Leave me in the dark. I'm happy there. It's quiet, and I have snacks.

I like my innocence intact, exactly the way it is. The naiveté that believes in the goodness of grandmothers is all I've got. I don't know what to do with a felon in cushioned orthotics.

For all I know, she might be offloading her guilty conscience on her doctor right now. So, I'm happy to let this particular subject lie. And anyway, we have other things going on. My inquisition about her confession will have to wait.

Thankfully, I know the hospital fairly well, since I've visited enough times over the years — between my own patients who've been admitted and my husband who works here. Ben is on the next floor up, and since I'm already scampering around in search of the perfect beverage for my picky grandmother, I figure it wouldn't hurt to check the staff room and see if Ben is between surgeries. I have no idea of his schedule today, but it's worth a shot.

I miss him.

Between his busy work schedule and Gammy's broken ankle after her fall, I've barely seen him in days. When I'm not visiting Gammy, I'm usually passed out fast asleep in bed or in front of the television on the couch with a thin blanket pulled up over my enormous belly.

He's doing his best to get as much work out of the way as he can before the baby comes, since he's taking six weeks of paternity leave to help me and Peanut get settled. I'm excited, since we've never had six whole weeks together. Of course, I'll probably be completely exhausted by motherhood. Still, maybe we can finally sit down and talk about all the things we never seem to have time to discuss — like hopes, dreams and the future.

He's not much of a dreamer. That role falls to me. But my dreams tend to be bite-sized. Small things really, but big in the scheme of life. Me staying home with the baby seems like an enormous dream after the childhood I had, with the relentlessness of my parents' ambitions for me. But it's those kinds of dreams that fill me with a deep contentment. Maybe even a family trip to visit all the worldwide landmarks that've piqued my interest over the decades. The Eiffel Tower, the Sistine Chapel, Big Ben, and the pyramids. So much of the world I haven't explored. Even though my parents dragged me from place to place when I was young, it was never to the famous tourist spots. They considered those to be beneath us in some way — we were the family who lived and worked in Dubai, Singapore, Canada and Malaysia. And as grateful as I am for the experiences I had in those places, there's still so much I want to see.

But not on my own. I want to go with Ben and little Peanut someday, when he's old enough to appreciate it. It'll be something we can share for the rest of our lives.

Remember that time we were in Florence?

We'll laugh together and reminisce over photos. That's what I'm looking forward to, what I'm dreaming about as I traverse the hallways and take the lift up to the fifth floor of the Royal Brisbane Hospital. I stop outside the staff room and take a deep breath. I'm puffing hard from the short walk and feel as though my entire uterus might lose traction and slip out into the floor. My hips ache, my neck aches, my feet are twice their usual size and hurt all the time. If Peanut doesn't make his entrance soon, I'm not going to make it.

Once I've caught my breath, I push open the staff room door and poke my head through. I'm looking around when I see Ben in the small kitchenette on one side of the room. He's stirring a spoon in a cup of something hot and staring at the beverage in a daze, as though not seeing it at all.

"Ben," I whisper.

He jolts, looks up at me, then grins. "Hey, what are you doing here?" He strides to me and kisses me with both hands cupping my face. His eyes glow with joy. "I wasn't expecting to see you."

"I'm visiting Gammy, so I thought I'd surprise you."

"Well, you did." He runs his fingers through his black hair, mussing it in the best possible way. I love this man more than I can describe; it's a feeling that shifts something in my heart and makes it ache with bliss as I stare at him and drink him in. His dark brown eyes are warm and sexy.

I shimmy into his embrace and rest sideways against his chest. "It's nice to see you."

He sighs. "You too. It's been a — a day."

"Bad one?"

He shrugs, stroking my hair. "Not anymore. Hey, I was thinking, we should get away before the baby comes. Just the two of us. We haven't had a holiday in a while."

It sounds amazing, divine even. The idea of lazing in a swimming pool, making love in a luxury holiday unit, and strolling along the beach front to eat at a seafood restaurant is exactly what I need. But thoughts of impending labour and Gammy's broken ankle disturb my idyllic imaginings.

"I'd love that. What about Gammy?"

"Gammy will be fine for a couple of days while we have our baby-moon. Who knows when we'll get a chance to holiday, just the two of us, again?"

I lay a hand on his chest. "I know you're busy, so I understand if it's too much."

"That's okay—this is important. So, what about do you think?"

"I think we should do it. It's the perfect time. I can't promise I'm up for much walking, but if you're looking to float, hippopotamus-like, in a swimming pool, then I'm your gal."

He throws his head back and laughs, then kisses my forehead. "That sounds perfect to me. We'll be hippos together."

I grunt, studying his lithe frame, muscular arms, and thin waist. "Nice try. You don't qualify."

"We can work on fattening me up this weekend."

"Perfect." I grin.

"I'll book something as soon as I get the chance," he says.

"You're busy. I'll do it," I object.

He kisses my lips, soft and sweet. "No, I'm being romantic. Let me do it."

I swoon, literally swoon. Maybe it's the hormones, I'm feeling extra warm and fuzzy towards Ben these days. But it makes sense— we're on a journey together, sharing something so special no one else will ever be part of it. We're becoming parents, just the two of us.

It's scary and wonderful and completely out of control, and I can't wait.

"Paging Doctor Sato to Surgical Five, paging Doctor Sato..." The voice booms through the staff room's loudspeaker system.

Ben looks at his watch. "Sweetie, I've got to go. Have a good visit with Gammy, and I'll see you at home."

He kisses me again, takes a swig of the tea from his cup, and sets the cup in the sink before hurrying from the staffroom.

I tell him goodbye, that I love him, and watch him leave. Then, I'm huffing back down the hallway to the lift. I find the soft drink for Gammy, but now my stomach is grumbling, followed by a flash of nausea. Great. It's time for another snack or I might upchuck the last one I ate into the nearest rubbish bin. One thing about this pregnancy that has frustrated me to no end is the amount of food I have to eat if I don't want to be constantly nauseated. I've stopped weighing myself. I don't want to know how much bigger I am than what I should be. I've simply got to make it through these next few days and worry about getting back into shape later.

Gammy is lying on her bed under a cream blanket and white sheets, eyes shut, when I enter her room. So, I'm quiet and do my best to tiptoe to the chair in the corner and put her drink on the small bedside table on wheels that also serves as her meal table. Her skin is pale, there are blue veins on the backs of her hands, crossed over her abdomen that are protruding more than they used to. Her grey hair stands on end around her face, splayed out across the mound of pillows propping her up. One leg has no pale, cream blanket over it — it sticks out, with a pink plastic boot wrapped from her toes to just below the knee. The pink complements the polish on her perfectly shaped toenails. Still, she looks older than usual, and the reality of that is like a sucker punch to the gut.

I know I won't have her with me forever, but this hospital visit is a reminder of that. Of the thing I try not to think about, that I push to the back of my mind most days since I can't picture a world without Gammy in it. I sit slowly, grunting my way into a semi-comfortable position, and lean my head to one side to watch my grandmother. I'd found a vending machine while out and about and bought a Mars bar to help stave off the nausea cramping in my gut. Now I pull it out, unwrap it and take a bite. Thoughts slink across my conscious mind as I chew, thoughts I've been ignoring but which keep rising to the surface like bubbles from a crab hole in wet sand.

She killed a man. There it is again. The same thought as before, unbidden. It jumps into my mind like a compulsive thought-rabbit.

Gammy confessed right before the paramedics arrived. I didn't have time to ask her about it and after we got to the hospital, she was in and out of scans and X-rays, then getting her boot fitted, then loopy on pain medication. I want to pry, to ask her all the questions I've been bottling up inside. But at the same time, I'm nervous. If I find out what she's talking about, perhaps I'll discover that either Gammy has lost her senses and will need to go into full-time care with Gramps, or she really did kill someone and I'm not sure how I'll cope with that knowledge. I'm having these circular arguments with myself every hour or so, while I'm with her and when I'm waddling through the halls in search of a drink or a jelly cup or on one of my many trips to the nearby toilet to pee.

I sigh, and as I do, her eyes flicker open. She blinks a few times, then catches sight of me in her periphery and swings her head around to look directly at me.

"Mia, you're still here," she says.

"Of course, Gammy. I went to see Ben and find something to eat. But I told you I was coming back. You fell to sleep."

She nods, smiling. "That's right. Silly me, it must be the medication they've put me on. I thought you'd left."

I stand with effort and sidle over to her, wrapping up my chocolate bar. "Would you like some?" I hold it aloft, and she shakes her head.

"No, thank you. My metabolism hasn't allowed me to indulge in one of those for forty years. And anyway, they're too sweet for my tastes now."

I laugh. "All the more for me."

With it safely tucked into a pocket, I reach for Gammy's hand and hold it softly. "Are you in any pain? Do you want your drink? I found your lemon, lime, and bitters."

"Water would be nice. And no, not in pain."

78

There's a cup of water on the table beside her, and she slurps it up through the straw as I hold it to her mouth.

Gammy's orthopaedic surgeon—Doctor Doug, as he makes us call him—pushes open the door to Gammy's room and walks inside. He's holding a clipboard with some paperwork on it, and there's a stethoscope around his neck. Could he be any more of a cliché? Then he opens his mouth and the deep booming voice confirms it — he's the picture-perfect surgeon, brimming with confidence and compassion. I can't help liking him.

"Good to see you awake. How are you feeling?" He checks Gammy's blood pressure and listens to her heartbeat while she tells him she's feeling fine but for a little dizziness.

His brow furrows. "That's not good. I think we'll do a few tests to make sure you don't have a concussion before we let you go home. How does that sound?"

"Fine with me, Doctor Doug," she says with a chuckle. "*The Bold and the Beautiful* is about to come on the telly, and I'm dying to find out whether Dwight's evil twin will fool everyone into believing he's his brother or not."

Doctor Doug laughs, his brown eyes sparkling. "Don't tell me what happens. I'd hate to spoil the surprise."

I want to laugh along with them, but there's something buzzing in my mind around and around like a bee. I try to catch the thought, but it's just out of reach until —

"Doctor Doug, Gammy says she's dizzy, but maybe it's not a concussion. I mean, she fell for a reason. Could she have been dizzy before the fall?"

The doctor's smile fades, and he checks his notes. "Hmmm...it's possible. We'll run the gamut of tests to be sure. Don't worry—most likely everything will be perfectly fine. But we like to be safe."

He leaves, and Gammy crosses her arms over her chest. "I told you I tripped over the carpet. Why are you bothering the doctor with all that?'

I sigh. "I worry about you, that's all." I cup her cheek with one hand, and she smiles.

"You don't have to worry, love. I'm perfectly fine, apart from this ridiculous boot." She flicks her eyes in the direction of her foot, disdain clearly written across her features.

With a chuckle, I sit back in my chair and cradle my stomach. My mind is full of all the things I want to ask her.

"That photo you were holding when you fell, Gammy — are you in it? There's a little girl looking directly at the camera. She looks like I did when I was that age."

The photo is in my purse, so I draw it free and hold it out to Gammy. She takes it in her hand, which shakes a little as she studies the faces in the image. One finger trails over the children, her knuckle swollen and knotted with arthritis.

"Gammy?"

She doesn't respond.

"The caption says, 'Children at Fairbridge Farm in Molong' — what were you doing there?" I've never heard her talk about her parents. Why didn't I realise this before now? No anecdotes, stories, or yarns about the good old days living on the farm in Molong. And who were all the other children in the photograph with her, scattered across a field and grinning at the camera?

"You don't have to tell me anything if you don't want to, but I'm curious about your past, Gammy. I love you so much, but I'm suddenly very aware that I know very little about you from before I knew you. Everything I know of you comes from Dad or from my childhood. Nothing from before that. Clearly, you're from England—you've still got the accent and we've talked about it. But even Dad doesn't discuss why or how you came to live in Australia, or what your life was like before that."

Gammy lets her hand drift down to her chest, the photograph resting on the cream blanket. She inhales a slow, deep breath, squeezes her eyes shut for a single moment, then meets my gaze with glistening eyes.

"Your grandfather and I came to Australia together on a boat when I was nine and he was eleven."

"Together? You knew each other when you were so young. What about your parents? Where were they?"

Gammy ignores my question and glances up at the television set.

Then she scans the bedside table, the floor, the bed. "Where's my remote? The show is about to start, and I'm going to miss the beginning. If I miss the beginning, I might as well forget the whole thing."

Her brow is furrowed, and her cheeks are flushed.

The remote is on the bedside table, so I pick it up and hand it to her. She switches on the television set and flicks between channels, finally selecting one.

"You said something when you fell. Something about killing a man?" The words rush out. I don't want to say it, not here like this. But I have to know. Is Gammy a murderer? It isn't possible, I know that. If she'd killed someone, we'd have heard about it before now.

Gammy blinks. "What?"

"After you fell, you mentioned it to me before the ambulance arrived."

"I don't know about that. I was in a lot of pain, love. You can't put any stock in the ramblings of an old woman in pain."

She laughs and settles back against the pillows a little deeper. "What do I have to do to get a nice cup of tea around here?" she continues, eyes narrowing.

"I'll get you one, Gammy. Relax—I'll be back in a few minutes."

"Thank you, love." She smiles, her frown gone.

After I fetch her the tea, I gather my things to leave. She's not going to answer any questions now, not with her attention firmly glued to the television screen levitating above her bed. And besides that, I'm tired. Bone tired. I kiss her goodbye and head out. I've got plenty to do before Ben gets home from work, so I might as well get started on it. The doctor will call me when Gammy's tests are done and the results are in, so there's no point in me sitting there all afternoon.

It's a long trek to the car park, and I'm doing my best not to think about how much my ticket is going to cost. I'm standing beside the car, ferreting around in my purse for my keys and mentally attempting to calculate how many hours I've been at the hospital, and how much my credit card is going to suffer from the parking fees.

I climb into the car and switch on the air-conditioning, but I'm not leaving yet. I have to find my ticket and my credit card. As I'm searching for those in my purse, I grab my phone and check for

LILLY MIRREN

messages. There aren't any, but suddenly I want to find out more about that photograph. I do a quick internet search for Fairbridge Farm and Molong, and there are dozens of search results with photographs very similar to the one Gammy has resting on her chest while she watches *The Bold and the Beautiful*.

The articles are provocative to my imagination and all of the unanswered questions floating around in my brain. So, I read one, then another, until an hour has passed and my car is still idling in the parking lot, my parking fee ticking over. I should go, but my heart is pounding against my rib cage, my eyes full of tears. I've learned more about Gammy's past in an hour than throughout my entire life. Was she really one of these kids? Gramps too? Sent from home, across the ocean, to a far-off land to work on a farm. Even more questions join the throng I'm waiting impatiently to ask — where were their parents? Why haven't I heard about this before now? How long were they at the farm? More and more questions and no way to find answers. At least not right now, since I'm in desperate need of something to eat and a nap. I'll have to put off the investigation until later.

Then something happens — water dripping, soaking my car seat, and it's coming from me. My waters have broken and I'm sitting in my car in a car park, exhausted and alone, about five hundred steps away from help. My phone battery is low, but there's enough of it to make a call to Ben. The signal is weak in the undercover parking garage, but I dial his number and it rings. It goes to voicemail, because of course he was headed into surgery when I left him. So, I leave him a message and then gather myself for the trek back to the hospital. It's time. Our baby boy is on his way, and I'm impatient to meet him.

❧ 8 ❧

MARY

The living room was cosy. A small fire crackled and hissed in the stove, fuelled by sticks Mary and Lottie had fossicked for throughout the neighbourhood and in a small wooded area a mile away from home. A lump of coal sat in the middle of it all, but they were almost out of it completely and since Mam had already packed most of their things to leave, they hadn't bothered to buy more.

Candles flickered in the dull morning light. The sun hadn't yet risen beyond the tops of the row of houses to the east of them. Instead, a thick fog lingered in their street. Mary stood by the front window, holding the curtain back to look out into the blackness. She couldn't see much beyond their front stoop, fog heavy in the air.

Mam clanged a pot full of water from the stove to a large tin tub on the floor of the small kitchen. She poured the water into the tub, then went back to the sink for more.

"Lottie, bath time!" she called.

Overhead, Lottie's footsteps thundered across the ceiling, then down the stairs.

There was a time when they'd bathed every Saturday night. Back in the early days when Mam had a job at the munitions plant and ration coupons for everything they needed. Mam had smiled a lot more then. Mary had hoped that when the war was over, Da would come home. He'd been part of their lives once. Even if he and Mam weren't married and he'd been gone more than he was around, they'd been a family of sorts. She remembered it, that feeling of giddy hope. She'd been two years old when the war finally came to an end, so the memories weren't really memories at all, but feelings she could still recall. There were images in her mind, vague and blurred around the edges, of what their life was like.

Then Da didn't come, and they made excuses. They couldn't help it —all they wanted was to see him again, and Mam's friends reassured them that plenty of men were still finding their way home. It was bedlam over there, they'd said. People everywhere and not enough boats to get them back across the channel. He'd be on his way still, no doubt about that. Mam had told her and Lottie this story many times when she had a bottle of Scotch to warm her by the fire.

But after two years, Mam gave up on that hope. Da still hadn't come. There were no letters, no telegrams. He'd simply disappeared. The official word was that he was missing in action, but after waiting for him for so long, it was obvious he wouldn't return, and when the munitions plant closed, everything changed for them. That was when the Saturday night bathing ritual became a once-in-a-blue-moon ritual. In fact, Mary couldn't recall the last time she and Lottie had scrubbed themselves raw in that small tin tub.

"Got to get you two girls looking clean and pretty for the fancy folks over at the *John Howard Mitchell House*," muttered Mam as she stripped Lottie free of her clothes.

"What's that?" asked Mary.

"That's the place where them Fairbridge ladies are gonna meet us."

Lottie hugged herself, shivering as Mam went in search of a bar of soap. Her eyes found Mary's, and there were tears in them. Mary wanted to reassure her, to tell her everything was going to be okay.

They were going on an adventure, that was all. But she couldn't find the words. They stuck in her craw, and wouldn't be dislodged. Nerves boiled in the pit of her gut and travelled up her spine, down her arms, and made her hands shake. She was excited, anxious, and sad all at the same time. But it was too late to do anything about it now. Mam had made up her mind, and Mary knew that was that, when Mam was determined.

While Mam washed Lottie, Mary carried the full potty from the bedroom upstairs down to the ground floor below where Mr and Mrs Badeaux lived, through their living room and kitchen to the outside toilet. She emptied the potty into the toilet and washed it clean under the tap. The nearly frozen water splashed her face, and she sucked in a quick breath. Then she carried the empty potty back up the stairs with a wave to a harried-looking Mrs Badeaux, who was chasing a half-naked toddler with rosy cheeks and blue eyes, and put the potty away.

After washing her hands in the stone sink in the kitchen, Mary fixed them all a pot of tea. There was nothing in the house for breakfast, but Mam had promised to take them out for their final meal together as a family. A lump built in Mary's throat thinking about it — why would Mam do this? It made no sense for them to be split up this way. Even if Mam did manage to follow them, what would they do? She couldn't picture what it might be like in the sunny wonderland the Fairbridge ladies had described. But it had to be better than where they were.

Perhaps that was Mam's purpose all along — maybe she wanted Mary and Lottie to have more in life than she could give them. But no, it wasn't like Mam to think about what they needed. She never thought of Mary or Lottie other than what they'd done wrong, or how much it cost to raise them. The complaints rolled off her tongue from the moment she woke until the girls crawled off to bed at night. She'd made it clear from the day she realised Da wasn't returning from the war that they were nothing but a burden inflicted on her by a cruel world to make her life a misery.

A more likely explanation for her sudden chipper mood and determination to send the sisters away was that she wanted Stan to take her in. Mary shook her head as she poured out three cups of tea, adding milk and sugar. If Mam cared so little for them that she'd get rid of them for a man she'd only just met, then they were better off without her. If they were such a burden to Mam, then they didn't need her. Mary would take care of Lottie, and they'd be a family without her.

Anger boiled in her stomach, pushing the nervous, sick feeling aside. In that moment, she hated Mam. Hated her with a passion she could barely control. Her entire body quaked with it. Lottie sniffled in the bathtub as Mam poured water over her head, washing the soap suds from her hair. Lottie wouldn't understand. Her baby sister wanted to stay with Mam, and it was breaking her heart to leave. The sobbing only made Mary hate Mam all the more.

Mam helped Lottie out of the bath, holding her tenderly in a way Mary had never witnessed before that morning. The anger inside shivered and hardened, forming a rock in her gut.

"Your turn, love," said Mam, facing Mary with a smile.

While Lottie dried herself and Mam dressed her in her best stockings, woollen frock and a jacket with too-short sleeves and holes in the elbows, Mary undressed and climbed into the tub. She slipped into the water, leaning her back against the hard tin. The water was tepid, not warm enough to stave off the cold morning, and she shivered from top to toe.

"Want any help?" asked Mam.

Mary shook her head. "No, I don't need it."

Mam eyed her with a frown. "Such a big girl now."

Mary didn't reply. Her throat ached and her mouth was dry. She washed quickly as the water cooled, then climbed out and dried herself by the fire. She dressed in her best clothes — a woollen skirt, matching cardigan and a scarf. She didn't have a winter coat that fit her, so she would have to make do by pulling on two pairs of long woollen socks over the top of her stockings.

Mam reached for her and pulled her close, then got to work combing the snarls from her long, wet hair. "I know you don't understand why I'm doing this, but one day you will." Her voice was hesitant, quiet.

Mary's eyes flashed. "No, I don't understand. You're sending us away. Lottie's heartsick over it."

Mam tugged at a particularly difficult knot, then spun Mary to face her. "It's for the best, love. Truly it is."

"Will you follow us?"

Mam's gaze dropped to the comb in her hands. "I plan to."

"But will you?"

"I can't predict the future any more than you can, love. But I'm gonna do my best, see if Stan will be up for it. He'd love it there, I'm sure he would. What's not to love?"

"You're sending us away so you can be with Stan," stated Mary. It wasn't a question, but an accusation that she spat out as though the words were poison.

Mam's cheeks coloured. "He says he don't want kids. Can't afford to feed the lot of us, not to mention buying your school things and such."

"Then stay here with us!" cried Mary. "We do all right here on our own—we get by."

Mam's lips pursed. "I can't live this way no more. It's too hard. You're so skinny and pale—your sister's sick all the time. I work myself to the bone and I can't get ahead. Don't you see that? Stan's giving me a chance to get out of here, start over, and I'm gonna take it."

Mary's bravado deflated at the look of panic on Mam's thin, pale face. There was nothing left to discuss. All she could do now was step into the future with confidence so that Lottie wouldn't be afraid.

They gathered their things and stood together by the front door. Lottie and Mary each had a small shopping bag with a few personal items inside. There were bags and boxes strewn around the living room where Mam was packing for her move down the road to the row house where Stan lived.

Mary looked out over the small, dark council flat that'd been home to her for nine short years. She blinked back the tears as Lottie's little hand slid into hers and squeezed. Then, with a quick intake of breath, she turned her back on the past and marched through the front door out into the cool morning fog where the gasman was extinguishing streetlamps with a hooked pole as the cold, dull rays of the sun inched up the shadowy street.

AFTER A BREAKFAST OF FRIED EGGS AND CHIPS AT THE LOCAL PUB, Mary was feeling decidedly more positive. The anger and angst of the morning had been replaced by an oily sick feeling from eating too many salty chips and buoyed by a tingling excitement over what was to come. She had no idea what to expect, but hoped the coming weeks would bring the changes to her and Lottie's lives that she'd prayed over for years.

Lottie sat across from Mary in the dingy booth, red-eyed and chewing on the ends of her fingernails. Mam chattered nervously about anything and everything, as though anxious to fill the emptiness with the sound of her voice.

They finished up, and Mam scurried ahead of them. Mary and Lottie held hands to follow her, ducking and weaving through the crowded streets. They climbed hills, the uneven pavement tripping Lottie several times. They traversed down footpaths that wound and curled between shops, offices, pubs, and markets until finally, they reached the train station. A train sat still alongside the platform; its engine in the distance was dark and snub-nosed. The carriages were painted a deep red and had windows all along both sides. Mary could see right through to the platform beyond.

Mam purchased tickets through a small window, and the three of them climbed on board the stationary train.

"Where are we going?" asked Lottie as she sat beside Mam on the slippery vinyl seat across from Mary.

Mam looked down at the paper tickets gripped tight in one hand. "Knockholt, in Kent."

Mary sat in silence, her hands folded in her lap as the train clicked, clacked, and shuddered, picking up speed. She watched out the window at the landscape flashing by: row houses, town houses, washing lines with pegged clothes hanging limp in the cold, damp air. Everything still half-hidden in the cloying fog. Finally, they left London and the scenery changed to lush green fields, hedgerows, and country roads as the fog lifted. Trees dotted the fields and lined the roads and laneways, their foliage a rainbow of orange, red and yellow, half hung from thin black branches, half scattered on the ground around them.

"It's beautiful," she murmured, leaning her forehead against the window. It was cold on her skin, her breath fogged the glass, and she raised a finger to draw a circle in it, then two eyes and a smile.

Lottie giggled at the picture, then shuffled closer to the window. "I want to draw too."

They drew bridges and trees, flowers and clouds. And all the while, Mary's worries were pushed to the back of her mind where she could deal with them later. The train ride was too much fun, the scenery too beautiful to feel down about anything at all.

They reached Knockholt station just as the dull morning became a bright sunny day. White bulbous clouds hovered overhead as though sunbathing. But the air was frosty against Mary's cheeks as she climbed from the train, a shopping bag full of her things in one hand. Mam helped Lottie down the steps to the platform, then they all walked past the ticket counter and down to the street. It was a long walk to the house, down village lanes, past quaint shops, two-storey white-washed houses and long, green hedgerows. There was a sign on the street announcing *John Howard Mitchell House*, and Mam led them along a curved drive.

When they reached the house, it took Mary's breath away. She'd never seen a mansion so large, so regal or so beautiful. It was two stories high with an enormous rectangular chimney on one end. Countless windows lined both stories, the pale brickwork seeming to reach to the sky, topped by a dark roof. Mary strained her neck to look up and admired the green vines climbing their way to heaven above the imposing front entrance.

They took the stairs to the front door, where Mam raised the knocker with one ungloved hand and tapped out a quick rhythm. A woman answered the door dressed in a sensible navy frock, her grey-streaked hair tucked back from her face with pins.

"Can I help you?"

Mam introduced herself, then Mary and Lottie, to the woman who took them in with a warm smile, her fingers laced together.

"Well now, welcome to *John Howard Mitchell House*. I'm pleased to meet you all. I'm the matron here, Mrs Hannity."

Mam turned to face Mary. Lottie's hand crept into hers. It was cold and small.

"This is goodbye, girls. I'll see you when I get there. You be good now, you hear?"

A stone of emotion caught in Mary's throat, and she couldn't do more than nod. Mam kissed them each on the forehead, a quick, dry peck. Then she spun on her heel and hurried back the way they'd come, her coat swirling around her stockinged legs.

Mrs Hannity watched her leave with raised eyebrows. Then she offered Mary and Lottie a bright smile. "Come, girls. Let's get you inside out of this freezing weather."

9

OCTOBER 1953

HARRY

"Do you think they'll let us bring our slingshots?" asked Davey in a whisper as he shoved a pair of charcoal-coloured pants with patches on the knees into a small rucksack.

Harry shrugged, picking up his favourite slingshot and weighing it in his hand. "Maybe, but we should leave the rocks behind."

They had a little pile of them hidden beneath their mattresses. The best stones they'd found in the yard—small, round, and hard. Harry could hit a chestnut from a tree branch with one of those.

"We'll find new ones when we get there."

Harry finished packing his own rucksack and set it on his bed. His heart hammered against his rib cage. They were really going. He and Davey had packed their things and would be heading off on the epic adventure within minutes. Almost as though they were heroes in a book of their own. He hoped they wouldn't be shipwrecked. The thought sent a shiver down his spine.

Mr Wilson was taking them on the train himself to wherever the

Fairbridge ladies were waiting. Nerves jittered in his stomach, clenching it into a knot.

He, Davey, and the other boys who were going said their goodbyes to the rest of the children, who gathered to watch them walk through the dormitory and down the stairs. A few called out best wishes. Jamie jeered, but his words didn't bother Harry any longer. It was the last time he'd have to listen to Jamie's taunting, and he had to admit that was the one thing that helped him keep his feet moving out the front door and down the steps. Mr Wilson waited for them outside with the long blue bus. He opened the bus door and Harry climbed in, with Davey following on his heels. The rest of the boys piled in after them, laughing and chattering with excitement about the odyssey ahead. A dozen girls from the Home were already seated in the front of the bus. They sat in quiet, hands folded in their laps.

Harry leaned back in his seat as Davey slid in beside him. He looked out the window at the place he'd called home for so many years. At eleven years old, he was ready for a new adventure. Especially now that his mother was gone. There was nothing holding him back, and he'd had enough of the Barnardo's Children's Home. More than enough.

"Good riddance," muttered Davey beneath his breath as if echoing Harry's thoughts. His friend stared out at the three-storey structure with its foreboding high windows and angular roof with his lips pursed and a furrow in his brow.

Harry couldn't feel quite so confident as Davey. It seemed nothing bothered his wiry, rosy-cheeked friend. But still, he was anxious to get moving and put distance between himself and the past.

They rode the train together. Mr Wilson sat at one end of the carriage, and the boys found places dotted throughout with the girls and their chaperone at the other end. Harry and Davey sat together at the front of the group. Harry wasn't in the mood to join in the rowdy conversations or raucous laughter. Mr Wilson usually kept the boys in good order, but he seemed to be lost in thought, seated on his own, staring out the window and ignoring all of the noise.

When the whistle blew, splitting the air with its shrill call, Harry couldn't help grinning at Davey. They laughed together. Excitement buzzed in Harry's gut. They disembarked together at the Knockholt station in Kent and walked through the village. The air was cold with the sun setting beyond a tall hedgerow and throwing them into shadow. They walked quietly now, in pairs. Mr Wilson led the way, and soon turned into a long driveway. The house they came upon was surrounded by expansive, well-manicured gardens. It loomed ahead of them in the gloaming, pushing Harry's excitement away and replacing it with a pit of dread.

Davey edged closer, but didn't say a word.

When they reached the front door, Mr Wilson addressed the group. "Best manners, children."

A woman answered the door. She was plump, with rosy round cheeks and sparkling blue eyes. She wiped her hands on a dish cloth and then flung it across her shoulder before smiling at them one by one.

"Welcome, welcome! Come on inside. Aren't you a handsome lot?"

She ushered them into the house, the boys completely silent now as they removed caps and shuffled through the front door after the girls.

Mr Wilson said a quick goodbye, then shut the door behind him. Harry blinked at the place where he'd stood a moment earlier. Mr Wilson was gone. He swallowed around a lump in his throat, then shook off the feeling. There was no looking back now.

🕸

"THIS HOUSE HAS A TRAGIC HISTORY OF SORTS." MRS HANNITY'S greying hair was pulled back from her face into a round bun. Her hips swayed beneath a full charcoal skirt. "The Fairbridge Society purchased it from a woman whose son parachuted into German-occupied France during the war. He was part of the British Secret Service, you know." She grinned at Harry, making him blush. "But alas, he disappeared, and she never heard from him again. So, she named this place after him. And now the house is used to help boys and girls like yourselves begin a new life."

She fell silent as she led them into a large room off the main hallway. "And here we have the library. As you can see, quiet reading is permitted as long as you've finished your assigned tasks."

Harry leaned around the doorway and peered into the library. It was an enormous room with bookshelves lining each wall. Books filled the shelves in every size and colour. A ladder leaned against one wall. Plush leather chairs were dotted throughout the space, along with lamps and small round tables that gleamed in the warm light glowing from sconces set into the walls.

A few girls sat in chairs or perused the shelves. One girl looked up at Harry as his gaze fell on her, and their eyes met. She was petite and thin, her skin pale, and her large blue eyes seemed too big for her gaunt face.

He offered her a half smile, and she grinned in return. Then she let her gaze fall to the book held in her lap. A small girl who looked like a miniature of the one in the chair sat at her feet, legs tucked up beneath her skirts, a book held in one hand as she studied the page with impressive focus.

"Let's keep moving. There's more to explore, children," said Mrs Hannity, clapping her hands together loudly. "Wait until you see the billiard room and the squash courts."

"Have you ever seen anything like it?" whispered Davey as they walked.

Harry shook his head silently, gaping at a giant oil painting on the wall beside him.

"We'll be serving three meals a day — breakfast, lunch and tea. Make sure to listen for the bell —you don't want to miss it. Trust me on that one. Our cook is a wonder, truly she is." She patted her rounded stomach. "I was two sizes smaller before I came here. I have an assistant, who you'll meet later on, as well as a gardener and a cleaner. You'll be well taken care of here. If you need anything at all, simply ask. We want to make sure you are happy, healthy, and safe. That is our priority."

Harry's eyes narrowed. He'd never heard a speech like it before in his short life. Nor had he been inside such a luxurious home. Barnardo's was a large house, beautiful to look at, but inside it was simply furnished and although every boy there had what he needed, it was nothing like this Fairbridge extravagance. If this was anything to go by, his new life in Australia might be even more wonderful than he'd imagined it could be.

When they were shown to their room, Harry pushed his bag beneath the bed and sat down on it, feeling exhausted. He sighed and glanced around the room. It was smaller than the rooms at the Home had been, but still spacious. The one he was assigned to was shared with five other boys. He and Davey had freshly made beds with white sheets pushed up to walls in one corner of the room. Darkness was falling, and one of the boys flicked on an electric light that buzzed to life overhead.

A bell jangled downstairs, and several of the boys wandered to the doorway to peep out. Someone called, "Teatime." They all tramped down the stairs and found the banquet room. Several long tables filled the space, as well as a buffet at one end. Steaming dishes filled the buffet, and a delicious aroma greeted them as soon as they'd found their seats.

Harry's stomach grumbled, and his mouth filled with saliva.

"I'm starving," muttered Davey, sitting in the chair beside him.

"I could eat a horse."

"And chase the rider," agreed Davey with a giggle.

All the children sat, and quiet descended on the room. Then Mrs Hannity bowed her head and said the prayer. Harry bowed his head as well, but peeked out to look around the room. Children were smiling with eyes closed. There were boys and girls of all ages. The entire room was warm, cosy, and filled with the scent of good foods — most of which he didn't recognise. His stomach growled so loudly, he was certain the rest of the room heard it, and his cheeks flushed with warmth.

When the prayer ended, the children lined up solemnly at the buffet, plates in hand. Harry and Davey followed, found their place in line, and chatted excitedly together over what was being served. Harry was anxious to get to the head of the line. What if the food was gone by the time he reached the table? Surely there wouldn't be enough to feed all of these children in those dishes, tureens and on the large silver platters he glimpsed every time he stood on tiptoe and craned his neck around the line of children.

Just as the thought crossed his mind, a woman dressed in a blue-and-white-striped frock with a long white apron tied over the top and a white cap on her head appeared through a doorway holding a large casserole dish between two gloved hands. She waddled to the buffet and set the dish down on the table, picked up an empty one, and carried it away.

Finally, Harry and Davey made it to the front of the queue. Harry piled his plate high with Cornish pasties, soused herring, thick slices of roast beef, ham, chipped potatoes, cauliflower au gratin, and a stream of thick brown gravy to cover it all. He carried the plate back to the table and set it down, his eyes fixed on the food. His taste buds tickled as he cut off a slice of beef and raised it to his mouth. With eyes shut, he bit down, and the flavour burst across his tongue.

He and Davey ate until their stomachs could hold no more. He leaned back in his chair, wiped his mouth with the back of his hand, and sighed.

"That was delicious."

Davey stared at his empty plate. "I wish I could eat another serving of that roast beef. It's officially my favourite food of all time."

"Me too," agreed Harry.

A group of bigger boys stood, empty plates in hand, and rough-housed behind them. One of the boys backed into Harry's chair, turned, and apologised with a laugh. Freckles smattered across a broad nose and his green eyes crinkled around the edges.

"Say, do they feed us like this every day?" asked Harry.

The boy grinned. "Aye, you'll be right fat before we leave."

"Are you going to Australia as well?"

"I'm off to Canada," replied the boy with a laugh, pushing a strand of red hair from his eyes. "Some of us are headed to South Africa. The rest will go to Australia — although there are a few different places there you could land."

Harry frowned. "I didn't realise."

The boy and his friends rushed away, setting dirty plates in a pile on a bench. Harry and Davey followed, adding their own plates to the growing pile. Then they headed upstairs to bed. It was eerily quiet as Harry lay in his bed staring up at the black ceiling overhead. The curtains blocked out any light from the moon and stars outside. The room was inky, the silence broken only by a few giggles and the rustling of sheets as boys turned over in their sleep. But Harry couldn't sleep. His thoughts whirled as images flashed through his mind — Mother waving goodbye, him leaving Barnardo's behind forever, pamphlets of happy children riding ponies and herding sheep. He didn't know exactly where he'd end up after the boy's laughing words in the dining hall, and the uncertainty kept a ball of nerves roiling in his stomach.

⬥

THE NEXT MORNING, HARRY WOKE LATE. HE'D FINALLY FALLEN asleep after the house fell into complete silence and the old grandfather clock downstairs had chimed eleven. When he woke, there were boys running in and out of the room. Most beds were already made, with only a few mussed heads poking up from beneath wrinkled sheets.

He climbed out of bed, immediately regretting the movement as he shivered in his undershorts and shirt. He pulled on his only other set of clothes, donned a jacket and stockings, then his shoes and patted his hair down with palms wet by his own spit, and headed out.

Davey was in the washroom talking to another boy. He smiled and waved when Harry walked in. He glanced around.

"Wow," Harry said.

"This is for everyone in our bedroom. Each room has its own lavatory and washroom. Can you believe it?" Davey's face glowed with excitement.

Harry shook his head. He couldn't imagine such luxury until that moment. A toilet and washroom for every bedroom. Who would think of such a thing?

When he was done, he and Davey went downstairs for breakfast. Again, they ate their fill — this time on ham, eggs, toast with marmalade and two large mugs each full of sweet, milky tea. His stomach satisfied, he meandered through the house, wondering if there'd be lessons or jobs for them to do. When no one gave them instructions, the two boys followed some of the others outside.

The air was crisp, and the sun shone dimly through the clouds overhead. Harry and Davey looked around in silence. Green fields extended as far as they could see in every direction. Around the garden, children played, laughed, chased, and explored.

With a laugh, Davey took off at a run and Harry ambled after him. They ran around hedgerows and past dormant garden beds filled with naked rose bushes. They found a tree covered in yellow and orange leaves and climbed its blackened branches. Then swung down to land in the soft piles of leaves below.

When he rose giggling from the midst of the crackling leaves, he found himself face to face with the girl from the library. She blinked once, then held out her hand. In her upturned palm there was a sweet biscuit, round in shape and sprinkled with sugar crystals on top.

He took the biscuit and bit into it. "Thanks," he murmured around a mouthful of the sweet pastry.

"We're playing hide and go seek. Wanna play?" Her voice was high-pitched, soft, and her accent transformed her words in a way that made him smile.

"I'm Harry," he replied.

"I'm Mary, and this is my sister Charlotte."

"That's Davey," he added, nodding his head in Davey's direction as his friend dropped out of the tree.

"You count to twenty first and we'll hide," she said.

Mary and Charlotte took off at a run. Harry leaned against the tree to count while Davey set off in the other direction. His search took him all over the gardens and around the circumference of the house. He found a squash court and some stables with horses inside that whickered and snorted when he poked his head through the door. The scent of leather and animal musk made him sneeze. He crept into the stables and found Lottie crouched behind a door.

She giggled when she saw him, and he tapped her gently on top of her head. "Gotcha."

He found Davey in the laundry, and they were both chased out by a woman in a grey apron. Laughing, they stumbled over Mary, who was crouched behind a hedgerow. Harry landed on the grass at her feet, still giggling.

She stood and pressed her hands to her hips. "You're supposed to find me, not run me over."

He wiped the smile from his face. "Sorry, I didn't see you there."

Her frown deepened, then she laughed. "Never mind. I'm not hurt."

They all sat in a circle to catch their breath. Harry lay back in the grass and stared at the sky, his chest heaving.

"Are you traveling to Australia?" he asked.

"We are. And you?"

"Yes," he replied.

"We're meeting Mam there," added Lottie.

"I don't have a mam," said Davey, linking his arms behind his head as he studied the sky.

Harry sighed. "Me neither."

"We can all look out for each other, then," said Mary, pressing a hand to Harry's arm.

He glanced up at her and found her smiling down at him, her blue eyes gleaming. His heart ached at the thought of how alone in the world he was.

❦ 10 ❦

NOVEMBER 1953

MARY

The bus lurched and wove. Mary pressed against the window, then flew into Lottie seated beside her as they rounded a bend. It seemed the driver had given up any regard for the safety or comfort of his passengers, taking corners at the same speed as the straights. She righted herself again, fixed her hat, patted her hair back into place and spun in her seat to face the back.

Behind her, Harry and Davey sat on the long bench seat that crossed the back of the bus. Harry wore a jaunty cap pulled a touch to one side. Davey's hung low over his brows. He held a piece of leather in his hands and was working on it. She couldn't quite make out what he was doing, but his mouth was pulled up on one side and the end of his tongue poked through as he concentrated on the task at hand.

"Where are we going?" asked Lottie, her gaze fixed firmly on the window to her left. She held onto the window frame with one hand, the other clutched the front of the seat ahead of her, knuckles white.

"Somewhere in London," replied Harry.

"Thanks. That narrows it down," quipped Mary with a roll of her eyes.

He laughed. "Well, you asked."

"We're gettin' fancy new clothes," piped up Davey, looking up from his work with a grin.

"I can't wait," added Mary. She'd never been clothes shopping before. Whenever Mam got her a new frock or a new coat, she'd simply show up at the house with some fabric or would come home with something used from the markets. Mary had no choice in what she received, and more often than not, the clothing would swim on her, or would have holes she'd have to mend.

She leaned against the seat behind her, lifting her knees beneath her skirts and letting her chin drop to her knees.

"I don't care about clothes," said Davey.

"What's that you're doing?" she asked.

He lifted the leather strap high enough for her to see it, letting it dangle in the air. "My slingshot. Ain't she a beauty?"

She admired the slingshot, and the stones Davey pulled from his pocket. Then Harry showed her his own creation, which she gave the same attention to. Both boys were clearly proud of their creations, and she couldn't help wishing for one of her own.

A sudden pothole lifted her into the air for a single moment, and when she landed again, somewhat painfully, on the vinyl seat, she figured it would be best to face the front after all. So, she spun around and massaged the back of her neck with her fingertips while watching the scenery through the window.

They'd reached the outskirts of London and buildings flashed by. Men on bicycles rode just beyond the window, caps pulled low over their foreheads. A double-decker red bus loomed alongside them, then turned down a side street. The footpaths on either side of the road were fast becoming busy thoroughfares the deeper into the city the bus took them.

Cars and lorries darted here and there; the noise of engines and horns became a constant backdrop to the hum of conversation in the bus. Finally, the bus pulled to a stop at the curb, and Mrs Hannity stood unsteadily at the front of the vehicle, one hand resting on a seat back.

"Ahem. All right, children. We're here. Please disembark in an orderly fashion and wait in line outside. I will lead the way. Follow me."

She climbed down the stairs, and the children filed out behind her, chatting in excitement about what was to come. Mary and Lottie held hands and stood in line behind the others. Harry and Davey came up the rear, shoving their slingshots and stones back into pockets.

The clothing store was large and packed from wall to wall with ready-made clothes in various sizes. There were coats, pants and shirts. Frocks, gowns, shorts and pinafores. Aprons, stockings and shoes. Everything imaginable, all found within one retail establishment. The children gaped at it all, then grinned and laughed as they pointed to this and that with delight. Still, they stayed in line. No one wanted to provoke Mrs Hannity to frustration, as they might miss out on the wonders of the promised new wardrobe.

Mary waited patiently for her turn. She couldn't help wondering if, when it came time for her to try on new clothing, Mrs Hannity would hold out a hand to stop her and shake her head and announce, "Not these girls, everyone else but them." But it didn't happen. When it came time for her and Lottie to follow the saleswoman into the changing room, no one stepped in front of them or brought them to a halt. No one objected, and so they followed the woman's sashaying hips with wide eyes and trembling legs.

By the time they were finished with their shopping trip and had returned to the house, Mary and Lottie each had a lovely new suitcase filled with everything they'd need for the journey, including a raincoat, a pixie hood, two gingham frocks, a coat, a tunic, a pair of grey flannel shorts, a woollen cardigan and jumper, a skirt with bodice, four pairs of knickers, two aertex blouses, two interlocked vests, a linen hat, three pairs of shoes (best shoes, sandals and plimsolls), two pairs of socks, three pairs of pyjamas, a bathing costume, face flannel, sponge bag, brush, comb, toothbrush, toothpaste and a Bible. Each of the boys had much the same, but with pants, ties, belts, and singlets instead of blouses and skirts.

Once home, they each took a bath. Mary scrubbed herself from tip to toe and shampooed her hair. She brushed the snarls from it carefully and pulled it back from her face with two hair clips, then donned one of the gingham frocks, socks, and plimsolls. She had never felt so pretty and clean in the course of her entire life. Her stomach was still full from tea and she couldn't help admiring herself as she turned this way and that in front of the bathroom mirror. Her body glowed with health, her cheeks pink from the warmth of the room, her skin pale and clean. She grinned at her own reflection, then spun on her heel to find Lottie.

She found her sister already bathed, with one of the plump, smiling women who worked there combing her still-damp hair and plaiting it gently into long braids. Mary watched for a moment, a shy awkwardness tiptoeing over her. How strange it was to find someone mothering Lottie, a job she'd done herself since her sister was born. But Lottie laughed and chatted with the woman good-naturedly as though it was the most normal thing in the world.

Mary packed all her new things away and slid her large fibreboard suitcase under her bed. She smoothed the sheets and folded the blanket again to make sure there were no wrinkles in it, then sat on the bed to wait until the woman was done. When she'd left, Mary spun around to face Lottie. She took her sister's hands in her own and lifted her to her feet, then turned her back and forth to inspect her.

"You look darling," she crooned, bending to kiss Lottie's cheek.

Lottie grinned, her cheeks blushing red. "Really?"

"Really," agreed Mary.

"You're a right lady," replied Lottie, blinking as she studied Mary.

"Can you believe all this is ours?" Mary beamed.

"I was sad when Mam left us here," began Lottie. She swallowed. "I didn't know why she did it. But perhaps it's because she knew they'd take such good care of us."

Mary's smile faded. She wouldn't forgive Mam so easily for the way she'd casually thrown the girls aside. Her own daughters, and she'd turned tail and run as soon as a man offered her a place in his rundown, rat-infested flat.

"I don't care about Mam. And I don't want to talk about her. We've got all the good food we can cram into our mouths, new clothes and a brand-new adventure coming up. That's all I'm thinking on. And you should too. Forget about Mam—she didn't care enough about us to try to keep our family together. But we still have each other, and as long as I can breathe, we always will." She wrapped Lottie up in her arms.

Her sister's small head rested against Mary's thin chest. "I know I should hate her, and I'll do it if you want me to."

Mary sighed. "I don't want you to hate Mam. I do, though, so you can if you like. But it's neither here nor there for me who you hate or like."

"Do you think she'll meet us there?" asked Lottie, raising her head to meet Mary's gaze.

"In the colonies?" Mary didn't want to answer the question. She knew how much Lottie longed for Mam to follow through on her promise.

Lottie's eyes brimmed with hope.

Mary couldn't understand how Mam could leave them. Walk away so easily and not look back. Facing her sister's doleful eyes, the hopeful pout of her small, pink lips, set a lump in her throat. "I don't know, and I don't care."

⚜

THE BUS CAME FOR THEM AGAIN THREE WEEKS LATER. THEY'D SPENT the past weeks playing in the expansive gardens at *John Howard Mitchell House*, eating the delicious food on offer, being pampered, and cared for, brushed, bathed and clothed by the women who worked there. It was a paradise. And now it'd come to an end. She was sad to say goodbye.

Some of the children had a mother or father visit them in the days leading up to their departure. The joviality of previous weeks had transformed to reddened eyes, sniffles, and morose countenances for those boys and girls who were leaving their parents behind as part of the One Parent Scheme. They'd see them again, or at least they planned to. But Mam hadn't come. Mary didn't think she could be disappointed by anything her mother did or didn't do any longer, but it'd still struck her like a knife wound to the chest.

She and Lottie had sat in the library, books in hands, but not paying attention to the words on the page — she couldn't read them anyway, and Lottie didn't know a single letter. They'd strained their necks to catch a glimpse of the front door every time it swung open, but there was no Mam. There were plump women in drab brown garb, thin young women in colourful gowns with bright pink lips, wiry men in factory worker clothes, or hunched men in suits. But no sign of the woman who'd been her only parent for nine years.

It was Lottie's doleful eyes that brought on the nightmares that made her toss and turn in bed in the hidden hours. Her sister needed Mam more than she did — she'd made an inner vow years earlier that she didn't need anyone, let alone a woman who wanted a snifter of Scotch more than she did her own child. But Lottie saw Mam in a different light — one with a rosy hue — as a woman who was flawed, but loved them through it all. A woman who'd do what she'd promised, even if it might be the very first time.

Mary told herself she didn't care, but the emptiness inside her grew a little more each day until it was a gaping black hole she had no idea of how to fill. Thankfully, she had Lottie, Harry and Davey. The four of them had become quick friends and spent every moment they could together frolicking in the sunshine or playing hide and go seek in the rain. But now it was time to leave their brief refuge, and for the first time, she wished she could stay in one place, with the very same people, for the rest of her days and never leave. But of course, that wasn't to be.

They climbed on board the bus, having handed their suitcases to the driver outside. He hunched over, a cigarette hanging from one corner of his mouth, while he lobbed each suitcase into the bus's dark underbelly. Mary and Lottie sat side by side, staring out the window up at the enormous house that'd so intimidated them three weeks earlier, but was now the home they'd never had. Mrs Hannity climbed on last, fixing her hat as she grunted into her seat. As the bus creaked and grumbled down the winding driveway, Mary spun in place to get one last look at the house where she'd learned what it meant to be warm, well-fed and cared for.

They drove to London, then under the Blackwall Tunnel and

through the East End. Mary and Lottie pressed their noses to the windows, taking in the familiar sights and sounds of home. Mary thought she might never see it again, and the lump in her throat grew. Beside her, Lottie sniffled quietly into her sleeve.

Then before long, Tilbury Docks rose up like a dark sentinel against the horizon. Mary caught glimpses of it through the front window by stooping low to look out. The bus slowed, bumping and grinding over potholes and through gravel along the side of the road as it eased to a halt. Rain pattered against the bus roof as the children reached for their raincoats and shrugged into them in silence.

Mary helped Lottie into her raincoat, and they followed the rest of the group out of the bus. Behind her, Harry trudged quietly. He hadn't said much in recent days. She noticed no one had visited him either and assumed his mood had something to do with that. He hadn't told her his story, and she hadn't asked. There was an unspoken agreement between the children that no one pried into anyone else's business. None of them had a happy tale to tell or they wouldn't have been there, and so they kept the stories of their woes to themselves, only sharing in the quiet spaces of friendships forged in the midst of their adversity.

Outside, the cold edged its way beneath her coat, stockings, and scarf. Mary shivered and reached for Lottie's hand. Ahead of them stood a tall building, immense and imposing. Beyond that, she saw the smokestacks of an enormous ship. There were gasps of surprise and awe from amongst the children, but Mary simply stared and squeezed Lottie's hand a little more tightly. Lottie sobbed quietly, and Mary couldn't think what to say or do to comfort her sister. Mam hadn't visited, and they were leaving London behind.

Excitement buzzed in her gut, and she hated the sound of her sister's tears as they pulled her back to reality, to the fact that their lives were changing forever. They may never come home, may never see Mam again. But Mary didn't want to think about that, so she focused instead on the tall, slanted smokestacks, the mainmast like a cross atop the deck reaching towards the sky, and the long, white sides of that glittering ship.

"You can have it, if you like." Harry's voice broke through Mary's reverie, and she spun to see him handing something to Lottie.

Lottie sniffled into her sleeve, then took the object and held it out in front of her. "But it's your favourite slingshot."

He grinned. "I know, but I want you to have it. I'll make another one, no trouble at all. This way, if you're scared, you know you can take care of yourself. No one can hurt you when you've got a slingshot like this one in your pocket."

He handed over three perfectly round, smooth stones. Lottie examined them one by one.

"You'll need these too. I don't know when we'll get to collect more, so Davey and I found all the best ones we could before we left."

Mary inhaled a quick breath. Harry's gaze rose to meet hers, and his eyes twinkled. She offered him a smile of gratitude as Lottie's sniffles faded, her attention instead focused on the slingshot and stones she was shoving into her pockets.

"Ta for that," said Mary.

Harry nodded.

"All right, children, let's get moving!" shouted Mrs Hannity. "Two orderly lines and follow me, please."

They clambered up the gangplank onto the ship, leaving Mrs Hannity behind with little fanfare. There was no one else to wish them farewell when Mary hesitated to glance back at the dock as a member of the crew, who were all dressed in matching uniforms, led them along the deck. There were twenty-one children in their group, plus two women who'd come from the House with them as chaperones. They looked just as nervous and out of place as the children did, lugging their suitcases along with both hands. Smart in navy-blue, the sailor leading them urged them forward, with a monologue about the ship and its history.

The ship was named the *S.S. Strathaird*. Built in 1932, the old P&O liner had been used during the war as a troopship to carry Australian and other Allied soldiers. It was a grand old ship, and after the war had been restored to its original beauty in order to become a passenger ship all over again. With oak-panelled walls, stained-glass windows, ornate ceilings, parquet floors, Persian rugs, and antique furniture, it was truly magnificent. It was hard to believe that Mary and Lottie would spend the next six weeks on board. Excitement bubbled up, and Lottie grinned expansively as they locked eyes. This was going to be great.

As the ship pulled out of port, Mary and Lottie stood on the deck, hand in hand, to watch. England drifted into the distance, rain clouds shadowing the island as they pulled away. The rain followed them out to sea, leaving divots in the glassy ocean's surface. Mary's heart squeezed as the last glimpse of home dissolved into the low-hanging clouds.

❧ 11 ❧

NOVEMBER 1953

HARRY

The cabins on D deck were large and well-equipped. The crew member described, as he ushered the boys inside and showed them around, how these cabins been a first-class state room that was converted into two rooms after the war to house the single-class passengers the ship now carried to Australia. The two cabins sat side by side. Harry and Davey joined four other boys in one. Mary and Lottie ended up in the cabin next door with two other girls, a younger brother of one of the girls, and a chaperone.

The rest of the group moved further down deck, along with the other chaperone and the crew member. His voice droned on, then faded away. Harry shut the cabin door and scanned the room. There were six bunks, and an adjoining lavatory and washroom. They seemed to have been left on their own, although he supposed there wasn't really anywhere for them to run off to. They'd be stuck on this ship, no matter what, until it arrived in port. The thought did little to buoy his already flagging spirits, although he couldn't help feeling a little bit excited at the prospect of so many weeks at sea. He'd read about explorers and adventurers, but never imagined he'd get the chance to sail to the other side of the earth at eleven years of age.

Harry put his things away in a compact cupboard beside his bunk bed, then sat on the bed, head bent so that it didn't hit the bunk above. Davey rustled around overhead, then slid down the steps to stand in front of him.

"This is aces. Can you believe how big this ship is? I can't wait to explore it all."

It amazed Harry how well Davey seemed to cope with whatever was thrown their way. No matter what happened in life, he took it in stride. Very rarely had Harry ever seen his friend down in the mouth. He'd been orphaned at a very young age and never held onto the hope of a family, the way Harry had.

Perhaps that was the key to finding happiness. Perhaps he should simply let it all go and forget he'd ever hoped that his mother would return and bring him back to a life full of love, warmth, good food, and fun. That maybe she'd remarry, and they'd all grow to be a family together. He had to push those thoughts from his mind forever. She was gone, she wasn't coming back, and he'd never have the family he'd longed for. He was on his way to a farm in New South Wales — a place where other orphaned and poor children would be his companions. They'd be his family. He wouldn't have one of his own. It was time he accepted it.

He offered Davey a half-smile. "It's dynamite. I wonder if they'll let us look around."

"We're aboard for six weeks. We're bound to feel right at home after so long. This ship'll be ours!"

There was no time like the present to explore, so the boys poked their heads out the cabin doorway. With no sign of either of the chaperones, Harry and Davey slunk along the middle deck past the cabins and suites. There were plenty of other children, as well as lots of empty rooms. The sea air was chill and brisk against his face, and Harry found himself smiling as he jogged after Davey.

They were out of sight of land, although Harry knew it wasn't far. The crew member had described how they'd sail across the North Sea to Cuxhaven in northern Germany first. There were six hundred passengers to take aboard, also headed to Australia. Then the *Strathaird* would steer back through the English Channel and south to the Bay of Biscay. Finally, it would leave England behind on its way to Gibraltar and the Mediterranean. Nerves wrestled with anticipation in Harry's stomach and made his head feel light.

۞

THE GERMAN PASSENGERS CAME ABOARD, BUT STAYED IN THE downstairs cabins. Harry heard two Englishmen muttering something about how that would show them who won the war. But he couldn't hear any more of the conversation even though his ears strained through the doorway from the promenade deck to the lounge where the men sat, playing a hand of cards and sipping snifters of brandy.

The reason his attention was so divided was that he was currently in the middle of a game of hide and seek, and he had yet to find a decent place to hide. The problem wasn't that there was nowhere suitable—it was that there were so many good hiding spots, he'd rendered himself frozen through indecision. And so, he stood beside the lounge, head swinging from side to side as he considered his options.

He pushed the hair back from his forehead, but the wind mussed it right back into his eyes. Then, with a squint, he chose a small nook in the lounge, behind the grand piano, for his hiding place. It wasn't as good as some of the other spots on board the enormous ship, but after one game had lasted two hours and the teacher from New Zealand, Betty Cousins, who was staying in Mary's cabin, had sent them all to bed in frustration when she'd been unable to find Davey in time for tea, they'd made up a set of rules that they each had to follow to ensure everyone was safely located before the game ended.

So, the nook would have to do.

He scurried into the lounge, around the outside with his back pressed up against the wall. He still wasn't used to being allowed the freedom they had onboard. He'd never been so pampered, trusted and respected before in his life. The two chaperones the Fairbridge Society had given them were young women who loved to have fun with the children. They dressed them, sang to them, bathed them, and read books to them before bedtime. He felt like a child for the first time in his life — or at least, what he thought perhaps a child might feel like who had someone to care for him.

Still, waltzing into the lounge wasn't something he could manage. Especially this time of the afternoon, when it was lousy with adults playing board games or cards and downing their first cocktails of the day. He was completely out of place and yet strangely at home all at the same time.

Armchairs dotted the space in clusters around small, round tables. There were thick Persian carpets lining the floors, and a bar, built of dark timber, set against one wall. The bartender was dressed all in black and white, with a tie tucked tight beneath his chin and an apron around his thin waist. The women seated throughout the lounge wore long, full gowns with tight, belted waistbands. Their hair was curled back from porcelain faces in soft waves, and their lips were various shades of red and pink. The scent from their perfumes and the men's aftershave filled the room with a heady aroma of florals and fruit that gave Harry a dizzy feeling.

His gaze fixed on a man with blond hair combed back with a neat side parting who leaned against the bar. Two women with thin waists and wearing stockings beneath their gowns with the black seams showing down the back leaned in close to him. At something he said, they threw back their heads and laughed — a tinkling sound that filled the room. They shook their shining manes as though unable to believe his words, and one of the women rested a hand on his arm. He smiled at them, reached for a pastry on a plate at the bar, and took a bite. The pastry crumbled and he caught the crumbs with his thumb, brushing them from the front of his black jacket.

Harry would be a man like him someday. He'd make jokes and beautiful, glamorous women would throw their heads back to laugh. He'd casually reach for a pastry and eat it whenever he liked. Maybe he'd even have two or three for good measure. His stomach grumbled, although not for lack of food. He'd never eaten so much in his life before as he had since he'd first arrived at the Fairbridge House in

Kent. And the meals on the ship were even grander and more sump-tuous than those had been.

With quiet footsteps, Harry glided behind the grand piano, an enormous instrument with shining black lines, and settled himself into the small cavity in the wall. He poked out his head to keep watch on the door, his heart rate thundering.

He waited there, with bated breath, for half an hour. How long would they take to find him?

When Mary appeared by his side, his heart leapt into his throat. Then he laughed when he realised it was her.

"Found you," she said with a glint in her eye.

"Are you it?"

She shook her head. "No, but I don't feel like playing anymore. I want to find something to eat."

"Me too," he replied, rubbing his empty stomach. "I'm starved. It must be time for afternoon tea."

"Scones with jam and cream," she said, her lips curling into a smile. "Or maybe bread-and-butter pudding."

"I'm hoping for chocolate cake."

"Oh, me too. Did you see the library yet?" asked Mary, her back sliding down the wall to sit beside him.

"Yep."

"I didn't know there were so many books in all the world."

"You gonna read some?"

Her gaze fell to her hands, twisting together in her lap. "I can't."

"You never learned?"

"Mam didn't want us going to school when we could be at home hunting for food or doing jobs around the house."

He gaped. He thought everyone had to go to school. There'd been plenty of times when he'd wished he didn't have to, but seeing the look of shame on Mary's face shook that right out of him. He'd hate not to be able to read his favourite stories, or the signs by the side of the road, or the menus in the dining hall.

"Come on," he said, reaching for her hand and pulling her to her feet. "I'll teach you."

Her cheeks coloured pink. "You can't. I'm too stupid."

He frowned. "Who told you that?"

"Mam. She said I should aim for being a maid, that it's the best I'll ever do. And that I didn't need reading for that. Besides, I was too stupid to learn anyway."

He shook his head. "I reckon anyone can learn to read if they try."

Hand in hand they ran across the promenade deck and down beside the cabins, finally ducking into the library. It was darker in there with the wood panelling on the walls and shelves holding countless books that seemed to glow. The scent of leather and paper filled the room. Mary dropped his hand and stood staring.

Harry knew where to go. He walked down one aisle, across the back of the room, then halfway up the next aisle, one hand held up brushing the books as he went. There he plucked a book from the shelf. Its blue leather spine contained gold gilt text that read *Charlotte's Web*. It wasn't an easy read for someone who didn't know how, but he figured he could at least point out some of the letters and words to Mary to get her started.

They found two small chairs against one wall in a stream of sunlight that came through a high round window. Harry opened the book and got to work showing Mary every letter in the alphabet, how they looked and sounded. Harry listened as she repeated the sounds back to him, her finger tracing the letters he'd taught her. A deep satisfaction crept up his spine and filled his heart with warmth at the sound of her voice. It wasn't much, this teaching of letters. But it was something. And the little, lost, and lonely boy deep inside of him clung onto that feeling with both hands.

🦋 12 🦋

CURRENT DAY

MIA

There's always some kind of noise in the maternity ward. Beeping of medical machinery, banging of doors. Then the lift arrives on my floor with another beep, shuffling of feet, the door whooshes shut again and off it goes. I shift slowly onto my side so I can watch the baby sleeping in the crib beside my bed, grimacing at the pain of movement.

He's there, our little peanut. So tiny. So cute and vulnerable, with a mop of black hair and eyes squeezed shut. He's peaceful now, sleeping with puckered rosebud lips. But this is the first time he's slept in twelve hours. He spent the night vacillating between feeding and crying. And I spent it either perched in my bed with him clasped to my breast or pacing the cold tiled floor, my dressing gown fanned out behind me.

I study him with a smile tilting at the corners of my mouth. He's perfect. The torture of sleep deprivation is pushed aside for a moment while I revel in the beauty of his cheeks, the tiny little fingers clenched close to his chin. The squishy sounds he makes as he breathes through his perfect little nose.

A nurse strides through the doorway and pushes aside the curtain that separates my bed from the three others sharing a room with me.

She smiles and glances at the clipboard attached to the end of my bed. "You should be sleeping."

I sigh. "I know. He finally got to sleep. But I can't help staring at him."

"You'll learn to sleep when he sleeps or you're going to be very tired." She's matter of fact, but there's a kindness behind her eyes as she takes my temperature, checks my blood pressure, and then examines my abdomen to see if my uterus is contracting back into place the way it should.

"Everything looks good," she says, tucking a brown curl behind one ear. "I'll be back in a few hours to do another check."

"How's he going?" I ask, dipping my head in Peanut's direction.

"He looks good. His Apgar score was fine. Let one of the midwives know if you have trouble feeding and we can come and help you."

Then she's gone and I'm left lying on my back, staring up at the high ceiling overhead. A fan spins listlessly, squeaking once on each rotation. It only adds to the cacophony of background noise. Somewhere a baby is crying, then another one joins in.

I close my eyes and wait for sleep to overtake me. But it doesn't. Even though I'm tired to the very core of my being, every part of me aching, I can't fall to sleep in all that noise and the baby so close by. I worry about him. What if something happens to him while my eyes are shut? He's so small and vulnerable. Is he breathing? My pulse accelerates, and my eyes flicker open again.

I turn my head and study his chest — it rises and falls in a steady rhythm, and my heart rate slows to its normal pace as I breathe out a sigh of relief. I try again, and this time I find myself sinking, sinking. Sleep comes, but the moment it does, someone else bursts into the room and speaks in a loud voice to one of the other new mothers in the bed beside mine. It wakes me with a jolt of adrenaline and I'm breathing in and out too quickly, making my head light.

This is ridiculous. I've got to get some sleep, since the baby will be awake again wanting to feed before too much longer. And I'm already operating on twenty-nine hours without sleep. The labour was long and intense. I managed to waddle back to the hospital after my waters broke and found someone to help me. The first nurse I came across fetched me a wheelchair, and before long I was in the maternity ward, waiting for contractions to begin.

Darkness begins to flood my consciousness again and I'm drifting until beside my bed, a phone rings. Another jolt of adrenaline and I'm semi-conscious, patting the bedside table with half-lidded eyes to find the offending mobile. It's buzzing and ringing, turning itself in a circle on the table with its vibrations. Then my hand settles over it and I pull it up to look, bleary-eyed, at the screen. It's my parents, and they're video calling me.

I sit up with a grunt at the pain, shuffling until my back is pressed against a mountain of pillows, and flick open the video call with a fingertip.

"Hi, Mum. Hello, Dad. How are you?"

"How are we — more like, how are you?" quips Dad, leaning in close to the camera until all I can see are his cheek and chin.

"I'm okay. Sore and sleep deprived, but fine really. The baby is sleeping next to me, and he's perfect."

I hold the phone so that the camera is angled at the crib, and my parents make all the appropriate noises about their adorable new grandson. I'm smiling the next time I gaze into the camera lens.

"Congratulations, darling," croons Mum. "He's absolutely beautiful. I can't wait to see him in person."

"Thanks, Mum."

We chat about the weather in Paris. About Dad's job at the consulate. How they attended a soiree the previous evening. Then, finally their plans to see us.

"When do you think you'll be able to come home?" I ask.

Mum's lips purse.

Dad leans forward again, speaking too loudly into the phone. "We've booked flights to Brisbane in two weeks' time. We figure that'll give you and Ben some time to get settled before we arrive."

I'm fine with that. In fact, I'm happy to have some time alone with

Ben and the baby before they fly in and unsettle everything in my life. They can't help it. It's their way. Everywhere they go, there's hubbub and rushing, anxiety and tension. I love them, and I'm glad they're coming. But I'm also happy to have two weeks before I have to deal with them.

"That's perfect. I can't wait to see you," I say with a smile. And I mean it.

They're my parents. My eyes fill with tears at the thought that I'll see them soon. It's partially the hormones, plus the lack of sleep. But also, it's the fact that I haven't seen them in months. I miss them. Even with all their craziness.

"I suppose we'll stay at a hotel," says Mum, her blue eyes bright.

"What about Gammy's?" I ask.

Mum and Dad exchange a glance.

"Well..." begins Dad.

"I didn't get a chance to call you and tell you she had a fall," I say, suddenly realising I'd planned on doing that when I got home from visiting her in the hospital. But I never had the time.

"Is she all right?"

"She broke her ankle. But the doctor says she'll be fine. I meant to tell you, I'm sorry — it's been a little hectic around here. It would really help me out if you'd stay at her place. Then I don't have to worry about taking care of her as well as the baby."

"That's fine, darling," replies Mum. "I suppose we could stay with her."

Dad sighs. "The hotel would work just as well."

I don't understand Dad's negative attitude towards his own parents. From what I can tell, he had a good childhood. He grew up in Brisbane, in the sunny suburbs, with a bike and a big backyard. Gammy stayed home with him and his sister. They had a vegetable patch next to the garage, and there are old photos of them running through the sprinklers in their undies during the hot summer months.

"Please, Dad, it would mean a lot to me. I hate that there's this tension between you, Gammy and Gramps. I don't get it. I mean, they're your parents. They're wonderful, kind and thoughtful. They've always been there for me when I needed them. What could you possibly have against them?"

His nostrils flare and he leans back away from the camera, crossing his arms over his chest. "It's complicated, Mia. I don't expect you to understand. You weren't there — my parents haven't always been the kindest, or the most considerate. They were often harsh to us kids, and we never had money for anything. It wasn't like it is nowadays."

I'm losing patience with this conversation, and it isn't heading in the direction I'd intended. I want to be focused on my new baby, to enjoy this special moment. Instead, we're heading into argument territory, and from previous experience, this discussion will go nowhere good. We argue, we can't come to an agreement, and we end up shouting at each other and hanging up the phone in anger. I don't want to do that today. I'm exhausted with the schisms that've torn my family apart over the years. Broken relationships I don't understand, can't comprehend. Family is everything to me — why won't they try harder?

"I'm really excited to see you both," I change tack. "And if you can stay with Gammy, that'll help us cope with everything that's going on."

"Of course we will, darling," replies Mum as she pats Dad on the arm. "And let me know if there's anything I can bring you from Paris. They have the most delicious croissants at the bakery on the corner."

"I don't know if you can bring croissants all that way..."

"Of course we can, darling. I'll make sure to buy some before we leave."

We hang up the phone, and I feel drained. There isn't an ounce of energy left in my body. A glance at Peanut shows he's still asleep, breathing peacefully. So, I close my eyes to sleep.

The door puffs open, and footsteps head in my direction. I sigh inwardly and blink my eyes open only to see Ben gazing silently at our son, a goofy grin on his handsome face.

He sees me and strides forward to kiss me, both hands cupping the sides of my face. "You're awake. I'm sorry, I didn't want to disturb you, but I finished handing over my patients. I'm officially on paternity leave."

I chuckle. "Congratulations."

"I'm so excited. A whole six weeks off to be together as a family. This is going to be epic."

His mood is contagious. I issue a gigantic yawn, then smile at him, feeling all gooey inside over everything we've done together and all we're launching into.

"I love you," I whisper.

He grins and leans over to kiss me again, reaching for my hand to hold between his. "I love you too."

"Should we pick a name?"

His brow furrows. "I still like Brody."

"You don't want something more Japanese?"

He laughs. "Nope. He's an Aussie. I'm happy to give him my Japanese middle name."

"Perfect."

"So, Brody Akio Sato?"

"Brody Akio Sato. I love it."

He smiles and carefully pulls the crib closer on its rolling wheels so we can both watch Brody sleep.

"Can I get you something to eat or drink?" he asks.

I sigh. "Do you know what I'd really love? A sleep. Could you take him for a walk around the ward and let me get a few minutes of shut-eye?"

He grins. "Of course, happy to. You rest —we'll be out here bonding. Might even try a game of soccer—see if he's got my natural ability with the ball."

I watch them leave, a smile lingering on my face. Then I shut my eyes and let sleep sweep me up in its warm, dark embrace.

❧ 13 ❧

MARY

The bang of a door swinging shut drew Mary from a deep slumber. She rubbed her eyes and yawned. When her eyes blinked open, she saw their cabin stewardess, a woman dressed all in blue and white, with a white apron and a blue and white cap, striding across the cabin. Her brown hair was tucked neatly into a chignon, and she set down a tray of glasses filled with orange juice and a plate of biscuits on the small table set between the bunks. The ship rolled a little and the stewardess caught the tray, setting it back in place.

She handed a glass of juice and a biscuit to Mary with a warm smile. "Good morning, Sunshine. Up you get. Time for me to make this bed. And while I'm doing that, you can check your things for dirty wash."

The stewardess bustled around Mary, who stood and took a sip of juice. The woman made Mary's bed in a flash, then moved onto the next bed. Mary gulped down more of the juice, enjoying the rich flavour as it filled her mouth. She couldn't have imagined how good orange juice would taste and how much she'd revel in drinking a glass every morning when she rose from bed. Even having her own bed to sleep in was a luxury. One with clean sheets and a warm blanket.

With a grin, she tossed a soiled blouse into the dirty wash pile, then hurried to the bathroom to get dressed for breakfast. The floor beneath her feet lurched, first one way, and then the other. Gale force winds whistled around the cabin, howling as they clawed at the windows. In the bathroom, one of the girls was bent over the toilet. Lottie stood at the bathroom sink, hairbrush in hand. Her skin had a greenish-yellow hue, and her mouth was turned down at the corners.

"Feeling sick?" asked Mary.

Lottie blinked. "Is it going to be like this the whole time?"

Mary shrugged. "I hope not. It's hard to play any kind of game when the ground won't sit still." The ship's movements didn't bother her much. She wasn't entirely sure why, since she'd never been on board a ship before. But the lurching and the heaving, the wailing wind and the crashing waves against the ship's sides that sprayed over the bow didn't bother her. It was exciting more than anything. Though she didn't dare say too much to that effect, since it seemed as though everyone else on board was suffering immensely from the wild weather in the Bay of Biscay.

She dressed, then sat on her bed to brush her hair while watching Betty read to a cluster of young girls. Some of the others from a cabin down the corridor were there as well. All of them gathered around Betty's feet, legs crossed as they listened intently to the story. Some of the bigger girls sat at the table together, writing letters home on the ship's stationery.

Mary didn't know how to write a letter, but even if she had known, she had no desire to write one to Mam. She was still angry at her mother and besides, Mam wouldn't care one jot whether she wrote to her or not. She knew her own mother well enough to realise that. All of the false warmth Mam had shown before she dropped them off at the House, buying them fried eggs with chips and fussing over how badly their clothes were patched, wasn't within her character. It was guilt, pure and simple. Mary recognised it easily, since it was the only emotion that'd ever prompted maternal concern from Mam.

A small bell sounded in the cabin, and all of the girls looked up in unison.

Breakfast time.

Mary smiled to herself. She spent a good part of each day looking forward to the next meal. She wasn't hungry, perfectly satisfied most of the time, a state which was completely foreign to her. But the food was so delicious that she could hardly go an hour without imagining what they might serve next. It was food that pushed her through each day — eating it, longing for more of it, thinking about how well it filled her stomach and how wonderfully it tingled her taste buds. That and the fact that Lottie had stopped coughing within a few days of them boarding the *Strathaird* and had pink cheeks that weren't from the cold. She'd plumped up as well. Her cheekbones didn't protrude quite so badly, and when she hugged Mary, her sister couldn't feel her ribs poking through the fabric of her blouse as much as before.

The bell rang four times per day, for breakfast, luncheon, tea, and dinner. It was confusing for her at first, since she was used to eating breakfast, dinner, and tea. But they no longer followed the working-class order for meals, and it suited Mary just fine. When she'd discovered that dinner now represented a five-course, silver-service meal every evening at eight o'clock, she'd been delighted and had stuffed herself to the brim with medallions of succulent veal jardiniere, crispy roast quarter of lamb, cream pompadour, fillets of plaice, and an impressive cold sideboard, followed by sweet plum apple tart and unlimited servings of ice cream.

Lottie held tight to the bed rail with her wispy blonde hair carefully combed back into a long plait.

"Ready for breakfast?" Mary asked as she fixed her own blonde waves into a plait to match Lottie's.

Lottie's lips pressed tight together. "I'm not hungry, but I'll come with you just to get out of this blasted cabin."

Mary frowned. "I think it's a lovely cabin."

"It is lovely," agreed Lottie, nostrils flaring slightly. "But I feel like I'm tucked inside a football being kicked about the green by Jimmy Myer and his friends."

Mary kissed Lottie's forehead. "Well then, let's go."

They struggled along the corridor between the cabins as the ship rolled from one side to the other, throwing them off balance each time. Then they made their way to the dining room. They didn't dare walk on the deck in this weather, as they might be thrown into the raging ocean. The thought of that sent a chill down Mary's spine.

In the dining room, some of the usual crowd was there, although there was a decidedly lower number than most mornings. Mary figured it was due to the weather and the constant lurching of the ship. She found Harry and Davey seated at one of the small, square tables. Each table was set with a white tablecloth, four places of china and silverware, along with crystal glasses that all seemed somehow to stay in place. Several people seated at tables slid a few inches to the left as the ship leaned. They laughed and pulled themselves back into place.

The wait staff, all from Goa, served their tables proudly, dressed in starched white uniforms. They brought out plates piled high with succulent slices of flaking white fish and mounds of buttery mashed potatoes, steamed peaches, scrambled eggs, lamb's liver with brown gravy, bread with butter and jam, as well as pots of tea, coffee and cocoa, which they poured into the children's mugs as often as was requested. Mary's stomach grumbled at the sight and aroma, and her mouth watered.

Lottie's plate held only a piece of toast with marmalade and a spoonful of scrambled eggs. Mary eyed her sister with concern, then pushed a forkful of potatoes into her mouth, almost moaning with delight but catching herself before she did. All around them, adults laughed and chattered, ate and drank. No one paid them any mind. They could take as much food as they pleased. They could eat from the intricately painted china plates with the gleaming silverware. They could drink from the crystal glasses. And no one would stop them. No one would frown or demand a payment they couldn't produce.

Mary kept waiting for someone to step in and send her and Lottie from the room. It'd been that way ever since they first boarded the *Strathaird*, this lingering sense of imposition. They were imposters in a world built for the posh, the gentry. But it never happened. No one demanded to know who they were or how they'd got there. They were welcomed in every part of the ship, left alone to eat and play as they pleased most of the time. It was paradise. At least, it had been before the lurching and rolling, the shrieking winds and the battering rain had forced them all indoors. But since it hadn't made her sick, she could still enjoy the many luxuries of the trip. Still, she hated to see poor Lottie suffer.

Lottie sat beside her at the table, carefully placing a cloth napkin across the lap of her new frock. She ate a bite of toast and surveyed the room, quiet as a mouse. Mary watched, a smile tickling the corners of her mouth. It was strange to see her little sister eating silently, with refined manners, at a grand table.

Mary leaned over and whispered, "Aren't we the little lords and ladies?"

Lottie's cheeks flushed pink, and she grinned. "Aye."

After breakfast, Mary wanted nothing more than to lay about. Her stomach distended, she wandered from the dining room with Lottie by her side. Harry and Davey trotted after them.

"Want to play a game or something?" asked Davey.

Mary sighed. "Too full."

"We could find a deck of cards," replied Harry with a shrug.

They all agreed that cards was the perfect game to play in bad weather and with full stomachs. They found a corner in one of the sitting areas on the ship with some spare seats and settled around a table with a plate of biscuits and glasses of cold lemonade. The lurching wasn't so bad there. Lottie said she felt a little better.

As they played, Mary studied Harry. He was a slight boy and seemed skinny beneath the layers of clothing. He had a mop of brown hair that hung low over his eyebrows and against his collar. His brown eyes were deep and dark. There was something about them that made her think of a small dog who'd begged at every home in their council housing estate the previous summer. She held her hand of splayed cards in her lap, glancing over at him every now and then to take in everything she could about him. She was good at sizing up a person from head to toe, figuring them out so she'd know whether they were a friend, foe, or a mark for extracting something she needed.

"So, where are you from?" she asked, meeting his gaze.

He shrugged. "Nowhere."

"Everyone's from somewhere."

"I guess that's true...London, I s'pose."

"Anywhere in particular?"

"Can't recall. My mother left me at the Barnardo's Children's Home in Essex when I was three."

"Me too, only I was younger," added Davey.

Mary didn't recognise the name, but she knew all about those kinds of places. Hadn't she and Lottie been threatened with being sent to a Home a thousand times over? Whenever Mam didn't like something they did or was sick and tired of taking care of them, as she said often enough.

"Oh."

"You?"

"Me and Lottie are from the East End. Lived there with our Mam."

"Where is she now?" asked Davey, his green gaze fixed on the stack of cards between them as he extracted a card to place on top.

Mary exchanged a look with Lottie, whose face seemed even paler than it had been. "Um...she's coming after. To meet us when we're settled."

"Really?" questioned Harry. "Lucky."

For a moment, she really felt lucky. "Yeah, I guess."

"Where are your mams?" asked Lottie, still fiddling with her cards. She was only seven, so though she tried her best to fit into conversations and games, Mary was protective of her when she couldn't manage it.

Harry's cheeks reddened. Davey examined the laces on his shoes.

Mary leaned over to look at Lottie's cards, her face flushing with warmth. "Here, put this one down," she said in an attempt to deflect her sister's questions away from the one thing she could clearly see the boys didn't want to discuss. They'd both come from a Home. She knew what that meant, although Lottie seemed not to.

Lottie's forehead creased. She took the card and threw it on the pile in triumph.

"I wonder what'll be for dessert tonight," mused Mary. "Bread-and-butter pudding, or canned peaches with custard?"

Harry's reddened cheeks faded back to their normal colour. Davey looked at his friend's face, then back to the cards in his hands, as the two of them studiously avoided letting their gaze meet. Harry's eyes seemed to glisten in the weak daylight that sifted through an overhead window.

"Oh, I hope it's the pudding," replied Lottie, oblivious to the boys' discomfort. "It's my favourite."

❧ 14 ❧

NOVEMBER 1953

HARRY

The sunshine warmed Harry's face as though he stood by a roaring fire. He stared out over the deck at the sparkling ocean. Sunlight glinted like diamonds on its surface as a small boat chugged towards their ship. The Mediterranean had been a welcome sight to the entire group onboard the *Strathaird*. Suddenly, they were out of coats and into shirts. They were promenading on deck rather than huddled in their cabins and over lavatory bowls. People smiled, strolled and laughed. And Harry was excited — he could spend all day staring out over the deck rail at the sights beyond.

"Mail boat! Mail boat!" shouted one of the crew as he strode along the deck.

People hurried out with letters and postcards to send to loved ones, whether at home or elsewhere around the world. It made no difference to Harry. Who would he write to? He couldn't think of a single person he might write a letter to except perhaps Mr Wilson. Although he didn't have a penny to his name, so he wouldn't be able to post it anyway.

Harry wandered back inside the ship to find his friends. He'd begun to feel quite at home onboard the *Strathaird* and couldn't help wishing the journey might continue indefinitely. Stopping at the door to Mary's cabin, he rapped it with his knuckles.

Mary answered, her blonde hair pulled into two tight plaits on either side of her head. She grinned at him, glanced back over her shoulder, then stepped aside to let him in.

"Betty's not here, so if you're quiet, no one will object, I'm sure."

He tiptoed into the cabin, scurrying quickly to where Lottie sat on Mary's bed. He'd sneaked into the cabin enough times, he knew where everyone slept.

"No one else is here," said Mary, coming along behind him. "They're all watching for the mail boat."

Lottie greeted him with a smile, then stuck a book in his hands. "We're up to chapter four."

"I know that well enough." He settled down on the bed between the two girls with his back against the wall and began to read. They'd discovered a copy of *The Magician's Nephew* in the ship's library and had been reading several chapters a day. Although he knew how to read, he found his reading skills were improving on the voyage since he had access to what seemed to him like an unlimited number of books.

He pointed out various words to Mary as he went, and already she'd learned to read a simple text. She'd picked up the things he taught her quickly and easily, although Lottie was another matter entirely. The younger sister seemed to have no interest in learning, and in fact declared that she wasn't clever enough. And indeed, she was so much younger that it took her longer to learn her letters. So, he'd focused his efforts on Mary.

He hadn't been reading for long when he glanced over at Lottie to find her fast asleep. She lay back on the bed, one arm draped over her face. He shook his head and continued reading. Mary sat beside him, a slight smile on her face as she listened to his words.

After a while, he paused and glanced over to find Mary staring at him, her eyes gleaming.

"My throat's a bit dry," he said. "I might take a break there."

"It's a wonderful story. Isn't it?"

He agreed, but then he loved almost any kind of story he could get his hands on.

"What a thing — to be able to read the way you do."

He shrugged. "You'll be there soon enough."

"It's hard for me to believe I could…"

"You can."

Mary's hand slipped into his, and she squeezed gently. "I'm glad you're my friend, Harry."

His throat tightened. "Me too."

"Let's make a pact," she suggested.

He figured he might as well. He'd never made a pact with anyone before, but he felt safe to promise anything to this slight girl with the wispy blonde hair. "Okay."

"Friends forever," she replied.

He grinned. "Friends forever."

❧ 15 ❧

MARY

The hum and bustle of life on board the *Strathaird* had built a steady kind of contentment that soothed like warm honey inside Mary's very core. She didn't recognise the feeling. It was new, foreign, and yet deliciously like a homecoming to no kind of home she'd ever known.

After three weeks, she recognised most of the passengers and crew from their part of the ship. On her way through the narrow corridors to the port-side games room, she'd exchanged pleasantries with a friendly elderly couple from Scotland, a shy young Englishman with a drooping moustache and a matronly woman from Wales. The passengers came from all over the United Kingdom and Europe, each looking for an adventure and happy to be sailing aboard their shared luxurious new home.

She skipped into the games room and found Lottie was already there with Harry and Davey. Lottie and Davey were seated cross-legged on the floor, a checkers board in between them. Lottie's blonde hair was pulled into a braid. Her pale cream frock was clean and ironed, and it fanned around her legs with dainty ease. Harry sat in a wingback armchair with his elbows pressed to his thighs as he surveyed a chessboard on the small round table in front of him. She slid into a chair opposite him with a grin.

He looked up and met her gaze, his eyes sparkling. "Wanna play chess?"

She shrugged. "Don't know how."

"I'll teach you."

She often thought it strange that a boy from a Home would know so many things she didn't. She knew what a Home meant, that he didn't have any parents. She at least had Mam. But Harry knew things like how to read, historical stories she'd never heard of before, and how to play chess. There was other stuff too, things that surprised her.

"Where'd you learn to play?"

He grinned. "One of my teachers at Barnardo's taught me."

"They had lessons?"

He shook his head. "Nope. He taught me in his free time."

"When he didn't have to?"

"That's right. He read to me as well. Me and some of the other boys who loved to listen to stories — he read to us before we could read. Helped us learn to read. He could've been home with his own family if he had one. I never asked him about that. But he was a good teacher."

He moved the chess pieces around as he spoke, sliding them across the board as the words tumbled out.

"I wish I'd had a nice teacher like that. Mam wouldn't let me go to school. Said I had to stay home to care for Lottie."

"Couldn't Lottie go too?"

"Mam couldn't afford for us both to go."

"Never mind. I'll teach you now."

In one corner of the room, a group of four men dressed in black coats and tails began setting up instruments. One held an enormous instrument with strings running down the length of it. Another carried a violin—at least, that was what Mary thought it was. She'd seen a violin before. One day she, Lottie and Mam had caught the train to the centre of town at Christmas. Mam wanted to show the girls Big Ben, as she'd had a dram of whiskey and was feeling the yuletide fever, or so she called it. When they'd stepped off the train and climbed the stairs in the midst of a driving crowd, Mary ran into a man. He stood under the cover of the station doorway with falling snow as a backdrop and an instrument tucked beneath his chin. His black coat was buttoned tight around his thin frame. A scarf ran around his neck, covering his ears and chin, and his bright red nose was long and hooked beneath a set of round spectacles.

She remembered him still — everything about him. The way he looked, the scent of soap and cigar smoke that lingered around him. But most of all, she recalled the music that filled the air. Most passengers fanned around him, finding their way beyond and into the snowy street. But not Mary. She stood, stock still, to watch him play. The notes teased her senses and soothed her spirits. She wanted to stare, to spin and to laugh as his bow danced across the violin strings.

"What's that?" she'd whispered.

Mam had pushed her behind the shoulder, making her stumble forward. "Just a violin. Keep moving—we'll catch our death if we stay still in this weather."

Harry cleared his throat. "You ready?"

She shook the fog of memories from her mind and focused her attention on the board in front of her. He taught her the names of each piece, what they could do, how they could move and what the ultimate aim of the game was. Checkmate. It reminded her of the way Mam could be when she'd finished the bottle of Scotch — one wrong move would put Mary and Lottie in the path of the switch that was never far out of Mam's reach. It was a threat she knew well, and she'd learned how to survive in a world ruled by an unpredictable queen who might strike at any time.

Her mind spun in knots trying to work out how to play, but after a few quick matches, which she lost in spectacularly rapid succession, she began to understand what she might do differently to help the game last and for her not to lose quite so soon after it had begun.

A waiter attended their table with a tray of ice-cold lemonade. He handed a glass to Mary and one to Harry. Her glass contained a red-

and-white-striped straw, along with several cubes of ice. She took a sip and let her eyes drift shut as her mouth delighted over the flavours — sour and sweet.

"Want to play again?" asked Harry, rearranging the chess pieces.

With a quick nod, she set down her glass.

"Can I ask you something?"

He quirked an eyebrow. "Fine by me."

"Do you have any brothers or sisters?"

"Nope. None I know of."

She inhaled a slow breath. "I'm sorry to hear it. I'd hate to be without Lottie."

"It's not so bad," he replied. "I've got Davey."

"That's true. You're lucky to have a good friend."

"And there's you." He flashed her a smile.

"And me as well."

He intrigued her, this gentle boy from a boys' home. This orphan with the deep brown eyes full of compassion and sparkling with life. He wasn't like the other boys on board — rowdy, uncouth, and ready to tease the girls in the group whenever they had the chance. Every day, he taught her new words from a book in the library and sat patiently as she sounded out a few more lines. Every day, they played together: board games, catch, hide and seek, or spot the whale. There was so much to do on board.

The weather was warmer now and they were all dressed in short sleeves. The girls wore skirts and the boys, shorts. The sailors had switched their uniforms from navy blue to white. Now that the days were fine, they'd spent every afternoon in the swimming pool. She wore a circular float around her waist that she clung to whenever her feet couldn't reach the bottom. But she loved it—the cool water splashing against her skin, the baking sun overhead that warmed her hair, the way her skin had developed a healthy glow.

One hand rested on her lap, and the other found a place on her stomach. She massaged it gently, intrigued at the roundness. She was growing, filling out in ways she hadn't before. Lottie too. Both of them had rosy, plump cheeks, and their clothing had grown firm around their shoulders and stomachs. Their weeks at the House and now on the

Strathaird had given them a full feeling that was pleasant and safe. She smiled as she studied her sister's face, creased in a frown as she considered her next move on the checkers board. Her skin glowed; her hair was no longer lank and frizzy, but soft and clean. She no longer coughed and her nose was dry. She seemed a different girl than the one she'd been.

The quartet of musicians in the corner struck up a song, spinning Mary's head towards them. Her lips parted in delight as music filled the room.

When they'd had enough of chess the four children made their way out onto the promenade deck. Sunshine radiated bright across the deck, glancing off the white handrails that surrounded it. They wandered over to those rails and leaned against them to stare out over the brilliant blue water. Mary raised a hand to her forehead, squinting at the horizon.

"I wonder how far away that is."

Harry's nose wrinkled as he peered in the direction she pointed. "What?"

"The end of the world."

He laughed. "It's not the end of the world, only the horizon."

"You don't know for sure."

"'Course I do. I've seen a globe. It's round. The whole earth is like that. It spins slowly, and the horizon is all we can see, but there's more beyond it."

She tried to understand, but it seemed impossible that anything could balance beyond that distant line.

"Haven't you seen a globe, or a map of the world?" he asked.

She shrugged, then spun in place to lean her back against the railing. "I don't care."

He swallowed and turned with a sigh to mimic her stance. "It's not your fault."

"Didn't say it was." She sniffed, raising her chin. "It's silly anyway."

He was silent then.

Betty and one of the sailors slipped out of a room nearby, laughing as they made their way to the railing. Betty leaned over the railing with a shout. The sailor stood close, his body matching her angle.

Betty flipped her shining hair over her shoulder and pouted in the sailor's direction. He grazed the back of his hand down the length of her cheek.

Mary's cheeks flushed with warmth, and she looked away. "What's going on?" she muttered as she caught sight of one of the small girls from their cabin.

The girl was sobbing, pressed up against the wall. Her legs were tucked against her chest, hands connected around them. Mary hurried over to her, with Harry lagging behind. She squatted beside the girl and rested a hand on her shoulder.

"What's the matter, Beth? Are you sick?"

Beth shook her small head, brown curls tumbling over her shoulders. "I miss my mam."

At that moment, Lottie stepped through the nearby doorway, her gaze landing on Mary and Beth.

"I know you do," soothed Mary, returning her attention to the little girl on the floor in front of her. "But everything is going to be right in the end. You'll see."

She sat beside the girl, back pressed to the wall, and took Beth's hand in hers to squeeze it softly.

Beth sniffled. "I don't wanna be here. I wanna go home."

Lottie slid into the space on the other side of Beth, her eyes already red.

Words of comfort stuck in Mary's throat. Soothing words, kind sayings, anything to help Beth through the pain she felt — but Mary couldn't bring herself to say it. Nothing would help to ease the girl's suffering. There was nothing to be done. They were in the middle of the ocean, halfway around the world. It wasn't likely Beth would see her mam ever again. But of course, those weren't the kinds of things Mary could or should say to the girl whose cheeks were streaked with the remnants of tears.

"I miss Mam too," whispered Lottie, taking Beth's other hand.

The three of them sat that way in silence for several long minutes. Harry squatted at a distance, counting the stones from his pocket and measuring the way they weighed down his slingshot.

Then Beth's sniffles abated, and she ran off on chubby little legs to play with some of the other girls. Lottie shuffled closer to Mary, resting her head on her sister's shoulder. Mary patted her cheek lovingly.

"I wish we could see her...just for a while, mind," said Lottie.

Mary's lips pursed. "I know."

"Who will take care of us, do you think? You know...when we get there?"

Mary faced Lottie with a fierce intake of breath, her nostrils flaring. "I will. That's who. I'm always going to take care of you."

Lottie's eyes glistened with tears.

Harry joined them then, shuffling feet moving him back and forth as his gaze darted from one face to the other. "You alright?"

Mary smiled. "We're right as rain."

Harry sat beside her, adjusting his cap so that it hung low over his eyes. He bent his knees up and rested his arms on them, juggling stones in one hand. "I miss my mother as well."

"Where is she?" asked Lottie, squinting at him.

"She died."

Mary's throat constricted. Her words stuck there. Nothing to say, again.

"Do you think it's going to be like this?" she rasped finally.

"What?" Harry's brow furrowed.

"The place we're headed...will it be like living on this ship? With the clothing, the meals, the bedrooms, people taking care of us and looking after our every need?"

He shrugged. "I don't know."

"I hope so," she added. "It's like heaven."

He smiled, a lopsided kind of smile that tugged at her heartstrings. "Heaven? But there are no angels."

"I don't mind that," piped up Lottie, "as long as they keep serving ice cream for dessert."

Harry and Mary burst into laughter. Soon Lottie joined them. They giggled together, clutching at each other for support as the hilarity took them over. And soon they'd forgotten about Beth's tears, their missing mothers, and that ache in their chests whenever they thought of home.

❧ II ❧

Troops of straight-trunked gums,
Rolling hills of green;
The unrelenting heat drums,
Unravelling azure seams.

— *AUSTRALIA,* BY BRONWEN
WHITLEY 2021

✨ 16 ✨

CURRENT DAY

MIA

The hospital room stinks of bleach and lemon-scented disinfectant, and I've had enough. We're going home. Brody is three days old, and he's sleeping wrapped up like a caterpillar in a cocoon beside my rumpled bed. His swathe of straight black hair swirls onto his forehead down to the black crescents of his eyelashes against his pale cheeks. His lips have a tinge of purple to them, and I wonder if he's cold. I tuck another blanket around him. Careful not to wake him, I move gently and slowly. He finally got to sleep at seven o'clock this morning, and I feel dead on my feet.

I've barely slept more than two hours together over the past three days. My entire body hurts, but there's a euphoria keeping me going that I can't explain. The problem is, that euphoria is coupled with a fairly intense onslaught of emotions just now. The book I'm reading tells me it's to do with my milk coming in.

My breasts are full and tight—enormous, in fact. Brody's little head is dwarfed by them when I feed him. I worry it's too much for him.

But the midwife assures me it's perfectly natural and he'll grow like a little trooper in no time at all. I keep the tears at bay with deep breathing and focusing on Brody's adorable little face.

I'm excited to go home. My bed is calling my name. Along with the blackout curtains and the sounds of the ocean I often play on my clock radio to drown out any neighbourhood noise when I'm taking a daytime nap. The hospital is full of noises—the clacking of heels on tiles, the ding of the elevator, the comings and goings of midwives, breastfeeding specialists, physiotherapists, the tea lady. There's always someone knocking on our shared door or poking their head through the curtains I've drawn shut around my bed in an attempt at some degree of privacy, and I feel as though my eyelids are permanently fixed open. It's a torture I'm ready to put behind me, just as soon as my loving hubby walks through that door to take us home.

My half-packed bag is on the floor. I grunt with pain as I bend to pick it up and set it on the foot of the bed. I pack the few things scattered around the room into the bag — my nightgown, maternity clothes flung over a chair back, a book I ambitiously thought I might get the chance to read but whose pages are still new and crisp, a magazine I haven't had any desire to flip through, a few sets of baby clothes gifted by friends who've visited us in the hospital over these past few days, a couple of burp cloths and blue teddy bear wraps.

There are three vases of flowers on the bedside tables either side of the bed. The largest is from Ben. He gifted it to me the day Brody was born, along with a white gold necklace with a white gold figure of a diamond-studded woman cradling a baby in her arms. My push present, he called it. I smile as I finger the necklace, then slip it around my neck and fix it in place.

Ben will have to help carry the flowers. Otherwise, I'm all packed and ready to go. I zip the suitcase shut, set it on the floor and open the curtains around the bed.

A woman knocks on the open door and walks towards me. She stops at my bed. "Mia Sato?"

I nod. "That's me."

She smiles, her brown eyes deep and soft. Her brown hair is pulled into a high ponytail that bounces as she moves. "I'm Doctor Siwa. I'm a paediatrician, here to check on little Brody before you leave."

"That's great because we're ready to get out of here."

She chuckles. "I'll be quick, I promise. Then you can leave and take this beautiful little bundle home with you."

I sit on the bed and watch the doctor work. Brody's not happy to be woken. His face is twisting into funny expressions, and he's making an *oh* shape with his lips as he wriggles and waves his arms about. She's taken off his wrap and is checking his heart rate and other things. But she's taking longer to check his vitals than I thought she would, and she's looking at his little puckered lips with their blue-purple tinge.

"I noticed his lips looked a little blue earlier, so I added another blanket," I say.

She glances up at me and nods. "Good idea. They're still a little blue, though, so I think we're going to have to run a few more tests before I can let you go home."

My heart skips a beat. More tests? That sounds ominously like she thinks there's something seriously wrong. I know the language, I use it myself when I'm meeting with patients.

"Do you think he's okay?" I ask. I'm beating myself up already for not picking it up sooner. I'm not a specialist, but I know what to look for in newborns. I've been so sleep deprived, I can barely put my thoughts into words.

She smiles, wraps Brody again and slips his medical clipboard back into place on the end of the crib. "I'm sure he's fine. We like to be thorough before you go home. I'll take him with me, and we'll be back soon. Okay?"

"Okay, thanks, Doctor."

She leaves and I wriggle onto my bed and lie on my back, staring up at the ceiling, my heart fluttering against my rib cage. My head feels light and my breathing is shallow. I focus on breathing deeper. The last thing I need right now is for my poor, fatigued, overtaxed body to pass out from a panic attack. I have to stay focused, alert. There could be something wrong, and if there is, I've got to be ready to deal with that.

Ben strides through the door, a grin on his face and the brand-new car seat in one hand. "Sorry I'm a little late. The traffic was horrible this morning. I guess everyone in the entire city is headed to work and school all at the same time for some reason."

He embraces me, kisses my cheek, then glances around. "Where's Brody?"

I reach for his hand and take it in mine, holding on tight. "The doctor wanted to take him for some more tests before they'll let us go home."

"Oh?"

"You just missed her. I wish you'd been here..."

"I'm sorry," he says again.

"I know, it's not your fault. But I didn't ask her enough questions. I'm so tired, and my head is dizzy."

He strokes my hair back from my face. "I'm sure everything's going to be okay."

Having him here calms me instantly. He's like a warm salve on my exposed nerves. It's hard for me to focus too much on anything that's happening —emotions threaten to swamp me if I do. I'll panic and only make things worse, so I do my best to think about how wonderful it will be to go home and be in our own space as a family. Besides, it's most likely I'm anxious over nothing and Brody is perfectly fine.

We talk about Brody. About how I'm feeling. About Ben's work and how we'll fill the days now he's going to be at home with us.

Then Dr Siwa is back with Brody, and she tells us we're free to go home. They won't have all of the test results back for a few days, so we should call her if we have any concerns. We thank her and gather our things. Then I slip Brody into his car seat, and Ben carries it by the handle with one hand, pulling my suitcase along with the other. I'm left with the flowers after all, and ask one of the nurses for a cardboard box to carry them in.

At the car, it takes us a moment to get Brody strapped in properly, but I'm still nervous. Have we done it right? Did the car seat click the right way when we pushed it back into place? There's a lot going on in my head. Every thought has something to do with Brody. Nothing else makes its way into my consciousness. I have no space or energy for anything but him.

MY EYES BLINK OPEN, AND I FEEL RESTED FOR THE FIRST TIME IN days. The room is dark, but when I glance at the clock on my bedside table, it tells me it's four o'clock in the afternoon. We've been at home for most of the day. I've showered and changed and had a three-hour nap. I'm feeling almost human again. A surge of joy brings a smile to my face as I swing my legs out of bed and tramp to the kitchen.

Ben is in the dining room with the bassinet beside him. He's reading and offers me an ample smile when he sees me.

"Brody's still sleeping," he whispers.

I put the kettle on to boil and search the pantry for something to eat. I'm suddenly ravenously hungry. I find some chips, then a container of French onion dip in the fridge. It's the perfect carb-loaded treat, and I sit at the table to eat it while Ben tells me all about the book he's reading.

A knock at the door startles us both. We weren't expecting anyone this afternoon. When I pad to the door and open it, I find Gammy and Auntie Char standing there. Gammy's orthopaedic boot looks out of place beneath her blue linen skirt. I cry out and throw my arms around Charlotte. I haven't seen her in months and missed her more than I've realised.

"You're here!" I say.

She laughs and kisses my cheek. "I wouldn't miss this for the world. Let me in. I've got to see this perfect little cherub."

Her hair is cut in a fierce grey bob, with angles around her face. She has the bluest eyes I've ever seen, besides Gammy's, of course — they share the same shade. She bustles into the house, exclaiming all the while over the new couch, the art on the wall she hasn't seen before, and of course Brody as soon as she reaches him. Gammy follows, hobbling slowly behind us both.

"He's perfect! The spitting image of you when you were born," says Charlotte with tears in her eyes.

"I don't know how that's possible, since he's exactly like his father," I reply. "But thank you, Char." I wrap an arm around her waist and pull her close to my side.

"It must be your aura," she replies with a wink.

"Well, he certainly doesn't have my hair." Mine is a red and wavy, whereas Brody's is jet black and straight, like Ben's.

I sit on the couch with Charlotte and Gammy, catching up on everything that's happened — the birth, Brody's possible smile that was most likely wind, but I'm convinced means he's advanced for his age, and also what's been happening in Charlotte's life in New Zealand since I last saw her.

"I'm taking an art class," she says.

"That's a great idea. I'm sure you'll enjoy that."

"I've always loved photography. So painting is the next logical step."

Gammy huffs. "Please, you don't have an artistic bone in your body."

"Gammy!" I admonish. "No need to be rude."

"It's not rude if it's true."

Charlotte laughs. "It's okay. She always gets jealous when I have your attention." Charlotte reaches for Gammy's hand and squeezes it. "Don't be jealous, Virginia. You have her the rest of the time. Let me get some loving in."

Gammy's eyes roll. "I'm not jealous —how absurd. I'm seventy-seven years old, not some pimply-faced teenager."

The two of them always fill my heart with joy. I love seeing them together, even when they're bickering. They're like a picture-perfect postcard of how life in your seventies can look — stylish grey bobs, piercing blue eyes, red lipstick, fashionable but tasteful clothing choices in subdued summer colours.

"So, tell me how Brody is doing," says Gammy out of the blue.

It makes my heartbeat hitch for a moment because the reality of not knowing hits me again as though it's the first time. "Well, he seems fine. But the doctor ran some extra tests, just to make certain."

"Why?" asks Charlotte.

"Because his lips were a little bluish when she examined him. I'm not sure if there was something else that made her concerned because she didn't say. But she told me not to worry, so I'm doing my best to follow doctor's orders." By that I mean I'm not obsessively testing

Brody's vitals myself. I'm waiting to hear back from the paediatrician, although it's almost killing me.

Gammy's smile fades and her eyes narrow. "Yes, well, you're probably right. Most of the time these things turn out to be nothing at all."

"Of course, he looks perfectly healthy to me," replies Charlotte. Although I can sense the hesitation in her words.

Ben and I exchange a look. His eyes tell me not to read anything into it —mine tell him I'm worried. I swallow.

"I'm sure you're right. I have to think about something else, though, or I'll go crazy."

I walk to the bassinet, gazing down at the sleeping baby. He's beautiful and perfect, and my heart is wrapped up in him in a way I've never experienced before in my life. I can't contemplate anything being wrong with him —it's too much. He stirs, begins to cry, and I lift him quickly from the bassinet and carry him to the couch and begin to feed. His perfect fingers with their ten perfect crescent-shaped fingernails rest on my hand. I leave them there, studying them through a veil of tears.

Ben gets up to make a pot of tea for our guests.

"I know just the thing to distract you," says Gammy, settling herself deeper into the couch.

Charlotte arches an eyebrow. "I don't know if I like where this is going."

"Oh hush, you," retorts Gammy with a snort.

"Anything that can distract me would be very welcome," I say, fighting hard not to cry.

"I'm going to tell you a story, one I never thought I'd tell anyone. But I think the time has come. Many years ago, your Auntie Char and I boarded a ship bound for Australia called the *Strathaird*..."

Panic flits across Charlotte's face. "Gina...what are you doing?"

"What I should've done years ago."

"But there are things —"

Gammy rests a hand on Charlotte's arm. "I know, dear. Things I've kept secret for far too long. I want to get them off my chest, so to speak."

"We made a vow," begins Charlotte, her eyes glassy.

Gammy sighs. "They're all dead. What will it matter now?"

She tells me a story of a mother who sent them away, a father they didn't remember and a family they left behind. A tale of a luxury ship and four friends who found their way to each other throughout a journey into an unknown future. A farm school in Molong, New South Wales, where those four friends found a way to survive in a harsh and unforgiving environment. And a principal who couldn't be what they needed him to be — a protector, a confidant, a father.

She's interrupted by my mobile phone ringing. I set the ringer to the loudest volume because I didn't want to miss the doctor's call. I hand Brody to Ben and answer, breathless, my heart in my throat.

"Can I speak to Mia Sato, please?" says a woman's voice.

"This is Mia."

"Mia, it's Doctor Siwa. I have the results of the tests performed on Brody."

My tongue sticks to the roof of my mouth. I reach for Ben and grasp his shoulder with my hand until my knuckles are white against his blue shirt.

"Yes?"

"We've found an atrial septal defect. It's a birth defect in which there is a hole in the wall that divides the upper chambers of the heart."

My throat closes over. I feel the breath leave my lungs. I recognise the words she's saying —I've studied it all at some point in my medical journey. But it's escaping my recollection — my head is light again, and something squeezes like a rubber band around my chest. "How big?"

"We're not sure yet. The hole can vary in size and may close on its own or may require surgery."

"Surgery." My voice sounds empty as I repeat the word. It has no strength. My chest is full to bursting now, pain, sorrow, anxiety — my heart thuds with the fullness of it.

"We can't say for certain whether Brody will require surgery at this stage. What I recommend is that we monitor his symptoms for a few weeks, see how he goes, then we can decide whether medication or surgery are necessary. I'll need you to bring him in every day for testing for now so we can stay on top of it and make certain he's getting the care he requires."

Every day. To the hospital for testing. I nod mutely, but she can't hear that, of course, so I squeak my agreement, thank her, and hang up the phone. The others are staring at me, waiting for me to tell them the news.

I swallow, glancing at Ben. His eyes are deep dark pools of worry, fixed on mine.

"They said it's an atrial septal defect."

His nostrils flare and he stares down at our perfect boy. "Okay. That might not be so bad."

I nod. "Not sure if he'll need surgery yet. We have to take him for testing every day."

Gammy waves a hand in my direction. "In English for the rest of us, please?"

"Sorry, it's a hole in his heart."

"How can he have surgery? He's so tiny," adds Charlotte, pressing a hand to her mouth.

"Let's not jump to that conclusion yet," replies Ben, ever the steady voice of reason. "It might close on its own."

I inhale a deep breath. "That's right — we'll hope for the best."

"He's going to be fine," says Ben, leaning forward to kiss me. "Perfectly fine."

❧ 17 ❧

DECEMBER 1953

HARRY

Seagulls cawed beside the ship, soaring overhead then away again. The splash of water against the ship's hull drew Harry to lean over the side to watch. Water washed white against the bow, frothing and glimmering beneath the sun's harsh rays.

It was December, and the heat of summer was unbearable. Harry wasn't used to the strength with which the sun bore down on top of his head. His hair was hot to the touch as though he'd been baked in an oven, and his skin was reddened where he'd been burned a few times over recent days. And yet, he couldn't help smiling into the wind.

They were in Sydney Harbour. At least, that was what one of the German passengers had told him before heading back to his cabin to pack. Harry didn't need to pack. He'd done it already that morning, and his suitcase sat now at his feet. This was the day they'd finally disembark from the ship. He'd never wanted to leave when they first set out, but after six weeks, he was bored and fidgety. He shouldn't be bored, Mary kept reminding him. There was so much to explore on board the *Strathaird* that it seemed never-ending — there were eight decks, lifeboats, a cinema, smoking rooms, and of course the swimming pool and library. But he'd been fed a steady diet of delicious meals for so long now that energy fairly burst from every limb and each cell in his body. He simply couldn't sit still to watch another movie or read another book.

He longed to get his feet on the ground, to run and leap, to play and shout. Of course, they'd had plenty of room to gad about on the ship, but it wasn't the same as having the grass beneath his feet. How he missed climbing a tree to sit in its branches and ponder the minutes away alone, with no one to interrupt his thoughts. Or to fling his slingshot over his head, knocking bottles from a wall with his collection of hard, round stones. He wanted his two feet to be on solid land. Every part of him craved it.

On either side of the ship, there was land. Not like any land he'd ever seen before. There were short, stout cliffs in various shades of orange and brown. Waves beat against black rocks scattered at their base. Above the cliffs, it was green, but not in the lush way of England. It looked dry and baked, the way he felt himself.

The ocean glistened a blue that cooled him down just by looking. The ship passed through a narrow strait, then the harbour opened up into a calm blue ocean. The waves that'd crashed against the ship dissipated and a quiet descended, only broken by the call of gulls and the thrum of the wind in his ears.

"Can you believe it? We're almost there!" Mary stepped up beside him to rest her arms on the railing. Lottie lingered behind with her arms crossed over her chest.

Nerves pulled taut in Harry's gut. "Hmmm."

"What do you think it'll be like?"

He shrugged.

There was no way of knowing. This land looked so strange, so foreign. He'd tried a million times to picture in his head where they were going. All he had were the images in the brochures the women had shown them on the day they came to Barnardo's to sell the boys on the idea of a new start. There'd been black-and-white images of smiling children, ponies, and fruit trees. He tried his best to reconcile those images with what he saw now and couldn't make them stick.

Mary linked her arm through his. She trembled against his side.

"It'll be grand. That's what I think. Don't you recall the pamphlets?"

She agreed. "You're right."

"Well, there you have it, then."

They stood, side by side, in silence as the ship cruised through the harbour. Lottie sat by Mary's feet and played with a handful of marbles one of the other passengers had given her. The ship slipped through the calm waters as passengers gathered on deck, wearing their best clothes with caps and hats to shade them from the sun.

After a while, there were buildings dotted here and there around the shoreline on either side. Soon the structures clustered down along the water's edge, some several stories high. Small boats ducked and chugged across the surface of the harbour around and before the *Strathaird* like water striders. Then the Sydney Harbour Bridge rose like the back of an enormous reptile. Its curved hump arching gracefully over the deep blue water built a pool of excitement inside Harry, which welled up and up until his head was light and a grin spread across his lips.

"Wow," he whispered.

Mary's hand slipped into his and she squeezed. Lottie stood as well, pressed herself against the railing and held Mary's other hand. Before long, Davey joined them, resting his arms on top of the railing.

The enormous bridge loomed before them, and the ship made its way directly towards it. Harry's chest tightened at the sight. Would the *Strathaird* fit beneath those long steel beams? Or would its tall smokestacks be struck down to scatter in pieces along the deck? It seemed impossible, yet suddenly they were through and on the other side. Traffic hummed by on the bridge behind them, and Harry craned his neck to look up and watch as cars whizzed across it.

Crowds lined the edges of the marina. The ship pulled slowly up to dock at pier thirteen. Passengers bustled around the edges of the boat, waiting to disembark. Excitement buzzed and conversations hummed. All the while, Harry shuffled from one side of the top deck to the other, unable to stand still, but unwilling to go anywhere without his friends.

"We've got to stick together," he said.

Davey stood on tiptoe to attempt to peer over the crowd. "Let's not get separated."

So, all four of them clasped their suitcases in one hand, then reached out to take hold of one another by their other hand, Mary with Lottie, and Davey with Harry. They waited like that until their chaperones finally emerged and led the entire group of children from the ship. The chaos of disembarking made Harry's head spin. He didn't know where they were going or what was expected of them. But before long, they found themselves standing before a giant of a man. The chaperones skipped away without so much as a backwards glance and their small group stood clumped together, waiting for some indication of what was to come.

The man's voice boomed, shouting that his name was Mr Forrest, and for the children to follow him. So, they did. People shoved them one way and the other as they hurried about their business. There was so much noise, it was hard to hear whenever Mr Forrest addressed them with a no-nonsense, barking style. Before long, Harry had to let go of Davey and Mary's hands. Davey clung close by him as best he could, but someone called his name, and he was separated from the group. Harry shouted after him, his face red, but Forrest grabbed his arm and pulled him away. Davey was gone, part of another group that was headed in a different direction.

It couldn't be happening. It must be some kind of mistake. They'd both been travelling to the same place. Why was Davey taken by another group? Surely the adults would fix it all up in a moment. Harry kept walking, but his attention was fixed on the place where he'd last seen his friend. That space was filled with a group of scared-looking girls in white pinafores with sashes tied around their middles. There was no sign of Davey.

Mary and Lottie followed behind, still connected. Lottie's face was pale. Harry wished he could offer her some comfort, but he was shivery and hollow inside. Besides that, his legs were all wobbly and he found it took all of his attention to simply walk in a straight line and keep pace with their leader.

One last glance over his shoulder showed the ship, tall and proud, still docked where it'd landed. He wished it goodbye with a hurried thought, then they moved on, pushing along in the line where nurses and doctors waited to check them with stethoscopes and thermometers.

What followed was a whirlwind tour of a zoo, which surprised the entire group and shifted their nervous tension, replacing it with amazement and excitement. There were elephants, emus, koalas, and monkeys. Everywhere they went, there was something even more exotic for the children to exclaim over. By the time they'd hurried their way through the park, the anxiety Harry had felt over his new life was replaced with a burning anticipation.

By the time they were seated on a train bound for their new home in Molong, Harry's eyes had drifted shut. He blinked and yawned, then leaned against the window. Davey hadn't shown up. He kept expecting to see his friend on the train platform, or while they waited in the office for the train to arrive. But he hadn't come. Harry asked Mr Forrest about it, and the man shouted something about keeping their luggage close by them at all times, then shook his head.

"Sorry, lad." And that was that.

The train clacked and rattled along the rail lines as it climbed through a dark and shadowy mountain range. Across from him, a boy stared at the ceiling, glassy-eyed. Mary and Lottie were seated on the next row. Lottie's head lolled against Mary's shoulder while Mary leaned on the window, her eyes shut but still flickering open every few moments.

Harry sighed. They'd made it to Australia and were only hours away from their new home. Mr Forrest had announced to the group at the station that he was their new principal, that they were to do as he said without asking questions first. The group by then were so tired, they could do no more than nod in mute acceptance. A few of the smaller children cried after boarding the train, but were comforted by some of the older ones. Some children lay on the bench seats, staring into the distance red-eyed. It seemed they'd been parted from their siblings at the docks and their groups whisked in different directions. Would they ever see their brothers or sisters again?

For the first time in weeks, he experienced a pang of regret over all he'd left behind. He was tired, anxious, and even though other children sat so close to him, he felt alone in the world. His mother was gone — Mr Wilson was thousands of miles away across a vast and unforgiving ocean. Everything familiar had been replaced by a rapid succession of foreign and strange experiences that, although exciting, brought an intense exhaustion as adrenaline spiked through his veins and was gone again as quickly as it'd come.

He shifted in place, lying down on the seat and spreading out across the open space, his cheek cold on the vinyl cover. He considered again what his future held and whether he'd live to see his homeland again. Then his eyes fell shut and he drifted into a deep and dreamless sleep.

❧ 18 ❧

DECEMBER 1953

MARY

The fire crackled in the stove, and Mary bent over it to lift the kettle free. Its whistling stopped and she set it on the kitchen table, steam rising from its blackened spout. She glanced up in surprise at a loud bang overhead, followed by a shout and the sound of running feet. Dust loosed from the ceiling, falling in wafting clouds around her. She grimaced, sneezed, and her brow furrowed. What could be going on up there?

In a moment, Lottie scrambled down the stairs, her feet barely touching each step as she ran. She skidded to a stop beside Mary, moving behind her and taking a hold of her nightgown from the back. Mary yawned, covering her mouth with a fist.

"What are you running from? Was it the mouse again? You know you're too big a girl to still be fearful of a wee mouse, Lottie."

Lottie whimpered. "It's Clem."

Mary's stomach flipped over inside her. "What did you do?"

"I didn't do a thing. He thinks I stole his pound note. I didn't, I promise you. I was only sleeping."

Mary had left Lottie in bed a few minutes earlier to come downstairs and stoke the fire in the stove and get the kettle boiling for breakfast. She knew her sister well enough to believe her — Lottie would never steal money from Clem, the latest man Mam had brought into their lives. She was terrified of Mam's boyfriend ever since Mam brought him home the first time and he'd threatened to tan Lottie's hide if she didn't go upstairs and leave them be.

"Never mind. I won't let him harm you." Mary straightened herself up to her full height and lifted her chin. Clem would have to go through her if he intended to lay a hand on her sister.

The steps grunted beneath his weight as he shuffled slowly down them. He wore nothing but a pair of undershorts and Mam's house robe, which swirled around his hairy body with each step he took.

"Come back here, you blasted guttersnipe!"

Mary swallowed. Lottie tucked herself right up against Mary's back, doing her best to be invisible behind her sister.

"Would you like a cup of tea, Clem?" asked Mary in a high-pitched voice.

She cleared her throat as he glared at her, his eyes seeming to bore a hole right through her to where Lottie cowered, shivering.

He growled with his hands clenched into fists by his sides. "Where's that little urchin you call a sister?"

Mary pressed a wobbly smile to her face. "I can add cream if you like. Mam bought some home yesterday, so you're welcome to it."

His piggish eyes narrowed. Red-rimmed, they studied her face. There was a darkness behind them that made her shudder. He stepped closer, then closer again.

"You didn't answer my question."

"What do you want with her?"

"None of your blighted business, you scamp!" he snarled. "But if you must know, she stole from me. She's a little thief, and if you take up for her, you're just as bad as she is, and you'll cop it the same."

Mary crossed her arms over her chest to stop them from shaking. "She's not a thief. If you're missing money, likely you lost it."

He got down in her face and sneered, revealing a set of yellowing teeth. The stink of his breath hit her like a sledgehammer. "I nabbed a pound note. Had it all ready to go for a bet and a pint down the pub today. Now it's gone. Your mam hasn't seen it. That leaves the two of you. Now, speak up or you're for it."

He slammed one fist into his open palm, making Mary jump.

Mary inhaled a quick breath. "I'll help you look for it. Lottie and me both will."

As the words left her mouth, Lottie took the chance to peep out from her hiding place. Clem's eyes widened at the sight of her.

"There she is!" he shouted, lunging for her.

He grabbed her with one meaty hand, his fingers clenched tight around the top of her arm. Lottie yelped in pain, her voice rising to a squeal as it yowled from her lungs.

Lottie's cry sent a bolt of rage running through Mary's body. She reached for Clem's arm, set her teeth around his flesh, and bit down as hard as she could.

MARY WOKE, SWEAT BEADING ON HER FOREHEAD. SHE STIFLED A cry. Then, as her eyes flickered open, she scanned her surroundings, doing her best to comprehend. Where was she? On a train. The rhythmic clacking of the tracks beneath the vehicle alerted her to that. One arm was numb. She glanced down to see Lottie's head resting comfortably there. She shifted to set her arm free, clenching and unclenching her fist as a tingling ran through her veins, bringing life back to the limb.

Then it all came to her in a rush. They were in Australia, headed to the farm in Molong where she and Lottie would live. Nerves tramped over her like a herd of cattle, taking her breath from her lungs for one brief moment.

The train squealed on the tracks, jolting Lottie out of her sleep. She rubbed her eyes and grasped for Mary's hand. Children all around the compartment were waking. They sat up on the bench seats, on the floor, wherever they'd found a place to lie. The air had cooled since they left Sydney, and goose bumps prickled along Mary's bare arms.

Mr Forrest strode through the carriage on tree-trunk legs. His enormous arms waved as he barked out orders.

"Line up here —we're getting off at Molong station. Gather your things, please!"

When the train stopped, they all stood in a raggedy line down the centre aisle and filed out one after the other, carrying their belongings as best they could. The biggest kids helped the smaller ones with their luggage. Harry followed Mary and Lottie from the train. They stood in a clump on the platform as the train chugged away. Harry missed having Davey by his side to tell him things would be okay or make a joke to let him know it was all right.

"Follow me!" called Mr Forrest, heading towards one end of the platform.

The children followed in dribs and drabs, some still rubbing the sleep from their eyes.

They'd landed in a small town. Smaller than Mary had expected it to be. She saw only a few scattered buildings. Beyond them, sunlight glowed orange against the dark horizon.

Mr Forrest led them to a corner. Across the street was a two-storey building with the words *Mason's Arm Pub* etched above the doorway. It was a grand old building with a wide verandah wrapping around the second level and a hitching post for horses outside.

A canvas-covered truck waited nearby. A woman climbed out of the cab and waved to Mr Forrest, who ushered the children towards her. He ordered them into the back of the truck, and they climbed in to sit along two long bench seats. The seats were hard, and when the canvas flap at the back swung shut, it was dark inside the back of the truck. The engine revved to life and Mary reached for Lottie's hand. Her sister scuttled closer to her, pressed up against her side. Lottie's thin frame shook, and Mary rubbed circles on her hand with a thumb to calm her. But she didn't say anything — she couldn't bring herself to speak. None of the children did. They sat in silence, backs stiff and straight.

Harry sat directly across from Mary. As the truck growled down the road, Mary exchanged a glance with him. Her own furrowed brow elicited a warm smile from him. It soothed her nerves, and she inhaled a long, slow breath, her eyes fixed on his.

The truck turned onto a bumping, winding road. Then finally it ground to a stop, and the canvas flap was pulled back.

"Out you get," came Mr Forrest's booming voice through the gathering light of dawn.

The last pale stars clutched at the shifting darkness. Rays of sunshine reached across the cavernous sky. Mary's head swung one way, then the other, as she took in her new surroundings in silence.

They'd pulled up at what looked to be a kind of village. Buildings clustered together on a flat and grassy landscape. Joined by winding dirt roads, each building was ringed with wispy evergreens. In front of them stood a two-storey house, and the woman from the truck shooed them inside, where she introduced herself.

"I'm Mrs Forrest, and this is our home. Welcome to Fairbridge Farm School."

She poured hot chocolate into mugs and handed it around to the children, who drank as quickly as the scorching liquid would allow. Mary touched the drink to her lips, then took a gentle sip. The chocolate was milky and sweet and soothed her empty belly.

The group stood around, sipping their drinks and chattering quietly amongst themselves. Mary, Lottie, and Harry kept to themselves, their eyes asking questions their mouths didn't dare to utter while Mrs Forrest hovered so close.

What came next?

Where would they sleep that night?

Who would take care of them?

There were so many unanswered questions. Mr Forrest was gone, and Mrs Forrest didn't seem inclined to share anything more than she already had.

Soon, a tall, gangly boy appeared at the doorway. Mrs Forrest offered him a nod, then she pushed Harry in his direction. Mary quickly waved a goodbye at Harry, then he was gone, trotting after the boy.

The rest of the children left in much the same manner. A scruffy child with a lopsided haircut and tattered, too-small clothing would appear in the doorway, and two or three more children would leave with them.

Finally, it was Mary and Lottie's turn. A tall girl with knobbly knees poking out below a well-worn pair of shorts, a shirt that pulled tight across her torso and a crooked fringe with short-cropped hair waited in the doorway as Mrs Forrest ushered the girls in her direction.

Mary pondered the question of where her suitcase had gotten to.

It'd been in the back of the truck, and she'd climbed down with it, but Mr Forrest had told them all to leave their suitcases there while they went in the house. Now she seemed naked without it, after so many weeks with it by her side. Perhaps someone would bring it to her room for her. She wished she could fetch her cardigan out of it; the chill morning air made her shiver.

As she held Lottie's hand and jogged along after the girl through the gathering dawn, Mary's shivering travelled into the depths of her soul. They were so far from home. Mam didn't know where they were or how to find them, did she? And if they wanted to go home, if they didn't like it here, there was nothing they could do. She knew that now. They'd travelled such a long way, there was no going back. What had they done?

❦ 19 ❦

DECEMBER 1953

HARRY

"This is Brown Cottage," said the tall boy, leading him through a doorway and into a simple structure. It was a timber building that stood on brick piers with a red corrugated roof. Inside, there were large square open windows along the walls of a dormitory, letting in the cool morning air.

Harry followed him inside and took in his surroundings with a sweeping gaze. It'd been a long day of travel and it wasn't over yet. Everything was foreign to him, he took it all in with trepidation, his gut in a tight knot.

"I'm Devon, but you can call me Dev."

"Like the devil!" shouted a boy who looked a little younger than Harry, perched on the end of a bunk against one wall.

The beds were made of metal tubing. Harry could see a diamond wire mesh beneath each thin mattress holding it in place. There were no pillows on the beds, but each was angled slightly upwards at one end. A small table on the far side of the room held an oil lamp that emitted a warm glow. Harry looked around. The lamp seemed to be the only lighting apart from the weak sunshine glimmering through the windows.

Dev rolled his eyes and waved a hand dismissively at the boy. "And that's Max. Ignore him —we all do."

Max grinned and leapt down from the top bunk to the floor below, pushing his thumbs through the belt loops around his thin waist. "Come on, I'll show you 'round."

Dev nodded his agreement, and Max beckoned the way forward. "This is the bedroom. That empty bed over there is yours."

There were boys everywhere, scattered throughout the cottage. It was hard to say how many since they were all in motion, but Harry guessed at about eight or ten. Some were in a half state of dress between ill-fitting and unmatched pyjamas and threadbare, stained work clothes. Everything they wore seemed to be either khaki, grey or blue, and even the girls he'd seen throughout the camp so far wore the standard shirt and shorts combination.

Boys scampered barefoot past them and out the door. Most paid no attention to Harry, but a few made eye contact, and one or two offered a brief smile. All had similar lopsided, scruffy haircuts. None wore shoes, and all had various cuts, scrapes, bruises, and stains covering their exposed skin. Every boy was bony, with knobbly knees beneath his shorts and skinny arms poking from his sleeves.

"The village is made up of fifteen cottages, like this one, with up to fifteen kids per cottage. Then there's Nuffield Hall, which is where we eat our meals. It houses the bakery and so on. In the village, we've got a dairy, hospital, school, principal's house, staff quarters, laundry, work-shops, chapel, sports fields, chook pen, piggery, slaughterhouse, plus shearing sheds, grain silos and a garage." Max walked backwards through an internal doorway as he spoke. "I'll take you to the Hall soon as the bell rings for grub. In here's the locker room, and back there's the matron's quarters — she's the cottage mother. You'll meet her soon enough."

He stopped and waited for Harry to catch up. They walked through the doorway and into a room with open lockers and bench seating. Dirty clothing hung from shelves and lay on the floor. There was a closed door that no doubt hid the matron's quarters, then beyond that, Harry spotted a kitchen.

"There's our kitchen and common room. Every cottage has one. We eat lunch and tea together here sometimes if we're not in the Hall."

Harry poked his head through the doorway. A black Victorian-style iron range stood in the centre of the room, along with a split timber dining table and sturdy chairs. He considered briefly whether he'd stepped into a time machine by mistake and been transported back several generations.

"Well, I never..." he muttered to himself.

❦

THE NEXT MORNING, WHEN THE BELL RANG, HARRY WAS SEATED ON his new bunk bed, shivering, and wishing his suitcase would show up so he could find a jumper or something warm to wear. His slingshots were gone as well. Everything he'd packed to bring with him had been in that bag.

"Where's my blasted suitcase?" he whispered.

A boy from the bunk next door answered him. "I don't know. Mine's not here either. And I don't like it one bit."

"Me neither. To think, all that luxury on the ship, and now this..." Harry waved a hand at the half-made beds, each with only one thin blanket, the scattered clothing and the open windows where a frigid breeze could blow through unhindered.

"Come on, you layabouts!" called Max, poking his head through the front door. "Time for breakfast. We eat in the Hall each morning. Forrest shuts the door, so if you're late, you miss out."

Harry rose with a sigh and followed Max. They trotted along a dusty path between evergreen trees, short, pale shrubs and in the midst of scattered groups of children, all headed in the same direction.

Where was Mary in all of this? What did she think of their change of circumstance? She'd begun to look happy on the ship. She wasn't the pale, skinny street urchin she'd been that first day he came across her at the Fairbridge house. She'd grown taller and fuller. Her sister had as well. They seemed like different girls. He hated to imagine them with their shining blonde locks cut in the short, off-kilter style the girls at Molong all sported.

"How long have you lived here?" asked Harry, catching up to their guide.

"Since I was four. They told me we were going on a picnic."

"How old are you now?" Harry jogged alongside, then slowed his pace to match Max's.

"Ten."

He didn't look ten. More like eight in Harry's opinion. Still, he seemed sturdy enough.

"When will you leave?" Harry asked. How long would they all be forced to stay in this godforsaken place?

"Sixteen or so. You'll attend school with the rest of us until about fifteen. The primary school is at the back of the village. That's where you'll start. Then you'll be a trainee and learn how to farm. After that, you'll be sent to a farm to work for a farmer."

"We're all to be farmers?" asked Harry. He'd known it was a farm school, but hadn't fully understood what now seemed a stark certainty — his dreams of working with books, in an office, would never come to pass if he couldn't finish school. He was to be a labourer, a farm worker.

"Of course. Farm labourers, anyway," shot back Max with a puzzled look in Harry's direction. "What'd ya think — you were coming here to study ballet?" He laughed to himself as he climbed the steps to a long building. A clamour emitted through the doorway when he pulled it open. "Welcome to Nuffield."

The noise in the dining hall was deafening. Fifty or so children scurried about, finding their seats at rows of tables. More filed in through the large timber door every moment. Max led Harry to one of the tables. Each table had a strip of stained and wrinkled linoleum along the centre. Tin plates and bowls were scattered along each side of the table, clearly thrown in place by someone with little regard for order.

"This one's for Brown Cottage boys," said Max, sitting on one of the long bench seats. Harry sat opposite him on another long bench seat.

One by one, seven other boys found their way to the same wooden table, and the rest of the group settled at the other tables. It was easy for Harry to pick out the other children he'd travelled with on board the *Strathaird*. Their clothing was newer, tidier, and of higher quality with a variety of colours and cuts, unlike that worn by the Fairbridge kids.

At the end of the hall stood one long, horizontal table. Behind it sat the adults, including Mr and Mrs Forrest. Their table was covered with a white tablecloth, china plates and cups, silverware, and glasses. Girls hurried from the kitchen with steaming plates of food to set before them.

Devon sat at one end of the Brown Cottage table, the tallest of the group, and the children on either side sat in order of height with the smallest boy at the other end. Max disappeared, then returned soon after, hefting a large steel bowl. He carried it down the line of boys, spooning porridge into each individual tin bowl. Another boy followed him with a hard piece of bread slathered in butter and honey, and still another boy trotted after him with mugs of milk for each child.

A buxom woman in full skirts waddled to the head of the table. She sat at the end of their table where it was set with a white tablecloth, china plates and silverware. A teenaged girl brought her a covered tray and placed it on the table in front of her, then flicked open a napkin to set in the woman's lap. The tray held a plate with strips of crispy bacon, soft-boiled eggs, and toast, along with a bowl of cereal and a small pot of tea, with a china cup and saucer beside it.

The principal, Mr Forrest, stood to read a prayer of thanksgiving. When he finished, all the children chanted, "For what we are about to receive, may the Lord make us truly thankful, through Jesus Christ's sake. Amen."

Harry's stomach grumbled and he stared at the cold, watery porridge in his bowl with a hint of suspicion. It'd been months since he'd eaten the gruel at Barnardo's. His system and taste buds had grown accustomed to the finer life. His stomach dropped as the realisation dawned that his time of living in opulence was well and truly over.

※※※

HARRY'S CURIOSITY OVER HOW HIS LIFE WOULD LOOK AT THE Fairbridge Farm School didn't take long to be satiated. After breakfast, most of the children marched off to different parts of the village, according to Max they all had work to do. He and Max were assigned to the garage. He still wasn't sure exactly what they expected him to do at the garage, and since there were no adults on duty there to tell him, he wandered around and did his best to look busy.

The bigger kids were hard at work on an old bus and seemed to be tinkering with its engine. The garage was an old, weathered timber shed with a rusted tin roof. It also housed two tractors, several pieces of farming equipment that Harry didn't recognise, the canvas-covered truck that'd brought the children to the farm the day before, several cars in various states of repair, a few rusted-looking motorcycles, bicycles, and gardening implements.

Harry had never looked inside an engine, let alone fixed one before, so he thought it best if he stayed out of the way. Devon stood bent over, his torso half hidden from view by the side of the bus. Harry watched out of the corner of his eye, curious about the boy who stood two heads taller than him and had thick, muscular arms on full display, as he'd taken off his shirt to work.

"How old is he?" Harry asked Max.

Max shrugged. "Fourteen, I guess. He'll be a trainee soon."

"What does that mean exactly?"

"It means he'll be leaving school for good and learning how to manage a farm. Then, it'll be goodbye Devon. All the better for the rest of us." Max lay back in the dirt and picked at a piece of grass.

"I thought we were supposed to finish school and get a good education. At least, that's what the ladies who told us about this place said."

Max laughed out loud. "Yeah, not gonna happen. If you're as lucky as the rest of us, you'll be able to write a letter to your sweetheart by the time you leave school, but not much more than that. Education isn't exactly a priority for them when it comes to us Fairbridge kids. They want us for farming, so that's what they push us into."

They lazed in the bleached grass outside the open garage doorway surrounded by rusted machinery and pieces of farm equipment or the remnants of engines long since fallen silent. Harry scanned the landscape through half-lidded eyes. Flat farmland stretched away from them in every direction. Brown and dusty, it baked under the relentless heat of the sun. Trees clustered in clumps, their leaves dust covered. Bent and squat, they seemed to shrink away from the pale blue sky so bright that Harry could barely look up for a single moment without blinking. It was a harsh land, so dry that the blades of grass at his feet crackled when he crushed them between his fingertips as Max prattled on about an upcoming athletics carnival, and how he planned on winning the fifty-yard dash this time around with a training schedule that involved regular sprints throughout the day. Just as soon as this blasted heat let up.

Max was thrown into shadow, making him sit bolt upright. Harry squinted to find Devon standing over them, hands pressed to his hips. His face was masked by the light behind him, but Harry recognised impatience in his stance.

Devon levelled a kick at Max's leg. The boy winced. "Get up, lazy bones. I'm not doing everything by myself."

Max climbed cautiously to his feet. "Isn't that how you like it best?"

Devon loomed over Max, and his eyes narrowed. "Might as well be, with useless louts like you on service with me." He clouted Max over the back of the head. Max ducked, but not far enough, and Devon's fist sent him sprawling. Devon leapt on him then, striking him over and over in the stomach, the jaw, the nose. Blood spurted from Max's nose, and he began to sob.

"Hey!" shouted Harry, bounding to his feet. Anger heated him from within like fire in a pot-bellied stove.

Devon's gaze shifted to Harry's face as he stepped away from Max. "Yeah, you got something to say, newbie?" Max scuttled like a crab out of Devon's reach and behind a burned-out car chassis overgrown with grass.

Harry had spent most of his life in institutions. He'd known boys like Devon, and he understood the dynamics of the situation. If he didn't take a stand now, he'd regret it for the rest of his time at the Fairbridge farm. He'd be known as a coward, a wuss, the kind of boy who could be pushed around. Besides, he hated the way Devon had bullied Max, even if somewhere deep down, he knew Max should've been pulling his weight. The beating reminded him of the countless other bullies he'd faced in his short life.

"Leave him alone," he snarled, squaring his stance and readying himself as heat and adrenaline thrummed through his veins. His heart beat impossibly loud in his ears, every one of his senses magnified.

The punch, when it came, seemed out of the blue. It struck in him the jaw and sent him staggering backwards as stars danced before his vision.

"You've gotta learn your place around here, newbie." Devon shook his head, the briefest smile lingering over his lips before he spun on his heel and marched back to the bus.

Harry pressed a fingertip to his lip, and it came away covered in blood. He straightened his back, stuck out his chin and watched Devon retreat into the shadows of the garage. Max rushed over to him with his eyes red-rimmed.

"You okay?" he asked, wiping the blood from his nose with the back of his hand.

Harry dipped his head. "You?"

"Fine."

Harry inhaled a quick breath. "Seems like he's got a temper."

Max tipped his head to one side, his lips pulling into a wide grin. "I guess he's not the only one, huh? You're crazy. You'll fit in bloody well around here."

Harry noticed the pull of swelling in his lips as he smiled. He fingered the place gingerly.

"Thanks," added Max. "For stepping in. Not sure how long he'd have kept it up." He grimaced, pressing a hand to his rib cage.

Harry shrugged. "No bother."

Max threw an arm around Harry's shoulder as they walked back into the garage together. "Come on, mate. Let me show you around the inside of an engine."

❧ 20 ❧

DECEMBER 1953

MARY

A kookaburra perched on a tree branch nearby eyed Mary and Lottie as they worked in the garden. In the distance, a crow cawed. The kookaburra took flight, flapping away over the sun-bleached grasses where sheep grazed idly, their woolly coats clipped and dusty.

Her bare knees smarted, buried as they were in the rocky soil. She wore the khaki uniform of shorts and shirt that all of the Fairbridge children wore. She'd found them on her bed that morning after a cold shower that stole the breath from her lungs and woke her up quick smart. A frantic search revealed her new clothing from London was gone. Her suitcase full of all of the wonderful things they'd purchased on their trip to town all those weeks earlier had never made it to the cottage from the back of the truck. Neither had Lottie's. The loss left a gaping hole in Mary's heart — she'd been so excited to own a suitcase full of beautiful new clothing, things she'd never thought she would have. She could only hope the clothes she'd taken off that morning would show up again, freshly washed and pressed. Although she had her doubts, given the state of dress of every other child at the farm.

She plucked a weed from the garden bed, tossed it aside and wiped the sweat from her brow with the back of her hand. Beside her, Lottie pushed a trowel into the dry ground, turning it over to reveal the dark brown soil beneath. She glanced up at Mary, streaks of dirt on her forehead and cheeks.

Mary smiled and reached out to wipe Lottie's cheek, but left a darker streak of mud instead. "Oh, sorry. I made it worse."

Lottie rolled her eyes. "Never mind. I'm covered from top to bottom."

"Me too. And I've never been so hot in all my life." Mary sighed as a trickle of sweat wound its way down her spine. "To think we were frozen to our depths only a few short months ago, longing for some sunshine."

"Well, we've got sunshine," replied Lottie with a giggle, swatting away a dozen flies that'd landed on her the moment she was still.

"We certainly do."

A blond-headed boy drove a horse and cart up to the edge of the fenced garden. He halted the horse, then he and another boy leapt down, pulled shovels from the back of the cart, and shovelled manure from a towering heap in the cart to a pile at one end of the garden bed. She watched as she worked, wondering at their wiry, tanned frames. They were all that way — the Fairbridge kids. Wonky haircuts, wiry tanned limbs, freckled faces. Finished, they threw their shovels into the wagon. As one of the boys spun around to climb onto the driving seat, he winked at Mary, then headed back in the direction from which he'd come. Her face flamed at the attention, and she forgot for a moment what she was doing as the horse plodded off, dragging the cart and the boys behind it.

"Stop your lollygagging! Get back to work," shouted a tall, wiry girl, her eyes boring holes into Mary.

Mary arched an eyebrow but returned to her weeding, waving at flies listlessly every few seconds. The flies were relentless— that was the first thing she'd learned after sunrise. They were inescapable, like a never-ending swarm that followed her wherever she went. Inside the cottage, in the dining hall, outside in the garden—it made little difference.

Already she'd learned to wave a hand in front of her face regularly to dislodge the ones buzzing around her eyes, nose, and mouth. The rest she left alone unless they stung her, which the largest ones seemed intent on doing. The sting was painful too, and it didn't fade until long after the fly was gone. She did her best to swat those ones. Lottie was already deathly afraid of them and had run circles in a panic the last time one landed on her small, pale leg.

Her younger sister adjusted her position where she sat, clutching at the too-loose shorts that kept shimmying down her hips every time she moved.

"My knees hurt," she whinged.

Mary shushed her.

"But I don't want to sit in the mud, and my nose is getting sunburnt —I can feel it. Besides, my head is kind of funny, wobbly or something. Can't we go back inside?"

"What do you mean, your head is wobbly?" asked Mary with a frown. She threw another weed on the growing pile.

"I don't know. I can't think properly, and my eyes hurt." Lottie whimpered and pressed muddy fingertips to her temples.

Mary scanned the garden, looking for the wiry girl who seemed to be in charge of the group. The girl wasn't in sight, so Mary led Lottie over to the side of the garden shed and sat her down in the shade of the tin roof where it hung over the edge of the shed. Lottie leaned her back against the shed's wall with a sigh. Mary fanned her face with both hands.

"Wait here. I'll get you a cup of water."

By the time Mary returned from the kitchen with a cup of water, Lottie's colour had improved. She gulped down the water and offered Mary a smile.

"Better?"

"Much," she replied.

Mary helped her sister stand. The girl in charge was back and watched them through narrowed eyes, her hands pressed to her thin hips. Long, spindly legs stuck out of too-short shorts, and her kneecaps knocked together as she walked. She marched in their direction and hissed when she came close.

"Get back to work before the gardener, Crew, sees ya. He's coming this way, and you won't wanna attract his attention if you know what's good for you."

The girl kept walking as though she hadn't spoken a word to them, making her way down the length of the garden and shouting a word here and there to the girls who squatted in the dirt. Mary shoved the cup into her shorts pocket and hurried Lottie towards their place in the garden. But it was too late. A man strode from behind the garden shed and shouted at them.

"Hey, you two layabouts. Come here!"

Mary hesitated, drew a deep breath, then glanced over her shoulder. He stared directly at them. There was no mistaking whom he'd addressed. He was a tall, lanky man with short-cropped brown hair. A cigarette dangled between thin lips, and small piggish eyes glinted black in the sunlight beneath a battered wide-brimmed hat. He beckoned her over. She took Lottie by the hand and led her sister slowly to him, taking his measure as she went. Her experience living in council housing, navigating the streets of London's East End virtually on her own since she could walk, gave her a sense of people. And she didn't like the look of him.

"Yes, sir?" she said, being sure to keep a respectful tone to her voice.

"Why are you two shirking? I saw you there, sitting in the shade like lady muck, sipping water while everyone else works."

He leaned forward, and the ash from the tip of his cigarette narrowly missed landing on Mary's nose as it fell.

"We weren't..." She drew a step backwards, pulling Lottie with her. Crew reached out and grabbed her by the shoulder as he leaned down, hauling her up to his level.

"Don't you dare talk back to me. Do you hear?"

She nodded, mute.

"I asked you a question."

"My sister felt faint. I thought it would do her good..."

"You thought you deserved to rest when you've not long since started. Let me show you how it is around here, little girl. Every last one of you needs to learn the same lesson when you get here. All start out lazy and irresponsible. But you soon learn." His eyes gleamed as he spoke.

He unbuckled his belt, and Mary took a step backwards. Her heart leapt into her throat as he removed the belt from the loops around his waist in one quick flick. She turned to run, but his gravelly voice stopped her in her tracks.

"Move one more inch and I'll make sure your sister won't be able to stand tomorrow."

Mary spun to face him. "Don't you touch my sister."

He glowered with his lips pulled back into a snarl. "What did you say?"

She pushed Lottie behind her, blocking her sister from his wrath with her own thin frame. "I said, don't touch her."

His face turned a dark shade of red and one weathered claw clenched around Mary's forearm. She released her hold on Lottie as he dragged her through the garden. The first slap of the belt strap against her thighs stung. The next forced a grunt from her lungs. Soon, the pain all melded into one long ache that she refused to acknowledge. She simply stood, bent over, while he landed blow after blow against the back of her bare legs.

Finally, he stopped, wheezing from the effort. She straightened and faced him, her eyes bright and clear, her mouth firmly shut. She crossed her arms over her chest and regarded him with as much disdain as she could muster. He seemed taken aback and unsure of how to respond as he tucked his belt through the loops on his pants.

"Now, you mind what you're told and no more lazing about, or I'll take it out on that sister of yours." He puffed as he fastened the belt in place.

"Don't touch my sister," she said again. This time her voice was cold and low.

He startled, then his eyes narrowed. "Do you need another reminder of who's in charge here?"

She stood tall and straight, unflinching under his gaze, her chin jutting out.

His breathing slowly returned to normal as he watched her. Then, with a brief nod at his own sense of victory, he spun on his heel and marched in the direction of the garage. Mary watched him go. The stinging on the backs of her legs made her gasp, although she wasn't going to let him see how much he'd hurt her.

Lottie rushed to Mary's side and threw her arms around her sister, sobbing. "I'm sorry, Mary. I'm sorry."

Mary patted Lottie's head. "It's fine, I'm not hurt. It wasn't your fault."

"I shouldn't have sat in the shade. You were only trying to help me. I'm sorry."

She grasped both of Lottie's cheeks gently between her hands and stared into her sister's tear-filled blue eyes. "Don't worry about me. I'm all right. See? Perfectly fine. I'm here to take care of you, not the other way around."

She pulled Lottie to her chest and patted her back slowly, in a circular motion, as Lottie cried into Mary's shirt. "Hush now, Lottie. We don't want them to see us cry. We're stronger than that."

Lottie snuffled into Mary's shirt, then pulled away, her tears already drying. "Yes, Mary. I'll be strong, I promise."

The knock-kneed girl wandered closer, eyeing Mary's legs. "I told you to keep out of his way. You'll need to put some iodine and a wet cloth on those legs of yours—he really gave you a walloping. Come on, I'll take you back to the cottage."

"But don't we have to keep working?" asked Mary.

The girl shrugged. "I won't tell anyone. Besides, Forrest will be upset if he sees those bruises, and Crew will make sure you get the blame for it somehow. Like I said, you don't want to get into Crew's line of sight, and if you cause him trouble with Forrest, that's exactly what you'll do. If you make an enemy of him now, you'll regret it."

Mary smiled. "Thanks, I think some salve would help. It burns..."

"I'm sure it does. Follow me."

Mary and Lottie fell into step beside the girl, trotting to keep up with her long strides. "I'm Faith, by the way. I'm the head girl at Evelyne Cottage."

"Pleased to meet you. I'm Mary and this is my sister Lottie."

"I know," replied Faith. "I really hope you two won't cause me this much trouble every day."

"No, we won't," promised Mary.

"Good to hear. You were impressive. No tears, not even a whimper." Faith smiled at Mary.

"Thanks," replied Mary. "Not my first time."

Faith grinned. "I think you'll fit in just fine around here. Although, try to stay out of Crew's way. Most of them aren't so bad apart from our cottage mother. Keep your head down when she's around as well."

"Thanks for the warning," replied Mary.

Lottie had her thumb firmly stuck in her mouth as they walked and she'd fallen silent, the way she often did when she was upset. Mary hated that she couldn't protect Lottie from all of this. But at least she'd managed to keep Crew's attention on herself rather than the hiding he'd promised to Lottie. She wouldn't have been able to control her rage if he'd thrashed Lottie the way he'd done to her.

Back at the cottage, Mary lay stomach down on her bunk while Faith found the first aid kit. It was comprised of a tin box with a few Band-Aids, a bandage, and some iodine. Faith applied the tincture, then wet a cloth which she lay on Mary's legs. She waved goodbye and told them to get some rest and stay out of sight until the others returned that afternoon.

Lottie climbed into Mary's bed and faced the wall, her thumb still in her mouth. Mary inched closer, wrapping her arms around her sister and holding her close. Lottie sniffled softly, but didn't speak. Mary stroked her hair with one hand and blinked back her own tears, the pain intensifying as her adrenaline abated. She'd be bruised in the morning, but would have to hide that fact from the staff on site in case it caused trouble for Crew.

"It's almost Christmas. Did you remember?" said Lottie all of a sudden. "I wonder what Mam is doing."

Mary swallowed hard, then dashed the tears from her eyes with the back of her hand. "I forgot all about Christmas. But I suppose you're right."

"I wish we were home with Mam," said Lottie, her voice full of tears.

"Best not to think about Christmas, or about Mam," replied Mary, her throat aching. "But one day, I promise, I'll give you the best Christmas of your life. We'll have plum pudding and custard, turkey with gravy, and the biggest slice of ham you've ever seen."

Lottie sighed. "Oh, I'm so hungry. I couldn't eat that slop they served for breakfast. There were wee black creatures in it — did you see?"

Mary agreed. "Aye, weevils. I'm famished as well. So, let's think about Christmas dinner with all the trimmings, like in that magazine picture I showed you last year. The one we saw on that stand outside Flannigans the day it snowed, and Mam forgot about us, and brought us nought for tea."

"I remember," replied Lottie. "It had a big ham on the front of the magazine, with apples baked in cinnamon."

Mary's stomach rumbled, and for a moment she forgot about the ache in her legs. "That's right — when we celebrate Christmas one day, there will be crispy baked potatoes and slices of roast pheasant. Plus, a big ham with those cinnamon apples you saw. Just like in the magazine."

"Oh, don't. I'm going to faint of hunger," complained Lottie with a giggle, one hand pressed to her stomach.

"Then we'll follow it up with slices of custard pie, apple crumble, and ice cream." Mary let her eyes drift shut as she imagined the delicacies all lined up on a table.

"And Mam will be there, as well as Grandma and Grandpa," added Lottie with a sigh.

Mary's stomach cramped. She didn't want Mam to be there. Mam was the one who'd sent them away. She didn't care to see Mam ever again. But she couldn't say so to Lottie. Her sister still held out hope that Mam would follow them, would meet up with them and they could all begin their lives afresh together someday.

"Yes, we'll be together. One big happy family," agreed Mary. "You'll see."

🦋 21 🦋

CURRENT DAY

MIA

I'm sore in so many places, it's become a sort of general malaise. But that's okay because despite the aches and pains, I feel good. Really good. Like I could conquer the world, if only I could get some sleep.

Brody's awake, but he's happy enough lying on his back on a bunny rug on the floor. There's a colourful mobile hanging over him, and he's watching it carefully and pumping his arms and legs in a haphazard fashion every now and then.

He's adorable and I'm falling more in love with him every day. I can't get over his deep, dark eyes, his black hair, the cute little dimple in one cheek. He's still skinny and lanky, but he'll fill out in no time. I've already read all the books about the baby years — I'm a bit of a nerd when it comes to pregnancy and parenting books.

I scoop him up gently and tuck him into his removable car seat. We're going to visit Gramps. Gammy is still not up to it, so I promised her I'd check on him whenever I could. Ben is at the shops picking up groceries for the week, and Brody is more settled than usual. So, it's the perfect time for me to try an outing on my own with Brody. Nerves flutter in my stomach, but I'm a capable, independent woman. I can do this. At least, I think I can. Other people seem to manage it all the time, anyway.

It takes me about half an hour to get everything we need packed into the nappy bag, Brody belted carefully into his seat and the seat snapped in place in the car. By that time, he's screwing up his face in preparation for a massive meltdown because he's hungry again. I've taken too long, and I have to start the entire feed, change, burp, sleep routine all over again, which means it'll be after lunch before I'll make it to see Gramps, if I do at all. And he's always better in the morning. Plus, I promised Gammy. So, I decide that Brody can wait the ten minutes it takes to get to the nursing home and start up the car.

He screams the entire way there. It's not so much that the screaming is loud, which it is, but there's something about the tone of the scream that makes my spine tingle and my hands itch and my head go all nutty. I do my best to ignore it, changing the stations on the radio until I find something soothing and turning up the volume so he can hear it over the sound of his own voice. But he doesn't seem to notice or care. He only wants to scream.

By the time we reach the nursing home, I've sweat through my maternity shirt and yoga pants. I can't take the crying anymore. I have to do something about it. So, I pull into the parking lot and feed Brody in the car, leaving it running. He settles immediately, and I breathe a sigh of relief as the air-conditioning washes over my roasting body.

After a quick change and a burp over my shoulder, I strap him into the pram. It should only take two minutes, but it doesn't because I'm not used to it yet and I only have one free hand. I heave it out of the car boot and my finger gets jammed in one of the joints, drawing blood. That makes me drop the pram on the road, and I'm now not sure if it's upside down or the right way, or if I've just broken the darned thing. There are so many different parts, and knobs that could be levers, but that I soon realise aren't when I press them.

The shop clerk showed me how to use it when I bought it, and it seemed so easy. Just a quick press of a button and pop, you have a wonderful pram with all these amazing features that are so very necessary for every new mum. But now, it's a mass of metal and fabric, and every part of it looks the same as every other part until finally I press something and it's the right button. The pram springs into shape and pinches the flesh on my thigh at the same time, making me yelp. My shout scares Brody, and he bursts into tears against my chest while I hop around the parking lot doing my best not to let my baby hear his first swear words at one week old.

When I push Brody in his pram through the automatic doors, I'm overwhelmed by an urge to cry with relief at having managed what I believe is probably a feat of human accomplishment worthy of some kind of medal.

It only takes a few moments for me to compose myself, check in at the front desk, and head to Gramps' room. He's sitting in the garden just outside his sliding door. It's a beautiful little rose garden with colourful flowers, dragonflies, and bees buzzing around as residents wander along a brick path, or sit in their wheelchairs, or doze on any number of chairs and park benches in the shade.

Gramps is staring into the distance, and when he sees me he gives me a big grin that lets me know he recognises me. It's going to be a good visit with him.

"Well, hello there, Mia-Moo," he says, kissing my cheek as I bend to hug him.

"Hey, Gramps. I brought Brody to see you."

He peers into the pram, touching under Brody's chin with his fingertip. "Well, how about that. What a handsome lad he's going to be."

"How are you feeling today, Gramps?"

He shrugs. "About as good as I can. I miss Gammy, and all of you. I don't want to be here, you know. But that's life, right?"

I squeeze onto the park bench beside him and wrap an arm around his narrow frame. He's smaller than he used to be. He was a big, strong man in my youth. The kind of man who could do, build, or fix anything. I thought he was invincible. Now he's shrivelled and hunched around the shoulders. It hurts to see him unhappy.

"I'm sorry, Gramps."

"I know, love. Not your fault. But I miss the outdoors, the bush. I miss farming and gardening. Being around my family. Working. Ah, it's no fun growing old, my dear. I don't recommend it."

"I didn't know you were a farmer," I say.

But he brushes my words away with a flick of the wrist. "Oh, well, it was a long time ago."

"Did you live on a farm in England?"

"No, my mother was from a small beachside village. Of course, I didn't live there though, since she moved to London before I was born."

"You've never spoken much about your mum, Gramps. What was she like?"

His eyes gleam as he meets my gaze. "She was quite beautiful. Long brown hair that shone in the sunshine. Brown eyes that were like molasses. And she could sing. Oh, she had a wonderful voice. Her laugh was contagious too. We had a lot of fun together, she and I."

I can't help smiling as he talks, imagining him as a boy with his beautiful songstress of a mother, walking hand in hand by the beach. It's a pretty picture.

"When did she die?" I ask, brushing a fly away from Gramps' face.

His smile fades. "A long time ago. She was in England—I was here. I wish I'd spent more time with her before...well, never mind. None of us can change the past."

His words hit home to me because I find myself often thinking that I should make more of an effort to spend time with my parents. No one lives forever, and I've hardly seen them in recent years. Usually only at Christmas, and maybe one other time during the year. Sometimes, not even then. We spent last Christmas with Ben's family in Kyoto while Mum and Dad went to St Petersburg. They said it was the trip of a lifetime, but I can't help wondering if they missed seeing family. Dad would never admit to it. He seems to take pride in not needing anyone, or at least that's my impression.

"Well, she didn't come to Australia, so I suppose I had to build my life here without her," continued Gramps. "Life is strange — sometimes it's cruel, sometimes it's kind. But we never know which mistress it'll be at any given time."

"And you met Gammy on the ship, right? She told me about that." I want to ask him more about Gammy, but when I look into his eyes, I can't bring myself to do it. *Did she kill someone, Gramps?* That's what I want to say. But this time with him is precious, so I'd rather get to know him some more and tell him how much he means to me. I don't want to upset him. Besides, even thinking it — the words sound ridiculous in my thoughts, let alone saying them out loud.

"I met her before we left England. But it's here we fell in love."

My heart melts. They'll share their sixtieth wedding anniversary next year. And yet he still talks about their courtship as though it's fresh in his mind.

"How did you know she was the one?" I ask.

He smiles. "It wasn't any one thing. We spent a lot of time together over many years, and I knew I couldn't be without her. She was a strong, brave, and kind girl. She became a wonderful, loving and compassionate woman. But I didn't know all that at the time. I only knew, I couldn't face the idea of living without her. So, we got married."

I adore hearing these stories. Especially told by Gramps, since he doesn't often engage in deep conversation much with me anymore. The sun is shining, and noisy minors dart and call as they chase a crow from a tree in the garden while Brody is drifting off to sleep in his pram. And my heart is full of warmth.

"I wish Dad could see just how amazing you and Gammy are," I say, my joy faltering.

Gramps pats my knee. "It's okay, love. He's got reason to be angry with us."

"No one will tell me what it is. Why he's so mad."

"Well, when he was a kid, we were pretty distracted. I worked a lot to pay the bills and wasn't home much. He and Gammy clashed. Especially when he was a teenager. He had an idea of how his life should look, the types of things he should be allowed to have or do, and your grandmother had a different perspective. Of course, they're so alike that it often ended in fireworks."

"What was he like as a teenager?" I've often mused over this question. My strait-laced father is the height of responsibility and maturity these days. It's hard for me to imagine him being rebellious and wayward.

"He had his moments. But he was a good kid at heart. Still, there were hard times — he drank, got involved in drugs for a while. Oh, nothing too serious, but it meant he was angry, difficult and didn't like being told what to do. Thank goodness, he made it through all of that. But it put a strain on our relationship. Gammy thought tough love would be the best approach, but now looking back I wonder if we did the right thing."

I didn't know any of this about my father. How is it possible he was a drug-addled teenager? Surely Gramps is talking about someone else. Although, the number of talks Dad gave me about avoiding drugs and alcohol when I was a teenager make much more sense now.

"So, he and Gammy fought even then?"

Gramps whistles. "All the time. They're both as strong-willed and stubborn as each other. Both want to be in charge. And when your grandmother called the cops on Patrick...well..."

"She called the police?" I'm gaping at Gramps, unable to comprehend who these people are he's describing. Little sweet Gammy, and uber-responsible Dad? Surely not.

Gramps chuckles. "Yep. She sure did. I was at work, and I came home to my son being led away in handcuffs. They didn't charge him with anything, but he spent a night in a cell and did community service for drug possession."

I don't know how to respond to that. So, I sit in silence next to Gramps, twisting my fingers together over and over.

It all makes much more sense now. Dad's resentment towards Gammy. Gammy's stubborn resistance to giving in to his demands. The conflict is still there. It hasn't gone away even after all these years.

"He still blames her, you see. Thinks she betrayed him. Of course, in the end it was the right thing to do because he gave up the drugs and eventually got back into studying and focused all his attention on building a career. He's got an obsessive kind of personality, a singularity of focus. He's always amazed me with the way he can put his whole mind to something and never give up. It's why he's been so successful, but it can cause him problems with his relationships."

"Were you like Dad?" I ask.

He shakes his head. "Not really. Sonya's more like me. But Patrick is like his mother, and possibly my father. I don't know much about him, but I believe he was a very successful businessman."

"You didn't know your dad?"

Gramps offers a sad smile. "I never met him."

"I'm sorry." As much as Dad is difficult to get along with at times, I know he loves me. Having him in my life makes me feel a sense of safety and security that I wouldn't have if I didn't know him. Gramps never met his father. And all I can do is complain about mine. I hang my head just a little bit, pick a daffodil from the grass at my feet, and pluck the petals from it one at a time.

"It's fine. I learned to come to terms with it long ago," he says. "I'm glad I've got you and Brody here with me. It means so much to me that you visit. I know you're busy."

I swallow around the lump in my throat. He deserves so much more than I give him. "Well, I love you, Gramps."

His eyes fill with tears. "Love. That's a special thing to hear. I didn't know about it, you see."

"What do you mean, Gramps?"

"Love. I didn't know what it was for the longest time. Not until I met your grandmother. Oh I loved my mother, don't get me wrong. But I spent so much time without her, I didn't know what love looked like in practice rather than in my mind."

A shiver runs down my spine at his words. They're painful words, but spoken with a matter-of-fact tone that's oddly emotionless.

"You didn't know what love was?"

"No. I was so young when Mother took me to the orphanage. And after that, no one loved me or gave me the slightest affection for such a long time. I didn't know how to love or be loved. It took me a while to learn the skill of it, you see. It's probably why your dad struggles with his feelings for Gammy and me. The two of us were loveless waifs for most of our lives until we found each other. It's a hard thing, to live without love. Like a tree without sunlight, or a flower without water. And when you don't understand something, it's easy enough to pass that confusion on to your children. Although Gammy taught me more about love than I ever thought I'd know. We did okay in the end, the two of us."

I squeeze his hand, my eyes brimming with tears. "I didn't know," is all I can manage to say as my throat closes over.

He pats my arm. "Never mind. It's all in the past now, Button."

I wait until the lump in my throat dissipates enough for me to talk, then cough to clear it completely. "Mum and Dad are coming to Brisbane to see Brody soon," I say. "So, you'll get to catch up as well. I'm hoping Dad and Gammy will be able to mend fences while he's here."

Gramps smiles. "That'll be nice. But don't hold your breath for a reconciliation, Mia-Moo. Your dad is a stubborn man when he sets his mind to something."

22

DECEMBER 1953

HARRY

"How's your lip?" asked Max when he and Harry were back at the cottage.

Harry shrugged. "Fine." His heart was hard and dull. The last thing he wanted to do was to talk to anyone about what'd happened. It was nothing. All part of living in institutions. Part of his life. He hated conflict, didn't want to fight, but he didn't have a choice. It was fight or die. At least, that was how it felt. As though he'd die on the inside if he let the bullies win without giving them something to think about first. In that moment, he missed Davey. Missed his friend having his back. Davey would know the right thing to say to make him feel better, or to have a laugh at himself.

No doubt Max understood as well. He wasn't so very different to Davey. He'd lived in institutions longer than Harry had. He knew what it was like to fight his way through life.

"Where you going?"

Harry pointed ahead. "Evelyne Cottage. I haven't seen Mary and

Lottie all day. Have you?" He'd spotted Mary early that morning, sitting on the verandah of one of the cottages that crouched in an arc around Nuffield Hall, staring into the distance. The sense of relief that'd filtered over him to know where she was, which cottage was hers, almost stole his breath away. He hadn't seen her again since then, and a fluttery feeling twisted in his gut.

"Nope. But I wouldn't know them if I did."

"I hate this place," Harry said with sudden savagery. His hands clenched into fists at his sides. Even Barnardo's was better than this. He never should have agreed to leave in the first place, only there wasn't a thing left to stay in England for anyway. At least now he had Mary, but he'd lost Davey along the way.

"It's not so bad."

Harry shot Max a disgusted look as they trudged along the dusty track between cottages and by clumps of dusty bushes. Beneath the glaring sunshine, his head burned hotter than ever. His skin was already red from a morning outdoors.

"Not really. I mean, it could be worse. We're pretty much left alone. And we've got a chance to go to school, to learn how to farm. I've already decided, I want to do accounts though, no matter what they say. I've got no desire to work out in the hot sun all day everyday chasing sheep, or whatever else they expect us to do. Bookwork is much more suited to my peaches-and-cream complexion." He winked at Harry, and Harry couldn't help laughing. Max had a way of helping him feel better when things seemed to be at their worst just like Davey had.

"I can see you doing bookwork," admitted Harry.

"Well, it's not gonna happen, but it's a nice dream anyway. We're all bound for farming, like it or not. What about you? What's your dream?"

Harry shrugged. "I haven't thought about it much," he lied. It seemed easier. "I like to read, but I'm not sure that's really a job."

"Maybe. You never know." Max squinted at the cottage ahead. "But one thing I do know—if you start out here full of anger, you're not likely to make it."

Max's words hit him hard.

"You're right," agreed Harry. "I won't make it."

"Not if you're angry. Trust me."

"I don't know how to be anything else. Why aren't you angry?" asked Harry.

Max grinned without looking at his friend. "I was. For a long time. But all that did was make me a target — for the principal, the teachers, the big boys. No one wanted to be my friend, no one cared about me, I was all alone in the world, and it didn't change anything for the better. So, I decided to laugh at life instead. When anything bad happens, I make a joke of it. It helps."

"Makes sense," admitted Harry. Although he didn't know how to get rid of the tight ball of emotions that seemed permanently lodged in his chest. He'd learned to accept it as a normal part of his life ever since Mother left him at the Home the first time.

"Besides, you're not much of a fighter. So, you'll have to make people laugh if you want to survive here."

"Oh, yeah?" Harry play-punched Max in the shoulder.

Max stumbled away, grinning. "Oi, ya greaser." Then punched him back. And Harry laughed before chasing Max along the path until they reached the steps leading up to the front door of Evelyne Cottage. Two girls sat on the steps in threadbare blue shorts and khaki shirts two sizes too small for them. They sported the same crooked hairstyles as the boys. One had dirt smudged across her cheek. Both were barefoot and eyed the boys with suspicion.

"What do you want?" asked the taller one, standing to her feet and pressing her hands to narrow hips.

"I'm looking for Mary and Lottie."

"They the new gals?" she asked, chewing the end of a fingernail.

"That's right."

She dipped her head in the direction of the door. "They're inside, but you can't go in. No boys allowed."

"Can you ask 'em to come out?"

"Nope. They're sleeping. Got into some kind of trouble, from what I heard. Tangled with Crazy Crew and got a walloping."

"I heard she stood up to him," piped up the smaller girl as she swung back and forth on the porch railing.

"Is she okay?" Harry's nostrils flared. He wanted to check on Mary, but there was no way the girls would let him through, and he wasn't about to make an enemy of Mary and Lottie's cottage sisters.

"Don't know. Seems fine."

"Can you tell them Harry and Max came by, please?"

"I guess. If I remember."

Harry gave up his attempt to see Mary and Lottie and returned to his own cottage. Max left him there to play a game of cricket in the field next door to the village. It would be teatime soon—they had a little while to rest before their evening showers. Harry and Max had worked on a car engine all afternoon, although he wasn't sure they'd done anything constructive in all their tearing apart, oiling and greasing of the various bits and pieces. He had a better idea of how the engine fit together now and found the process interesting. He wasn't entirely convinced Max knew what he was talking about when he described the role and function of each of the parts as they set them on the dirt beside the broken-down vehicle, even though he'd detailed each with complete confidence. He'd be surprised if the engine ever turned over again once they put it back together.

Inside the cottage, Harry threw himself down on the bed and linked his hands behind his head to stare at the wire mesh supporting Max's mattress overhead. He lay there for a while, then took a shower and returned to his bed as soon as he'd dried himself and dressed again in the same clothes.

"You lazy bugger, still in bed," remarked Max, swaggering into the cottage with a wide grin on his freckled face. "Should've known."

Harry rolled onto his side to face the wall. "Shut up."

Max poked his fingers into Harry's rib cage. Harry laughed. "Stop it."

"Come on, it's a beautiful day. No time to lay about in bed."

"What else is there to do?" asked Harry, rolling onto his back to look up at Max.

"You're right, you should rest. It won't last. They'll have you working your arse off in no time. But, we *could* sneak up to the girls' cottages and throw freezing water on them through the windows."

"Won't we get into trouble doing that?"

Max's nose wrinkled. "By who? If the cottage mother isn't in, who will ever know?"

"Don't they dob?" asked Harry.

Max shook his head. "Nope. They're likely to get in more trouble than we are if they do that. Boss doesn't like dobbers."

Harry processed what Max had told him, then sighed. "No, thanks."

"Or we could see if the kitchen has some scraps to feed the horses."

Harry sat up in bed as three other boys traipsed into the cottage. He recognised Devon, but didn't know the others by name. Their bare feet left a muddy trail and they jostled with each other and laughed, knocking Max out of their path like a ball on a ping-pong table as they made their way to the shared dining table at the other end of the cottage.

Harry followed them and stood at a distance to listen to what they were saying. He made himself busy filling a cup with water from the sink, then sipped it slowly. They were talking about an outing they were planning for the following weekend, from what he could gather. A trip to the movie cinema in a place called Orange. Devon noticed him standing there and arched an eyebrow.

"Hey, newbie, what happened to your face?"

Harry raised a hand to his mouth self-consciously. "Get lost."

Devon laughed. "Sorry about that. Can't help myself sometimes."

The other two boys laughed, along with Devon.

"Forget it," replied Harry. "I already have."

Devon slapped him on the shoulder. "Good to hear, mate."

"Why do you all have the same ugly haircut?" asked Harry.

"Hey, watch it. I happen to like my style." Devon ran his fingers through his hair.

"It's because we have to cut each other's hair, and we're not exactly hairdressers," replied another one of the boys, whose sandy blond hair had a particularly crooked and jagged fringe.

Max sidled up to Harry and stood beside him, watching the older boys ragging on each other's cuts for a few moments. "You'll look like us soon enough."

Harry peered down at the work clothes he'd donned that morning.

When he'd emerged from bed he'd found the cottage mother, Elsa, had replaced his clothing with what appeared to be the school farm's uniform — a second-hand outfit in khaki with a hole beneath one of his arms. His suitcase full of clothes had never arrived after being loaded into the truck at the train station, and now all he had was this pair of worn shorts and a shirt, along with another set Elsa said was for outings.

"I'm already halfway there," said Harry. "Hey, when do we get to go to school?"

"You'll go in February," replied Max. "Classes are finished now for the summer holidays. Devon and his mates are lucky — they'll go into town to the high school next year. Sometimes they can nick a lunch off one of the town kids instead of eating the slop we get in our lunchboxes."

⚜

HARRY PEERED DOWN AT HIS WELL-WORN SHIRT, PUSHING THE crumpled fabric flat against his rib cage with the palms of his hands. There was a grease stain on the front pocket, and he shivered as the cool evening air breezed through the open windows. He tried shutting one of the windows, but it didn't budge when he pulled at it with all his strength.

He found most of the boys gathered around the dining table. Some played a hand of cards. Others set the table or filled a jug with water. Elsa stood at the stove, stirring something in a pot. She oozed warmth and good-natured fun, teasing boys or laughing with them over a joke they told. All of the boys hovered around her like bees at a hive. She was the centre of their world, that was clear to Harry.

When she noticed him and Max standing a little to one side of the group, she beckoned them over. She checked behind Harry's ears for dirt, parted his hair and examined it, then rested a hand on his shoulder. "I hope you're hungry, Harry. I'm cooking mutton and potatoes for tea. Do you like mutton?"

He shrugged. "I guess."

She laughed, and it was a sweet, gentle rumble of a laugh that set him immediately at ease. "Good to hear. How about you help me get the lumps out of these potatoes while I pull the mutton out of the oven?"

He took the wooden spoon from her hand and did his best to whip the potatoes until they were creamy, adding a dollop more butter to the mixture before considering it finished. He'd never cooked anything before in his life and felt a twinge of pride when Elsa peered into the pot and smiled in approval.

"Well done. They're just about perfect, I reckon. Take a seat, lad. I'll dish up and we can eat."

He found a seat at the table. The seats filled quickly with boys, and what followed was a hearty mealtime filled with raucous laughter, conversation, and ribbing. Elsa reigned over it all with a warm smile, a ready word of encouragement, and the occasional gentle admonishment. All the boys seemed to love her, and each sidled up to her on occasion for a hug or a quiet conversation as the evening progressed. Harry longed to have that kind of relationship with her, or with someone. His own mother had loved him, embraced him, kissed his forehead, and told him how handsome he was, or how well he helped her around their small flat. He remembered those times vaguely, but it'd been so long ago. The pain of missing her, of missing affection and encouragement, swamped him.

It took all his strength to hold back the tears that threatened to spill down his cheeks as he helped to clear the table.

Elsa thanked him and gave him a one-armed, brief hug as he set his plate on the sink. It was all he could do to keep from crying then. Instead, he ran to his bed, burying himself beneath the blanket so that even the top of his head was hidden from sight. He rolled onto his side, facing the wall, and tucked his legs up against his chest.

It was then the tears came, pouring down his cheeks until they soaked the blanket and he fell to sleep.

❧ 23 ❧

JANUARY 1954

HARRY

"Out of bed, lazy git," spat Devon, slapping Harry up the side of the head to wake him.

Harry startled, grabbed for the place where his head stung, and scuttled up the bed and out of reach. He blinked away the sleep and glared at Devon, who laughed.

"Come on, we're milking today. I'm rostered on for the dairy, and you might as well learn the ropes because it'll be your turn soon enough."

Harry didn't bother arguing. He climbed out of bed, shot the sleeping Max an envious look, then followed Devon out the door of the cottage and into the dark. The sun didn't rise until about four thirty on summer mornings, so it must've been earlier than that, but Harry didn't own a watch so wasn't sure exactly what time it was. Rain pattered on the verandah roof, and when it hit Harry's face and neck as he skipped down the front steps, it elicited a gasp. The cold rain soon soaked his shirt and shorts and ran in rivers down his spine. His hair was plastered to his head and he had to blink away the raindrops so he could see where they were going.

Devon strode with long, purposeful steps through the village. Harry had to jog to keep up with him. They walked in silence. The rain prevented conversation, but Harry didn't have anything to say even if the weather had been fair. He was sound asleep thirty seconds earlier and his brain still struggled to catch up. He yawned and shoved his hands deep into his shorts pockets, hunching his shoulders against the rain.

As they climbed the sloping hill beyond the edge of the village, the downpour increased in intensity, pummelling the crown of his head. It slapped against the muddy ground, forming creeks that snaked downstream through the grass.

The boys ducked through a barbed-wire fence, then crossed a paddock to where a herd of fifty dairy cattle stood waiting patiently. Their internal time clocks had them ready for the morning milk, and they'd clustered together along the fence line in the rain, heads down as they huddled together. Harry was grateful for the white patches on their black coats that fairly glowed through the darkness. Heavy clouds hung overhead, obscuring any light from the moon and stars above them. The entire landscape was obliterated from sight. It was as though they were the only two people left on earth. Loneliness curled in Harry's stomach like a snake in a pit.

Devon shouted at the cattle, herding them towards the gate at the end of the field. They moved slowly, with short, lumbering steps. A few shook their heads at Devon, but none made too much of a fuss. They knew the routine and were ready for the morning ritual that would release the tension from their udders.

Harry wasn't sure what he should do, so he copied Devon's movements, following along close by. He shouted at the cattle, waved his hands, clapped and generally pushed them forwards by moving in that direction. His efforts at herding seemed to work, and after a while they had driven the herd up to the dairy entrance. He slipped and fell in the mud twice along the way, the black muck caking itself to his rear end, legs and hands. He tried wiping it away on his shorts, but that only made matters worse. The rain did a better job of dislodging it. And by the time they reached their destination, most of the mud had been washed free from Harry's clothing and skin.

The dairy was a long, squat timber building. The timber had aged in the sun and rain, and had rotted in spots. Inside, the cattle wandered obediently to their places. Four other boys were there already, shepherding cattle into bails to be milked. There were six bails, four with shining new milking machines. The machinery glistened in stark contrast with the walls of the tired, musty building.

Harry stood against one of the long walls, unsure of what to do next. Devon beckoned him over. The older boy sat on a stool in one of the bails that didn't have a milking machine. The stool was pushed up close to a cow. The animal kicked a hind leg towards its stomach, then waved its tail. Harry's heart thudded against his rib cage. A kick from one of those hooves would do serious damage. Yet Devon was pressed up against the cow's side, his head leaned into its flank as though he was completely unbothered by the risk he was taking. His hands moved quickly, pulling, squeezing. Milk squirted into a steel bucket between his feet. Left, right, left, right. Harry watched in awe.

"Your turn," said Devon, rising to his feet.

Harry sat on the stool and lifted his hands to the animal's teats. He squeezed, but nothing happened.

"No, not like that." Devon leaned in to show him how to do it, closing his hands over Harry's and squeezing.

Harry copied the action, and milk trickled into the bucket. He grinned. "I did it."

"Great, I'll bake you a cake," Devon hissed. "Get on with it."

Devon left him alone and moved into the next bail. Harry continued milking. It took him a long time to finish, and by the time he was done, the rain had stopped and the faint glow of dawn shone through the dairy windows and open doorways. When he couldn't extract any more milk, Devon finished milking his cow for him. The bigger boy muttered under his breath the entire time over how slow Harry was, and how they'd be there all day at this rate.

When Harry sat to milk the next cow, he leaned his head into the animal's side the way he'd seen Devon do. His fear had waned, and he'd begun to enjoy himself and the cow's closeness. Her warmth soothed his spirits and he stroked her side gently before beginning to milk, whispering encouragement to her through his teeth so no one else would overhear him. This time, the milk streamed into the bucket more easily. But before long, his hands began to cramp. He pushed through the pain for as long as he could manage. Finally he had to stop work and stretch his fingers.

A swift punch to the back of his head sent him sprawling from his stool onto the hard floor of the dairy. He scrambled to his feet, spinning to face his attacker with a snarl.

"What was that for?"

A short, wiry man stood there, eyes dark and empty. A lit cigarette dangled from the side of his mouth, and smoke puffed out through a gap where his teeth should've been.

"You're slackin'. Nobody slacks off in my dairy. Get back to work, boy." His voice came out as a growl, and the threat in his eyes was barely veiled. Harry hurried to sit on the stool, the back of his head still smarting with the pain of the assault. There'd be a bruise, no doubt. But he didn't dare complain.

When the man left, Harry leaned beneath the cow to whisper through the slats to the next bail. "Who was that?"

Devon whispered back. "Bronson. He's the dairy manager. You don't want to cross him."

"I figured that one out," he replied, rubbing the back of his head gingerly.

"If he thinks we're not moving fast enough, he turns off the milking machines and makes us milk the entire herd by hand."

Harry swallowed hard. At the pace he was milking, that would make for a long day. From then on, regardless of how his hands cramped, he kept milking. By the time they were finished, he could barely move his fingers.

Harry wanted nothing more than to climb back into bed and sleep for hours. But it was time for breakfast, and after that would be a full day working with the rest of the children in the village to gather in the oat harvest. He didn't know how he'd have the energy. They'd gathered wheat the previous week, and oats for several days so far this week under the blazing summer sun. The children over eight years of age came from the village and followed the harvester all day long, picking up the sheaves of oats and stacking them in vertical *stooks*. They'd be doing the same again after breakfast, and he didn't know how he'd manage it with hands that he could barely curl into a fist.

"Let's eat," said Devon, as he headed out the door. "Don't dawdle, I've got to get back here fast or Bronson will have my hide. I still have twelve hours of work left in my day."

Devon stared at his hands where blisters had become callouses, beneath a layer of grime that the slimy brown soap in the cottage washroom wouldn't be likely to shift. He rubbed them together then shoved them into his pockets as they passed a horse drawn cart and a slight boy with an overbite loading ten gallon milk urns for delivery to the village.

"Sixteen hours?" asked Harry, doing the sum in his head.

"Every day, even on the weekends, for the month I'm rostered on at the dairy. I'm fourteen, so at least I'm going back to school soon and I'll only have to pitch in before and after, and some on the weekends. The trainees have to work everyday, all year long. That'll be me next year. But don't fret," said Devon as they walked back to their cottage. "You'll get used to it soon enough."

JANUARY 1954

MARY

THE JARRING RING OF THE BELL CUT THROUGH MARY'S PERFECTLY good dream about eating ice cream in the dining room on board the *Strathaird*, making certain not to get any drips on her beautiful blue frock. Her eyes blinked open and the disappointment of not being back on the luxurious ship overwhelmed her.

She didn't let the feeling hold her hostage. A lifetime of disappointments meant that she allowed herself only a moment of self-indulgent pity before embracing the new day. There was work to do, things to accomplish, and besides that, it was the school-wide athletics day.

Not that she was one for athletics. Truth be told, she wasn't exactly sure whether she was or wasn't, since the only athletics she'd ever participated in had been running through the streets of London with the corner grocer in hot pursuit, a loaf of still-warm bread tucked beneath her skinny arm. She'd managed to evade many such attempts to catch her, so perhaps she was better at racing than she thought. But still, the idea didn't give her the level of excitement that the rest of the group seemed to experience.

Lottie bounded out of bed, clear-eyed and with a smile on her face. As she climbed into her shorts and shirt, she toppled over onto the floor in her excitement, with one foot caught in the leg.

Mary giggled. "What are you doing?"

"It's the carnival today!" cried Lottie, her bright blue eyes gleaming.

Mary shook her head. "You're stark raving mad. It's not an actual carnival, just an athletics day. What, are you expecting clowns and fairy floss?"

Lottie crossed her eyes and poked out her tongue. "Of course not. I know what it is, but I'm excited about it anyway."

"I don't know why," continued Mary, setting her bare feet on the cold timber floor. "It's going to be hot as Hades and you'll be galavanting around an open field under the sun."

Lottie shrugged. "I don't know why exactly, either. But it's something — a little different to the normal. All we ever do is work and wander around. It's summer, so we're not even able to go school for a change of scenery."

Mary couldn't argue with that. They'd managed to get through Christmas without too much difficulty. They'd even been fed a special Christmas dinner with sliced ham and gravy. But it wasn't the same as it'd been back in England — the lunchtime temperature was so high they ended up wiping their limbs down with damp cloths and fanning each other while they lolled about in the shade, chasing flies. It hadn't seemed like Christmas, and now January was even hotter than December had been.

They'd been at the Fairbridge Farm School for a month now and Mary had begun to feel more at home. She was used to the heat, or at least she was coping a little better than she had when they first arrived. She'd figured out the routine and how to stay out of Crew's way. She'd even managed to garner a kind word from Forrest when he saw how well she washed the dishes one day in the kitchen. Some of the kids they'd arrived with hadn't fared so well as she and Lottie, especially the younger ones. They missed home, missed their parents, and there was no one here care for them.

Mary and Lottie had been caring for themselves for as long as Mary could remember and this new way of living suited them. At least, for now. She had no intention of going into domestic service, which was the only thing they trained girls for in this place. But it was a safe place for she and Lottie to live, where food and clothing were provided and they weren't at risk of freezing to death for another few months.

All in all, when she thought it through, she and Lottie were better off than they'd been. Even if it wasn't remotely akin to their life onboard the *Strathaird*. It'd seemed too good to be true because it was. That wasn't real life for girls like her and Lottie. And she'd come to terms with that on the second day after they'd arrived at the farm. Harry, however, seemed determined to hold onto the life he'd left behind. She hadn't been able to shake him out of the doldrums he'd fallen into the moment they'd stepped off the ship, although she didn't see him now as often as she had then. They only saw one another by accident around the farm, or during shared mealtimes. Sometimes he came to visit her at the cottage, but if their cottage mother, Ingrid, was around, he had to stay out of sight or she'd report him to the principal for a caning.

Ingrid was one of the many things Mary had steeled her resolve against. She wasn't about to let a mean old woman like her cottage mother ruin things for her. Instead, she simply kept out of Ingrid's way and did her best not to antagonise her. Once, during Mary's first week at the farm school, Ingrid had caught the smallest girl in the cottage by the collar and shoved her head into the toilet because she'd wet the bed. Mary knew then to keep Lottie out of the cottage mother's way.

German speaking from South Africa, the grey-haired old lady did her best to inflict misery on the girls in her cottage. That was the general consensus, anyway. But Mary understood what a life of hardship could do to a person. She'd seen it often enough in her life, though it didn't give her any more sympathy for the woman. It did make her wary because a wounded animal was unpredictable. And there was pain behind Ingrid's dour demeanour, regular canings for the girls, and her lack of interest in providing them with edible food.

Mary dressed quickly, washed her face with cold water, then tied her hair back with a piece of old rag. The girls filed in twos and threes out of the cottage to do their various jobs around the village before breakfast. The sun was already high in the sky and the earth was heating up beneath its unforgiving rays. Outside, a chorus of kookaburras resounded in the distance, then gradually petered off to be replaced by the titter and squawks of the variety of other birds that populated the area. Since their arrival, Mary had been struck by the abundance and variety of birdlife around the village.

She and Lottie filled a bucket with warm water and soap. They took two mops from the broom cupboard and got to work mopping the cottage floor. It was marked with dirty footprints from one end to the other, but it didn't take them long to leave it reasonably clean. By then, the water in the bucket was brown and cold, so they threw it out and carried the empty bucket to the next cottage, where they began the process all over again.

A group of young boys stood around a woodpile, bare-footed. They took turns swinging axes to split the logs into firewood. Two of the boys carried the split timber to a pile, where they stacked it up against the side of Nuffield Hall, across from the cottage where Mary and Lottie mopped. The boys looked to be about six or seven years old, yet they wielded the axe as though they'd been doing so for years. Mary wondered how many had lost a toe that way.

They finished mopping the next cottage and headed out to move on. A horse and cart came trotting into view, and Mary and Lottie had to step aside to let it pass. Two boys who appeared to be eleven or twelve sat atop the cart. One held the reins loose in his hands. The other leaned back and offered Mary a grin as they went by. They stopped in front of the cottage, and the boy leapt down and carried a jug of milk up to the doorstep, where he set it down. He looked again at Mary, his brown hair flopping across his forehead. He was tall, skinny, and freckled, like so many of the boys at the farm. She recognised many of them on sight now, but still didn't know all their names. He reminded her a little of Harry, and she missed him all of a sudden. Missed their time together unhindered, exploring the ship, hiding in various nooks and crannies or sneaking pastries from the kitchen when the staff wasn't looking.

"Have you seen Harry?" she asked.

Lottie picked up her mop as the wagon set off again, and they walked side by side along the track. "I saw him yesterday. He says he's going to compete in all the races today."

"I hope we get a chance to —" She was interrupted by the breakfast bell. With a sigh, she glanced at the cottage before them. "Well, I guess we can't mop any more floors."

"What a shame," replied Lottie with a grin. "Race you back!"

They ran, Mary outpacing Lottie by a few steps, but then holding herself back so her sister could keep up. They tumbled, all arms and legs, through the doorway and slipped on the wet floor, landing in a pile. Laughing, Mary put away the bucket and mops and the two of them skipped to Nuffield Hall arm in arm.

A line formed at the closed doors leading into the hall. Mary and Lottie stood at the back, waiting their turn. Principal Forrest soon arrived and unlocked the doors. He stood at the head of the line as the children filed past, inspecting their hands for cleanliness. Mary held up her hands, and he nodded her through. She and Lottie quickly found their seats at their regular table.

The hall was abuzz with discussion about the carnival. Children rushed between tables, full of chattering excitement. Boys blustered and swaggered, boasting about who would beat whom and by how far. Harry was there, standing beside his table with Max. She waved when she saw him and he waved back, a broad smile splitting his face in two.

It sent a thrill through her, seeing him like that — happy at last. She'd wondered if he'd ever recover his smile again. His good, kind smile. Somehow the three of them would make it through this and anything else that came their way, just so long as they could laugh about it together.

She grinned back at him just as the rest of the boys at his table noticed the exchange and broke into raucous jeering, whistling and laughter as they pushed him around and teased him. But when his face turned a dark shade of red, she couldn't help laughing as well.

✿ 24 ✿

HARRY

The scent of sweat filled the air. Children cheered and jumped in place along the sides of the unmarked track. Adrenaline pumped through Harry's veins. His head fairly throbbed with it. The noises of the carnival faded as he studied the finish line, knees bent, arms tucked to his sides, hands curled into fists. He'd run races before at Barnardo's, but something about this one seemed real and important in a way the others hadn't. This time he'd run in bare feet across a sheep pasture.

"On your mark, get set, go!" shouted Forrest, letting his raised hand drop towards the ground.

Harry jumped forward, his heart thudding with excitement. Then he ran as fast as his legs would carry him. His arms pumped at his sides, his legs like pistons. He leapt over a cow patty, ducked around a sun-bleached foxtail, and stumbled in a hole hidden beneath the crunch of summer dried grasses. He'd started out strong, ahead of the rag-tag group of boys by the twenty-metre mark, but it wasn't long before the group gained on him.

He pushed himself, reached deep inside for every extra drop of energy he could call upon, and crossed the line in second place behind Devon. Devon patted him on the shoulder, puffing hard, then bent to press his hands to his knees.

Harry smiled to himself, gasping for breath.

"Good one, Harry boy," said Max, coming up behind him, his face red from exertion. "Didn't know you could run so fast."

"Lots of practice escaping canings," Harry quipped with a wink.

"Too right." Max cocked his head to one side.

"I bet you've run from Forrest enough times over the years."

Max wrinkled his nose. "Eh, he's not so bad. Stay on his good side and he'll treat you fine. I never knew my father. Forrest is the dad around here for a lot of us. Don't get me wrong—he's tough on the kids who play up — but he's fair as well."

Sweat trickled down the sides of Harry's face; some got into his eyes and stung. Flies buzzed around his nose, and he swiped at them as he jogged to the next event. He pondered Max's words — Forrest seemed like an authoritarian. The kind of man who didn't have a good side. But Max had lived at the farm long enough to know him as well as any of the children could. If he thought Forrest was okay, maybe Harry had misjudged him. All he knew in that moment was how grateful he was for a day without harvesting, milking cows, or slopping pigs. His body had adjusted to the heavy workload well, and most of his aches and pains faded as quickly as they came after a few days working on a new task.

When he reached the long jump, he found the girls still taking their turn. Mary waited in line. He watched as she ran and jumped into a pile of sand, legs outstretched. Her blonde ponytail bounced as she trotted over to greet him.

"Hi, Harry."

"Hi," he replied, suddenly feeling a little squiggly inside. He didn't understand the feeling—he and Mary had been fast friends for months. But now when he saw her, it made his stomach tingle in a strange kind of way.

Her cheeks glowed with health, pinked by exercise and sunshine. Her hair shone, and she'd grown taller in the months since he'd known her. She wasn't the small, skinny girl with the pale face and oversized eyes he'd first met at the Fairbridge House any longer. She was the picture of health, even while wearing the oversized, stained farm uniform.

"I saw you won your race," she said, crossing her arms over her chest.

He liked that she'd watched him run. "Second," he replied.

"Oh, well, it must've been close because it looked like first from here."

"Yeah, it was pretty close."

"You sound Australian already," she replied.

"You too."

"Do you think we'll ever completely lose the accent?"

He shrugged. "Maybe."

"I don't care," she continued. "I don't ever want to go back there. I'm happy to put England behind me forever."

He studied her, his heart suddenly aching with the memories of home, as though a curtain was pulled back from a window into the past. "I'm going back there first chance I get."

"Oh?" Her eyes narrowed. "Why would you want to do that?"

"I'm getting out of here. And then I'm going home."

She arched an eyebrow. "Not me. I'm going to find a job — they say you can get any kind of job you like here. Doesn't matter where you came from."

He'd heard the same. Still, he couldn't help feeling disconnected from this place. It was so strange, so foreign, with such a barren landscape, harsh and unforgiving. He missed the green hedgerows and steady dripping rain of England.

A man with a camera wandered amongst the children, stopping now and then to squat and take a photograph of a race or an event. He stopped beside Harry and Mary, holding the black camera high. He wore a black hat and a black suit with a white shirt, buttoned to where a charcoal tie fit around his neck.

"Do you mind if I take a photo of you two?" he asked.

Mary exchanged a glance with Harry, who nodded imperceptibly.

"I don't mind," said Mary.

"Would you get a bit closer together?"

Mary shuffled closer so that her shoulder nudged Harry's. She looked up at him, laughing at the pink in his cheeks. He grinned back at her as the photographer snapped his shot.

"Perfect," the man said. "I'll send you a copy as soon as it's processed. This'll be great for the farm and help promote it to the community. Maybe we can help you folks with some fundraising."

After Harry did the long jump and the four hundred yard race, the cottage mothers showed up with buckets of ice creams on sticks. Harry rushed at Elsa with the rest of his cottage brothers, and they all got an ice cream. They sat around in the grass, finding shade beneath trees or against the sides of buildings where they could, licking and slurping at the rapidly melting treats.

Harry experienced a moment's contentment as he looked around the group. There were happy smiles and tired, blinking eyes. Sunburnt faces, sweat-streaked shirts and dirty knees and feet everywhere he looked. It'd been a good day, the best he'd had at the farm so far. It sparked a small flame of hope deep inside his heart.

⊗⊗⊗

BY THE TIME THE LAST RACE HAD BEEN RUN, THE CHILDREN WERE already packing up. Hay bales that'd been used as dividers and seating were loaded onto a trailer pulled by a tractor to take back to the stables. Rubbish was collected by the smaller children, who trekked back to Nuffield Hall with it piled in their arms. The three- and four-year-olds trotted bleary-eyed and tired through the sheep pasture, headed for home with ice cream and dirt streaked across their sunburnt cheeks.

Harry stacked hay bales to wait for the tractor and trailer. When it arrived, he loaded the hay bales into the trailer. Mary and Lottie ran over to say goodbye, then climbed on top of the hay bales to catch a ride back to the village. Devon drove the tractor. The older boy carried himself with a confidence Harry envied. Nothing seemed too hard for him. He was tall, sinewy, tanned and seemed capable of anything.

Harry watched as Devon drove the tractor, bumping over the uneven ground and through the iron gate, past the chook pen and around the other side of the stables to unload. With a sigh, he wiped the sweat from his brow.

The sun hung low on the horizon. The sky was a mixed pallet of pink, orange and yellow streaks. The heat of the day had passed; it no longer baked everything it touched. But it still left a trail of sweat down his back and under his arms. He fingered the tip of his nose gingerly. It'd be sore tomorrow, along with his entire face, arms, neck. He'd never been so sunburnt in all his life, but it was worth it. He'd loved every minute of the carnival.

It was past teatime, and his stomach growled with hunger. He hoped Elsa had something hearty cooking on the stove when he returned to the cottage. He set off across the paddock at a run. If he was quick, he might get a chance to shower before tea. Elsa wouldn't be happy if he showed up at the table looking the way he did.

When he reached the cottage, he climbed the stairs wearily and sat on the top step. He'd been limping for the past hour, with some bindis that got stuck in his foot. He'd tried to get them out, but there must've still been something in there because one side of his foot twinged with pain at every step he took.

He crossed one leg over the other and studied the sole of his left foot, rubbing fingertips gently across it. There. A prickle scratched his fingertip. He got to work pulling it free between two fingernails, his tongue poked out the side of his mouth in concentration.

"Whatcha doing?" asked Devon, traipsing up the steps beside him.

He grimaced. "Got a bindi."

Devon grunted.

Harry pulled the rest of the prickle free with a shout of exultation, then stood to his feet to test it out. No more pain. He grinned at Devon, who couldn't help smiling back in return.

"Hey, did you see whether Mary and Lottie went back to their cottage?"

Devon shrugged. "I don't know. Crew was there. Said he had a job for them to do."

Harry went cold. "What?"

"Yeah, something about cleaning up a mess the younger kids made."

"You left them there with him?"

Devon's brow furrowed. "What was I supposed to do? Crew would flatten me if I so much as squeaked. The other day he pummelled me for a full minute because I didn't get out of his way fast enough when he was walking by."

"You know what he's like, and you left them alone with him," replied Harry.

"What do you care?"

Harry wanted to punch Devon's nonchalant, tanned, confident face. But it would only slow him down. He had to find Mary and Lottie before Crew lost his temper again with them. He hadn't interacted much with the gardener himself, but Mary told him what'd happened when she and her sister had encountered him the first time. Since then, he'd heard snippets of other stories about him around the village. About the man's temper, his tendency to use his fists, or even a boot when a fist wouldn't do. Whether or not it was all true, there were enough stories to give him the creeps.

He descended the stairs in one giant leap and set out at a run in the direction of the stables.

"Hey, where are you going?" shouted Devon after his retreating back. "Elsa's gonna be mad if you miss tea."

Grey shadows lengthened across the dirt as Harry ran. Mosquitos hummed in his ear a moment and then were gone. There was nothing more than a whisper of breeze to lift his hair. The muggy heat squatted heavy over the golden glow of bleached foxtails mixed with green shoots of stubborn grass. His feet padded lightly along the dusty path. Sharp stones pricked and bruised his soles, but he couldn't stop now. Mary would be fine — he was overreacting. Crew wasn't likely to hurt her again, not so soon after the last time. But what if she spoke back to him, provoked him? He had a temper—that was what Harry had heard. And Mary didn't hold back if she had something to say. Besides, he'd heard other things about Crew he couldn't let himself consider. If he did, his head went light and his stomach lurched with fear.

The stable when he reached it was all lit up on one side by the brilliant setting sun. When he rounded the end of it, he found the other side in dark shadows. It was quiet. Too quiet. Where were the girls? Perhaps they'd already left and were seated at the dining table in their cottage.

A whimper caught his ear and he crept towards the sound, unsure of what he'd heard. A horse snorted, stamping its foot. Another crunched on a mouthful of oats. He held his breath, on tenterhooks listening. Another whimper and a sniffle, he was certain of it.

He found Lottie seated behind a loose box. Surrounded by hay, she was almost entirely hidden in the shadows. He reached her in a moment and squatted in front of her. Her red-rimmed eyes were translucent when she met his gaze.

"Charlotte, what is it? Where's Mary?" he whispered.

"Harry, help her."

"Where? Where is she?" he repeated, his heart thundering.

Lottie didn't respond. She only lowered her face to her tucked knees and cried against them.

Harry stood up and scanned the stables in desperation. Then he heard it — a scream that struck to the depths of his soul. It sent a shiver down his spine. It was muffled, as though covered by something or someone, but unmistakable in that dark, quiet place.

Then he ran, ducking into every loose box, stall, and storage room he found, wildly scanning for anything to indicate where the sound had come from. When he saw Crew's back, it filled him with a white-hot rage. Crew was on top of Mary in one corner of a tack room. Saddles and bridles lined the walls, and Mary was hidden away from his view behind a pile of saddle cloths. But she was there. Her small, bare feet were visible beneath Crew's dark jeans, her cries louder now.

With a scream of rage, Harry barrelled at Crew's back. All arms flailing and legs pumping, he rammed into Crew with a grunt and a shout.

"Stop!"

Crew spun his head around, his eyes narrow. He spotted Harry and flung out one arm, sending Harry sprawling through the air. The boy landed hard against the wall. His head made an empty cracking sound with the impact. Then he crumpled to the dusty, hay-strewn floor without a word.

❧

HARRY'S HEAD POUNDED. IT WASN'T THE FIRST TIME HE'D RECEIVED a concussion — he'd hit his head when playing football when he was five years old at Barnardo's. He shouldn't've been playing with the older boys, but there was no one to tell him not to, and the big kids curried him into it.

"Don't be a baby," they'd taunted. He didn't want to be one. He wanted to be big so he could work and pay the bills so that Mother would want him to come home.

"I bet you'll cry like a little sook." He wouldn't cry. He'd given up crying in front of other people by his second week living in the Home. It brought nothing but more pain and endless taunts from the boys who'd lived their whole lives without compassion or comfort.

It wasn't his first time blacking out, but it was the first time he couldn't recall why. It was quiet — well, almost. Someone was crying nearby. His eyes blinked open, then shut again as the pain in his head rushed in like a train pulling into the station. With a grimace, he pushed a palm against his temple and let his eyes flicker open again.

He was in the stables. He remembered everything now. The memories flooded him as his stomach lurched. He fought the urge to be sick, instead crawling on hands and knees to where Mary lay huddled on her side in the hay. Her legs were pulled up beneath her chin, her head bowed to meet them.

"Mary," he whispered, resting a hand on her knee.

She startled and looked up at him with wet eyes the colour of a spent storm.

"It's me, Harry. I won't hurt you."

She pulled away from him, scuttling further against the wall and into a mound of scattered hay.

He wanted to hug her, to comfort her the way his mother used to do with him when he scraped his knees playing chase or fell from the porch railing onto the pavement below and knocked out a baby tooth. He wanted to be everything she needed in that moment, but he couldn't. She shrank from him as though he was to blame. And maybe he was — why couldn't he stop it? He should've come looking sooner. Should've done more to stop Crew.

Instead of comforting her, he squatted beside her, throat aching, and watched in silence. Waiting for some sign from her about what to do next. Lottie joined him then, shuffling across the dusty space to sit beside Mary. She curled up behind Mary, her smaller body curving around her sister's. Mary's frame relaxed imperceptibly, then the tears stopped. She sniffled, wiped her nose with the back of her hand and stared ahead, blank-eyed.

It seemed like an hour before she finally moved. But it was probably only minutes. Harry couldn't tell anymore. It wasn't fully dark when they emerged from the stables together.

Mary had her arm around Harry's shoulders, and he took as much of her weight on his frame as he could manage as they walked side by side. Lottie came along with them, clutching tight to her sister's hand.

"I'll take you to your cottage, then I'm going to see Forrest," he declared, his voice steeped in anger.

Mary whimpered, wild-eyed. "No, you can't tell Forrest."

"What?" His nostrils flared, his head still pounding.

"You can't tell anyone."

"We've got to. That monster hurt you. He could do it again."

She shook her head violently. "No, don't say anything. Not to anyone at all. Please, promise me you'll keep quiet."

His throat tightened, and anger bubbled in his stomach. He couldn't do that. He would do anything for Mary, but not that. He'd die before he'd let Crew harm her again.

"Why? It doesn't make any sense. Why'd you want me to do that?"

She inhaled a slow breath, her face lined with the pain of it. "He said he'd do it to Lottie if I told."

Harry cursed and shook his head. "I'll kill him."

"No, you can't. You'd be the one in trouble. They'll never believe us over him. Who are we to them? Street Arabs, rubbish...that's how they see us. It's how they've always seen us. You should know that as well as anyone. They won't listen to us over him. It's how it is, and we've simply got to bear it. I won't let anything happen to Lottie. We're all going to keep this to ourselves. Do you hear me?"

Her piercing gaze shifted from Harry to Lottie and back again. Both gave their miserable agreement, then continued on their way back to the cottages. The aroma of roasting mutton and boiled vegetables drifted through the still, dank air. Harry's stomach churned with nausea. He watched Mary and Lottie climb the stairs and walk into Evelyne Cottage. Then, with tears in his eyes, he spun on his heel and wandered back to Brown with his hands shoved deep into his pockets, head hanging low. He missed Barnardo's. Missed his mother. Missed the cool trickling rain falling on his head and the deep green hedgerows that marked lush grassy fields dotted with brilliantly coloured wildflowers. He missed England, his home. And a hopeless sense of how far away from that home he now was settled over his soul.

❧ 25 ❧

MIA

My head nods against my chest. My eyes are heavy, like something is weighing down the lids. I can't keep them open. The air-conditioning blasting from the vents around the airport is soothing. It's cooled my overheated body, I'm sleepy and the armchair I found nestled in a corner is comfortable. There's a head rest, and I lay my head back on it, struggling to keep my eyes open. I fail and they shut immediately. My head bobs back up again and I blink, then glance at my watch. My parents should be arriving in about thirty minutes. I probably shouldn't have come to pick them up so early, but I wasn't sure what the traffic would be like at this time of day, and I didn't want to be late. There isn't much Dad hates more than tardiness.

It's been two weeks since Brody was born. Brody hasn't been sleeping well at night. Daytimes are a breeze — he spends hours sleeping soundly on his back with his fisted hands raised high, either side of his head. But at night, he wants to feed and be held, and he won't settle for anything less. He cries, fusses, and his face turns red, so I spend hours every night pacing around the house, rocking him in my arms — it seems like the only thing that works to keep him content. If Ben tries rocking him for a little while to give me a break, he screams the house down. So, it's fallen to me to do the night shift, and Ben lets me sleep during the day.

What that means now is me sitting in an airport unable to keep my eyes open. The airport carpet is a jagged pattern of blue and red, with straight-edged shapes bumping into each other. I assume it's to confuse the eyes enough we won't notice any stains or food crumbs. I'm seated outside a café, and it's crowded. There are people seated at every table, drinking coffee, wine, eating plates of chips or toasted banana bread. Perhaps they're waiting to go somewhere, or maybe they're waiting to meet someone. Either way, everyone here is doing the same thing: waiting.

There's a young woman in stiletto heels with a phone attached to the side of her perfectly coiffed head, striding fast and pulling a tiny black suitcase behind her over the carpet. A man seated in an armchair matching my own, but across the way, dressed in sports clothes, with bulging muscles and headphones over his ears, eyes closed and one foot tapping out a rhythm. Plus hundreds of other people, each unique, all with somewhere to be and something important to do. I'd love to sit here and watch them all, but I'm intrigued by Gammy's story, and I have to know more.

I yank my phone from my purse and flick through various websites. I search for the Fairbridge Farm School and find there are dozens of search results with images of smiling children on the farm, or with suitcases boarding a ship in England. I'm still processing it all, even now. She hasn't raised the subject of the Fairbridge Farm School again since that day she and Auntie Char came to visit Brody, when she told us about how she, Charlotte and Gramps travelled to Australia on board a big ship and ended up at the Fairbridge institution. I've rifled through this information before, but I want to know more.

She was matter of fact, the way she described it all. I'm still reeling. How could it be that the three of them went through something so far-fetched, so horrifying, and yet none of us have ever heard of it? Do

Mum and Dad know about it? That was something I wanted to ask Gammy, but didn't have the heart. If they know about it and they're still willing to be so hard on Gammy and Gramps, I'll struggle to understand my own parents — although that's nothing new for me. I've spent many an hour in tears over the decisions they've made or the things they'd said that've cut me to my core.

But today, I'm determined things will be different. I'm going to be patient, understanding and kind. There's going to be a kind of Zen to my personality they've never seen before. I'm a mother now—doesn't that mean I should have everything under control? I'm not a kid anymore. I'm an adult and I'm going to act like one. Nothing they say or do will control me, I'm going to control myself — or something like that, anyway.

Perhaps I've been reading too many self-help books.

Regardless of all that, I've got to know more about Fairbridge and what my grandparents endured. Gammy paused her story before Brody's doctor called. Then, we were all so focused on Brody's health, that it was an hour before she got back to it. She described the first sports carnival they held at the school. How she was assaulted. And I still can't believe she never told anyone. But that's what she said — apart from Gramps and Charlotte, we're the first people, me and Ben, to know what happened to her that day, and it's breaking my heart into little pieces. It doesn't make sense, but I wish with all my heart I could've been there for her, to comfort her, hold her, to make it all okay. I'm glad she had Charlotte. I've always wondered how the two of them could be so close after so many years — but it makes sense to me now.

I wipe the tears that've found their way down my cheeks with the back of my hand and scroll through the search results. It's a rabbit hole and I'm burrowing down into it, reading articles, studying photographs, learning everything I can about the Fairbridge Society, the *Strathaird* and the life my grandparents lived all those years ago.

One of the articles stands out to me — it's recent. A quick scan reveals there's a reunion of Fairbridge kids coming up at Molong. My heart quickens as I read through the details — some of the children from her time will be there. Maybe this could be a chance for Gammy to come to terms with what happened to her, how it impacted her life and made her who she is.

When I dial her number, she answers after ten rings. I'm about to hang up when finally, I hear her voice. She's out of breath and I imagine she's left her phone in her purse in the bedroom again. I don't know how many times I've told her to keep it with her. There's no point having a phone hidden in her purse if she has another fall. Thankfully, Charlotte is staying with her, so at least she has someone watching over her for now.

"Gammy, it's Mia. How's your ankle?"

Gammy sighs. "Oh, it's fine, but this dratted boot is driving me crazy. It's like dragging a pot plant around on the end of my leg."

I chuckle at that thought.

"How's the baby?"

"He's fine. I left him with Ben so I could pick up Mum and Dad at the airport."

"Of course, I forgot about that."

My lips purse. Gammy is nothing if not passive aggressive. She knew the time of Mum and Dad's flight—I pinned it to her refrigerator door. But she's playing their game — the one they all play so well. Where they pretend they don't care, because it hurts too much when they argue or push each other away.

"Gammy, I was looking up all this Fairbridge stuff, and it seems there's a reunion coming up at the farm in Molong."

"A reunion?"

"That's right. What do you think? Would you like to go? It's a few months from now, so I could possibly go with you. I'm not sure, though. It would depend on how Brody's doing."

Gammy hesitates. "I don't know, love. I don't really care enough to show up to something like that. I probably wouldn't recognise anyone. And Gramps isn't likely to be able to make it."

"Well, it's up to you," I say, although I'm hoping she'll change her mind. It could be the very thing she needs to find closure and healing after all this time. "It might be good for you."

"Maybe... I suppose it could be fun to go back there after all these years. See what the place looks like now. Of course, most of the people

I knew from that time are probably dead by now. Certainly the cottage mothers would be, plus a lot of the older kids, the principal and his wife, the gardener... On second thought, I don't think I will. But thanks, anyway."

I squirm in my chair when she mentions Crew. That's what she called him, only this time she doesn't say his name, and I can't blame her. How she can even think about him, recall what happened, without crying, screaming, or shouting is beyond me. I want to do all those things, and it wasn't me he hurt.

It sits hard and heavy in my gut, this feeling of anger mixed with pain. That she didn't tell anyone, didn't report him, or get him in trouble only makes it worse. The person inside of me who likes to fix everyone, to help, to make things better can't stand the lack of resolution. There should've been justice, him in a jail cell or at the very least fired and reviled.

But he didn't get any of that. He walked away free, with no recrimination or revenge. Just him and his evil, out there in the world. If he was still alive, which Gammy assures me he's not, I'd fly to wherever he lived and confront him. But I can't do that. All I can do is be here for Gammy now. The reunion might be a way I can help her come to terms with her past and let go of it all. She's held it so tight to her chest, this dark secret that's shaped so much of who she is.

And there's a hint of a whisper in the back of my mind that maybe it's been the cause of the schism between her and Dad all these years. He's accused her of not being a loving mother, of not caring about him the way he needed her to when he was young. Maybe that's why. If he only knew what she'd been through, perhaps he'd understand. Or not. Dad isn't the emotional type. Everything's about rationality and logic with him. Except when it comes to Gammy and Gramps — for them he's held onto an irrational resentment that keeps them at arm's distance.

I finish the phone call, tell Gammy I love her, and hang up. I'm scrolling again when someone clears their throat in front of me.

Suddenly Dad's there, standing over me with his large hand wrapped around the handle of a roller bag. Mum's there too. She's puffing along behind him, tugging her aqua roller bag all crooked and bumping.

I jump to my feet and embrace them both, the emotion of everything I've been thinking, of my conversation with Gammy, still lingering in my heart and wetting my cheeks. Mum pulls out of my hug and studies my face.

"You've been crying. Is everything okay?"

I nod and squeeze her hand. "Fine, Mum. Looking forward to seeing you, that's all."

Dad shifts uncomfortably, standing a little at a distance. He doesn't like public displays of emotion. So, I wipe my cheeks dry and press a smile to my face.

"I'm so glad you're here. Come on, I'll help you get your luggage into the car." I take Mum's suitcase by the handle, and she falls into step beside me.

"Good to see you weren't late," mutters Dad, back straight as he marches ahead of me.

He has no idea where I've parked, but doesn't let that stop him from leading the way. I want to roll my eyes at him, but I've decided to be Zen. So that's what I'm going to do. Be Zen.

"Of course. I know how much you hate it when I'm late."

"And how is Brody?" asks Mum.

"He's fine, so far. I take him to the hospital every day for tests. They haven't told me anything new yet, just that they're monitoring him. I'll be taking him today after I drop you at the hotel."

Mum offers a brief nod. "I can't wait to meet him."

I grin and fight against the lump in my throat. I've missed them so much. There's nothing that means more to me than having my family together — all of them in one city. Soon, I hope they'll all be in the same house, maybe even the same room. My dream would be for them to get along, to put the pain and conflict of the past behind them and move on. To be a family.

"You should ask the doctor to give you more information when you go today. They must know more than they're letting on. You have to fight for your health when it comes to doctors. Sometimes they hold back when they shouldn't. You know how it is." Mum's lips are pulled into a tight pink line — she's wearing a glossy lipstick. Her blonde hair is pulled into a chignon at the nape of her neck. Her pink suit perfectly matches the colour of her lipstick, as well as her three-inch pumps. Mum looks as though she's stepped off the cover of a mature women's magazine. She makes me feel frumpy, but that's nothing new and it doesn't really bother me. Her immediate reversion to the pushy, controlling woman of my teenaged years, however, does. I ignore the insinuation about my profession. I know she doesn't mean anything by it.

"It's fine, Mum. We'll work it out. Have you and Dad reconsidered staying with Gammy instead of at the hotel? Gammy would love it, and she has plenty of space. I know you said you changed your mind—you don't want to be a burden to her—but really, she wants you there with her. And I'll help when I can."

Mum and Dad don't respond. We reach the car and I help them load their luggage into the boot, then climb in to start the engine. The heat has sweat running down my spine and I immediately put the air-conditioning on full blast while I wait for Mum and Dad to get settled into their seats.

"Ugh, I'd forgotten how awful the weather is here," says Dad, wiping his forehead with the back of his long sleeve.

"You're dressed for Paris, that's all," I reply. For some reason I feel like I've got to be the mediator between my parents and my hometown — I want them to love it the way I do. To move here eventually, make it their home. But it's probably a pipe dream, one I should give up — that's what Ben tells me every time I raise the subject.

Let it go, Mia. They don't want to live here and you're never going to convince them.

He's right. I should let it go.

Mum is in the back seat. Dad's beside me, waving hands in front of his face, I assume in some effort to fan himself as he leans into the blast from the vents. Eye rolling is so difficult to avoid at this point I'm on the verge of pulling a muscle, and we're only a few minutes into their visit.

"We can't stay with Mum," he says out of nowhere. "We don't want to put extra pressure on her to take care of us, and besides, I think we'll all do better with our own space."

I can't argue with that point. Space is probably a good thing, in their case.

Throughout the entire car ride to the hotel, Mum gives me advice on how to take care of Brody, how to feed him, burp him, wrap him, rock him, what colic looks like and how to set up a sleep schedule—which I should do as soon as possible, according to her sage wisdom. All the while, Dad complains about the heat, the car's lousy air-conditioning, the state of Brisbane's roads and the insanity of having so many one-way streets in the centre of a major city — a shameful thing, according to him.

By the time I drop them off, there's a twitch in my left eyelid and my stomach is in knots. I drive home, listening to an AM radio station that claims to play relaxation music, and I have to admit I'm feeling slightly better when I pull into the garage.

That doesn't last long, though. Right before I step through the garage door and into the house, I hear the wail of a very unhappy newborn emanating through the walls. My inner peace is gone, shattered by a screeching that to me feels something similar to the noise of nails down a chalkboard. I hurry to the nursery and find Ben rocking Brody back and forth, back and forth, in his arms, with a stricken a look of panic on his face. He sees me and the panic is replaced with utter relief.

"You're home! I didn't realise it'd take so long."

He hands Brody to me, and I pat his back gently as I carry him to the feeding chair. It's an armchair that glides back and forth in a rocking motion. It's probably my favourite purchase for the nursery. I spend hours every day in this chair. I sink into it, and Brody is feeding within moments.

Ben kisses my forehead, then strokes Brody's cheek before backing towards the exit. "Sorry, honey, I've got to go."

My brow furrows because I know he's on paternity leave, which means there isn't anywhere else he has to be right now. Nowhere more important than here. Nothing more pressing than this. But still, he's shuffling backwards in the direction of the door. "What do you mean? Where are you going?"

His cheeks pink. "There's an emergency at work. Sorry..."

"What? You're on leave."

He shrugs. "I can't help it. There was no one else to help and they need me. I'm the only anaesthetist in the group who's available this weekend."

"But you're not available," I protest as he slips out the door.

He blows me a kiss. "I know, and I promise I'll remind them of that. But this time...gotta go!"

And he's gone.

My head is pounding, and I realise I forgot to eat lunch and haven't had a thing to drink in hours. When I finish feeding Brody, I'm tired, drained, head-achey, thirsty and in pain all over. I stop in the kitchen to grab a glass of water and a banana, then carry him to the car. We'll be late for our hospital appointment if I don't hurry.

He cries non-stop from the moment I strap him into his car seat until we pull into the hospital parking lot. I try rocking him at the stoplights by tapping the brakes gently over and over, but it doesn't help much. He stops screaming for a moment, but starts up again as soon as the rocking finishes.

We sit in the waiting room for what seems like hours. I spend the entire time pacing back and forth with him up against my shoulder, soothing him with soft crooning words and gentle pats on the back. Finally, he settles after an enormous burp, and the doctor calls us into his office.

I'm nervous about this visit. We've come to the hospital every day for testing, but we don't usually see the doctor. We see nurses and receptionists and other patients. But the doctor, in his blue scrubs, half-moon glasses perched on his nose and stylishly flicked salt-and-pepper hair, has an imposing presence that gives me a chill.

I realise it's because he holds the power of life and death over my son. Is he going to tell me something else is wrong? Or that the treatment is working and everything is fine? Every possible scenario is sailing through my head as Doctor Harris examines Brody from top to bottom with various implements and machinery, then looks over his file.

The truth is, I already know what he's going to say. I've checked Brody over myself so many times it's clear — things aren't going well. I'm poised, on edge, waiting for his doctor to confirm my fears.

He sits at his desk, spectacles on the very tip of his nose, and clicks away at his computer in silence for a few minutes. Finally, he faces me and removes the spectacles, setting them on the desk in front of him. I sit across from him with Brody wrapped and snoozing in my arms.

"Mia, I'm afraid the medication isn't doing what we'd hoped it would. We'll have to proceed with the surgery."

❧ 26 ❧

JANUARY 1954

MARY

T he scent of fresh-baked bread filled the air. Flour dusted every surface and coated Mary's hands. Someone had left it behind on the bench after mixing a batch of bread dough. The scent of it tickled her nose. She resisted the pull of a sneeze and instead held her breath until the feeling passed. Beside her, Lottie drew the outline of a doll in flour on the bench. Her nose was dusted with white, and her hair had a white tinge. Mary giggled.

"You look like an old woman," she said.

Lottie's nose wrinkled. "So do you."

"Don't make a mess," admonished Faith, traipsing into the kitchen with two loaves of bread and hoisting them onto the bench. Both had partially blackened tops and they made a hollow thud as they hit the bench.

"We weren't," replied Mary.

Faith rolled her eyes. "Okay, I'll bring in the rest of the bread the boys baked in the bakehouse this morning. Your job is to clean up this mess and make two sandwiches each for sixty kids for our lunch bags. We all take turns—today's your turn."

"How do we make a sandwich?" asked Lottie, eyeing the bread with suspicion.

Faith sighed. "Haven't you two ever made sandwiches before? What have you been doing all your lives — waited on hand and foot, huh?"

"We usually had nought but butter for our bread," replied Mary.

That seemed to shut up Faith, who inhaled a quick breath. "Fine, you slice these loaves, spread butter on one of the slices, then look in the cupboard on the cold shelf for leftovers." She strode to the cupboard and plucked one door open, then bent to scan the shelves. "If there aren't any leftovers, we usually have Vegemite." She pulled a large tray covered with a waxed cloth from the cold shelf and shoved it onto the bench beside the bread. "Lamb's brains from last night's supper."

Mary's stomach heaved at the sight of the cold brains. She swallowed. "Is that all?"

"Be grateful. Some days there's nothing left over. When you run out of the brains, there's a jar of pickles in the fridge you can use."

"Pickle sandwiches?" questioned Mary.

"Yep."

It was the first day of school after the summer holidays. The summer had been a long one, longer than any Mary experienced in her life before. Living with Mam in London, the warm months came and went in a mad dash. Summers were short and sunny days infrequent. This summer, she'd experienced a kind of heat that zapped every ounce of energy from her body and left her with a consistently reddened tan on her face, arms and legs.

She hadn't attended school back in England, though Mam often promised they would. So, the prospect of attending now both excited her and twisted a ball of nerves that ground in her gut.

What if she couldn't keep up with the other kids? She hated to be stupid in front of the class. She was nine years old, and the only reading she'd done was with Harry in the library on board the ship from England to Australia. She was bound to be the worst reader of the group. Not to mention all the other important things children learned in school that she knew nothing about.

As she and Lottie sliced the loaves of bread, she thought about all the things that could go wrong at school, and how much she longed to know things, to read, to write, and to learn. She wanted so badly to be the kind of child others could look up to, but she knew it was impossible. She'd always be Mary Roberts, a gutter child from the East End whose own workhouse mother didn't want her.

The bread, when sliced, was only partially cooked. Hard and burned to charcoal on top, but doughy and undercooked in the centre of the loaf. They did the best they could putting the sandwiches together and packaging them in brown paper bags that they lined up along a set of tables at one end of the kitchen. Before long, children filed into the room in dribs and drabs to collect their paper bag.

When, finally, they were done, Mary wanted to take a long nap. Her arms ached, her head throbbed—her legs wanted to crumple beneath her. But the breakfast bell rang. So, they dusted themselves off and hurried to Nuffield Hall to eat, their own lunch bags under their arms.

"When Mam comes to meet us, I'm never going to eat lamb's brains again," said Lottie with a shudder as they found their place at their table. "Or those wee black creatures in my porridge. More like splodge than porridge, if you ask me. That's what some of the other kids call it."

Mary frowned. "Mam isn't coming." She'd been avoiding this conversation. But she was tired and hungry and not looking forward to the weevil-filled mush that passed as a breakfast food at the farm.

Lottie blinked. "She is too. She told us she was coming."

"She's not coming. You might as well get used to it."

Lottie's eyes filled with tears. "Don't say that."

It was too much. Everything she'd been through, all the lies she'd told herself for so long about why they were alone, why Mam didn't love them. She couldn't take any more. And she couldn't face Lottie's tears. Not now, after spending the entire morning bent over half-cooked lamb's brain sandwiches that she'd be expected to eat on her first day at school.

"Don't bring her up again, or I'll give you something to cry about," she spat.

It was one of Mam's favourite sayings. She'd used it when Mary was upset — whether over a scraped knee or an empty cupboard when her stomach growled so loud, she was sure it'd wake the neighbour's baby and then they'd never hear the end of it.

Mam hated the sound of a wailing baby more than she hated to be interrupted when she was with one of the men she brought back to the flat after an evening out. She couldn't get into the pub, where only men were allowed, but in the warmer months she'd spent her evening waiting around outside the off license for *gentlemen friends,* as she called them. When it was too cold, she wouldn't stay, but passed by to see if any of the men would shout her a bottle of drink or walk her home.

Mary and Lottie spent many an evening tiptoeing around the living room so as not to wake the neighbours' baby. The woman seemed to have a new one every single year that they lived next door. There was always someone crying, it seemed to Mary.

Lottie's attempts to bite back her tears after Mary's harsh words irritated her further still. So, she sat on her hands waiting for her bowl to be filled with splodge and stared directly ahead at the wall. The chatter and din of children around her blocked out Lottie's sniffles and she forced herself to think of something else, anything else, other than her sister's pain. By the time she'd finished her bowl of porridge, which she ate without once thinking of the weevils, the knot of resentment in her chest had loosened and she slipped her hand into Lottie's as they walked with the other children to the schoolhouse.

❧ 27 ❧

HARRY

The sun hung over the horizon. It climbed steadily through the bright blue morning sky, chunks of sunshine slanting golden over the sheep paddocks and into the slaughterhouse. Harry pressed against the timber fence, arms folded and one foot propped up on the lowest railing as he watched the sheep traverse the chute. A group of fifteen- and sixteen-year-old boys pushed the sheep up the chute, bleating and kicking to where two boys waited to butcher them. They would serve as dinner for the children and staff that evening.

Beside Harry, Max studied the sheep with a cigarette between his lips. He pulled it free, exhaled a cloud of smoke and squinted into the sun. He turned to lean his back against the fence as he took another drag.

"That'll be us in a few years."

"Trainees?" asked Harry.

Max shrugged. "Yep. No more schooling, no more history books or maths problems. Just butchering sheep, milking cows, feeding chooks, harvesting wheat, baking bread and picking peaches in the orchards."

"It's not so bad, I guess," replied Harry. "What else would you do with your life?"

"What do you mean?"

Harry peered up at the sky and watched a fluffy white cloud billow into various different shapes, transforming in slow motion. "I dunno. If you could do anything at all, what would you do?"

Max glanced at him, his eyes dark. Then he looked away. "Don't laugh."

"I won't."

"I've given up on the idea of accounts. I'm terrible at maths. I'd make films."

"What?" Harry faced him with narrowed eyes.

"You know, like at the cinema. I saw one once, on that big ship that brought me here years ago. It was in black and white and there wasn't much to the storyline, but still... it made me feel good. Every now and then, Forrest takes us all to Orange on a Saturday and lets us watch a reel at the pictures there. The room is all red velvet and plush seats, we can eat popcorn until we're sick from all the salt, and I feel for a little while as though I'm somewhere exotic living someone else's life. I can be someone different, someone who's got a family, someone with a future other than —" He waved a hand around at the village. "This."

Harry knew what he meant. There was something special about watching a film. He'd seen two in his life, and both had left an impression on him. "I think that'd be grand."

"Yeah?"

"Yeah, you should do it."

Max didn't look up. "I'll get right on that. I'm pretty sure they let high school dropouts make films. Right?" He laughed, pushing away from the fence with a heel on the railing. "Come on, let's go before we're late for cricket practice. Forrest will have a kitten if we lose this game to the town kids."

Max flicked the butt of his hand-rolled cigarette to the ground, then picked up a rock to smash the end into the dirt. They jogged together back through the village, laughing and joking, stopping to chat along the way. Max knew everyone, and he introduced Harry whenever they came across someone new. He felt more at home now. The farm was familiar to him, the birdcalls and bleating of sheep less mysterious and foreign. The buildings had names—he'd tramped every path and knew where they led.

When they reached Brown Cottage, they found it empty. Max double-checked every room, but there was no one around. He set off at a trot. "They've already left and we're late."

Harry jogged beside him, and before long they arrived at the front paddock, which Forrest had made two of the senior boys mow into a cricket field with a slightly crooked pitch. Max seemed tense, but Harry didn't pay attention. He was more interested in the game already underway. He'd played cricket occasionally back in England, but never anything serious. The game that'd been set with the team from Molong sent a thrill of anticipation through his veins. The hope of winning made his gut squirm with nerves.

Forrest stood at the gate, a cricket bat in one hand. He pulled the wire gate shut and was looping a chain around the fence post when Max arrived with Harry behind him.

"You're late, Max," barked Forrest, his face red.

"Yes, sir. Sorry, sir," replied Max in a cheerful voice, stepping through the opening.

The bat, when it connected with Max's back, surprised Harry. Forrest swung it with all his might. Harry jumped away from Forrest's swing and stumbled over a tussock of grass, thudding to the ground on his rear. Harry gaped as Max collapsed in front of him with a yelp. The principal stood hulking over Max where he lay, his giant muscled arms and chest heaving with the aftereffects of what he'd done.

"Don't be late again," he growled. "Now get up and join in with practice. We're gonna need all the help we can get with this lousy team."

He marched back to where the rest of the children played. One boy was running back and forth on the pitch. Another was bowling. A few had witnessed the attack on Max and stood watching, shock written across their features. No one moved towards Max or said anything to him or to Forrest.

Harry scrambled across the grass to where Max lay on his side, his eyes shut and his mouth open as he gasped for breath.

"Max, are you okay?"

Max didn't move, but his hazel eyes blinked open and focused on Harry's face. They were dark with pain. "Harry, I can't move."

His words were expelled on a gasp.

Harry's heart battered against his rib cage as adrenaline surged through his veins. His thoughts clouded with fury. "I'm gonna get him for this..." He rose to his feet, but Max's voice cut through the tumult of blood thundering through his veins.

"No, Harry. Don't do it. You won't win. He's a brute, and he doesn't take any backchat or misbehaviour. Help me up, okay?"

Max reached out a hand and Harry took it with both his own. With a grunt, he leaned back and did what he could to help Max to his feet. But Max cried out, agony lacing his voice with tears. Harry lowered him slowly to the ground again. He rolled onto his back and stared up at the sky, breathing hard.

"I can't do it. I can't get up."

"Wait here, I'll get help."

He rushed over to where Forrest was showing one of the younger boys how to grip the cricket bat.

"Mr Forrest?"

The principal spun to face him, his bulbous nose red from the sun, his hair askew in the wind. "Yes?"

"Max can't move. He can't stand up."

Forrest's gaze wandered to where Max lay still in the distance. "Huh? Oh. Run up and find the nurse, will you?"

Harry offered a brief nod, then waited until Forrest made his way over to Max's side before sprinting back up the hill to the village. And as he ran, the anger that'd stirred inside him built and grew until it consumed him.

THE NEXT DAY, HARRY SPENT THE MORNING LAZING ON THE FRONT verandah at the cottage. He didn't have any morning chores that day, and with Max in the hospital in Orange, he had no one to talk to either. All he wanted to do was get away from this place. To go home to England and never think about Fairbridge Farm School again for the rest of his days.

He plucked a smoke from the packet he'd found in Max's belongings when he'd lain on Max's bed staring up at the wire mesh beneath the bunk overhead earlier that morning. He couldn't sleep thinking about it all — the memory of what'd happened, the way Forrest had struck Max kept playing over and over through his thoughts. He lit the cigarette with a match, then gulped in a great lungful of smoke. He coughed and hacked, his eyes watering.

"You gotta take it slower than that the first time you have a drag," offered Devon as he sat beside Harry on the timber slat floor.

Harry coughed again and offered a quick nod. "Thanks."

"Can I bum a ciggie?"

Harry handed Devon a cigarette, making a mental note to pay Max back the next time he had a chance. Devon lit up and dragged coolly, blowing the smoke in a line straight over his head. "Sorry about what happened to Max."

Harry didn't respond. Instead he took another drag, this time more carefully, not letting the smoke into his lungs. He puffed it right back out again.

"Have you heard anything?"

"Nope. They're not gonna tell me what's going on, are they?" He hated this — not knowing, having no power to find out how Max was, whether he'd ever walk again or if he was coming back to the farm.

"I'm sure he'll be fine."

Harry grunted in response, but he wasn't convinced.

When Forrest brought Max home later that day, he carried the boy in his arms to the cottage with a stern expression on his broad face and sat in a chair beside the bed, hat in his hands. Harry stood at a distance, watching, as anger burned hot within.

"Are you comfortable, lad?" asked Forrest, massaging his hat with both enormous hands until it was flat.

Max sat propped up by pillows behind his back. His legs stretched out before him. "Fine." He didn't look at Forrest, but stared at his toes protruding in two lumps beneath his blanket.

"Well, that's good. I could get you something to eat, if you like."

Max glanced up at Forrest and sighed. "That might be nice."

Forrest stood to his feet, still squeezing the hat. "Right. I'll get you a nice plate of something and a glass of milk. That should help you feel better."

Max didn't contradict him, although Harry wanted to shout that Max would never be all right again. He'd cared for Forrest, thought of him as a father figure. And the principal had betrayed that trust. Harry wouldn't trust the man again either. In fact, he hated him. Hated all of them — the masters, matrons, leaders, and officials — for what they'd done to Max, Mary, and everyone he'd ever loved.

Forrest strode from the cottage, and Harry sidled over to Max with his hands pushed deep into his shorts pockets. A lump formed in his throat at the pitiful frown on his friend's normally gleeful face.

"You okay?"

Max met his gaze and offered a half smile. "Didn't you hear? Right as rain in a jiffy."

"Does it hurt?'

"Yep. It kills, but the doctor said once the swelling goes down, I'll be up and about again in no time. At least they think so—of course they don't really know. It's a bruised spine. They kept saying they want me to stay positive."

Harry rubbed both hands over his face, willing the lump in his throat to dissipate. He didn't trust his voice with the pain of it tweaking at his emotions.

"I'll get him back. I promise you."

Max's brow furrowed. "What? You mean Forrest?"

Harry dipped his head.

"No, don't do that. I don't want you to do anything."

"What? Why not? He deserves it. I should kill him for what he did..." His hands balled into fists at his sides, his head hot.

Max let his eyes drift shut, his face growing pale. He shifted in place, grimacing as he manoeuvred into a more comfortable position.

Then he spoke again in a pained voice. "Promise me you won't get back at Forrest over this. Please."

That made no sense. Forrest should've been reported to the police. Prison was too good for the man. He couldn't get away with it. Crew had gotten away with hurting Mary. Now Forrest would walk away from injuring Max. "I don't understand. Why don't you want him to pay for what he did? He should've been arrested."

"Like I told you before, he's not so bad. Most of the time, he's a decent guy. He's getting me something to eat and some milk because he feels sorry for what he did. I don't want..." Max swallowed, and his voice cracked. "I don't want to lose him. He cares about me—really, he does. He told me so on the way home from the hospital. Promised it wouldn't happen again. Said he's working on his temper."

"And you believe him?" Harry fumed.

"Yeah, I do. And, besides, if he goes, who else is there? Elsa's the only other family I have in the world. It's okay for you. You had a mother, so you know what it's like. I've never had anyone but Forrest and Elsa."

"You've got me," replied Harry.

Max grinned. "Glad to hear it."

Harry paced to the other side of the room and slapped a hand against one of the bunk beds. "It's not right."

"It's what I want."

"Fine, I'll keep my cool for you."

"Thanks, mate. You're a good friend."

The bell rang. Harry hesitated, then waved goodbye and plunged through the cottage door, headed out to do his evening chores. His thoughts in turmoil, he broke into a jog and before long found himself sprinting through the village. When he reached the stables, he slowed to a jog, then stopped at the fence to watch the horses graze. Animals gave him a sense of peace, even when his emotions threatened to overwhelm him. He wanted to punch someone, to hit something until it broke apart under his bloodied fists. Instead, he slapped the fence. One of the horses, a grey animal with black mane and tail, looked up with a start, then loped over to see him. No doubt hoping for a carrot. He held up his hands as if in surrender.

"Sorry, mate. I don't have anything for you."

The horse stuck its muzzle through the railings. Harry shook his head in disbelief. Horses were amazing creatures. He'd mostly only seen them from afar before. Now, on the farm, he could watch them up close, even pat them occasionally. This time, he stroked the horse's nose. It puffed out a hot breath that whispered over his face, making him laugh out loud. Then his hand worked its way up to the long hair between the horse's ears, and he scratched the spot gently. The horse seemed to enjoy it, pushing a little further through the fence until its lips nibbled at Harry's shirt.

He spent a few more minutes with the horses, petting them, whispering to them, and walking around the yard alongside them as they grazed. By the time he left, his thoughts had calmed and he'd forgotten his anger, at least for the moment. As he headed off to do his chores, he considered that there were some good things about living at the farm — the friendships he'd made, the horses, the sports carnival. Max's perspective challenged him — how could he forgive and forget so easily? It wasn't something Harry was ready to do. Something within him clamoured for justice. But he could keep his mouth shut about the things eating at him from the inside, for now. For Max and for Mary.

❧ 28 ❧

MARY

After two months living at the farm, Mary had grown accustomed to the Fairbridge way of life. Weekends were her favourite part of the week. Although they were almost as structured as the rest of the week, there were often fun activities for the kids to participate in. She found herself pushing the memories of her own pain and trauma down deep into the darkest recesses of her mind and moving on as though nothing had ever happened. She'd managed to completely avoid seeing Crew in recent weeks and at the same time avoided thinking about him. Instead, she embraced the best parts of their new world: attending school, evenings in the cottage with Lottie and the other girls, the Weekend Notice which was pinned to one of the doors at the entrance to Nuffield Hall on Fridays and outlined the activities for the weekend ahead.

"I still don't understand...ouch...why I can't simply have long hair." Mary's face squeezed into a grimace as Faith yanked a brush through the knots in her hair. They sat on the verandah outside Evelyne Cottage. A pile of hair in various shades curled and knotted at her feet.

It was Mary's birthday. She was ten years old. She hadn't told anyone. Lottie hadn't remembered—she was too young to keep track of things like dates and birthdays. Anyway, Mary didn't want to celebrate. Celebrating birthdays seemed wrong — besides, there was no one to celebrate with her and she didn't feel much like it anyway. And she had a feeling that the reminder of time passing would only make Lottie pine anew for home. Mary couldn't bear listening to Lottie's muffled sobbing or her stuttering grief.

It was wrong of her to feel that way. She was hard-hearted like Mam had told her a hundred times, she knew that, but she couldn't help it. No more grief. No more tears. They'd both shed enough to last them a lifetime, and Mary could only stand so much of it. She wanted to laugh and have fun, to enjoy each day regardless of how many trials came because in all truth, it was still better than life had been when they'd lived with Mam. Although Lottie seemed unable to recall the worst of it. Some kind of rose-coloured lenses seemed to embellish her recollections of their lives in England.

The worst of it was getting her beautiful hair cut off on her birthday. But it couldn't be helped, and she'd made a vow not to cry over anything that didn't warrant it. So, she pushed her chin out and bore it.

"You're getting a haircut because you let it get too tangled. I can barely get the brush through it. Besides, Ingrid told me you look as though a hive of bees set themselves up to make honey on your head."

Mary crossed her arms over her chest and glowered at her own reflection in the hand mirror Lottie held before her. "I don't much care what Ingrid thinks." She had no love for their cottage mother, a woman who'd leave them to fend for themselves at suppertime if she had a date in town. Ingrid's temper was legendary around the farm, and most of the children cowered in her presence. Not, Mary though. She didn't let Ingrid bother her the way the others did — Ingrid couldn't hold a candle to Mam when she was in a rage.

"You will care when she gives you a walloping for having messy hair."

Mary didn't think that she would care. Not one bit. She'd dodged

Ingrid's paddle many a time already. Besides, she hated to think of herself with the lopsided style the other girls wore. But she also knew the importance of fitting in and not making waves. She'd spent her young life slipping beneath the radar and staying out of trouble even while stealing a handful of toffee right from under a shopkeeper's nose. And so, she sat still on the rickety chair and held her breath to ward off the pain.

Lottie's hair was already cut, and it maddened Mary to see it. A thick, slanted fringe, along with a lopsided, blonde, boyish bob that tickled her shirt collar. Her beautiful full waves were gone, leaving only straight hair in their place. She wasn't the baby-faced girl who'd cried herself to sleep in Mary's arms at night after a row with Mam any longer. Her face had lost its soft curves, her legs were long and lanky, and her arms tanned brown.

A snip felled one side of Mary's long blonde curls to the slatted floor below. She glanced down with a pang of regret. Faith lifted her head with a finger beneath her chin.

"Don't move or you'll lose an ear."

Mary crossed her eyes and poked out her tongue. The mirror shook as Lottie laughed silently.

When the haircut was finished, Mary regarded her reflection again. She didn't recognise herself anymore. A full-cheeked, tanned face with freckles over the bridge of the nose, hair darker than it had been and cut short above her collar and with a full, blunt fringe hovering over blue eyes. For some reason, it brought a lump to her throat.

"It's not that bad, is it?" asked Faith. "I tried to get it just right."

"No, it's not bad. It's fine," replied Mary, swallowing down the lump. "I look different, that's all."

Faith shrugged. "I think you look nice."

"Thanks."

"The Weekend Notice is up!" shouted a small girl as she ran along the track from Nuffield Hall and bounded up the stairs in two strides.

All the girls moved at once. Faith threw down the scissors, Mary leapt from the chair, and Lottie placed the mirror, glass up, on the floor. They hurtled down the path to Nuffield Hall, where a small pink sheet of paper fluttered against one of the doors in the afternoon breeze.

Mary could read most of it, and Faith helped with the words she didn't understand.

WEEKEND NOTICE

FRIDAY
>*4pm: Muster for all children not needed for work on septic tank.*
>*7pm: Bus to the pictures in Molong.*

SATURDAY
>*8am: Breakfast.*
>*8:30am: Cottage coke supplies from coke yard.*
>*10am: Pony Club in Molong.*
>*11am: Sunday School picnic, followed by handing out of the week's pocket money.*
>*1:15pm: Tuck Shop.*
>*2pm: Swimming in the dam.*
>*6:30pm: Dinner.*

SUNDAY
>*8am: Breakfast.*
>*9:30am: Report to the dining hall for church.*
>*11am: Sunday School.*
>*Noon: Lunch.*
>*2pm: Cricket.*

"DO YOU THINK MRS FORREST WOULD LET US JOIN THE PONY Club?" asked Lottie after Faith read through the items in the notice.

Mary shrugged even as excitement buzzed through her veins. Ever since they'd come to the farm, the thing she'd longed most to do was ride the horses that grazed in the paddocks just beyond the village. Some of the boys used the horses to pull wagons around the farm, but the rest of the time they were ridden by the Pony Club kids. And Mary desperately wanted to be one of them.

"I don't see why not," said Faith. "You'll have to ask this afternoon, though. If you want to go tomorrow."

Mary and Lottie exchanged a look, then spun on their heels and sprinted in the direction of the principal's house. There was a small office space on the ground floor, and Mary knocked on the door, still puffing.

"Come in," called a feminine voice.

Inside, it took a moment for Mary's eyes to adjust to the dim lighting. Mrs Forrest sat behind a desk at one end of the room, a pen poised above a ledger book. She regarded the sisters over half-moon glasses.

"How can I help you, girls?"

Mary swallowed, hands clasped together in front. She shuffled forward with Lottie close to her side. "Good afternoon, Mrs Forrest. I'm sorry to bother you, but Lottie and I were hoping we might join the Pony Club tomorrow."

Mrs Forrest stood to her feet, smoothed her frock, and stepped out from behind the desk.

"I suppose that would be fine. Although I have to warn you, there's a lot of work involved in keeping horses, exercising them, currying and feeding them. Do you think you'll be up for the challenge?"

Both girls nodded in unison. Mary could barely stand the anticipation. It didn't seem possible they might have horses of their own to care for and ride.

"Then I'm happy to offer you both a place on the team. Two of our older girls have moved into trainee positions and their horses are available. They're good horses, nice and quiet. They'll be perfect for beginners. How does that sound?"

"Do you mean it?" exploded Lottie, her mouth pulled into a happy grin.

"Yes. If you want to join the club, you're welcome to do so." Mrs Forrest had a warm, open expression with kind, dark eyes.

"Yes, Mrs Forrest," said Mary in the politest voice she could manage. "Thank you, Mrs Forrest."

She offered an awkward curtsey, then took Lottie by the hand and dragged her back out through the door. They ran behind the nearest building, then threw their arms around each other as they squealed and danced in place.

"I can't believe it," said Lottie breathlessly.

"It doesn't seem real—that's the truth." Mary caught her breath through a laugh, and kissed Lottie on the forehead. "Let's go and meet the rest of the club. They'll be at the stables getting the horses ready for tomorrow."

LOTTIE'S HORSE WAS A GREY WITH DAPPLED COAT WHOSE NAME, Slim, bore no reflection on the horse's rotund frame. Mary's horse was named Glitter. She wasn't sure why either, since the animal was a dull bay colour with black mane and tail. She didn't glitter and seemed half asleep most of the time with hooded eyes and only the occasional swish of her tail against the flies to indicate consciousness. Which suited Mary perfectly well, since she was terrified to ride a horse that might bolt and throw her.

They'd prepared their saddles and bridles the night before, with Faith's help. Faith was one of the older girls still riding with the club, although she'd have to finish up after her fifteenth birthday when she'd become a trainee.

"Won't you be sad to leave the Pony Club?" asked Mary as she, Faith and Lottie rode side by side along the road to Molong.

Faith shrugged. "Nothing I can do about it. When we become trainees, we're working for the farm. The fun is over." Her voice had a forced cheerfulness to it that Mary didn't believe.

The ride was hot, the landscape quiet other than the clip-clop of horse hooves on the bitumen verge. The scent of horses and dust drifted through the air. It'd rained the night before, but the only evidence was the greener grass that pushed its way in new shoots through the dry earth along the sides of the roads and through the fields that banked their way.

"I'm glad you're riding with us today," added Lottie.

Lottie had been giddy with delight all morning while they'd brushed and saddled their horses. They stopped at a stream outside town to let the horses drink. The animals thrust reaching muzzles into the cool, bubbling water and sucked greedily. Mary climbed down and used her hand to scoop some water into her own mouth. It was fresh and sweet, so she patted it over her face, neck and arms as well.

The Pony Club was held in a large show ground located just before they reached Molong. The town girls were already there on their posh ponies, trotting in circles, heads held high. The Fairbridge girls rode in on bedraggled horses, wearing their khaki uniforms and bare feet in the stirrups. The town girls looked them over but didn't address them. Mary urged Glitter into line to listen to the club leader welcome them and explain how the day would progress.

They started out by riding in group circles around the various adults who'd shown up to run the club. Mary assumed they were parents. The woman in the centre of her circle wore pale jodhpurs and riding boots. The woman called out to them to straighten their backs, push their heels down, gather their reins. Mary tried to follow instructions the best that she could, but found herself bouncing from one side to the other until it seemed her teeth might chatter from her head to the earth below.

After that, they tried jumping their horses over crisscrossing white timber poles. Glitter wouldn't jump, and Mary was glad. She wasn't sure she'd manage to stay on the horse's back if it sailed over those logs. Lottie was in a younger group, and they didn't try the jumps. She seemed to be having fun with the young town girls, riding up and back in a line.

By the time they finished and headed for home, Mary was exhausted but happy. She'd never had so much fun in all her life. Horse riding was an immediate passion for her, one she hoped she'd be able to do again and again. She stroked Glitter's neck as the animal plodded along the side of the road.

Lottie lolled a little to one side on Slim's wide back, her head dipping every now and then as though she was falling to sleep. Mary called her sister's name to make sure she didn't drift off and fall.

As they rode through the village, some of the smaller children jogged alongside the horses, excited to see them. By the principal's house, Mary saw Harry and a dozen other boys climbing into Mr Wood's station wagon. The boys were dressed in matching striped shirts and black shorts and wore cleats on their feet with long socks pulled up to their knees. He'd mentioned rugby tryouts — he was hoping the team would get into the A-league for the winter season in Orange, although he didn't like their chances. She waved at him, and he gave a quick wave back, along with a smile as he ducked into the vehicle. The entire team squeezed into every inch of the rust-bucket before it lurched bumping down the driveway.

Back at the stables, they unsaddled the horses and brushed them down. Then led them to the water trough and spread some hay near the trough for them to eat. Everyone was tired, but spirits were high all the same. They'd had a great time, the horses had behaved, no one had hurt themselves even though two of the girls had fallen when jumping, and Lottie had tumbled from Slim's back when attempting a trot, but she'd climbed right back on with a smile on her vibrant face.

"You go back to the cottage. I'll pack everything away," said Mary.

Lottie yawned. "No, I can't leave you with it all."

"Of course you can. You're tired and it's not much — I'll put the saddles, bridles and curry combs away. You have a shower and I'll be there soon."

One by one, the girls drifted off to their cottages as they finished tidying up. Mary stood for a while leaned up against the fence railings to watch the horses lip at the hay and nose the water, tails flicking at flies.

Finally, she sighed and carried one of the saddles into the saddle room. She collected the rest of the items and put them away as well. The last things were the curry combs, which she set on top of a barrel in one corner of the room where the grooming supplies were piled.

"Had a nice ride?" His voice paralysed her.

Slowly she turned to face him, heart thudding against her ribs. "Get away from me," she hissed.

Crew lolled against the door frame with his arms crossed over his chest. A lazy smirk stole across his face. "Oh, come on. You don't mean that."

"I do mean it. Don't you dare touch me."

"But you didn't tell anyone…" He straightened, then stepped in her direction, his movements languid but his eyes clear and bright.

Anger blurred her vision. Fury rose up through her chest and thundered through her veins. She rushed at him and kicked hard, her foot landing between his legs with all her ten-year-old might. It threw him off balance for a moment and she ducked past him, out the door into the brilliant afternoon sunshine.

"Hey!" he shouted, rage deepening his voice. "You come back here right now."

She didn't wait to listen to the litany of swear words that streamed out of the saddle room behind her. Instead, she ran as fast as her legs would carry her. Arms pumping, she sprinted along the path back to the cottages. One of the cottage mothers was there, carrying a bundle of laundry beneath one arm. Elsa was Harry's cottage mother and had always seemed like a kind woman, but Mary didn't have time to stop. She had to get away from Crew.

"Mary? What's wrong? What's happened?" called Elsa, concern etched across her face.

Mary didn't reply. She ran along the path without a word, then stopped and spun about to look back the way she'd come. Her chest heaving, her lungs fighting for air, she checked to see if Crew had come after her. He emerged from the stables, set his hands on his hips, and stared after her, his face hidden in the shadow of his ever-present hat.

"Mary, are you hurt?" asked Elsa again.

Mary faced her, puffing hard.

Elsa's gaze drifted from Mary's face up the path to where Crew's menacing figure stood, legs planted wide. Understanding hardened her features.

"Did he hurt you, Mary?"

Without saying a word, Mary broke into a run again. She streaked past Elsa, down the path, not stopping again until she reached Evelyne Cottage. She barrelled inside and plonked down on her bed, pulling the blanket up over her head even though sweat streamed down her cheeks and back from the heat of the day. She lay there, legs tucked up against her chest, shivering in the unwavering heat and wishing she had someone to protect her from the darkness that lurked in the shadows.

❦ 29 ❦

FEBRUARY 1954

HARRY

An ache in his legs pulled Harry out of a deep slumber. Outside the cottage, birds trilled and cawed in the cool morning air. Although it was early, sunshine slanted across the floorboards. There were no curtains to keep it at bay, and the windows stood open as they always did to let in mosquitos and flies in equal numbers at different times of the day and night.

He hurt in various parts of his body from the rugby tryout the day before. He'd never played before, so he didn't know the rules. But he could run, and Forrest seemed happy about that.

The ache in his legs was mirrored by the one in his heart. His body hurt, but it was the pain of grief that tore him apart the most. He'd woken from a dream in which he'd lain in his mother's arms while she told him her favourite story — about a prince and a girl who'd fallen foul of the king over their love and had to hide away in a cave in the forest until the king finally died and the prince, his son, rose to power. It was a sad tale. When she told it and reached the ending where the prince and princess finally wed and lived happily ever after, there'd often be a tear or two on her cheek. He didn't understand her sorrow then, but felt it now with the last remnants of the dream fading in the reality of the breaking day.

With a great swallow around the lump in his throat, he swung his legs from the bed and pressed his feet to the cold floorboards. There were chores to do, and already his stomach grumbled with need. He'd been so hungry lately. Hungrier than ever before in his life. He'd grown as well, and his waist had shrunk as his legs lengthened.

He hurried about his chores, glad for the distraction from the gnawing in his gut. Finally, the breakfast bell chimed across the village, and he hurried for Nuffield Hall.

The morning routine was embedded in his brain. He didn't have to think about it at all anymore. It was no longer strange—he'd adapted, the way he had at Barnardo's. He looked around the dining hall and spotted Mary seated at her table, deep in conversation with one of the older girls. She caught his eye and sent him a smile over the sea of children that filled the gap between them. His heart warmed at the sight of her. Even after months at a distance, he couldn't shake the feeling of connection he had with her. It drew him to her every day. He thought about her often and wished they were back on the *Strathaird* together playing hide and seek or reading in the library.

When the prayers were said and the splodge ladled into every bowl, the children stared at it in dismay. A few poked at it with spoons, others wrinkled noses, but most pushed their bowls to the centre of the table. Harry stirred the soupy cereal with his spoon, noting that there were as many weevils in this batch as there were flakes of oats. He swallowed back the bile that rose in his throat and pushed the bowl away.

His stomach grumbled, but there was no amount of emptiness that would induce him to eat a porridge so black with weevils that it appeared grey from a distance. Several of the boys from his table carried their bowls to the pig bins that sat against one wall of the dining hall. They'd carry the bins to the pigpens after breakfast. At least someone would get a benefit from the forsaken meal. They scraped the porridge into the bins using spoons, laughing and whispering amongst themselves as they did. Harry followed them. He had no intention of eating, even if his stomach had flattened against his spine. He stood in line for the bins, waiting his turn.

"Stop that right this moment!" bellowed Forrest from his seat at the long staff table.

He stood to his feet and marched down the steps from the stage to where the boys all stood around the pig bins.

"What's going on here?"

"It's full of weevils," complained one of the bigger boys, his cheeks red.

Forrest's nostrils flared and he peered into the bins one by one. "This food costs good money. Do you think we have money growing on trees around here? Because let me inform you — we do not. A little extra protein will do you all some good. You will spoon that porridge back into your bowls and you'll eat it, or so help me..." He didn't finish his sentence, but every child in the dining hall, who all sat at attention in silence, understood the implied threat.

Whatever the punishment was, Harry wanted to avoid it. He'd seen enough of Forrest's idea of discipline to know that he didn't want to be on the receiving end. Thankful he hadn't scraped his own splodge into one of the bins yet. He returned to the table with his bowl to eat his breakfast.

It was hard going, eating the now-cold mush. It was watery and tasteless. He swallowed it down as quickly as he could manage, doing his best not to look at it before plunging the spoon into his mouth.

Forrest stood over the other boys, watching as they foraged around in the bins for their share of the discarded cereal. As soon as their bowls were full again, he made them eat the watery mess. The porridge was now mixed in with carrot peelings, eggshells, apple cores and anything else the children had thrown into the bins for the pigs. The boys did their best to pick the pieces out, but Forrest was impatient and began rapping them over the knuckles until they used their spoons to shovel the mixture into their open mouths.

One of the boys, a small lad with ginger hair and a button nose, heaved and threw his splodge back up directly into his bowl. Harry looked away, pushing down a heave of his own at the sight. He stared at the wall, breathing deep and fighting his stomach's desire to rid itself of the cold, watery porridge.

"I'm sorry, sir," whispered the ginger-haired boy, wiping his mouth with the back of his hand. His face grew pale when he saw the look of fury on Forrest's face.

"I said eat it!"

The boy's brow furrowed. "But I…"

"Eat it, or you will regret your decision for a very long time, son."

The dining hall was silent. Someone dropped a spoon on the floor and the echo reverberated around the cavernous space. The ginger-haired boy began to cry. Giant tears trickled down his freckled cheeks. His eyes reddened as he stared miserably at the bowl in his hands.

Forrest remained unmoved, so the boy began to eat. Around him, children looked away — staring at their hands, their feet, or the ceiling overhead. The rest of the staff continued eating their hot breakfast without showing the slightest concern over what took place in front of them.

Mrs Forrest stood to her feet and cleared her throat. "Children, if you've finished your breakfast, you may be excused."

There was a thunder of feet as dozens of children hurried to take their dirty dishes, cups and spoons to the washing tubs along the side of the room next to the kitchen. Harry joined them, shuffling forwards as fast as he could. He wanted to get out of there. To breathe deep in the morning air and forget about the congealing splodge and weevils in his gut, to push the image of the ginger-haired boy from his mind's eye.

Outside the hall, a farmer sat atop a wagon loaded with peaches. He wore long brown pants, with an oversized belt cinched tight around his waist. His buttoned shirt was stained and worn with the sleeves rolled up to his elbows. He wore a dirty scarf tied around his neck and a wide-brimmed hat atop his head. Around him, children buzzed and laughed, grabbing at peaches and shoving them into their pockets, down their shirts and piling them into their arms.

The farmer laughed good-naturedly as he climbed down from the wagon. "I thought you might like some of my fallen fruit. I can't sell them anyway, and it would be wasteful to let them rot on the ground.

Looks like I was right about that. Hold your horses. I'm gonna take these into the kitchen—you can eat your fill then."

But the children didn't listen. Harry rushed at the wagon, eager to fit as much of the fruit into his own clothing as he could. He pushed a juicy peach into his mouth, then filled his pockets. As he was piling peaches into the front of his shirt down through his collar, he noticed Mary alongside him. Her shirt was tucked into the waistband of her shorts and was full to the brim with peaches too.

He laughed at her around the peach in his mouth. Her eyes sparkled back at him. Beside her, Lottie filled her own pockets. Max hobbled up behind him and reached for a peach, his eyes gleaming.

"I've never seen so many peaches in all my life," said Mary, laughing.

"Get away from that, you rascals!" shouted Forrest, coming out of the dining hall behind them.

The children scattered with clothing stuffed full of peaches.

"Put that fruit back. We'll share it out equally amongst the group!" Forrest did his best to grab for a child on his left, then one to his right, but they ducked out of reach and scampered away into the village.

Harry ran as fast as he could manage without dropping fruit in the direction of the garden shed. Mary, Lottie and Max ran beside him. Max's back had improved enough for him to get around now. Harry was grateful that when the swelling subsided, the doctors discovered that Max's back was healing well, and he would eventually regain the full use of his legs. For now, he shuffled or hobbled around with an awkward, leaning gait, although it didn't slow him down too much. He straggled behind them. Harry spun to beckon him on every few seconds, and to make sure his friend could manage.

"Let's go inside. No one will see us in there," said Mary, puffing as she ducked into the shed.

Harry waited for Max, then helped him shuffle through the doorway.

They settled inside the garden shed against a wall, letting the fruit tumble out onto the ground around them from pockets, shirts, and arms.

"How wonderfully delicious," said Mary, letting her eyes drift shut.

Harry agreed, but didn't stop chewing to say so. Juice dribbled down his chin as the tart-sweet flavour burst over his tongue. He spat out the pit, then began on another peach.

"One day, I'm going to grow my own peaches. I'll have a tree in my backyard, and I'll eat them whenever I like," said Lottie, her face covered in the pinkish juice.

"Me too," replied Harry as he reached into his shirt for another. "And I'll never eat porridge again."

Laughing, the friends ate as many of the peaches as their stomachs would hold, and the feeling of emptiness inside Harry faded a little more with each discarded pit.

30

MARCH 1956

MARY

The thin piece of paper fluttered with the rush of the wind across the cottage verandah. Mary held it in place with the heel of one hand against the seat of the chair, her tongue poked out the side of her mouth.

"Ask her when she's coming," suggested Lottie, hovering close by.

"I will," replied Mary.

The letter to Mam was slow going. Mary had learned how to form the letters of the alphabet, but spelling wasn't her strong suit. She was doing her best to phonetically sound out the words she wanted to use, but had a feeling it wouldn't be easy for Mam to decipher. Besides that, Lottie continued to harangue her with suggestions for entire paragraphs about their new living arrangements, and questions that Mam wasn't likely to answer.

Mary had never seen Mam put pen to paper in her entire life. She hardly thought Mam would begin now. Besides that, she didn't know Mam's new address. The last time they spoke to her, she had plans to leave their council flat and move in with Stan. But she didn't give Mary his address. So, she'd send the letter to the old address and hope it found its way to Mam's new residence. Although by now, she and Stan could've split up and she might've moved on to somewhere else entirely.

She leaned forward and pressed the pencil hard against the paper as she formed another word. It would take her until suppertime if she kept going at this rate. Frustrated, she set down the pencil and slumped against the wall, her back aching.

"I'm never going to finish," she complained. She hadn't wanted to write a letter at all, but had given in when Lottie looked at her with those big blue puppy-dog eyes, begging to do it. All of the other girls in the cottage who had a living relative back in England were writing, why shouldn't they write too? Lottie was adamant. Mam was coming to meet them, so they should stay in touch or she wouldn't know where to send them word when she arrived.

Mary hated to break her sister's heart. So, she wrote the letter and would give it to Ingrid to send to their previous address, knowing that someday Lottie would have to face the fact that Mam wasn't coming.

She finished up the letter and strode inside to give it to Ingrid, who sat at the dining table with her feet up on a chair reading a copy of the *Women's Weekly* magazine and eating from an open bag of salted chips.

"Here's the letter from Lottie and me," said Mary, handing it over.

Ingrid took it, the grease on her fingertips transferring to the paper as she scanned over the words.

"Crap spelling," she muttered.

"I know," replied Mary, swallowing.

Ingrid met her gaze, then waved a hand. "Okay then, go away now."

Mary hurried from the room, biting on a fingernail. Outside, the morning sun warmed the still-dewy grasses. Mary and Lottie walked side by side in the direction of the stables. On the way, Harry and Max caught up with them. Mary's stomach tingled at the sight of Harry. Ever since the incident with Crew, he'd been particularly attentive to her, going out of his way to check on her every day, even when he was busy with school and farm work.

"Did you write to your mother?" he asked.

"Yep."

"I wrote to Davey. I don't know if he'll get it, though, since I only have the Fairbridge headquarters address."

"He'll get it," she assured him with a sympathetic smile.

"Where are you going?" asked Harry.

"To the stables."

"We'll come too," he replied.

He didn't want her to go there alone. He'd said as much several times. The fact was, Harry couldn't always be with her, and she hated to let Crew cause her to live in fear, but she rarely went anywhere alone anymore.

"Fine with me," she said.

"When you're finished with the horses, let's go mushrooming," said Max.

"Oh, yes, let's." Lottie's eyes gleamed, and she rubbed her hands together.

Mary loved mushrooms as much as Lottie. Every now and then, they'd managed to scavenge for some around the bomb site near their home in London. They'd beg the neighbours, one by one, until they found someone who could spare a dab of butter, then they'd fry the mushrooms with butter and onions, if they had them, and eat them on toast. Mary's mouth watered at the thought. It'd rained the day before, and the ground was wet. Perfect weather for mushrooms, although they were best if found in the early morning before the day grew too hot.

They hurried through their chores at the stable. Mary and Lottie removed Slim and Glitter's rugs and brushed them until their coats shone. Then they spread hay over the ground, along with the other Pony Club girls, for the horses to munch on, and filled the water trough.

By the time they were done, it was almost time for the breakfast bell. The four children ran from the stables up the length of a sheep field to the paddock beyond that was being rested and had only a lone bull as an occupant. The bull grazed at the other end and paid them no attention. They slipped through the gate, careful to shut it behind them. Then began the search for mushrooms.

It wasn't long before Mary found her first dozen nestled beside a cow patty. The mushrooms were short, stout and round, completely white and easy to pluck from the ground. She filled the front of her shirt with them, then continued the hunt. The children passed over the tall, wide-brimmed gold-topped fungi, which would make them sick, instead sticking to the small, white button mushrooms that looked like little fairy dwellings. Mary imagined fairies building their homes beneath the shelter of the mushroom caps, with tiny windows on the stems and baby fairies sleeping in bunk beds inside the caps.

When the breakfast bell rang, they all had a decent number of mushrooms stashed in their upturned shirts. They hurried back to their cottages to hide their treasures until they could fry them.

After breakfast, it was time for school. Mary looked forward to it every day. She enjoyed learning, and the teacher was kind to her. It was far better than spending her days scavenging the streets of London for something to eat. At least in this place if she was hungry, she could find mushrooms in the field nearby, or pluck peaches from a tree alongside the road on the way to town. There was always a way to find something to line their stomachs, even if it only kept the hunger at bay for a few hours. She seemed to always be hungry these days. Harry had grown in recent weeks, his legs had lengthened, and he towered over her now. He seemed never to have a full stomach, no matter how much food he ate. She'd helped him steal some of the stale, day-old bread from the kitchen before bedtime on more than one occasion to help stave off his hunger pangs until morning. It helped her as well.

When school finished, Mary and Lottie went straight to the stables to ride with the other girls. They practiced lunging their horses in a circle at the end of a long rope. They saddled them and rode around in a circle, this time focusing on how to sit straight, to cling on with their legs, to grip the reins firmly but not too firm, and so on. Mary improved her technique every time they rode. She'd managed to push herself up in the stirrups, then back into the seat again, in time with the horse's steps while trotting, which meant she no longer feared her teeth would be jolted from her head.

They brushed the horses, fed and watered them again, then put their rugs on for the night and headed back to the cottage for tea.

When they arrived, the girls were seated around the dining room, feet up on chairs. No one had set the table. And there was no sign of Ingrid.

"What's going on?" asked Mary, searching through the cupboard for some fresh milk to drink. Her stomach grumbled with an emptiness that seemed as though nothing would satisfy it. Plus, her head swam and throbbed, as she'd barely had anything to drink all day.

"Ingrid has a date," said Faith as she spun a spoon around on the table.

There was no milk, so Mary downed two full glasses of water. She leaned against the kitchen bench and studied the group.

"What's for tea, then?"

Faith tipped her head in the direction of the stove. A pot sat on one of the cold burners with a lid balanced askew on top. Mary wandered to the stove and pushed the lid aside to sniff at its contents. She reeled back and gagged against her hand. It was a saucepan full of cold stew, with maggots inching their way up the sides and falling back into the murky grey mess once they reached the halfway point.

Some of the girls tittered with laughter.

Faith grinned. "I can't believe you shoved your face in that thing."

"I didn't know," replied Mary, rubbing her nose. "You should've warned me."

Lottie slumped into a chair, her expression morose. "Is that truly what she's left us for tea? I'm half-starved."

There was a general consensus among the group that it wasn't fair they were stuck with Ingrid as their cottage mother. Some of the other mothers made decent meals for the children, but Ingrid never seemed to bother with much. This pot of congealed, maggoty stew was by far the worst tea she'd delivered since Mary arrived, though. Mary leaned over the stove and firmly pushed the lid back into place, then slipped the saucepan into the sink.

"Never mind, girls. I've got just the thing to cheer you all up." She went into the bedroom and found the stash of mushrooms rolled up in her spare shirt. She carried it to the kitchen and set it on the table, opening the shirt for the girls to see. "Lottie's got a shirt-full as well. I'll bet between us, we'll all get enough to cover a piece of toast. All we need is a bit of butter for frying them, and some bread."

The girls cheered up immediately at the sight of the mushrooms. Lottie hurried off to find her mushrooms to add to the stash. Faith ran in the direction of the kitchen to search for some bread. And one of the other girls pulled a wedge of butter from the almost empty cupboard. Before long, the delightful scent of mushrooms frying in butter filled the cottage. The girls laughed and chattered as they set the table and straightened the cottage. Then they all sat down at the dining table to eat together. Without Ingrid there to spoil the discussion, they talked about anything and everything. And for the first time since they'd trundled up the long drive in the back of the canvas-covered truck, Mary and Lottie had a family again.

⌘

THE CIRCUS WAS IN TOWN. EVERYONE AT THE FAIRBRIDGE FARM School was in a tizzy over it. Mary hadn't heard anything at all about it until Harry came home from Orange High School with the news. He'd heard it from some of the other boys—the circus would be in Orange for three days. When he told Mary, she thought she'd burst with excitement and disappointment all at the same time. There was no way she'd get to attend. Perhaps she could've snuck out to see the performers through a peephole in the tent if it was in Molong. But how could she catch a ride to Orange?

Then Forrest called everyone to attention after breakfast and announced that they'd all be attending on Saturday. It was more than Mary could've hoped for. She went about her usual chores and school-work with joy in her heart, marching straight-backed to and from the stables, and between cottages with the mop and bucket. She even smiled her way through making sandwiches for school lunches out of cold kidney and onions on hard, stale bread.

It seemed as though Saturday would never come. But finally, it did, and the farm released a collective sigh into the fog that clung over the landscape and lingered into late morning. By noon, however, the sun was high in the sky. White fluffy clouds swam across its reaching blue expanse. After lunch, the children all dressed in their best clothes — blue and khaki shorts and shirts, with shoes and socks pulled up to their knees. It seemed strange to wear shoes again. Mary found her feet had grown since they arrived at the farm, so she had to barter with the other girls in her cottage to find a pair that fit her. Lottie did the same. Finally, they were ready, with their hair slicked back and parted on one side. Mary wanted to braid her hair, but it was too short now, and besides Lottie had never learned the skill. So, she settled for a comb and water to style her unruly bob.

The children all climbed into the school bus, and it set off, bumping down the long driveway. Once they reached the road, the jarring smoothed out and they were able to talk to each other. Harry and Max sat behind Mary and Lottie. They discussed what they thought they might see. None of them ever having gone to a circus before, it was all wild guesses and wishful thinking. Still, they agreed there was likely to be a clown at the very least. Perhaps even an exotic animal like an elephant if they were really lucky.

When they pulled into Orange, evening was fast approaching. The town fell into shadow and the cool night air listed over the fields, filling the town with a growing chill. The bus driver parked in a dirt parking lot on the outskirts of town beside a series of other vehicles all lined up bumper to bumper. An enormous rainbow-coloured big top tent stood in an empty field dotted with foxtails and wispy grasses. Fluffy sheep grazed all round it, seeming oblivious to the intrusion on their territory.

Mary could hardly contain her excitement. She jiggled in place on her seat until finally Forrest shouted that they could all file out in a single line. They matched themselves into pairs and followed Mr and Mrs Forrest to the tent. A clown with white makeup and a red nose stood atop a pair of towering stilts. He met the children with a shout, then blew on a horn and stepped lightly between them, never once losing his balance as the children squealed with delight and jumped out of his way.

Soon they were surrounded by a troop of clowns juggling. One of the men rode a tiny bicycle and a small, white-spotted dog leapt from his head to the ground, to his back and then up again to his head as he rode.

Lottie walked slowly beside Mary, beaming as she watched it all. Mary's stomach jittered with anticipation over what was to come. And it was everything she'd hoped for. They found seats along one side of the tent, and the show began. There were dancing white horses with feathers on their heads that performed tricks she'd never imagined any horse could do. There were clowns who made fun and joked with the crowd while falling over their own feet. Acrobats who dove through the air, spun, twirled and flipped in ways that made the crowd gasp and shout in amazement. There was even an elephant who plodded around the circular stage, his enormous feet kicking up clouds of sawdust as he went, his trunk swaying from side to side while a beautiful woman in a sparkling gold outfit performed stunts on his head.

Beside her, Harry laughed, shouted and applauded with the rest of the crowd while Mary watched quietly. When the horses finished their performance and completed a bow to the crowd, she thought she might cry at the sheer beauty of it all. Then Harry slipped his hand into hers and squeezed. She looked at him, and he grinned back at her. He knew how she felt—she could tell from that one look. It was everything, and it was perfect. Only Harry understood just how perfect it was and how it made her throat ache, her heart sing, and her entire body tingle all at the same time. He knew what she was thinking without her saying a word. He dipped his head in her direction and squeezed her hand again. She shuffled a little closer to him on the bench seat until their arms touched softly against one another through their shirt sleeves, their fingers entwined.

✦ III ✦

Young hearts are drawn to muster,
Young love finds its own way;
Strength built upon the shoulder
Of the brave who dare to stay.

— *AUSTRALIA,* BY BRONWEN
WHITLEY 2021

❦ 31 ❦

CURRENT DAY

MIA

I'm frantic. And it's all my own fault. I thought it would be a great idea to invite my family over to our house while caring for a newborn. I'm not sure what kind of high I was on. It's very likely I wasn't thinking clearly at all, considering my constant state of sleep deprivation. Also, I'm worried about Brody. The strange thing is, he seems fine. So, I can't help hoping that maybe the doctor was wrong and everything's okay. Or that the issue isn't as bad as they thought, and we won't need to worry about medication or surgery. That's what I think about when I stand over his bassinet, watching him sleep, his glorious black hair swept into the cutest pompadour on top of his perfect newborn head, his eyelashes two black curves on pale cheeks. He's an angel when he's sleeping, and I can't imagine there's anything wrong with my perfect cherub. But he doesn't sleep long, and the crying gets to me sometimes.

Brody is two months old, but he's still not sleeping much during the night. So, my sleep schedule involves an hour or two, here and there, throughout the day and night. Ben is back at work, so that means it's quiet during the day, which gives me a much better chance of sleep than when he was there wanting to talk, watching television, or listening to his music on full volume while he braised pork shanks or rolled salmon sushi. It was great having a gourmet chef in the kitchen every day as he prides himself on his cooking. But I'm glad for the peace and quiet now that he's occupied by his work again. And we're back to my simple attempts at comfort food in the kitchen — chicken and dumplings, meatloaf and mash, sausages with gravy.

I feel badly for not missing my husband more. In fact, I was anticipating him going back to work for at least a month. Does that make me a terrible wife? Don't get me wrong—I love Ben, and I'd never get sick of his company. But I'm tired. So tired.

"Did you find the tablecloth?" I call through the back door.

Ben's on the verandah stringing twinkle lights and grumbling beneath his breath that it's overkill to have twinkle lights for an autumn afternoon, since no one will ever see them twinkle. But he's hanging them anyway, to please me.

"I did," he replies, sending me a wink.

"Thank you. And what about the punch?"

"I'll get the ice in a minute."

"You didn't get the ice yet?" I'm in panic mode already. The last thing I need is for my mother to complain that the punch is warm and if only we'd thought to get ice, it might be perfect.

"I'll get it—don't fret. It's only your family coming over. We're not entertaining the queen."

He's right, I'm overthinking this whole thing. But I know how tense it can be when my family spends time together, and I don't want any conflict. "I'm sorry. I get a bit crazed when it comes to them."

He chuckles, meets me at the back door, and kisses the tip of my nose. "It's fine. I'll make sure everyone is nice and has a good time." His dimple lights up his smile, and I'm smitten with him all over again. I'll never forget the first time I met him, as first-year students at the University of Queensland. He was new to Brisbane, but I'd lived here my whole life. We hit it off right away, and I offered to take him to Southbank on the weekend. We swam, joked, laughed, and talked until the sun went down, then he kissed me with the cityscape behind him, a towel around my shoulders and the scent of salt water in our hair. We'd been together ever since, inseparable and head over heels.

"If only you had that superpower," I complain as butterflies merge into a mini tornado in my stomach.

He kisses me again, rolls his eyes in mock frustration, then releases me. I rush back into the house and check the baby monitor. There's an image on the screen of Brody sleeping peacefully in his cot. My heart explodes with the love I feel for him, and the feeling brings things back into perspective. He's been with us such a short time, but he's everything to me. To both of us. I want my entire family to reconnect, to rebuild the bridges between us that've been in disrepair for so long, for Brody's sake.

My iPad sits unlocked on the bench top, a fresh page of search results on the screen. I've been looking for something, anything, to suggest that Gammy really killed someone, that those rushed words after she fell weren't a figment of my imagination. I've searched on her name, her maiden name, and there's not much there. She doesn't have social media, and she's never been in the paper. So other than a letter she wrote to council once about a drainage problem in the local park, she's a digital ghost.

Gramps is featured in more stories, but mostly about his work as a solicitor over the years. Nothing about either of them living at the Fairbridge Farm School, and definitely nothing to link them to a murder there. And on that subject, I couldn't find anything about a murder. Nothing during the time period they would've lived there. Surely something like that would've made it into the news — yet there's not a single news item, obituary or announcement. Maybe Gammy was having an episode of some kind when she made the confession. Perhaps it's just as she told me—she was in a lot of pain and not thinking clearly. Still, it's a strange thing to say, even in those circumstances, if it's not true.

The house is a disaster. I haven't had the energy to clean, but it will have to do. I shove some clean laundry from the couch into a basket and push it through our bedroom door, then pull the door shut.

There's a knock at the front door, so I hurry to answer it, smoothing my hair back with both hands as I go.

Mum and Dad are here. They've stopped along the way to pick up Gammy and Gramps. Auntie Char returned to New Zealand a few weeks ago, and I miss her happy demeanour and the cheerful ice breakers she is so skilled at inserting into awkward conversations. But we'll manage. At least, that's what I tell myself.

Mum hands me a casserole dish encased in a towel. "Here you go. Gammy made her famous apricot chicken with rice."

Dad's holding a shopping bag. "And I've got Turkish bread, a salad and some ginger beer. Where can I put the salad together?"

I kiss cheeks, then lead the way through the house. "Thank you! Follow me, Dad. I'll set you up in the kitchen."

I find a space at the kitchen bench for Dad, and get him a cutting board and knife, along with a salad bowl. He hauls the ingredients for a fresh garden salad from the shopping bag and gets to work turning it into a masterpiece. He and Mum aren't much into cooking. So, whenever their cook was out of town or off sick, we always ate BBQ chicken and salad, homemade pizzas baked on a tortilla, tacos, or pasta with pesto for dinner. Whatever could be thrown together easily in about ten minutes —that was my mother's specialty.

Now that they're older, she seems to have given up her attempts entirely, leaving Dad to pull something together if they're not eating at some fancy restaurant or diplomatic function.

"Gramps, it's so good to see you," I say as I embrace him.

He encloses me in his arms, squeezing me tight. "You too, Button." I'm so happy to see him outside of the nursing home. He looks happy and strong, and for a moment I can forget just how much of a fog his mind operates under most of the time.

Mum's already mixing ginger beer with juices and ice cubes she's found in the freezer into the punch bowl I set out on the bench.

"Thanks, Mum. I was about to do that, but this is a big help."

"Of course, honey. Let me know if I can do anything else."

There's a squawk on the baby monitor, and Mum immediately sets down the apple juice bottle and grins. "Somebody's awake!"

"I'll change him and bring him out to see everyone," I say.

When I get to Brody's bassinet, he's squeezing his eyes together and red-faced, about to burst into a wail. I call out his name, his face relaxes, his eyes blink open, and he's instantly calm. With careful hands I lift him from the cot, talking to him in a soft voice the whole time.

He's pumping the air with his fists and his feet as I change his nappy. Excited to be free, with the air on his skin, for at least a little while. I dress him in one of my favourite navy outfits which has pretend buttons down the front as though he's wearing a suit, then carry him out to the kitchen.

Mum takes him from my arms immediately, crooning and ah-ing over his every movement. Was she was ever like this with me when I was young? I can't recall her being so motherly, although perhaps I'm being too harsh.

"He's getting some chubby cheeks," says Dad, peering over Mum's shoulder as he pulls faces at Brody.

"I know. He's growing," I reply as I gather together the plates and cutlery we'll need to carry outside.

Finally, all of the food is arranged along the bar out on the back porch, like a buffet. The table is set, and everyone is outside, talking amicably amongst themselves.

"Thanks for coming," I call out, loud enough to stop the conversation. "I wanted to get us all together to celebrate Brody, and to enjoy this time we have together with Mum and Dad before they head back to Paris."

"Hear, hear," adds Ben, smiling openly as he raises a glass of punch above his head.

Mum and Dad look appreciative, if a little uncomfortable.

"We're glad to be able to get together like this," says Dad. "It's good to be back in Oz."

The meal goes swimmingly. I'm feeling rather smug about it all when I see Dad and Gammy talking together over pieces of Turkish bread dipped in apricot chicken sauce. It must bring back memories for Dad, since Gammy has made her signature dish for more years than I can count.

Gramps is deep in conversation with Ben. I'm always grateful for my husband's compassion when it comes to Gramps — he has so much patience and love for the man who means so much to me.

Mum hands me a glass of punch and sits beside me. "Lovely meal, Mia."

"Thanks, Mum. I'm so happy you're home." Although it's not really their home. They haven't lived long-term on Australian soil since I was tiny. I feel tears welling up in my eyes, and a lump forms in my throat. My emotions are still in turmoil, what with the hormones and lack of sleep. I'm not in control of myself these days. So, I do my best to pull it together. No need to weep over the slightest hint of sentimentality.

"Your dad and I have been talking, and we think that once this posting in Paris is over, he might finally be ready to retire from the Department, and we'll move back to Brisbane permanently."

I'm gobsmacked, but try not to show it. This isn't something I thought Dad would do for a while yet. He's sixty years old, but I expected him to work for the Department of Foreign Affairs and Trade for a least another five years. He loves his work, and everyone knows and respects him. It's been such a consuming part of his life that I can't imagine him without it. Who will he be if he's not the consul-general, or Ambassador Patrick Evans with the ice-blue eyes? The diplomat who always knows exactly what to say in every situation, except with his family. "Oh, wow. That's wonderful, Mum. How long does he have left for this posting?"

"About six months."

"So, you could be back in Brisbane in six months?" Tears are threatening again. I'm doing my best, but my eyes are stinging, no doubt reddening by the moment.

"That's right."

Gammy overhears Mum and joins in the conversation. "Brisbane? Wow, I didn't think you'd ever come home again, Pat."

Dad is chewing on a piece of bread. He nods in response, although I can tell he's bristling at Gammy's insinuation. It's been a point of contention between the two of them that Gammy feels Dad has prioritised his work over his family, and that he should make more of an effort to be present. Dad doesn't want Gammy's input into his life and has told her so on more than one occasion. He wants me to focus more on my career, says it's truly the only thing that'll bring me satisfaction in life — I disagree, and Gammy backs me up.

We've had this conversation so many times, but usually it goes something like this: I say, *I want a family.* He says, *You have one.* I say, *But I want a real family, the kind that eats meals together, spends time together. I don't want to work all the time.* He says, *There's no reason you can't do both. I did.* But then I have to bite my tongue because I want to point out to him that I hardly saw him when I was young. To me, he was the man in the suit who scared me more than a little bit with his brusque voice and shiny shoes, but who I only saw on the occasional evening when he'd remind me to behave and to study hard. But I don't want to say any of those things because I want us to get along and not have a fight — just this once.

"I'm so excited," I interject. Ever the peacemaker, I try to smooth down the rough edges of this well-worn discussion. "We'll be over the moon to have you back here full-time. Won't we Gammy?"

Gammy pulls off a warm smile. "Of course. I can't wait."

"And Brody will love having you around. It will be amazing for him to have a set of grandparents close by," says Ben. "I know my parents wish they could be closer." We aren't sure when Ben's parents will visit. It saddens Ben to think about it, so I usually try to distract him by making fun of my family's dysfunctions. Now my parents will be the ones living close by, possibly even as engaged and involved grandparents — neither of us saw that twist coming.

The sun cooks the edges of the porch, reflecting off the floorboards. The glare is too brilliant to look at directly. The orb sinks into the horizon, sending golden streaks across a cotton-candy sky. The air hints at an evening chill. Two magpies trot along one of the porch railings, heads dipping one way, then the other, as they survey the food on the table with beady black eyes. Brody's lying on his back on a rug just inside the back door. I can see his little legs kicking as he bats a hand at a colourful mobile overhead. I think about how much it will mean to him over the coming years to be able to see his grandparents whenever he likes.

Gammy walks inside with her empty glass, no doubt looking for a bottle of sherry. I should follow her to let her know we don't have any in stock. I know she loves it, but I didn't get a chance to go to the Bottle-O before they got here. Thankfully, I see Ben hurry into the house after her. He'll offer her a glass of the Moscato in the fridge. I relax with a sigh into my chair.

Dad finishes up the last of his apricot chicken and sets down his fork. There's a tension line in the middle of his forehead between his bushy salt-and-pepper eyebrows.

"Are you looking forward to retiring, Dad?"

He grunts. "I won't be retiring, not exactly. I've spoken to the general manager about a position in Brisbane. She thinks she could find me something at the state Trade Office."

"Oh, that's a good idea."

"No doubt Mum will have something to say about it," he grumbles, reaching for his glass of punch.

"She means well, Dad," I say.

"Does she?"

"Of course she does. She loves you."

"I don't know about that. She's my mother, so there's some sort of maternal attachment there. But she's never been one to show a lot of affection. That's something a child needs — affection."

"I know, Dad. But she had a difficult upbringing. Maybe you should cut her a little bit of slack."

His eyes narrow. "She was poor, but so was everyone back then."

I clear my throat. How much does Dad know about Gammy's background? It's hard to tell. Surely he would've gleaned a few things over the years. Even if Gammy and Gramps weren't completely open about everything that happened in their youth.

"You know about the Fairbridge Farm School. Right, Dad?"

"I suppose. I remember them saying something about it. Is that where Mum attended school? Somewhere near Orange, right?"

I don't know where to begin. It throws me how little Dad knows about his own parents. But then I remember that I barely know my own—at least it seems that way at times. We take our parents so much for granted that we forget to know them in any real way other than the little things like their favourite drink, or how easily they fall asleep on the couch, or their favourite hobbies. But we don't pry into the deeper stuff, the reality behind who they are as a person. We're too caught up in the mundane to dig for more.

"That's right — she and Gramps were sent over to Australia from England. They came here by themselves, with no parents. Grew up on a farm outside Molong. An institution for poor or orphaned children, where they learned how to work on a farm or in domestic service. They didn't receive affection or have anyone to love them — no one taught them how to love. So, I'm sure they did the best they could in raising you and Aunt Sonya."

Dad rubs his forehead with one hand and squeezes his eyes shut. "I should probably know more about all that. But the problem is, they both drive me crazy. I don't know why. Too much water under the bridge, I suppose."

"You can work on that," I say.

I pull my phone out of my pocket and scroll through the photographs of Brody to find the images of Fairbridge. I saved them to my camera roll: the image Gammy crumpled in her hand when she fell in her room and broke her ankle, along with the ones of wiry, smiling children I found online.

The seat beside Dad is empty, so I slide into it and show him the photos.

He flicks through them slowly, taking it all in. "I can't believe they never told me much about this place and how they ended up there. They went alone, you said?"

I nod. "That's right. I don't know how that happened exactly—Gammy didn't say. But somehow, they ended up on a ship that sailed from London to Sydney. Gammy with Charlotte, and Gramps by himself. You should ask Gammy about it sometime. She's told me a little bit, but I'm sure there's a lot more. Anyway, I thought you'd like to know what they went through. It might illuminate some of the things you've struggled with about your childhood."

He meets my gaze, does a quick dip of the head, then shifts gears to talk about work, the weather in Paris, and if I'd consider bringing Brody to see them before he retires.

When Gammy returns to the table, she sits across from Dad and listens to him describe the opera he and Mum attended last week. She smiles and laughs in all the appropriate places, although I can tell it pains her that there's a tension between them. Aunt Sonya lives in the United States, so Gammy and Gramps rarely see her, and I don't think she calls often. Gramps is out of touch with reality most of the time, so Gammy must be lonely. No wonder she spends so much time with me.

I want to hug her and tell her it's all going to be okay. But I'm the granddaughter, and it seems strange for me to take on that parenting role with her. She's tough, that much I know. She'll weather this, like she has the other storms in her life.

The wind picks up and whispers across the table, shunting a stack of napkins into Dad's lap. He grabs them with a start and sets a glass on top of them to keep them in place. Then he looks directly at Gammy.

"Mia tells me there are things about your childhood you failed to fill me in on," says Dad.

I groan inwardly. This isn't the way to go about it. She invited me to a private glimpse of her painful past, disclosing things she'd never told a soul before. Dad's words are like a barb, striking at her soft centre. I want to cry out. Gammy's cheeks colour.

The sun sinks suddenly, throwing the porch into shadow, and I suddenly wish I had a cardigan to wrap around my shoulders. At that moment, Brody lets out a cry, fussing and squirming on his play mat, and I scurry over to him to make sure he's warm enough. I gather him up and sit on the daybed behind the table to feed him while keeping an ear on the conversation. I can't quite make out what they're saying.

Gammy's voice rises. "I don't want to talk about it tonight. It's not the appropriate time."

"It's never the right time with you, Mum. We don't talk about anything meaningful because you don't want to. It's always been like that. I don't know why I bother."

Dad rises to his feet, sending his chair flying backwards across the porch. I'm stuck where I am, so I signal Ben with a head tilt. He stands awkwardly, clearly unsure of what to say or how to intervene in my family's drama.

Gammy steps away from the table, her chin jutting out. "I think it's time I went home. Ben, would you take me and Harry home, please?"

Ben jumps to help with her chair and offers her his arm. "Of course, Gammy."

Once they leave, Mum and Dad order a cab. I ask them to stay, but they're stubbornly refusing to listen to reason.

"Come on, Dad. It wasn't so bad. You approached it in a bit of a prickly way..."

"What? You're saying that was my fault? You heard her. She doesn't want to talk to me about anything. She'll tell you, but heaven forbid she talks to her own son."

I'm holding Brody against my shoulder, and he lets out a gigantic burp. I pat his back absently, my brow furrowed. "It's not like that. Mum, please tell him Gammy loves you both. I shouldn't have said anything today. This is all my fault."

Mum rests a hand on my arm as the taxi pulls up at the kerb. "It's not your fault, honey. Dad and Gammy have a sensitive relationship, that's all. There's nothing you can do about it. It's up to them to work it out."

They wave goodbye, and I stand there a few moments after the vehicle pulls away. Ben comes out and rests an arm around my shoulders. We both stare into the lamplit street. My heart hurts, but I don't know what to do. This dinner was supposed to be our chance at *rapprochement*. Instead, it's only made things worse.

Stars blink in the sky overhead as clouds shimmy across the inky black expanse. Ben kisses my hair, and I face him with tears clogging my throat. His eyes are black in the darkness. They're deep and full of love. It's warm when he wraps his arms around us. He shrugs against us with his head tilted to one side. I know exactly what he means by it. Then he kisses Brody's head, kisses me again, and we walk inside together.

✣ 32 ✣

AUGUST 1958

HARRY

The chatter of his own teeth woke him in the dark. He could barely move. Every limb was stiff with cold. Harry tucked his knees tighter beneath his chin. They didn't fit so well now they were the long and gangly limbs of a sixteen-year-old. He'd grown at least an inch every month over the past year. It seemed that way to him although he had no way to measure it. Before bed, he'd piled every item of clothing he owned on top of the single, worn blanket covering him, but the frigid wind blew in through the open windows and sliced through his covers as though they didn't exist.

He peeped out from beneath the blanket. It crackled as the ice that'd formed around his nose and mouth beneath the wool shifted and fell away. There was nothing for it but to get up quickly. Doing it slowly only made it all the worse. So, Harry squeezed his eyes shut, braced himself and swung his legs over the side of the bed. He'd slept in his clothes, so all he had to do was pull on his shoes, run his fingers through his hair and he was ready.

A glance in the cracked mirror above the bathroom sink revealed his pants were too short, his thin woollen jumper had a hole in it and his socks were in bad need of laundering (but since he only had one pair, he hated to give them up). Another swipe of fingers through his hair made very little difference to the dark brown mop that sat atop his head. He frowned at his own reflection, then jogged out of the cottage in the direction of the dairy.

He padded quietly along the pathway, noting a few older boys trotting out of cottages as he went. He was grateful for the shoes on his feet. The younger kids who didn't attend Orange High School didn't have shoes to wear, even though the ground was frozen solid and the grass crisp with ice. His body still hadn't thawed, so he hugged himself as he ran, his teeth grinding together as the frigid air seemed to burn his cheeks and nose. A fog hung heavy over the countryside so that he couldn't see more than a footstep or two ahead of himself. The occasional light from a cottage verandah shone dull when he drew close, but otherwise he was alone in a world void of anything but the damp fog, the freezing wind and hard muddy ground beneath his feet.

Some of the trainees were already in the dairy when Harry arrived. He got right to work, fetched a waiting cow from the yard, sat on his milking stool and warmed his hands with a breath on open palms. Then he set about milking into the large silver bucket beneath the cow's teats. He enjoyed the morning milking, even though most of the boys complained bitterly about it. The early hour, the freezing weather —he understood their complaints. But he liked rising early, watching the sun climb up the sky as it threw pink jagged streamers over the land. He loved the animals, so big and gentle with doe eyes. They waited for him with impatience, lowing into the dark for him to hurry. But most of all, he enjoyed the solitary monotony of milking.

He squeezed in a steady rhythm, enjoying the satisfaction of watching the frothy, creamy milk rising slowly up the sides of the bucket. It was his time to think, to ponder, to work through his problems. And today was no exception. He was almost finished school. In fact, Forrest had given him leave to continue his schooling for longer than any of the other boys had done. He'd excelled at Orange High School, and the principal had asked Forrest to allow Harry to finish.

Forrest hadn't wanted to, but the high school principal had pointed out how good it would look for Fairbridge to have one of their own graduate with such excellent results, and Forrest couldn't refuse.

Harry released that cow and took another. He could work his way through five before the breakfast bell. But today it seemed he had only three to milk.

Most of the boys around him had left school at fifteen and become trainees. They would remain on the farm all day, working in the dairy, the slaughterhouse, the fields. Their work didn't end on weekends, like it did for the rest of the children — they rarely had an afternoon off to do as they pleased. And when their trainee program came to an end, they'd be sent to a farm to work for the farmer, their time at Molong complete. He envied them that. It was his only regret. If he hadn't remained in school, perhaps he could have moved on and left this place already. Maybe he could've earned enough to return to England. He hoped one day to find his mother's grave and lay a bouquet of flowers and say a prayer for her. Something he'd never had the chance to do. He could look up her relatives and see if anyone remained — if he had family still living. The pull of that dream drove him forward.

"You finished yet?" asked an impatient Max as he leaned against the yard railing, his eyes gleaming with that mischievous look that'd never left him.

Max had grown even taller than Harry. He was gangly, awkward, and had a small fluff of hair growing in patches across his upper lip. He was a trainee, and the work left him skinny and lithe.

"Yep, finished now." Harry released the cow and slapped her on the hindquarters. She set off at a trot in the direction of the open gate that led to the pasture where she'd graze for the rest of the day.

"Great, I'm starving. Let's go."

Just then the breakfast bell sounded across the farm. The fog lifted over the village, but still clung to the lowlands. The sun emitted a dull glow that barely pushed back the darkness. As Harry and Max strode through the village, children erupted from cottage doors, flinging them down the stairs as they ran for Nuffield Hall and the breakfast that would satisfy their hunger for a few short hours.

Harry and Max both carried a bucket of milk in each of their hands. They reached the dining hall and ducked inside to leave the buckets on the kitchen bench. Mary was there, and her smile thawed the last of the cold within him.

"Good morning," she said.

"I've got the milk for you."

"Thank you. It'll be perfect heated up with some cocoa and sugar."

He wanted to say more, but couldn't think of the words. That was how he felt when he was around her much of the time these days. And it frustrated him, given how long they'd been friends. Why did his tongue seem to tie itself into knots and words fly directly out of his head when she was around?

Instead, he backed out of the kitchen, tripping over Max on his way into the dining hall.

"Hey, where are you going?"

"To sit down."

"You're an oaf." Max hopped on one foot, grabbing for the injured one.

"Shut up."

Max followed him to their table, laughing as he went. "Just admit it. You're keen on her and she doesn't feel the same way."

Harry slumped onto the bench seat, pressed his elbows to the table and rested his head in his hands. "Do shut up."

"The truth hurts, my friend."

"The only thing that'll hurt is my fist in your teeth," hissed Harry.

Max slid into the seat beside him, grinning. "I'd like to see you try. I'm half a head taller than you now."

Harry rolled his eyes. Max never let him hear the end of it when, finally, the scrawny little boy had grown taller than Harry and most of the other boys at the farm. But it didn't bother him really. He was glad for Max. It seemed to buoy his confidence no end and with everything Max had dealt with in his life, any little boost would help.

He ate the toast and jam without tasting it. All he could think about was Mary. The bouncing blonde hair that snuck out beneath her cap and delightful pink lips, plus the fact that school was almost over and he was set to become a trainee. Forrest had asked him to withdraw from school in two weeks' time. And he didn't know what he'd be able to say to change the man's mind since Max was leaving to go to a farm, and Forrest wanted Harry to take his place in the trainee program. It made no sense at all, considering Forrest had let him stay in school for an extra two years — it would be crazy to pull out only months away from graduation. But even though he'd grown to have a grudging respect for the man over the years, he'd also learned there was no reasoning with Forrest once he set his mind on something.

"Can I have your egg?" Max talked around a mouthful of food.

"No," replied Harry, brow furrowed. He boxed in his plate with one arm. "Keep your hands to yourself."

"I'm dying over here. My stomach's caving in on itself. At least you'll get to nick some kid's lunchbox at school today. I'm stuck here. Probably have to eat cold leftovers that make me want to puke, or half-cooked bread again."

Harry took another bite of toast. "I don't steal other people's lunches. I have to eat the same crap you do."

"You're not as big as me," grumbled Max, wiping the crumbs from his plate.

"And I won't be either if you keep taking my food. I've got to go." Harry stood to carry his plates to the bench as Max offered him a mock salute.

He was still chewing when he walked out the door and jogged back to his cottage, where he grabbed his books and pencil case. He didn't have a backpack or suitcase like the other children at the high school — the ones with parents who cared about them. He had to carry his things in his arms and balance his lunch bag on top. A letter from Davey sat on his bed. He shoved it beneath his mattress where there was a small pile of letters written in the same hand. Davey had been sent back to Western Australia to another Fairbridge farm. His letters came in the post sporadically. It seemed to Harry his friend was having a much harder time adjusting to their new way of life than Harry was. He'd fallen from a moving vehicle driven by one of the teenagers on his farm early on and injured his leg, so he had a difficult time walking and running the way he'd used to.

The crowded school bus was only a few minutes late, so Harry didn't have to wait long with the other children from the farm. He climbed aboard and found a seat near the back beside a younger boy who promptly turned his back on Harry to talk to his friends seated across the aisle. That suited Harry perfectly—he didn't feel like being social. Besides, he'd borrowed an exciting book from the library—*The Naked Sun* by Isaac Asimov—and he was dying to finish it. He fished it out of the pile in his lap and leaned against the window to read.

At school, he sailed through classes. He usually sat near the back of the room and kept to himself. The rest of the Fairbridge kids his age had stopped attending almost two years earlier, and the town kids didn't understand him. He hadn't made friends in that time, although he hadn't made much of an effort, either. Mary had attended for a while but had dropped out to become a trainee earlier that year, so he'd had to give up sitting next to her on the bus and during lunch. Sometimes he wasn't sure he'd made the right choice in staying.

With his lunch bag in his hand, he made his way to the edge of the hockey field to eat at lunchtime. Children played touch football, netball, soccer and handball across the various fields and courts that hugged the red brick high school building. Sheep grazed behind a nearby fence like balls of cotton that'd been sprinkled over a light brown carpet.

Nearby, a group of boys passed a soccer ball back and forth between them. Oliver, a thin boy with black hair, noticed Harry sitting by himself eating a Vegemite sandwich and sneered at him.

"Nice haircut, orphan boy."

Harry ignored him. He'd heard the taunts for years — all the Fairbridge kids had messy hair styles, and the town kids loved to tease them about it. It didn't make any difference whether he responded to them or not. There would always be children who'd go out of their way to make fun of the Fairbridge kids. It was one of the few constants of his high school career.

Oliver juggled the soccer ball on his knees, back to his feet, then kicked it up in the air. It landed in Harry's lap directly on top of his sandwich, sending it flying into the dirt.

He stood to his feet and brushed the crumbs and dirt from his lap. Now he was mad. He'd been looking forward to eating that sandwich all morning. It wasn't much, but it was all he had, and he wasn't about to let a runt like Oliver get away with that. Most of the time he kept out of the way of the town kids, but if they attacked him directly, he didn't hold back. He'd learned a long time ago not to let bullies think they could push him around. His face screwed up in anger, he marched over to Oliver and sucker punched him right in the mouth.

Oliver staggered backwards, shock registering on his face. Clearly, he was accustomed to the Fairbridge kids taking it without fighting back. But that wasn't Harry's style. He'd learned a few things over the years about boxing and crouched into the boxer's stance. Oliver charged at him, his friends egging him on from behind, momentarily throwing Harry off balance.

They scuffled for several minutes. Harry tore Oliver's shirt. Oliver scratched Harry's cheek. Harry landed a few more punches, and Oliver kicked Harry in the shins. But mostly they wrestled around in the dirt with a small crowd gathered around them, jeering, taunting and shouting with glee over the fracas. Fights were a common occurrence at Orange High, and they always elicited excited chants of "Fight, fight, fight!" that brought children running from every direction to watch.

Before long, the maths teacher arrived to break up the fight. He pulled Harry and Oliver up by the collars and marched them to the principal's office, his chastisement ringing in their ears as they went. Down the long concrete corridor, up the set of concrete stairs and into the spacious, if sparsely decorated, office where a secretary sat behind a desk, her hair curled neatly and a pair of horn-rimmed glasses perched on the end of her nose.

"Good afternoon, Mrs Cawley. These two young men are in want of a caning for fighting," said the maths teacher, a tall and gangly young man with blond hair that fell across his forehead and into his eyes before he blew it back into place with a huff of breath.

"Yes. Mr Jones will be right with you. I believe he's on a phone call."

"I'll leave them in your care, then."

"Thank you."

The maths teacher dipped his head and left after a parting glare at

Harry. No doubt he blamed Harry for the fight. Most of the teachers at the school had little patience for the Fairbridge kids.

The principal's door opened, and he stepped out to meet them. Mr Jones' rounded belly hung over a too-tight belt, and his white shirt was open at the collar, a tie loose around his neck. He peered at the two boys through reddened eyes, then sighed.

Mrs Cawley explained the situation. He stepped to one side.

"Come on inside, boys. Thank you, Mrs Cawley."

Harry liked Mr Jones. The principal was one of the few adults in his life who'd been kind to him, who'd taken enough of an interest in his future to suggest he stay enrolled and graduate. Suddenly shame sent a spike of adrenaline into his gut over what he'd done. He should never have let an ignoramus like Oliver get to him.

"Please, take a seat, boys. Let's hear it. What happened?"

The boys sat in seats across from Mr Jones' desk, and he leaned against it, arms folded over his chest. Neither boy spoke. Harry had no intention of dobbing on Oliver, no matter how much he hated the boy. It just wasn't done. Oliver seemed to feel the same way.

"Fine. Neither one of you is willing to talk, so you'll both be punished. There's to be no fighting in my school grounds. Do you understand?"

"Yes, sir," both boys spoke in unison.

They lined up and Mr Jones caned each of them smartly across their open palms three times. Then Oliver left, red-eyed, for class when the bell rang.

"Wait a moment, please, Harry," said Mr Jones.

Harry stood still, stinging palms hanging loose at his sides. "Yes, sir?"

"I can't help feeling this is out of character for you. It's been a number of years since I've had to break up a fight with you involved. Do you want to tell me what's going on?"

There was nothing for him to say. He was lonely. He had no one. He was passing the time until school was over and he could move on with his life. None of those things had caused him to throw that first punch at Oliver's teeth. But they'd all played a role in his mood. Still, how could Mr Jones understand?

"I see that you don't want to talk, so let me. I heard from one of your teachers that you're considering dropping out of school. Is that correct?"

"Yes, sir," replied Harry, his heart heavy.

"Can I ask why?"

"Mr Forrest needs someone to replace one of the other boys who's found a position at a farm out west."

Mr Jones swallowed, pressing his fingertips to either side of his nose. "Here's the issue for me — you're only three months away from graduating. I don't understand why, after all this time and effort, you'd pull out now."

"It's not really up to me, sir."

"Well then, I'm going to have to call Mr Forrest to talk to him about it. I'm not happy to see your efforts go to waste for the sake of a few months. And besides that, I've been meaning to call you up here to talk about next year. There's a scholarship being awarded for a disadvantaged student to study law at a university in Brisbane. I submitted your application a few months ago and they would like to offer the position to you."

Mr Jones' words didn't process in Harry's brain immediately. He'd never seriously considered attending university. Why would he? He didn't know anyone who'd gone on to higher education. Until recently, he hadn't thought he would even graduate from high school. "Really, Mr Jones?"

Mr Jones' face relaxed into a smile. "Yes, really, son. I didn't tell you about it because I didn't want to get your hopes up. But it turns out, they liked your application and your marks. I want you to seriously consider this offer. But it would mean remaining in school until you graduate."

"Yes, sir. I'd like to graduate and to accept the scholarship."

"I'm glad to hear it, son. Now go on to class, and let's have no more fighting."

❧ 33 ❧

AUGUST 1958

MARY

The dry grass crackled under Mary's black leather shoes as she walked. She wore a calf-length dress with a white apron over the top and a matching white cap. Beside her, Lottie, still clothed in the Fairbridge uniform, sighed.

"What happens to me when you finish your traineeship?"

Mary had thought about it a hundred times and still didn't have an answer. When she finished her traineeship, she'd be sent off to work as a domestic servant. The school advertised that the girls would become farmers' wives, but she had no intention of marrying the first farmer she came across. She would make her own way in the world, even if she had no idea where she'd go. Wherever it was, it wouldn't be with Lottie, who still had two years of school to complete before she started her traineeship.

"Well, I won't finish until at least next year, perhaps the year after, so we don't have to worry about it yet."

"I know, but I can't help thinking on it all the same. I can't imagine living here without you."

It was impossible for Mary to consider as well. Leaving Lottie wasn't an option. But what else could she do? She couldn't stay here, and Lottie must.

The pale sun lingered over the horizon, throwing cold shadows across the village. Children hung from the verandahs of the cottages or hid inside their frigid walls. There was nowhere to escape the cold. Two boys chopped firewood beside a pile of logs, their bare feet calloused and cracked as their toes clung to the timber, axes swinging down with a thwack.

Mary looked at her own bare feet. They'd stopped feeling the cold ground beneath them a month earlier. She'd never been so cold in her life. The temperature didn't drop so low here as it had in England, but at least there she'd worn shoes and stockings, no matter if they were an ill fit, and a fire to sit by. She hadn't believed things could be worse at the time. Although here she and Lottie had food to stave off the worst of their hunger pangs.

There'd been a light dusting of snow on the ground when they rose from their beds that morning, along with thick ice on the window-panes and on the blanket covering her nose and mouth. But the ice soon melted, and the snow was gone now after a day under the waning smile of a sallow sun. But the day was almost gone and the icy wind that'd picked up across the flat landscape sent a chill down her spine and set deep into her bones with a cold that she knew would stay with her all through the long night.

Cold and emptiness were her constant companions. She knew them so well she had forgotten how it would feel to live without them again, as they had on the *Strathaird* only a few years earlier. Those days gave her happy memories of a time of luxury, warmth and a full belly. Images flashed through her mind like a vapour, an impossible dream.

The stables were dark and cold. Horses in rugs milled about the yard, nibbling at the last remaining strands of hay. Mary and Lottie stood by the fence, leaning between the railings to stroke long, trembling noses and to scratch at scruffy, dusty forelocks. The Pony Club had been a sanctuary for them both over the years. They'd become adept riders since that first day and each had won a multitude of ribbons at the competitions in Molong and Orange. They weren't able to travel further afield because the school didn't have its own horse float for transportation. But any gymkhanas held nearby promised a day of excitement for the girls involved.

The boys preferred to play rugby. A few were involved in a local soccer team as well. Harry had done well at rugby; he was even selected for the district football team the year before. Although now he was more focused on his schoolwork. It was only a matter of time before they sent him away. He was sixteen, which meant he was likely to be placed on a farm within a year or so. There were no children older than seventeen at the farm. All of them left before they turned eighteen, most well before that.

She'd miss him when he was gone. She worried about it constantly. First Harry would leave, then she would. There was a time when it was all she could think about — leaving. After Crew came for her the second time, then the third. She'd lost count of his assaults over the years, even though she'd managed to fight him off at least half the time. She didn't tell Harry. He thought that by keeping an eye on her, he'd made her safe. But the truth was, Crew knew how to find her when no one else was around. Inside she was a ball of cold, hard emptiness. There was nothing except the love she had for Harry and Lottie. Everything else in her depths was black and hollow.

"We could leave together," she offered. The words came out as a whisper in the still afternoon air.

Lottie inhaled a sharp breath. "You know we can't do that. They'd catch us for sure. No one ever gets far. Then they're thrashed in front of the whole village."

"I know." Mary didn't have to be reminded. She'd seen enough of the public beatings for the memory to be fresh in her mind. She knew the risk, but it was a chance she'd take if it meant the possibility of escaping with Lottie by her side. "I can cop a beating. I've had plenty before now, and it won't make much of a difference. But I don't want to see you hurt."

That was the crux of it. Over the years she'd managed to protect Lottie from the worst of it — taking the blame whenever anything went wrong, jumping between Lottie and whichever cottage mother, teacher or worker had it in for her to catch the thumping herself. She'd protected Lottie with everything she could. There wasn't anything she could do to protect her sister from the pain of knowing Mam would never come — Lottie had come to terms with it two years after they landed in Australia. It'd left her in a foul mood for months. She'd emerged from her grief a sober, thoughtful, and quiet girl who kept mostly to herself. And as penance for not being able to produce their mother, Mary took it upon herself to ensure Lottie never went through pain again whenever she was able.

"I'll be okay. You don't have to protect me, you know," said Lottie as she tickled the nose of a chestnut mare.

"I'll figure it out, I promise. I'll find a way for us to leave together."

Lottie met her gaze, eyes deep with fear. "You can't promise that."

Mary looped her arms around Lottie's shoulders and pulled her into a fierce embrace. "We can't be apart. I won't survive it."

"I won't either. But I don't see how."

"There has to be a way, and I'll find it." Mary kissed Lottie's forehead as she stared out across the darkening village. Lights twinkled to life here and there. The sound of children's voices and laughter echoed across the frozen landscape. In the distance a crow cawed a mournful cry that it repeated over and over as it rose into the air, its great wings flapping in a steady rhythm.

This was her home, as much as anywhere had ever been. She was afraid to leave, and afraid to stay. She equally loved and hated the place. But wherever Lottie could be found was where Mary would be — no matter what they said, or where they sent her, she'd find her way back. That much she knew.

❧ 34 ❧

CURRENT DAY

MIA

The Ferris wheel looms skyward beside us. I look up, craning my neck to see the top of it. The stationary white wheel dazzles under the autumn sun, blinding me even though I'm wearing oversized sunglasses.

"Want to ride?" asks Dad.

"No, thanks. I think I'll keep my feet on the ground today."

"No worries. I've ridden it before anyway." He tucks his hands into his pockets as we walk.

The crowd along the Southbank shoreline is light today. Business people huddle over desks in the skyscrapers across the river from us, other people scamper about the suburbs ensconced in their daily tasks.

The river winds wide, lazy and brown through Brisbane, lapping at the foundations of the jagged cityscape. Tall buildings throw dark shadows over the swirling water even as ferries chug from one side to the other carrying pedestrians, commuters and tourists to the opposing docks.

The water is sluggish, confident, at peace. I'm not. Inside, I'm like a rushing brook, bounding over rocks and getting hung up in whirlpools. The one thing that consumes my thoughts is Brody and his impending surgery. What is else there to think about when my baby is going under the knife? Even the thought of it sends a chill through my body and I shiver involuntarily, though the weather is warm and the sun beats down on my hair until I can feel it burning my scalp.

"You okay?" asks Dad. He's studying me through narrowed eyes, as though I'm a specimen on a thin glass slide and he's a scientist with a microscope. He doesn't do compassion particularly well, although I don't hold it against him because I know he's trying.

"I don't know. I feel a bit funny." My head is light, spinning. My chest feels tight.

"What's on your mind, sweetheart?"

"I'm worried about Brody."

"The surgeon, Hugh Harris, is the best cardiac surgeon in the city. I checked him out right away. Brody is in good hands."

"I know." I'm flustered, swiping at a trail of sweat on my brow but wanting to cry instead. "I'm sure he's great. But this is my baby. He's tiny. Look at him." I wave a hand at the pram I'm pushing. Brody is in there, facing towards us under a shade cloth. His eyes are shut, and one tiny fist has escaped his wrap and is clenched tight. The nail on his thumb is so small and perfect, it makes my throat ache.

Dad sighs and looks older than I've ever seen him before. There are new lines on his face. A nick beside his mouth which speaks of carelessness. His grey hair flutters in the breeze, making it messy. My father never has messy hair. It's always perfectly combed, with a side parting just so.

"I know it's hard. But there's nothing else we can do. Right? He's got to have the surgery."

He's right. What else can we do? We've asked for three different opinions now, and all of the specialists we've seen agree that Dr Harris is right — Brody needs surgery. They also agree that Hugh Harris is exactly who they'd want operating on their child if they needed the same surgery. It helps me feel better, but only a little. The fact is, Brody will still be out of my control and under someone else's scalpel very soon. Ben doesn't seem to be struggling with the impending surgery as much as I am. He's calm and collected, at ease with the whole thing. At least, when he's around me, he is. It's more than a little aggravating. I can't fall apart when he's so pulled together.

"He needs the surgery," I admit with a shrug. But my head is swimming now, my legs feel weak, and I'm not sure I'm going to be upright for much longer if I keep breathing this fast.

We're wandering past a café. There are al fresco tables and chairs nearby and Dad guides me quickly to sit, with one hand beneath my elbow and the other at my back.

It's nice to have him with me, to feel his arms enveloping me. It's been a long time. The last time he held me this way was when I fell off my bike at the age of sixteen. I'd taken up mountain biking and had joined a race. There was a particularly rough patch where I'd chosen to jump the bike up onto a log rather than brave a pile of rocks on a downhill stretch, but the tyre had slipped off the log and I'd ended up with a broken wrist, plus a dozen bruises and cuts all over my body. Dad was amazing. I still couldn't believe he'd come to watch me. It wasn't something he generally did. He was stationed in Toronto, and I'd given up on inviting him to watch me race. But he came. And he drove me to the hospital in his town car. He didn't even get upset at me when I got blood on the passenger seat.

"Sit here and I'll get you a drink. Breathe slowly. Everything's going to be okay," he croons, hovering for a moment before trotting into the café.

I watch Brody sleep. He stirs, lifts his fist, and turns his head. Then he resettles. Dad returns from the inner sanctum of the café to sit beside me. He plucks the sunglasses from his face and folds them on the table.

"How are you feeling?"

"Lightheaded, dizzy..."

He reaches for my hand and squeezes it. "I ordered you some chamomile tea. That should do the trick."

"Thanks, Dad."

His compassion makes my throat squeeze against a sob. I'm on edge. The hormones, the lack of sleep. And now impending surgery on my newborn. I'm a mess. It doesn't take much to push me over the edge into full-blown tears these days. But I resist the urge. It'll make Dad uncomfortable, and I don't want to ruin this moment between us. I don't get many moments alone with him.

A waitress brings my tea, plus a coffee for Dad and two scones with jam and cream between us. I pour the tea, my hand shaking. Dad takes the pot from me and pours it instead. I take a sip and study the river. It's still moving at the same pace, unhurried and unaware of the turmoil I'm feeling. It's calming to watch the eddies and currents as they head out to sea beyond the crisscrossing bridges with their taut wires, sturdy brick pylons and angular steel girders.

"Sweetheart, I've told you this before, but no good comes of worrying about things that haven't happened. You can't control the outcome of the surgery by fretting over it."

I've heard it so many times. And even though it's irritating, and a little trite, to hear it in this moment, I breathe it in and let my eyes drift shut as I mull over each word. *Don't worry about things that haven't happened.*

"But Brody's sick. He needs surgery. It's my worst nightmare, and it's happening, Dad."

"This isn't your worst nightmare. Don't get me wrong, I know it's bad. But there's hope. There's still hope and a very good chance that everything is going to be perfectly fine. Don't lose sight of that, sweetheart. You're a doctor. You know that."

I scrub both hands over my face, groaning. "I know. At least, I should know. It's ridiculous. I'm the patient I always complain about."

Dad chuckles. "Don't they say doctors make the worst patients?"

Then I'm laughing too. "I suppose they're right about that. The problem is, we can imagine every possible scenario, and it does our head in."

"Will you and Ben both stay at the hospital?" he asks.

My heart skips a beat. "Dr Harris said we can. There aren't beds for us both, but Ben will sleep on the floor or in a chair or something he said. We both want to be there when he comes out of recovery. I can't imagine leaving him." I want to pick him up right now and kiss him all over his face, but he's sleeping, and he needs it. He hasn't been sleeping well lately. It's why Dad suggested we go for a walk. Brody sleeps best when he's moving, surrounded by noise, in the pram. I jumped at the chance to get out of the house and feel the sun on my face. My entire world has become very small since Brody was born.

"Let us know if we can do anything. We're headed back to Paris next week, but we could fly out again if you need us."

It's a kind offer and fills my heart. "I really appreciate that, Dad. But Gammy is here. Between her and Ben, I think I'll be fine. Don't get me wrong, I'd love for you and Mum to be here, but it's okay if you can't."

"Well, let me know."

"I wish you'd make things right with Gammy and Gramps. That's probably the biggest thing that would help right now."

Dad takes a bite of scone and chews it slowly. He wipes his mouth with a napkin, then sets it on the table. "Everything between me and your grandparents is perfectly fine. Don't worry yourself about us. You have enough on your mind."

The scone is delicious. It's so soft, it melts in my mouth. The strawberry jam mixes with the thick, smooth cream, and my mouth waters even as I bite into it. It's been a long time since I ate anything so decadent. I've been trying to lose the pregnancy weight, but it's slow going. It makes me think I might never fit back into my pre-pregnancy clothes.

I don't know what to say. Conflict is the last thing I need right now. But at the same time, this entire thing has reminded me how short life is and that holding onto grudges between family members is a completely pointless exercise. All we have is each other.

"Things aren't okay between you. Please, Dad, you've got to deal with this."

Dad sighs. "You had a good childhood, didn't you, sweetheart?"

Where is this coming from? "We're not talking about me."

"Just answer the question." He tips his head to one side.

"Fine. It was okay, I guess."

"Okay? It was just okay? You travelled the world, lived in exotic locations, learned different cultures and languages. You attended diplomatic parties with the wealthiest people and the most elite schools. Come on, sweetie, you were absolutely doted on."

I laugh. Not because it's funny, but because the word *doted* is so unexpected. It's certainly not the way I'd describe my upbringing. "Doted on? I don't know if that's exactly right, Dad."

"Okay, then. Tell me — what was so hard about your childhood?"

I shrug. This isn't exactly where I want to take the conversation, but the dizziness has passed and is quickly being replaced by a slow-burning anger that's lighting me up on the inside and making my words rush out, one after the other. Usually I'd stop them, push them down and pretend they weren't there bobbing beneath the surface. But today I'm raw, on edge, and I choose not to hold the emotion at bay. "How about moving to a new country every four years?"

"I know, an amazing experience. Right?"

"Wrong, Dad. I was always the new kid. I had to live in a brand-new country every four years. Learn a new language, make new friends, start my life all over again. I had no stability. I'd put down roots and it'd be time to move on. It was fine at first—four years seemed like an eternity when I was little. But by the time I was in primary and high school, it was torturous."

Dad smiles. "Don't you think that's a little bit of an exaggeration?"

"And then there were the nannies."

"Well, your mother and I had a lot of events and functions to attend. We didn't want you to be dragged from pillar to post."

I nod. "You were very busy. I get that. But I had a new nanny every year—sometimes they only lasted six months. One of them stayed with us for four years, and just when I thought I couldn't live without her, we moved to Peru and left her behind in Indonesia. Some of the nannies barely spoke English, but you stuck them with me all day long. I was in a big house, with a strange nanny who didn't know how to communicate in English, while you and Mum went to parties and played golf at the club. I had no one."

"We thought it'd be a great way for you to learn the local language — immersion. It's a proven educational technique."

"My life was one big educational program, Dad. I wanted family, friends — I wanted to be loved."

Dad's voice breaks around the words. "You were loved...are loved."

Tears glide down my cheeks. He's never told me that before. It's heart-wrenching and shatters me. "I know you love me, Dad. But it's nice to hear it, all the same."

He inhales a slow breath. "Sweetheart, you're the most important thing in our lives. I'm sorry we're not always good at showing that. Is all this the reason you've given up on your career?"

Annnnd we're back.

The good vibes sift out of my soul in a single moment as the hurts of the past come careening in to push them away in one big lump of emotion. "I'm not giving up on my career, Dad."

"But you studied for so many years to become a doctor. You're going to give that up to stay home with Brody? It's admirable, but Brody would want you to be the best doctor you can be."

"Don't say that, Dad. It's not true. Brody will want his mother with him, not some stranger. He'll want me to be there to read his bedtime story. He'll be happy that I'm the one putting the Band-Aid on his knee after he falls and scrapes it playing basketball in the driveway. He won't care about whether I'm a respected doctor—he'll care that I was there, with him."

Dad shakes his head. "I don't understand it." Then he sighs. "But I won't argue with you about it anymore. It's your life, your career. And I'm proud of you, no matter what you choose to do."

I'm ready with a retort burning in my chest. But my rage fizzes and dies. He's proud of me. Another first. "Thank you, Daddy." I reach for his hand and squeeze it even as fat tears trail down my cheeks.

"Everything's going to work out, you'll see. Brody will be fine. I'll make things right with Mum and Dad. I promise."

He wipes his eyes. I've never seen him cry before. It makes me cry even harder so that I'm sobbing now. I try to pull myself together by taking a deep breath, but all it does is result in hiccoughs.

Dad presses his hands together and stares at them. "I didn't have a childhood like yours. I tried to give you everything I didn't have. We were poor. Dad worked all the time. We were left alone and had to take care of ourselves a lot when Mum found work. I was the eldest, so I watched Sonya and made sure she had enough to eat, clean clothes to wear, that sort of thing. I know they did the best they could — but I guess I've held that against them for a long time. Then, well, Mum was pretty harsh on me as a teenager. I wanted her love, and she gave me discipline. They weren't there for me, didn't provide me with the kinds of opportunities I needed. I didn't realise what they'd been through themselves, just a selfish kid only thinking of myself. I'm glad you told me about the Fairbridge scheme — I think it'll help me to let all of that stuff go finally."

"I hope so, Dad. Gammy and Gramps love you so much."

He nods. Pats my hand. "I know you're right."

I rummage in the nappy bag hanging on the pram handle for tissues, then pass a few to Dad, who blows his nose and walks in the direction of the river — no doubt he needs some time to reflect and to calm himself. He hates public displays of emotion. I smile as I regard myself in a small hand mirror I keep in the bag — my entire face is red, my eyes bloodshot, there's snot — a lot of it—and streaks of tears and mascara on my cheeks. I've never felt more torn apart. But I'm happy too. Spent, but invigorated all at the same time. I wipe my nose with a tissue, stand with a smile and push the pram to meet Dad.

❦ 35 ❦

JANUARY 1960

HARRY

The white sheet fluttered for a moment midair, then floated down across the length of the table. Nuffield Hall was completely transformed. Every table was covered with a white sheet. There was a vase of fresh-cut flowers on the staff table. Children in their best clothes, with perfectly combed hair and shoes on their feet, scurried here and there carrying trays, plates, folded sheets, and bowls of steaming food.

The Fairbridge Council of New South Wales was coming to visit. Harry watched it all with a half-smile playing over his lips. He'd seen this charade performed annually for six years. The entire farm underwent months of preparation, a complete makeover from top to bottom, so that the council would see them at their best. At least, that was how Forrest termed it — didn't seem to matter to him that it was a fabrication of their best, since their best didn't include eating a whole roast pig at any other time of the year. Several of the trainee boys lugged the pig across the room. In the kitchen there were also a half-dozen roasted chooks, more vegetables than they'd seen all year, rice dishes, mashed potatoes and turnips, as well as several large fruit platters filled with fresh cherries, mulberries, peaches and oranges.

With an apple in its mouth, the pig was crisp brown all over, and the delicious aroma of roast ham permeated the entire space, making every child's stomach clench with hunger. Harry's stomach was no exception. He'd been hungry for much of the past five years, ever since he turned twelve and his appetite could no longer be satisfied by the threadbare meals provided at the Fairbridge Farm.

He was accustomed to hunger, and it no longer bothered him the way it had when he first entered his teen years. Now he was seventeen, he was the eldest child at the farm, and there were some perks to be had for that. He'd sneak a piece of ham when he was carving it, since the job had fallen to him. He'd even hand a few pieces to the smallest children who hung around the edges of the dining hall, their gazes firmly fixed on the delicious meat as they pretended to sweep and scrub the last scuff marks from the timber floor.

"Make sure you save me a piece," whispered Mary behind him.

"I'm not saving you anything. You didn't give me one of your apples yesterday."

"It was for Lottie," she protested, and he got a prod to the middle of his back that almost made him laugh out loud as he fought not to stumble forwards.

Mary, Faith, and the other trainee girls were busy in the kitchen helping the cook prepare the sumptuous feast that would be served for tea that night when the council members completed their inspection of the farm. It was the same thing every year.

He glanced over his shoulder and caught sight of Mary bustling back into the kitchen, a white apron tied around her thin waist. She caught his gaze and pulled a face, her eyes crossing and her tongue poking directly at him. He wished he could grab a hold of her and tickle her until she squealed, but there was no chance of that. The entire hall was full of children, teachers, cottage mothers and other farm staff.

Forrest was with the council members. He and his wife were no doubt showing off the cottages or the numerous farm gardens — the children had spent three months preparing them for this very inspection. There wasn't a weed to be seen in any of the large, rectangular gardens. Instead, they were each filled with either a cacophony of colourful flowers set amongst sturdy evergreen bushes, or the heady growth of summer vegetables: sweet green peas, beans on the vine held in place by stakes and wires, carrots with fluffy heads poking through the dirt, potatoes hidden beneath a bed of leaves, bright red berries peeking out of dark bushes, heads of lettuce, tall, dark silverbeet and a large unruly pumpkin patch.

Harry was caught in mixed emotions. Everything about this place spoke of home to him now. His memories of England were fluid, shadowy. It'd been such a long time ago, it seemed to him he was a different person then. Still, he couldn't help holding onto the promise of that time, that place. He'd be leaving Fairbridge tomorrow, and he couldn't wait to put it behind him. Yet, there were plenty of reasons he didn't want to say goodbye.

He strode into the kitchen to find the carving knife. There was Mary, settled in front of the stove, a large stirring spoon in one hand. Her blonde hair was pulled back in a jaunty ponytail with a scarf tied firmly over the top. Her blue eyes sparkled at the sight of him, and her full pink lips widened into a teasing smile.

Everything about her confused him these days. Their easy, comfortable friendship had been replaced by a longing need he didn't fully understand. He wanted more than anything to be around her, yet when he was, he couldn't find the words to express himself, found a heat traveling up his neck and across his face that he couldn't control, and he often ended up tripping over his own feet or dropping his dinner plate on the floor.

"What's in the pot?" he asked, edging closer to the stove.

She grinned. "We have mulberries simmering in this one for the mulberry pies. And this one has the potatoes. I'm going to mash them with butter and cream."

"I'm starving," he said, standing on tiptoe to admire the purple mulberries stewed with sugar and some spices he didn't recognise.

"Don't touch," she admonished with a swing of the spoon. "They're hot and you'll burn your tongue."

He settled back on flat feet and pushed his hands into his pockets. "I'm leaving tomorrow."

Her smile faded and she fixed her gaze on the mulberries, stirring slowly. "I know. Will you tell me goodbye before you go?"

"I will. If I can." His feet shuffled in place. "I want to."

"Good." She offered him a smile that lit him up on the inside and set his heart racing.

"After everything's set up, the staff will be busy keeping the council members occupied. I'll come to your cottage."

"Okay," she said.

He found the carving knife and walked with it out to meet the pig that'd been set up on a buffet table near the front of the hall. It sat on a long, silver platter tempting every child in the room. He'd been rostered on at the piggery all month, fed them slops every morning in the dawn's early light. He knew each one by sight, but he also knew they had a purpose and he understood by now how things worked around the village. No one had taught him how to raise pigs, it was something he'd had to figure out on his own, like most things the children did in the village. An older child led the way, then he was left to muddle through alone.

Bronson managed the piggery as well as the dairy and Harry learned early on that Bronson was known for the inventive ways he siphoned cash into his back pocket by selling pigs, calves, hay and grain on the side, with Forrest none the wiser. Any boy who spoke up about what he saw, had Bronson to deal with the next day. No one spoke up twice. Harry knew to keep his mouth shut. He did the work he was assigned to do and swallowed his anger at the way the younger children ran about the place in bare feet with collar bones protruding, shivering in the cold because there wasn't enough money to buy meat, bread, shoes or coats. That was village life, and there wasn't anything he could do about it. Now he'd was leaving, could put it all behind him and never look back.

His heart ached with the knowledge that it would be the last time he'd see Mary, Lottie, Max and all of the other children who'd become such an important part of his life — his makeshift family. Max's farm placement had been delayed. Forrest had kept him at the village longer since Harry remained at school after his conversation with the principal. Devon had left the farm several years earlier and they'd never heard from or seen him again. Every year, the older children moved on, then his peers, one by one. They'd each left a small hole in his heart. He'd say goodbye, and hoped they'd come back to visit, but they never did. And he supposed he wasn't likely to be able to either. He was going to Brisbane to study law at the University of Queensland. It was a long way from Molong, and he wouldn't have the money for a return trip.

Harry carved the ham, then hurried back to the kitchen to return the carving knife as Mr and Mrs Forrest led the council party into the hall and the children all stood by their tables at attention, hands flat against their sides. All he wanted to do now was to get out of the way. He didn't intend to stay for the meal. As much as his stomach longed for him to sit at the table and stuff his face full of the delicious and aromatic feast, his nervous energy meant he had to keep moving. He'd already packed, so there wasn't anything left for him to do to prepare for his trip north tomorrow. But he wanted to take one last walk around the farm, alone in the dark, to say his goodbyes.

He set off through the village. The cottages sat in darkness with only the occasional verandah light to bring the children home after tea. A full moon glimmered bright in the sky, illuminating the countryside with a golden glow that darkened shadows and exposed the rest. Sheep dotted the field beside the village. Some stood grazing, most lay in clumps and clusters, their coats newly shorn, cropped short against fat sides.

The small herd of horses clustered around the stables. They whinnied soft and low when they saw him, and two of them broke away from the group to come in search of treats. He handed them carrot tops from his pockets, stroked their soft noses and whispered his goodbyes into their long, tangled manes, inhaling the scent of them one last time.

On his way back to the cottage, Max came bounding to him through the darkness. He'd been placed at a farm southwest of Molong. He'd be leaving the following week and one of the younger boys would take his place at Fairbridge as a trainee. Harry hoped they'd cross paths again, but his experience so far had taught him hope was futile, and the thought left an empty feeling in his chest.

"There you are," said Max, falling into step beside him. "I thought you might be out and about. You missed a great meal." Max licked his lips. "I went for seconds."

Harry sighed. "I know. But I couldn't stick around and listen to all that tripe about how wonderful the institution is, and the opportunities it's providing for the children. Not again."

"I guess you're right. Seems to me you're getting a pretty great opportunity though." Max kicked at a stone, sending it skipping along the path ahead of them.

"That's true. But most kids aren't. You're not."

"I'll be fine."

They'd had this conversation before. Harry would never see the Fairbridge school the way Max did. His friend seemed to view everything in a positive light. He loved Mr and Mrs Forrest like they were his parents, even after all the times Forrest had hurt, shouted at and neglected him over the years. There was no point in arguing the matter with Max — he wanted to be happy, and there wasn't anything Harry could say to dissuade him from his perspective. In fact, Harry didn't want to. If Max could be happy with his childhood on the farm, Harry had no desire to take that from him.

"You're right about one thing," continued Harry. "I should be grateful for what I've got."

"You'd never be going to university back in the UK," added Max.

"I wish..."

"What do you wish?" asked Max.

"That you were coming with me. That's all. I want the same thing for you."

Max shrugged. "I didn't get the results you did. I can barely read to save my life. Don't know how you ended up so smart." He laughed and slapped Harry on the back. "Nope, that was never going to happen for me. But I can't tell you how pleased it makes me to see you reaching for the stars. When I'm lugging hay bales onto the back of a tractor, or herding cattle on dipping day in the blazing sun, I'll think of you huddled over your books, saving the world."

"I don't know about saving the world."

"Well, learning about it, anyway."

Something inside Harry leapt at the thought. He longed to learn everything he could about the world — its history, books, artists, architecture, laws and languages. But he'd settle for becoming a solicitor and representing the law. For now, anyway.

Max shook his hand and waved as he walked away. "See you back at the cottage."

Harry's heart squeezed at the sight of his lanky friend wandering into the gloaming. With a deep breath, he set his sights on Evelyne Cottage and Mary. She waited for him on the verandah, legs tucked up against her chest, chin resting on her knees with her back pressed to the wall. It was dark —she hadn't turned on the light. He slid down the wall and sat beside her, his leg pressed up against the side of hers.

She faced him, her eyes wet with tears. "I don't want to say goodbye."

"Then we won't." His heart raced and emotion welled up in his throat.

They sat side by side in silence, looking out over the moon-washed village. His hand brushed against hers where it lay on the floorboards by her side. He reached for her fingers, winding his gently through hers. She lay her head on his shoulder.

"It's not forever," he said.

She sobbed softly. "You'll come back?"

"Absolutely, I will."

"No one ever does."

"But *I* will. I won't leave you behind."

"You promise?"

"I promise. I'll come back as soon as I can earn money for a ticket. When you're old enough, we'll get married." The words tumbled from his mouth before he could stop them. They hadn't spoken of marriage. But suddenly he knew in the very depths of his soul that he wanted to spend the rest of his life with Mary. Living without her wasn't possible. He could hardly remember a time in his life when she wasn't there. He hated to leave her on her own, but it seemed Crew had forgotten about her over the years. The gardener had left the farm to care for his elderly mother months ago. She'd be safe at the farm, and it wouldn't be long until she'd finish her traineeship. Then she could join him, they'd be together again, and no one could keep them apart.

She faced him with her eyes red-rimmed. "You want to marry me?"

"Of course," he said. "Do you?"

"I don't know. I haven't thought about it. All I can think about is getting out of here with Lottie."

His stomach clenched. "Well, you don't have to decide right now. We're both too young. But we'll be together again soon anyway."

She studied the lines of his face in the dark. "Don't forget us, will you?"

"How could I?" He traced the lines on hers with the tip of a finger. He wanted to memorise every curve, every familiar freckle, the way her hair fell in blonde strands across her forehead and the depth of blue in her tear-soaked eyes.

"Send me a letter when you're settled so I can write to you," she said.

"I will."

Then he leaned forward to kiss her soft lips. Tentative, gentle. He was uncertain, and she seemed surprised. She gasped against his mouth, then pressed herself to him. Her lips were still, firm, and true. Her eyes fluttered shut. His arms found their way around her thin frame. His hands pressed to her back, and he shuffled closer, the taste of her teasing his tongue. The kiss opened him up in a way he hadn't expected — as though the world was full of possibilities now that he hadn't considered before. Love was real, and perhaps he could have a piece of it. Their embrace lasted only a few moments, but it changed everything.

❧ 36 ❧

MARY

With a needle and thread poised in one hand and a thimble on her pointer finger, Mary stared into the bucketing rain. Raindrops thundered on the tin roof over her head, poured from the verandah eaves and burrowed into the dirt, building muddy rivulets that crisscrossed the village paths between the cottages. Deep puddles formed here and there, and several of the smaller children ran through them, splashing and laughing as mud clung to their arms, legs and faces, streaking their skin brown.

She smiled at them without seeing, then focused again on her work. She was mending a pair of Lottie's shorts, but so far had been staring at the rain for half an hour and only had five stitches to show for her efforts. She couldn't concentrate. All she could think about was the emptiness inside now that Harry was gone. He'd left a few weeks earlier. Gone before she'd risen from bed. There was a note beneath her pillow — she didn't know how he'd put it there without waking her. The note promised that he'd write soon, and not to worry about him, since he could take good care of himself. There was a dried flower as well, and she'd pressed it to her lips before tucking it, along with the letter, into a notebook she kept hidden beneath her mattress as a journal.

So far there'd been no correspondence. Nothing from Brisbane to let her know he'd arrived safely, or where he was staying. Perhaps he'd forgotten them already.

Ingrid's heavy footsteps crossed the verandah behind her. "Get on with it, lazy bones." She kicked at Mary's leg with her booted foot. "I've a good mind to use the strap on your back. You can't seem to get nothin' done without some enticement, I guess. Ungrateful tramp that you are."

Mary bent over her sewing, pushing the needle through the fabric and stopping it with the thimble before repeating the procedure over again. She wasn't concerned about Ingrid. The cottage mother was full of bluster, but rarely followed through on any of her threats. Still, Mary didn't like to get her offside, since it generally meant going hungry at teatime. Although Ingrid's measly attempts at cooking were often better missed anyway, and she could sneak into the kitchen after lights-out to find something more nourishing and less likely to give her stomach cramps.

Lottie wandered onto the verandah and slumped down beside Mary. "I'm bored."

"You could learn to sew and mend your own clothes," mumbled Mary.

Lottie grimaced. "No, thanks."

It wasn't like Lottie to complain. But the rain had fallen for three straight days and everyone was sick of it. It was a different kind of rain to the drizzle that dampened the British landscape day after day. This was a downpour. Each drop was fat and heavy. It landed hard and eroded the dirt away until there was only mud, puddles, roaring creeks and swollen rivers. Sheep huddled beneath tree branches in clusters, tucked in as close to each other as they could manage, heads down and backs to the driving rain. Birds were hidden away out of sight, no doubt tucked into hollow tree trunks or roosting under eaves and gutters. The horses had barely left the stables in days, and the chooks had taken refuge in their pen.

"Don't you wanna run in the rain?" Lottie sighed as she watched the children shrieking and kicking water over one another.

"Not really."

"Come on, it'll be fun. You've done nothing but mope about the place for weeks."

"I'm too old to behave like a child."

"You didn't say that when I lobbed pieces of bread across the room and you caught them in your mouth last night." Lottie smiled.

Mary grinned as she pulled the needle through the fabric for one final stitch, then tied it in a knot and bit off the end. "I suppose it doesn't hurt to get a little muddy every now and then."

She carried the sewing inside and put it away. Then she tied back her hair into a stubby ponytail. With a shout, she and Lottie leapt from the verandah into the pummelling rain. The chill of the water down her back stole her breath for a moment, but she continued to run side by side with her sister, arms outstretched and face tipped skyward. Rain slapped against her skin. It soaked through her clothes. The other girls from the cottage watched them go, then jumped down to the muddy ground to follow them.

They found a hill just outside the village, and someone pulled a piece of torn old canvas tarpaulin from the garden shed. Before long, they were taking turns sliding down the tarp and landing in a mud bog at the bottom. By the time they trekked back up the hill to the top of the slide, the rain had washed the mud from their faces and eyes, and they could see enough to slide all the way back down again.

They ran in the rain, kicked water at each other, and slid down the slide into the bog over and over until they were each exhausted. When the sun blinked against the horizon and Mary's teeth chattered together, it was time to go inside. They washed themselves mostly clean in a rushing creek that'd jumped over its banks with eddies of cold, brown water hurrying loudly between swirling round ponds. They laughed as they washed, catching the strongest current from one pond to the next on a few quick kicks.

"Look at this frog," said Lottie, emerging from one of the ponds.

She held up a green frog that blinked in the rain, then leapt from Lottie's outstretched hand back into the creek, disappearing beneath the swift waters in a moment.

"Oh, no," complained Lottie, her brow pulled into a furrow.

"Never mind. I'm sure you'll find another in no time at all," said Mary.

She left the rest of the group there and wandered back to the cottage, where she took a hot shower and rinsed out her wet clothes. At least she'd managed to beat the rest of them back and the water heater was operating. The last girls would land a frigid shower, but it was far worse in winter.

When she returned to her bunk and flung herself down on it, a towel wrapped around her still-damp hair, something crinkled beneath her. She turned over and found a letter under the rags she'd sewn into the shape of a pillow for her head. It was a letter from Harry.

She sat up in a hurry and carefully tore open the envelope, her heart lifting at the sight of his neat, loping hand etched in black ink across the cream paper.

DEAREST MARY,

I'm writing to you from my room in the city. My very own room, and no one to tell me what to do or how to live in it. It's in an old boarding house on the edge of town. An elderly couple owns the boarding house and wanted someone to let a room who could help them in the garden every now and then. Which I'm perfectly suited to, as you know. Haven't we spent hundreds of hours doing just that?

The first thing I did when I arrived was secure the room, thanks to Mr Forrest's help. He's not so bad at times. Although I really do think he could give the kids a break now and then.

The second thing was for me to find work. I found a job as a foot courier. All it means is that I carry documents between businesses around Brisbane. It's fine work. I have a trolley, and I can walk for hours without getting bored. There's so much to see and so many people to watch. Besides that, I practice reciting legal precedents in my head while I'm walking and when I ride the bus to university. So, you see, I'm already on my way.

I hope you and Lottie are well. I haven't heard from Max since he left, although I have his address so will write to him next. You can reach me at the enclosed address. Please do—I'm anxious to hear from you, as I don't know a single soul here. It's very strange to be all alone yet surrounded by people. Still, I'm excited for this new life. If only you were here with me. I know you're safe there now though. I wouldn't have left you if I thought otherwise. So, don't fret my darling, I will see you again soon.

I look forward to receiving your letter.

With all my love and some more besides.

Yours,

Harry

MARY JUMPED TO HER FEET AND PRESSED THE LETTER TO HER HEART as it hammered against her rib cage. He sounded well, and it brought her so much joy to know he was happy and that he hadn't forgotten her. She'd missed him every single day since he left, but didn't realise quite how much until that very moment, when she'd spied the envelope bearing his handwriting. It hit her with such a force that she worried her heart might leap from her chest.

Hope furrowed a way through the darkness she felt in her heart. Perhaps they would all be together again. It didn't seem quite so impossible now that she'd heard from him. He'd promised they'd be married, that they would find a way to make it all work. She didn't know about marriage, hadn't ever seen a marriage other than Mr and Mrs Forrest, and she didn't want what they had. All she knew of those kinds of relationships were the ones Mam shared with the men who careened into and out of her life and her bed. And the violent way Crew cornered and mistreated her.

She knew that wasn't for her, had never considered that she might marry one day. Her entire goal for most of her life had been simple: as soon as she was able, she'd find work and pay for herself and Lottie to have a place of their own where no one could hurt them again. But Harry was different. A life with him could be good. He was kind, thoughtful, gentle, and loving. Maybe marriage to Harry would not be so bad. In fact, it might be wonderful.

With the letter safely ensconced between the pages of her journal, and the book hidden away again beneath her mattress, she stepped onto the verandah to see whether the rest of the girls from the cottage had returned. She plucked the towel from her hair and rubbed it dry as she wandered to the railing, then leaned against it to look beyond the stables. But she couldn't see them. They were hidden from view and clearly weren't on their way back to the cottage yet.

A deep voice startled her and drew her back to the present in a flash.

"All alone?" asked Crew, leaning on a long stick in the pouring rain just beyond the cottage steps.

His wide-brimmed hat funnelled rain down his back. His sodden clothes clung to his lithe frame. His piggish eyes squinted through the rain at her.

"No," she lied, lifting her chin.

He grinned. "Yes, you are. Guess you didn't know I was back."

"What do you want?" She ached to walk away. Everything in her screamed she should run. But she knew if she moved, he would pounce.

"What makes you think I want something?"

She shook her head. "Leave me alone, Crew."

"Or what?"

"Or nothing. Just leave me be."

He shrugged and crossed his arms over his chest, letting the stick drop to his side. "Maybe I will, but if I do, I might have to go see your sister. She's turning into quite the little beauty."

Anger flooded through Mary, the hair on her neck stood on end and she clenched both fists at her sides. "Don't you dare go near her."

"What are you gonna do about it? I'll do what I like. I always do."

He laughed, then uncrossed his arms, twirled the stick in the air and sauntered off towards the stables through the pouring rain.

Mary watched him go, adrenaline pumping from her heart through every nerve ending. She hated him. Hated him with every cell in her body. She quivered with it as he strode into the fading light. He'd hurt her too many times to count. But she'd fought back and given him plenty to be wary of. But Lottie was different. She was sweet, gentle, and naive. She didn't know how to fight, not like Mary. If he ever touched Lottie, she'd kill him.

❧ 37 ❧

MIA

Gammy is a neat freak. Her house is always perfectly put together. I didn't inherit that trait from her, although I wish I had. She doesn't own fancy or expensive things. All her furniture is well loved. That's what she says — better to buy something sturdy and love it well than cheap and plastic. The world has adopted a throwaway culture, Gammy rants whenever the subject comes up. It's better to fix things and keep them than to replace them.

She takes good care of her furniture, pots, pans, glasses and china, making sure everything in her home is put away in its proper place. She still has the same Tupperware she used when her kids were little, and the china plates she and Gramps bought for their ten-year wedding anniversary.

Throughout my life, from what I recall, very little at Gammy and Gramps' house has changed. Even though he moved to assisted living three years ago, his favourite rocking chair still sits in the living room right next to the kitchen and posed to look at the television set. Its brown patterned fabric is worn, and there's a knitted brown-and-cream throw rug folded neatly over the back. He likes to sit in his chair, watching cricket, with the rug over his knees. He still does it when he comes to visit Gammy on the weekend sometimes.

I'm sitting in his chair now, the rug behind my head, as I rock it back and forth and gaze around the empty living room. Gammy is visiting Gramps, and she's tasked me with helping her get the paper-work together for the Medicare office so she can be reimbursed for her medical expenses. But since Ben has Brody with him, it's the first moment I've had alone in weeks, and I'm taking the opportunity to pause and breathe. It won't last long because there are things to get done and I have to be home to feed Brody in an hour. But for now, I'm breathing. In and out, in and out. Looking around and remembering the childhood hours spent playing and colouring in this room, the time I fell and hit my lip on the coffee table. It split open and there was blood everywhere. There's probably still a small stain on the Turkish rug that Gammy couldn't get out even after all her scrubbing with bicarb soda and vinegar.

With a sigh, I get to my feet. There's work to be done and no one to do it but me. Mum and Dad are packing at the hotel, as their flight leaves in the morning. They don't have time for things like this. And besides, Gammy wants me to do it. I'm the only one she trusts completely to poke around her house and find the things I need to make it happen. Sometimes I wish it was Dad, though, since I've got my hands full with Ben and Brody. But I'll do anything for Gammy and Gramps, so I set my resolve and head into the guest bedroom Gammy also uses as an office.

The desk is tidy, with only the unpaid bills lying in an open and neat stack on one side. It's a timber desk that looks like it might be fifty years old. There are scratches and grooves in various places all over it. The sides have a lovely wave shape to them, and there's an old lid that slides down into place—or at least it did once, but it no longer works. There's also a groove along the top for pens, and I reach for one of them, turning it over between my fingers, then set it back in its place. Gammy said the Medicare paperwork was on top of the desk, and the receipts in one of the drawers where she stores the items ready for filing.

I find the Medicare paperwork quickly enough, but when I look through the drawers, I can't locate the medical receipts right away. The first drawer contains a sheaf of stationery with Gammy's name and address across the top, surrounded by tiny butterflies and swirly flowers. *Virginia Evans*

I've always loved Gammy's name. When I was a kid, I used to wish I'd been named after her. Then I could be Ginny or Gina just like her. Instead, I got Mia, and it pained me to no end that I couldn't shorten it. Of course, the kids at school found ways to lengthen it instead, to things like Mia-bo-bia, or Mia-Pia. There are really no good options for a nickname that rhymes with my given name. At least, no one thought of any when I was going through my prime teasing years.

Next to the personalised stationery is a stack of letters in envelopes held together with an elastic band. I pull out the letters to look through them. A flash of guilt holds me back for a moment, but curiosity gets the better of me. The envelopes are faded and with old-fashioned handwriting across the front. They're addressed to a Mary Roberts, and when I turn them over, the same handwriting lopes across the back of the envelope, announcing that the sender's name is Sylvia Roberts, and that she's from London.

I can't help questioning why Gammy has a stack of someone else's letters in the top drawer of her neatly laid-out desk. She's not the kind of person who hordes random old letters. They're in with her best stationery, a roll of the latest Australian animal-themed postage stamps, and the stickers I bought her to put on the back of envelopes with her name and address typed over a serene beach scene.

I'm about to put them back when I shake my head and wrest one of the envelopes free of the stack. I'm gentle, being careful not to tear the paper, since they seem as though they were written a long time ago. The paper is tinged yellow, and the ink is faded.

The letter is one single sheet, all written in that same difficult-to-read handwriting. The kind of handwriting people used years ago, back before I was born. This writing clearly comes from a different time.

. . .

DEAREST MARY,

THANK YOU FOR YOUR LETTER. I WASN'T EXPECTING TO HEAR FROM YOU since no one seemed to know where you'd gotten to.

I hope you and Lottie are well. I miss you both more every day. I've got some kind of illness now. The doctor talked to me about it, but I can't say I really understood what he told me. Something to do with my stomach and throat, and it's bad I believe.

I want to tell you I'm sorry. I broke my promise to come, and I know you probably won't ever forgive me for that.

All I can hope for is that you and your sister are well and happy. That you have a better life now than I could've given you. I always was a hopeless case. But you know that better than anyone.

If you can find it in your heart to forgive me, and maybe even visit some-time, I would love to see you both.

WITH LOVE,
   Mam

I'M STILL CONFUSED AS TO WHY THIS LETTER IS IN GAMMY'S DESK. I know she's from England, and it seems this person is as well. Is it possible they're from the mother Gammy and Auntie Char left behind in England? And if they are, why are they addressed to Mary?

Because I've already snooped, and I'm dying to find out more, I look through the other letters as well. They're all from the same person, and all express similar sentiments — *I miss you, I'm sorry, won't you please call or visit...*

They also have dates scrawled on the top right-hand side of each. The first was written on the second of February, 1971, the last on the third of December, 1972. They stop suddenly, although the last letter seems to indicate they'd spoken several times over the phone and tells the reader thank you. So, whoever they are, I hope they received the forgiveness they were looking for. It makes my throat ache to think about someone all that long distance away, hoping and begging for forgiveness from a loved one only to be turned away at the end. So, I'm choosing to believe there was a reconciliation, if only to stop my own tears from consuming me when I'm supposed to be looking for receipts and getting back home to my baby.

The elastic band goes back around the envelopes easily, and I tuck them into their place in the drawer. There are so many questions rushing through my thoughts. I wish Gammy was here so I could ask her. But how do I ask those questions without explaining my snooping?

⊗⊰⊙

A MAGPIE HOPS ALONG THE BACK OF THE BRICK BARBECUE. IT watches me slinging snags onto the hot grill. They sizzle as they hit the steel, and I step back, pleased with my work, wiping my hands dry on a paper towel. The bird takes to the air with a flap of wings and roosts above me in the branches of an enormous gum tree. It warbles, its song answered by another magpie who flies in to greet the first, sharing the branch.

I finish loading sausages beside rows of thinly sliced sizzling potatoes. "There you go. The rest is up to you," I say.

Ben gives me a mock salute with the barbecue prongs. Then he and Dad settle into their manly cooking stance, legs slightly apart, arms crossed, brows furrowed. I'm sure they'll talk about cricket and politics and all the things they love to discuss whenever they're together. It makes me happy that Dad and Ben get along. At least that's one family relationship I don't have to fret over.

With a sigh, I head back to the picnic table. There's a playground with colourful swings, a slide and a climbing wall behind the table. Gammy, Gramps, Mum and Brody are all there. Mum is holding Brody and blowing raspberries on the palm of his tiny hand. Gammy and Gramps are hovering, laughing and exclaiming over his delectable cuteness. I pause for a moment to snap a photograph and can't help smiling at the four of them. It's a moment I'll treasure after tomorrow when Mum and Dad are back in Paris. It'll be months until we see them again, and even though we've had some tense moments, it's been wonderful to have them here. They've been a big help—running errands, buying groceries, dropping by to cuddle Brody while I cook dinner. I'll miss them when they leave.

I sit at the picnic table and get ready to mix the potato salad, something I didn't have time to do before we left the house. But instead, I find myself staring at my blank phone screen. With a quick flick of a finger, the blank screen is replaced by a photograph of the first letter I read, to Mary Roberts, written by *Mam*. I can't get the letters out of my mind. Who is Mam? Why does Gammy have her letters to someone called Mary? Is this woman my great-grandmother?

With a shake of my head, I glance up at Gammy, who's completely absorbed in something Brody is doing. So, I return my attention to the phone and do a search for Mary Roberts. Even as I run the search, it dawns on me the name couldn't be more common and I'm very unlikely to find anything useful. The search results confirm my suspicion. There are hundreds of Mary Roberts in the world, and even if I did happen across a link to *my* Mary Roberts, how could I possibly tell? I know nothing about her except that she was alive in 1971 and most probably travelled from England to Australia some time before that.

Behind me, a child riding a bike slams into another child on a scooter. The screams, yelling and general pandemonium distract us all for a moment. My heart thuds against my rib cage. The adrenaline that's been keeping me functioning lately is never far away — it doesn't take much to spike my anxiety and the crying children do that admirably well, hormonal as I am.

So, between deep breaths, I scroll through the search results. There are social media accounts, smiling photographs of women, young and old. There are newspaper articles, award ceremonies and professional profiles — all women called some variation of Mary Roberts. And any of the older ladies could be *the* Mary Roberts I'm looking for. But I can't tell, and there's really nothing more I can do right now since I've got to prepare the meal before everyone revolts and eats their fill of the Tim Tams stashed in the bottom of the esky.

"Can I help?" asks Gammy, sliding onto the bench seat beside me.

"That'd be lovely. Thanks, Gammy. You could set the table. There's a tablecloth and paper plates in the basket over there." I point to a wicker basket covered with a red-and-white cloth.

Gammy walks over to the basket and gets to work. She's wearing a blue scarf over her white hair that brings out the brilliant colour of her light blue eyes. People tell me all the time we have the same eyes, and I love that we can share something so simple that ties us together in a special way.

"You look beautiful today, Gammy."

She grins, her full lips pulled wide. "Thanks, love. You're pretty smashing yourself. As usual."

I want to roll my eyes and make a quip about having had no sleep and that all I had time to do was put on lip gloss and pull my hair into a messy ponytail, but I'm practicing receiving compliments and not brushing them off. So instead, I tell her thank you and keep mixing the potato salad even as I'm squirming inside.

Dad sets an empty tray on the table. "I think we forgot the onion."

"Oh, right. We can't forget that. Gammy will never forgive us." I wink at Gammy and hand over the container of sliced onions to Dad.

Gammy laughs. "You can't have a barbecue without onion."

"I think you can," quips Dad.

"Not a proper one, anyway," Gammy corrects him.

He rests a hand on her shoulder, then bends down to kiss her cheek. It's a quick kiss, just a brush of lips against paper-thin skin. But her cheeks flush and she looks up at him in the most adoring way, with her hand on her cheek. "What was that for?"

He shrugs. "I love you, that's all."

She reaches for his hand and squeezes it. "You'll never know how much I love you, kid."

His eyes glisten. "And I'm sorry."

"Me too," she says.

"I don't mean what I say sometimes. There's something that happens to me when I'm with you and Dad. It's like I revert to my childhood, and I become an angry teenager all over again. But I'm working on it."

She pulls him into an embrace. "Thanks, darling. That means a lot."

"I know you did your best, you and Dad. I'm sorry I didn't ask more questions about your childhood and family. I could've phrased it differently the last time I asked. But I really do want to know."

She sniffles and drag a tissue from her cardigan sleeve to wipe her nose. "I'd love to tell you all about it sometime."

He squeezes her hand, then walks away. I'm overcome with emotion. It's everything I was hoping for when I held the family dinner. But their fight had dashed those hopes. I didn't know if we'd ever get to the place where they could stand to be together. But I've been talking to Dad about everything, and he seems ready to listen, ready to forgive. It fills my heart with a warm, heady kind of peace.

Gammy wipes her nose again, and then blinks back tears. "Well, I wasn't expecting that."

I wrap an arm around her shoulders, hold her close. "I'm so happy to see the two of you make amends."

"Me too, kiddo. He's my baby, and always will be. You've got your own baby now, so you understand how that feels."

I nod. I do understand. It would break my heart into a million pieces if Brody rejected my love the way Dad has with Gammy. But she's not going to hold that against him. I know that because I wouldn't either. We're similar in more ways than one, she and I.

❧ 38 ❧

MARCH 1960

HARRY

The earth turned over brown and moist beneath his trowel. Harry sat back on his haunches, puffing lightly, to survey his work. The garden bed was mostly dug now. It'd been back-breaking work — earth full of rocks, broken cement, weeds, and root systems. The Hobolts were proud of their boarding house and garden on Turbot Street, but it'd fallen into disrepair as they'd aged, and they hadn't had the energy to do anything about it. Now that he was renting a room from them, they were excited to see what he could do with the garden and had big plans for planting all of their favourites again. He was excited about the discount they gave him for it.

And truthfully, he didn't mind the work. Gardening had been a chore on the farm, but now it gave him a chance to step away from his books for a while and enjoy being outdoors. Something he'd never thought about much before, but now time in nature was hard to find. It refilled his soul to squat under the afternoon sun, dirt beneath his fingernails, butterflies and dragonflies humming around him as he pushed bulbs into the soft, dark earth.

He brushed his hands on his pants, pulled open his shirt pocket, and retrieved a folded photograph. It was the image the photographer took of him and Mary at the sports carnival all those years ago. In it, she stood by his side, a laugh on her pretty face as she stared up at him. The two of them were so young, she just as tall as him although she was two years younger. They were both skinny, with knobbly knees, and dressed simply in the Fairbridge uniform.

Their open countenance and grins belied the facts of their circumstances. They seemed not to have a care in the world, two children who'd never faced hardship or fear in their lives. The reality was something different, but the image captured the essence of the life he'd wished for himself. It brought him joy to see the two of them that way — naive, innocent and happy children. Even if it wasn't entirely true.

The back screen door slammed shut, and in moments a kelpie galloped across the backyard to him. The dog licked him right across the face before he'd had a chance to rise to his feet. He laughed, wiping away the wet kiss with the back of his sleeve before giving the dog a pat on the back.

"Come on now, Bess, give me a chance to get out of the way. I don't want slobber from chin to crown."

The dog wagged around him in a circle, her rusty brown coat gleaming in the afternoon sunshine.

The garden gate was shut, but beyond it the busy street held a steady stream of regal, rounded vehicles. A buttery-yellow Pontiac Chieftain with a white peaked roof, a black Standard Vanguard, an indigo Morris Minor and several Holdens chugged by while he stared out across the burgeoning young city, wondering where Mary was and what she was doing at that moment.

The dog pushed against his legs, keening for a walk. He laughed and rubbed her ears. "All right, let's go inside. I've got to get a drink of water before I can take you out."

Inside, he filled a glass with water from the tap and chugged it down in two gulps, then refilled it again. Sweat soaked his shirt. His hat tipped back from his forehead to make way for the glass. He finished it off again.

He and Bess walked around the city, as they did every afternoon. The dog had boundless energy and was too much for the elderly couple to handle. They'd mostly left her to her own devices, and she'd chewed holes in the walls and timber staircase in her frustration and boredom. By the time he got her back home again, she was huffing lightly and ready for her supper. He fed her, then took a shower before retreating to his room to study.

It was Sunday, so he didn't have classes or work to attend to. Most of Brisbane came to a halt on Sundays. Nothing was open, and people generally stayed home to rest after church. He'd learned that the time after church, which he attended with the Hobolts, was a good chance to catch up on his studies and the gardening, since the couple spent much of the afternoon visiting with friends or napping. And the few other men who boarded with them were usually out or shut in their rooms napping, listening to records or smoking cigars.

He discovered an unopened envelope on his desk and quickly slit it open. A single sheet of paper fell onto the desk, and he read it hungrily. Mary's handwriting was as familiar to him as his own, and he recognised it instantly. She wrote to him about how she longed to leave the farm, to get away from Crew and his constant harassment. It seemed the gardener was back, and the knowledge of that shifted into a ball of rage and fear in Harry's gut. She also wrote that she didn't intend to stay any longer than she had to. As soon as she could figure a way to bring Lottie with her, she'd leave. He held the letter to his chest, his heart rate accelerating at the thought of what might happen if she followed through on her threats. Every child who'd run away from the farm was found and returned. They were punished openly, and their life became far more restricted, something that would be unbearable for the freedom-loving Mary.

He despised Crew more than he could say. If only he could go back and rescue them both from that life. But how could he do it? He didn't have the money to pay his way to Molong, let alone to get all three of them out of there. And then what? Would he be arrested for taking them? It wouldn't do them any good for him to languish in prison, with the two of them back at the farm after provoking Forrest's ire. She should finish her time there—then they could be together again. He pulled a sheet of paper to the centre of his desk and wrote a response, his brow furrowed and his heart heavy.

❦ 39 ❦

MARCH 1960

MARY

"Let's go. We've got that gymkhana coming up on Sunday and I want practice for the barrel racing. I was so close to winning last time." Mary pressed her hands to her hips and tapped a foot on the cottage floor impatiently.

Lottie scrubbed the floor with the mop, leaving a trail of water behind her. "I'm almost finished. But if Ingrid comes in here and I haven't done it, I'll be in for a walloping."

Mary groaned. "We'll be the last ones there."

"Why don't you head up now and I'll follow you in a minute."

Mary took a moment to think it through. She'd stuck close to Lottie's side for weeks, ever since Crew made his threat. But they wouldn't be apart for long—Lottie would follow her soon.

"Okay, fine. I'll see you there." She reached for her boots and socks and ran out of the cottage. Ingrid stamped up the steps, her face thunderous. Mary hesitated and glanced back as the cottage mother stormed inside. What had Ingrid in such a foul mood? It didn't bode well for Lottie to be the only girl in the cottage when Ingrid looked like that.

She snuck back inside to follow Ingrid.

There was a shriek, followed by a thud. Mary bounded through the bunk room and saw Ingrid lying on her back on the common room floor, her skirts askew and legs in the air. She grunted, then groaned as she rolled over onto her hands and knees and huffed to her feet.

Mary's heart fell. Lottie stood close by, the mop still in the bucket.

"You idiot!" shouted Ingrid as she straightened her skirts. "The floor is sopping wet. Look what you've done." The woman waved her arms around as she yelled. From where she stood, Mary couldn't see her face, but could imagine it turning a dark shade of red as the veins in her neck bulged — it wasn't unusual for Ingrid, but never as a result of something Lottie had done. Mary did her best to protect her sister from Ingrid's fury, but there was nothing she could do now.

"I'm...I'm sorry, Ingrid," Lottie stuttered, stumbling backwards away from the approaching woman.

Ingrid's fists shook with rage at her sides. "I've told you a hundred times— you have to wring the water from the mop before you set it on the floor. I could've broken my neck."

Lottie stared at her bare feet with her hands clasped together.

Mary edged closer. Ingrid seemed about to explode. The woman stood beside the cast-iron stove in the centre of the room and reached for the poker that leaned against it. She wielded it in one hand as she rounded on Lottie.

"Your sister's not here to save you this time. You're all mine, and you'll finally get what you deserve," snarled Ingrid.

Fear rose like a snake up Mary's spine. If Ingrid hit Lottie with the heavy metal poker, she might kill her. As Ingrid brought the poker down, Lottie ducked, and it hit the floor with a thud, splintering the timber floor.

"Wait, Ingrid — I'll fix it. I'll scrub it all over again, make it as clean as you've ever seen," pleaded Lottie, her eyes filling with tears.

Ingrid had one hand on the small of her back as she limped after Lottie. She swung again, this time clipping Lottie's arm.

Lottie yelped and stumbled away from her pursuer. Mary couldn't take it anymore. With a roar of rage, she rushed at Ingrid, pushing her out of the way. The woman stumbled forward and fell to her knees. Mary grabbed for the poker and wrenched it out of Ingrid's hand, making her cry out in pain. Mary took Lottie by the hand and pulled her from the room. They sprinted, side by side, through the village to the stables. When they got there, they scurried into the tack room and collapsed on a mound of hay, puffing hard. Tears streaked down Lottie's cheeks in two dirty, winding trails.

The stables were empty. They smelled of leather, manure and hay. The other girls had already saddled up and left for their afternoon ride. The building was silent but for the twitter of a pair of swallows that darted in and out of the tack room carrying horsehair, sticks and mud to build a nest. Mary squeezed Lottie's hand once, her heart hammering against her rib cage.

"We've done it now," she gasped, setting the poker down on the floor in the midst of the hay.

"She's going to kill us," agreed Lottie with a hiccough.

Everyone knew Ingrid didn't put up with lip. But more than that, she hated being made a fool. And Mary had humiliated her. She wouldn't let them get away with that. There was nowhere for them to run or hide—they'd have to face Ingrid before the day was over. Dread piled up in Mary's gut. Not for herself—she could handle whatever Ingrid did, but for Lottie. She couldn't bear the idea of Ingrid hurting her sister in any way. She'd been mulling over the idea of herself and Lottie escaping from the farm together, and this only strengthened her resolve. It was time the two of them left Fairbridge and struck out on their own.

"Well, hello there. Did you two come to see me?" Crew's hulking frame filled the doorway, blocking out the sunshine.

Mary's heart fell. Her breathing more regular now, she pushed quickly to her feet and stood in front of Lottie. "Yes, we had something urgent to tell you."

He cocked his head to one side, his hat threw a shadow across his face so that she couldn't see his expression. "Oh?"

"That's right. They're building a new bridge on the other side of town, and I just had to find you right away so I could tell you to go take an enormous leap off it." She poised, ready to fight, even though she was half his size, and he blocked the only exit. Her entire body radiated with anger.

He threw his head back and laughed. "You're getting feisty in your old age. Does your sister feel the same way?"

"Stay away from my sister." Knees bent, she circled Lottie as Crew moved closer into the tack room and sidled around them.

He lunged at her, then stepped back and laughed. "Come on, we're having fun. Aren't we?"

Mary spotted the poker at her feet, where she'd left it. When Crew grabbed Lottie by the arm and wrenched her away from Mary, she reached for the poker and picked it up slowly. He paid her no mind, his attention firmly on Lottie's writhing frame.

Mary ran at him with a roar, raising the poker high over her head. She brought it down hard on the back of his skull. There was a hollow thud as the steel connected with his hat. He stumbled, grabbed at his head, shifting the hat over his forehead and eyes, and then crumpled to the ground, landing on his back.

But Mary didn't want to stop there. She was afraid and enraged after so many years of his torment. He'd threatened Lottie, and she couldn't let him walk away from this. If she hurt him, he'd come after them, and she couldn't let that happen. She raised the poker high over her head, but Lottie cried out.

"Mary, stop!"

She hesitated, her arms lifted skyward, then let the poker fall to the ground with a clang.

"Please, let's go," begged Lottie.

"If he's not dead, he's going to come after us," said Mary, her sides heaving as she gasped for breath, her heartbeat wild in her chest.

Lottie simply shook her head as tears spilled from her eyes, making new dusty trails beside those that already lined her cheeks. Her eyes were red, her countenance written with exhaustion.

Mary squatted beside the prone man and pressed fingertips to his neck. She'd seen a police officer do the same years earlier in the East End when an old beggar fell off his stool on the street corner one frosty morning. She wasn't sure exactly what she was looking for, so felt her own neck with her other hand at the same time.

"I don't think he has a pulse."

"So, he's dead?" asked Lottie.

"Maybe. I don't know for sure." She got down low and peered at his face, looking for some sign of life. His eyes were open, and there was a growing puddle of blood on the floor beneath his hat. Under his head sat a square made of hastily gathered bricks. The gouge she'd made with the poker had split further open against the edge of a brick. One of the Pony Club team must've pushed the bricks inside after using them to help someone too short to reach their stirrups to mount up. Mary and Lottie had utilised the same technique themselves plenty of times when they were younger to climb aboard their horses. Crew hit his head on a brick when he fell. In the exact spot where Mary had already wounded him.

"We should go," said Mary, rising to her feet, her stomach churning.

With a hand over her mouth, she looked wildly around the tack room. She spotted Crew's bottle of whisky in the corner. He often hid in the stables to take a swig. She'd seen him do it plenty of times. She rushed to the bottle, carried it back to where he lay, then poured some into his mouth, over his clothing, and dropped it on the ground beside him. The glass smashed open and whisky spilled out, soaking the hay around his body.

"What are you...?"

"Shh, come on. We've got to get back to the cottage."

"But Ingrid will be there."

"Come on," insisted Mary. She grabbed the poker and took Lottie's hand before leading her back down the path to the village at a jog. When they reached the first cottage, they slowed to a walk. Mary's thoughts raced, and she fought the urge to heave the contents of her stomach into the nearby garden bed. They couldn't do anything out of the ordinary. They should act as if nothing was amiss and go on with their day, beginning by returning the poker to the cottage and apologising to Ingrid. And if Crew was dead, they'd have to run away before the police came to arrest them.

◈⚜◈

INGRID DIDN'T RETURN TO THE COTTAGE. NONE OF THE GIRLS knew where she was. Mary and Lottie didn't say a word about what'd happened. But they were on tenterhooks the entire evening, wondering if Ingrid would show up or if Forrest would march through the door with the strap in his hand. The entire group went to bed with nothing for tea but some stale bread with jam and warm milk. Ingrid wasn't there to cook for them, and no one else came to check on them either. The other girls didn't mind—Ingrid often left them to their own devices. They seemed happy that they had the evening alone with no one to give them trouble over how loud they spoke, how dirty their fingernails were or who would wash the dishes.

They stayed up later than they should, playing marbles in the common room, and poker with the pack of cards Ingrid had hidden in her bedside table. When they finally went to bed, Mary and Lottie had been lying under their cover for hours. Lottie was fast asleep, but Mary's anxious thoughts and frantic planning kept her awake, along with the girls' rowdy games.

Finally, the cottage fell quiet. Cicadas hummed outside, their noise more deafening the longer Mary focused on it. Somewhere an owl asked a question, and a lamb called out to its mother. Mary's eyes fluttered shut, and her breathing relaxed as calm fell over the village.

Suddenly the cottage door flew open and slammed shut again with a crash, waking several of the girls. Mary bolted upright with a start, her heart racing. Forrest strode into the bunk room and flicked on the light switch.

"Mary Roberts, get to your feet," he thundered.

Mary blinked in the bright light, then gingerly climbed from her bed, her nightdress falling over her knees as she rose.

"Yes, sir?"

He stood glowering at her, a notebook under one arm, the cane he used for punishment tucked under the other.

"Come here, child. I've been at the hospital in Orange with Ingrid, who says you're the reason for her injuries. She's sprained her ankle and has a bruised tailbone, not to mention the headache you've caused with your antics."

"I'm sorry, sir," replied Mary, linking her hands together and keeping her eyes firmly fixed on the ground in front of her feet.

All around the room, girls rubbed bleary eyes, or sat with their blankets tucked under their chins watching the scene before them play out in disbelief. Lottie was huddled against the wall, her legs curled against her chest, her head entirely covered by her blanket.

"Sorry doesn't cut it. I've had a horrible night, what with the accident and everything else that's going on. And all you can do is make my life all the harder. Come here and hold out your hands, palms up."

She complied, stepping closer to him, and raising her hands. "Accident?"

He ignored her question and brought the cane down hard on her palms. The sting of it brought tears to her eyes, but she knew better than to pull them away. Palms hurt, but they healed. It was far worse for her to receive the strokes on her rear end, where the bruises would remain for weeks.

After three quick flicks of the cane against her hands, Forrest puffed a little, his cheeks a dark shade of red. "Now, let's have no more of this nonsense. Do you hear me? I have enough to deal with tonight. You girls behave!"

He marched out the door, letting it slam shut behind him again. As soon as he was gone, Mary hurried to the door and peered outside. The night was black, with heavy clouds covering the stars and moon. Trees and bushes hid in the shadows, and none of the cottages were lit. Forrest disappeared in the direction of the stables. She crept after him.

"Where are you going?" whispered Lottie after her.

Mary raised a finger to her lips, then was out the door and down the steps on bare feet. She padded quietly through the night up the pathway, past the last of the cottages and the garden shed, beyond the chook pen and rounding the corner, she saw the stables.

Blue-and-white lights silently flashed from a conical globe atop a white police vehicle. There was an ambulance there as well. A Dodge station wagon painted yellow with a red light on the roof that spun, sending a ray of light into the paddock beyond, over the bushes and across the timber slatted walls of the chook pen. Several men milled about the stable's doorway, then two of them pulled a stretcher from the back of the ambulance. They trotted inside, returning a few minutes later weighed down by a man held between them. They pushed the stretcher into the back of the ambulance. Forrest appeared in the doorway beside a uniformed police officer who held a notepad in his hands, a pencil poised over the paper.

They'd found Crew. It would only be a matter of time before they figured out what'd happened. Would she go to prison? She didn't know much about prison, but she wanted to avoid it all the same. She'd be separated from Lottie. That was enough to bring tears to her eyes. Before they saw her peering around the side of the chook pen, she turned on her heel and ran as fast as she could manage in the dark back to her cottage. She burst through the door, then caught it before it slammed and tiptoed to her bed, breathing hard and with her hands stretched out in front of her to feel her way forward.

"Mary!" hissed Lottie. "Where did you go?"

Mary reached for Lottie's hand and squeezed it. "We'll talk tomorrow. Nothing to worry about—sleep well."

Then she climbed into bed and rolled onto her side to stare at the screen door. She would wait for Forrest to return and when he did, she'd lose her freedom and her sister forever. She blinked the tears away, determined not to sleep. But before long, her adrenaline faded, and exhaustion overtook her young body.

❦ 40 ❦

MARCH 1960

MARY

"When are we leaving?" whispered Lottie.

They lay side by side, arms around one another, legs entangled, beneath Mary's blanket. It was still dark. In the distance, a crow cawed. The sun would be up soon, and the day would begin. Would it be their last together? Tears wet both their cheeks. Lottie reached out a hand to wipe Mary's.

"As soon as we can. I saw the police here last night. They were at the stable. If Crew wakes up, he'll tell them what we did. So, we have to get out of here before it's too late."

"Unless he's dead," replied Lottie, her blue eyes fixed on Mary's.

"Yes. But he wouldn't be. Would he?"

Lottie shrugged. She didn't know. Neither did Mary. The thought that she'd killed someone was too much for her to comprehend. But at the same time, if he wasn't dead, he'd tell, and she trembled as she imagined the police coming for her, their guns drawn and handcuffs glinting in the sunlight.

They lay quiet for a few moments, each lost in their own thoughts.

Mary inhaled a deep breath. "So, we'll pack our things now. Keep them under our pillows. That way, we can leave at a moment's notice. Okay?"

Lottie nodded. She scrambled out of Mary's bed and got to work packing the few things she owned into an old canvas bag Mary had found on the side of the road a few weeks earlier and stashed beneath her bed. They'd wiped it clean the best they could, and there was a tear along one side, but it would carry their single change of clothes and nightgowns, along with toothbrushes and a spare pair of underwear and socks when they left the farm.

It wasn't long before the other girls stirred around them. The bell sounded, and soon there were girls sweeping, scouring, and running out the door to complete their chores. The sound of water beating against tiles filled the cottage as girls ducked into and out of the showers. And before long they were all lined up at Nuffield Hall for breakfast.

Mary's heart was in her throat. She wanted to run. Everything inside her said they should escape, get away from the village and the police. But what if they didn't suspect her and Lottie yet? Running would make them look guilty. No, they had to stand their ground for now. Pretend nothing was wrong.

Beside her, Lottie fidgeted and shifted from foot to foot while they waited. Mary shot her a dirty look, and she stopped moving, her cheeks flushing pink.

"I'm so hungry I could keel over," said a girl at the front of the line.

The door popped open, surprising them all, and Forrest peered out. "Come on in."

He usually walked down from the house and unlocked the door in front of them all. But he'd beaten them to the hall this morning. That, and the fact that he didn't check their fingernails, behind their ears, or comment on anyone's dirty shoes was out of the ordinary.

When everyone was seated at their tables, he stood at the head of the room and addressed them as a group. With a cough to clear his throat, he clapped his hands together once, then waited for quiet to descend over the children.

"Thank you, all. I have some sad news to share with you. Last night, one of our staff, Mr Able Crew, had a fall in the stables and hit his head on a rock. I called an ambulance as soon as I found him, but unfortunately, he didn't make it. He passed away. I know some of you will be upset by this news, so please, come and see me or your cottage mother if you want to talk about it. We'll be holding a small memorial in a few days' time. His family wish to hold the funeral service in Bathurst, where they live, and I will be attending on behalf of us all."

As Mary listened to Forrest's speech, every nerve in her body was on high alert. The principal hadn't mentioned foul play, murder, or anyone else's involvement in Crew's death. And it was a death. A murder, in fact. The reality of that played out in her mind's eye over and over as the speech drew to a close and the children fetched their breakfasts in silence. Every face in the room was grim as people came to terms with what'd happened. Most of the children wouldn't be upset — they hated the man who lurked hidden around corners and shouted abuse at them whenever they paused in their work. Still, death was a toll that triggered uniform quiet contemplation.

She choked down breakfast quietly, unable to taste the toast and Vegemite or the glass of milk that followed. Beside her, Lottie ate in silence as well. No doubt pondering the same questions as her. When would it be safe for them to leave? Would they be arrested? How much did the police know? Would Mary spend the rest of her life in prison, or did children receive a different punishment for murder?

After breakfast, they wandered out of the hall. Mary couldn't think clearly. Her head was light and the breath in her throat was thin. In front of her, Forrest strode for his house. She followed. Lottie had stayed behind with some of the other girls and Mary was on her own. She trotted after Forrest, ducking into doorways, hiding behind cottage corners, and staying out of sight as much as she could manage. He didn't know she was there and seemed focused on where he was going.

When they drew closer to the house, she noticed a police car pulled up outside the front door. Mrs Forrest stood with a uniformed officer. Forrest joined them and Mary crept closer, keeping to the bushes in the garden that surrounded the house. She couldn't hear what they were saying, so ducked low and tiptoed through the newly laid mulch. A butterfly fluttered close, its orange-and-black wings flapping soft in the light breeze. It landed on a bright pink azalea, then took off again. Mary watched it, her heart beating a loud rhythm in her ears.

"We can't say for certain," said the police officer, his voice breaking through her reverie. "It seems to us that he'd had a bit much to drink, then fell and hit his head on a pile of bricks."

"So, it was an accident?" asked Mrs Forrest.

"Seems that way, Mrs Forrest."

"Can't say I'm surprised," added Mr Forrest. "He was known to have a few too many of an afternoon. I've had a word with him about it on more than one occasion, but he was a stubborn fella."

"I'm sorry for your loss," replied the officer. "I'll head back to the station and file my report now. Feel free to call anytime if you have something else to add to the report, or any questions you want to ask."

"What a senseless tragedy," added Mrs Forrest in a regal tone. "Thank you, Officer."

The police officer climbed into his car and drove away, leaving a cloud of dust in his wake. Mr and Mrs Forrest walked into the house, and Mary sat down in the garden bed with a soft cry. It would be deemed an accident. They wouldn't be charged. Her life wouldn't end in a prison cell.

Tears clogged her throat with a lump that wouldn't budge. It ached as she stood to her feet. There was no sense in them staying at the farm any longer. It would only give the police time to figure out what she'd done. And besides, she still had to face Ingrid — a confrontation she'd prefer to avoid. With resolve hardening her heart, she set off at a run to find her sister.

INGRID WENT TO BED WITH A HEADACHE SOON AFTER TEA. NO ONE in the cottage wanted to wake her, so the girls tiptoed around the cottage, whispering and laughing in hushed tones. There was a sock-sliding competition, followed by a quick expedition outside to see if any of the boys were about. The outing was soon foiled by Forrest, who brought the leader back to the cottage with her ear firmly clenched between his fingers.

"And stay inside!" he shouted, slamming the door shut behind him.

Mary and Lottie were tucked in bed already, hoping the rest of the cottage would drop off to sleep so they could make their escape. Everyone in the cottage flinched as the door crashed shut, but Ingrid didn't emerge, so before long they'd brushed their teeth and were in bed, whispering beneath the covers.

Most evenings in the cottage were quiet. The girls were generally exhausted after a hard day of work. But because of what'd happened with Crew, Mr and Mrs Forrest, along with much of the staff, had been busy for the day and left the children to their own devices.

Mary and Lottie spent the afternoon riding Slim and Glitter. Lottie had cried silently as she stroked Slim's grey muzzle and whispered her goodbyes. They wouldn't see the horses again if everything went according to plan. Mary's heart was a stone in her chest. She'd miss her horse, but more than anything she wanted to get away and couldn't risk being separated from Lottie. Besides, she'd already written to Harry, so he'd be waiting for them.

Finally, the rest of the cottage fell silent. Cicadas set up a steady hum, somewhere a fox yapped, and a dog howled, no doubt straining against its chain at the full moon. Moonlight slanted across the cottage floor, giving the beds and their sleeping occupants an ephemeral blue tone.

Lottie leaned down from the top bunk, her hair hung about her upside-down head like a halo. Mary gave her a quick nod. Then the two of them tore off their nightgowns and shoved them into the canvas bag, along with their makeshift pillows. They'd left their clothes on underneath to save themselves time and limit the risk of waking the others. By the time they'd donned shoes and packed their toiletries, Mary's heart beat wildly in her chest so that she had to strain to hear anything above the sound.

With a shiver at the cool nip in the air, the two girls slunk from the cottage, taking care not to let the door slam shut. They tiptoed across the verandah, avoiding the boards that squeaked, then hurried along the path, keeping to the shadows of the bushes that dotted either side as much as they could.

They stopped at the kitchen. Mary had broken into it many a time through the rectangular window that sat just above shoulder height. She pried open the screen, and Lottie helped to push her through with two hands beneath her foot as though she was mounting a horse. Mary found a loaf of bread, several boiled eggs, two apples and two small bottles of milk, wrapped them in a tea towel, and passed them out the window to Lottie, who stashed the meal in their bag. They'd each saved pocket money for months, and that was hidden in their pockets as well. Mary hoped it would be enough.

When they left the safety of the village, Mary stopped for a moment to look back over it. She'd spent a large portion of her life in its confines. It was home to her, and she could hardly remember another. Still, it didn't evoke any emotion in her other than an inner push to leave. She'd miss some of the people, although most of her friends had already moved on to other lives far away from Molong.

The driveway that wound from the village to the road was narrow. Gravel crunched with each footstep. The moon lit their way, which gave her peace of mind. The last thing she wanted now was to step on a tiger snake in the dark. They trotted down the drive and opened the gate, then shut it behind them again. As they traipsed along the side of the road, the moon rose higher in the sky overhead. Every time a car passed, they scurried into the drainage next to the road to hide from the sweep of headlights. They'd hitchhike when they were further from the village, from anywhere people would recognise their uniform. But for now, they'd travel in secrecy.

❧ 41 ❧

MARCH 1960

HARRY

There was a line at the post office. He'd come to the post office many times since arriving in Brisbane. He wrote regular letters to Mary, Davey and to Max. Max had settled on a farm outside a town called Hay. He seemed content enough, but he'd only written once. His writing was stilted, full of misspellings and difficult to read. Still, Harry loved hearing from him. Davey seemed to have been broken by his time at the farm school. He only wrote once a year now, at Christmas. His letters were full of darkness and gloom. He'd left farming behind and worked instead on a fishing trawler. It was hard work, but he'd made some good friends. Harry hoped they'd be able to see each other again someday, but Davey was like a stranger to him now.

The line moved slowly, inching forward. It wasn't usually this busy, today there were dozens of people waiting in line to buy postage stamps or mail packages. Harry stood at a bench off to one side, writing the last line of a letter to England. He'd written several letters in recent months, hoping to find some remnant of his family. He recalled his mother telling him they had family in Newquay, so he had written to the post office there in hopes someone would know of the Evans family and could pass on his communication to them.

So far, he hadn't heard anything, but he didn't want to give up yet. If there was an uncle or aunt, or maybe some cousins living in Newquay, perhaps they could write to one another and he could find out more about his parents lives. It'd been difficult for him to move on over the years, without any kind of closure.

"Can I help you, sir?" asked a young man dressed in a blue suit with white shirt and matching blue cap.

"Yes, please. I'd like to post this. Also, I want to check for mail addressed to Harry Evans, please."

"Of course, sir. Come with me, please."

He closed the envelope, with his letter inside, and licked it shut while he followed the man to the counter. Minutes later, he stood outside the post office with two different envelopes in his hands and sweat beading on his forehead. One was from Mary, the other from England.

The return address on the second envelope was a Marion Evans in Newquay. His mother's name had been Marion Evans. Was it possible she had a living relative with the same name? He glanced around the sandstone building down the narrow alley beside the post office with a view to the busy street beyond, feeling at a complete loss of what to do next.

He hurried out of the alley. Office workers dressed in suits and carrying briefcases rushed past in both directions along Queen Street. He skipped down the stairs, checked for traffic before dashing across the road to the parklands opposite. People sat about on the grass eating lunch from paper bags or lounged in the sun talking and laughing. Some ate hurried meals on park benches, their ties flung over their shoulders as they read briefings and reports balanced on their laps. A large statue of an earnest brass soldier on a horse looked over them all. Harry found an unoccupied park bench and sat to open the letter from England with shaking hands.

· · ·

DEAREST HARRY,

YOU DON'T KNOW HOW I'VE LONGED TO HEAR FROM YOU ALL THESE years, my darling boy. I regret every day leaving you at that place for so long. But I didn't know what else to do.

I went to see you at Christmas time, and they told me you were gone. I cried for a week, but there was nothing I could do about it. I didn't know how to reach you and they wouldn't tell me nought but that you were in the colonies. I moved back to Newquay to be near family and have lived here ever since.

I hope you will come to see me sometime.

Your loving mother.

TEARS BLURRED HIS VISION AND DROPPED ONTO THE PAGE, smudging the ink. He wiped the tears away and folded the letter back into the envelope. His mother was alive. It was too much to bear. He'd mourned her so long ago, given up the hope of having a family again. And now to discover that she'd been in England, that he could've chosen to stay behind to see her again, but didn't know.

Hands clenched into fists, he punched down on the timber bench, bruising his knuckles. A group of young women walking past shied away from him, clutching onto one another. He opened his palm and slammed it down again on the bench. The pain distracted him for a single moment from the wrenching in his heart.

They'd lied to him. His mother might've taken him away from the Home years ago and raised him in Newquay, with their extended family nearby. How different his life could've been.

Unable to stand the pain any longer, he leapt to his feet and shoved the crumpled envelope in his pants pocket. He took off at a run, sprinting through the park. He ran all the way home, pushed through the gate and past the dog who begged for attention before following him up the stairs and into the house. In his room, he threw himself down on the bed, folded his arms behind his head, and stared up at the ceiling, doing his best to hold back the tears.

So many times over the years, he'd been hurt but hadn't cried. He'd learned well how to push down his emotions, to shove them beneath the mask he wore each day. But now that pain threatened to break free. He drew a deep breath, then another, and slowly the threat abated. Finally, he swung his feet back to the floor and rested his head in his hands.

He'd see her again. As soon as he was able, he'd travel to England to see his mother. Perhaps Mary and Lottie would go with him.

Mary.

He remembered her letter then and pulled it from his pocket. It'd been folded along with the one from his mother. He separated them and opened it to discover she'd finally acted on her impulse to leave the farm.

"Silly girl," he muttered beneath his breath. "They'll catch you before you make it to Sydney."

If only she would stay put until she'd finished her time there. But he wasn't with her to make her see the stupidity of her actions. And he didn't understand why leaving was so urgent all of a sudden. Perhaps something had happened. Either way, she said she would leave before he was able to write back to her, so they should meet in front of the town hall at dawn. She didn't know anything about Brisbane, she said, but she presumed every city had a town hall, so it was as good a place for them to meet as any.

"But what day?" he asked, turning over the page and finding it blank. She hadn't specified when. He'd have to stand in front of town hall every single day at dawn until she arrived. And what if she didn't make it? What then?

He sighed and combed fingers through his hair, then lay back on the bed, his heart pounding. If she would only wait. He'd find a way to come to her. But it was too late now for his plans. He knew Mary well enough to realise she'd leave Fairbridge her way whether he liked it or not.

❦ 42 ❧

MARY

The car rattled along the road. Mary's forehead pressed to the window. She opened her eyes and yawned, then wiped the trail of saliva from her chin with the back of her hand. A moment of panic passed through her as she struggled to place where she was. And what about Lottie? But a quick glance around the vehicle revealed Lottie curled on the back seat beside her. Up front, a couple chatted about politics. The woman nodded and agreed with her husband who expounded the ideals of personal liberty and swift justice.

She blinked and rubbed the sleep from her blurry eyes, then yawned again.

"Oh, you're awake, love," said the woman. Mary vaguely remembered her saying her name was Jill and her husband Bill. Bill and Jill — she tried hard not to smile at the remembrance.

"Yes, I suppose I slept for a while," she said.

Jill laughed. "Sure did, at least two hours. Your sister is still out. I

347

hope your aunt and uncle will be glad to see you after all this time down south." Jill studied her, head twisted around to face the back seat. Mary could tell the woman wanted more information, was digging to discover anything she could about why the two girls were so far from their home and on their own. But Mary had chosen to be as vague as possible. The less information they shared, the better, as far as she was concerned.

"Oh, they'll be thrilled. Mum is so sick, and Dad has to work. They couldn't afford to buy us tickets, but we wanted to see my aunt and uncle before they move overseas. It could be our last time together, and we're so close."

"Not geographically," quipped Jill.

Mary offered her a conspiratorial smile. "No, not that kind of close."

Satisfied, Jill spun around in her seat, facing forward. Her ginger hair barely moved as it hugged her shoulders with perfectly formed waves. A brightly coloured headband separated the curls from her fringe that looped away from large brown eyes and a freckled nose.

Bill fell silent, his black horn-rimmed spectacles focused on the road, both hands on the shining steering wheel. The maroon Holden cruised along the highway, headed for Brisbane. The engine purred, and with the back windows down, the noise meant they had to shout to one another to be heard.

"How long until we get to Brisbane?" asked Mary.

Bill rubbed his chin with one hand. "About ten minutes, I think. Almost there. So, you want us to drop you off in the city?"

"Yes, please. We're meeting our aunt and uncle at town hall."

He glanced at her in the rear vision mirror with a hint of suspicion in his dark eyes. "Okay. Will do."

It didn't matter if he wasn't convinced of her story, just so long as he didn't report them to the police. The best way to make sure that happened was for them to be as forgettable as possible. So, she offered him a polite smile, then sank back into her seat to look silently out the window. She'd learned the art of invisibility at a young age. It'd served her well over the years.

The couple in the Holden dropped them off on Elizabeth Street, then pulled away from the curb bickering about the best way to get back to the main road from there. Mary watched them leave, while Lottie, still yawning, glanced around with sleepy eyes.

"Where are we?"

"Brisbane," replied Mary.

"I know that, but...how will we find our way around?"

Mary shrugged. "I guess we'll ask someone."

The city buzzed with activity. People hurried in every direction, with briefcases and purses clutched in their hands. The men wore cotton short-sleeved shirts and long pants, and the women wore cotton sleeveless dresses in various colours and patterns with tall high heels that clacked on the footpath. Everyone had somewhere they had to be, including Mary and Lottie.

They tried a few times to stop someone and ask directions before finally a woman pointed out the way to town hall.

"I think you mean city hall," she said.

Excitement buzzed in Mary's gut. They'd be there soon—maybe they'd find Harry. Although, she had begun to regret the idea of meeting him at dawn. It'd seemed such a romantic gesture when she'd written it in the letter, overwhelmed by the emotions of the moment. Now, the reality of that began to wash over her. Dawn — how would they find him? They'd have to sleep somewhere overnight and meet him the next morning. And what if he didn't show up?

"Do you think Harry will be there?" asked Lottie, as if reading her thoughts.

"I don't know. I hope so."

They hurried in the direction the woman had pointed. Up Edward Street, then down the Queen Street Mall. There were so many shops. The weather was fine, and people were out shopping, eating and sitting on park benches. Buskers were dotted along the mall, playing violin, or performing magic tricks while people wandered by or threw coins in small boxes at their feet.

The bustle reminded Mary of London — a vague memory that shifted around the edges of her consciousness. But it was different too — warmer, friendlier, more casual. She felt safe. People were kind and courteous. No one pushed them out of the way or shouted at them.

They asked for directions twice more, and both times were helped with a smile and ready answer.

By the time they found city hall, Mary's stomach grumbled with hunger. She was thirsty as well. City hall was a large sandstone building with striking columns and a clock tower that peered down from on high at its surroundings. The two sisters stood in front of the building, staring up at it in wonder.

"We made it," said Lottie.

Mary grinned. "It's beautiful."

They both glanced around. "I don't see Harry," said Lottie.

Mary's heart fell. He wouldn't be here. It was late afternoon. Their trip from Molong to Brisbane had taken them three weeks. They'd walked, hitched, and walked some more. They'd slept in cars, and on bus stops, in tall grasses beside the highway, and in cattle sheds along the way. They'd long since eaten the food they'd packed and had taken to drinking from streams, stealing what they could or accepting the kindness of strangers. And all the while, they'd looked over their shoulder for the police who must surely be pursuing them. But so far, no one had stopped them. They'd faced questions from some along the way, but most people ignored them or offered to help. Mary couldn't quite believe they'd found their way to Brisbane and that Harry was somewhere close by. It seemed like a dream.

Finally, the three of them would be together again.

⚜

MARY ATE THE LAST SLICE OF PIZZA AND LICKED HER LIPS CLEAN. Lottie lay back on the grass with a contented sigh. A passing businessman had seen them sitting there and handed them the box of half-eaten pizza at dusk.

"I'm not going to finish it," he said. "You might as well, if you like."

They thanked him and finished up by drinking their fill from a nearby bubbler. Finally, they lay back on the grass again and stared up at the sky. Mary linked her hands behind her head and counted the stars. The moon was no longer full, but it blinked from behind a cloud and cast a golden glow across the city. Most people had already left the business district or were on their way to catch buses and trains back home to the suburbs. Some walked to their homes nearby. Still others popped out of offices to pick up food and continue their slog in offices lit up ready for a late night.

Mary didn't know what she and Lottie should do. As soon as darkness fell, she figured they should find a quiet corner out of the way and snuggle down into it for the night. They'd spent several nights exposed to the elements, but had never slept in the middle of a bustling city before. And although they seemed safe so far, the encroaching night and sounds of traffic leaving the area filled her with an impending dread. She and Lottie were far too vulnerable as the streetlights blinked to life and illuminated the parkland in front of the building.

"Come on," she said, rising to her feet. "Let's find somewhere to sleep."

"But Harry won't see us if we leave," complained Lottie.

"He won't be here until dawn. If he comes at all," replied Mary, brushing the dirt and grass from her shorts.

"What do you mean? You don't think he'll come?" Lottie's voice rose an octave.

Mary sighed. "Don't worry, he'll be here." She didn't feel the same confidence within, but Lottie needed reassurance, so that was what she'd get.

They investigated the outside of city hall and found a place along one side that was hidden from most of the streetlights. They nestled down into it, pulling abandoned newspaper over their bodies to help with camouflage and to retain their body heat. It was a restless night. Every sound dragged Mary from sleep. Every rustle, every birdcall had her struggling back to consciousness. Finally, the sun climbed up the horizon and the sound of traffic rose again through the cool dawn.

Mary shook Lottie awake. "It's morning. We've got to meet Harry."

Lottie was shivering when her eyes opened, but she struggled to her feet, arms still clasped around her thin frame, and followed after Mary who jogged around to the front of the building.

The parklands were empty. A woman hurried up to the city hall front entrance and inside. But otherwise, there was no one around.

"It's still early," said Mary as they slowed to stand in front of the building.

"Yes," agreed Lottie, a tremor in her voice.

They settled onto the grass again in the same place they'd sat the evening before. Lottie's teeth chattered quietly, Mary tried to keep her still, although her arms and legs were covered in goose bumps. She wanted to cry, but it wouldn't help. There was no point crying over spilled milk. It was something Mam used to say. And it was true. Crying didn't make anything better. Still, she wished she could hide away and bury her head in their canvas bag to let the tears fall in private. But she wouldn't let Lottie see her that way. Not now, when they'd come so far.

Gradually, more people filtered into the city. They arrived on buses or climbed out of cars. They filed into city hall in dribs and drabs. And still there was no sign of Harry. Mary was ready to give up for the day and go in search of breakfast when she heard her name called.

"Mary!" It was a shout from across the street behind them. "Mary! Lottie!"

She spun around, a grin sliding over her lips. "Harry?"

He was there, jogging towards them and waving frantically over his head. She took off at a run, her heart leaping at the sight of him. He looked different — like a stranger, yet familiar at the same time. He was taller than she remembered. He wore long pants and a buttoned shirt. His hair was neatly cut and combed to one side. When she reached him, she didn't stop, but threw herself into his arms. He enveloped her, pulling her tight against his thin, muscular frame.

"You're here," she said against his chest, her face buried in his shirt.

"Where else would I be?" he whispered into her hair.

Lottie ran up behind Mary and joined in their embrace, knocking Harry off balance. He laughed and steadied himself. Mary didn't want to let him go. Nothing would ever be so bad again now they were together. Life would be happy and full, safe and good with no one to tear them apart.

THE THREE OF THEM SAT IN HARRY'S ROOM. IT WAS A SMALL SPACE and a little crowded. But they didn't care. There were three cups of tea, and a packet of chocolate biscuits Harry had bought with money he'd earned from his part-time job. Something so simple had never been so freeing and joyful to Mary before. There was no one to tell them what to do, or not to do. No one to cane them for being late, or to chastise them for dropping crumbs on Harry's bedspread. She took an enormous bite from the biscuit and chewed with her eyes closed, savouring the flavour.

"Sorry it isn't much," said Harry. "I'll find you something to eat just as soon as the kitchen is free. It gets pretty busy this time of day, but everyone will be off to work soon enough."

"It's delicious," mumbled Lottie around a mouthful.

"Mmmm, perfect," agreed Mary.

Harry watched them with concern. They were thin and glowed with sunburn. "You're hungry?"

"Starving. We haven't eaten in...how long has it been?" asked Lottie as she crossed her legs on the end of Harry's bed.

Mary stood by the window, staring out at the warm, bustling city. "We had pizza last night. But before that, two days."

"Well, I don't know how you two managed to get here all on your own. I was worried sick about you. But I'm glad you're here now, and everything's okay. Did anyone follow you? Are they looking?"

Mary sighed. "We don't know. We didn't see any newspapers. We tried to stay out of the town centres as much as possible. And none of the people who gave us a ride said anything."

"Who knew you were coming here?" he asked.

"No one. We didn't talk to anyone about our plans."

"Good. That's for the best. I still don't understand why you couldn't wait a little longer," he replied softly.

Mary knew he'd wanted her to finish her time at the farm, and she didn't know how to tell him what'd happened. He'd blame himself. For years he'd stuck close to her and Lottie, doing his best to protect them whenever he could. He hadn't wanted to leave them, but she'd assured him they'd be fine, that Crew would leave them alone now they were older. He'd take it personally.

She sat on the bed next to him, took his hand in hers and wound her fingers through his. Then her blue eyes found his brown ones. The connection set her heart racing as she looked deep into his soul.

"It was Crew," she said.

His eyes hardened. "What happened?"

She told him everything. Every last detail. What she could remember of it, anyway. Much of it had been pushed into the hidden recesses of her mind, some of it was emblazoned on her imagination forever. Lottie helped to fill in the blanks. Between the two of them, he got the whole picture.

He stood to his feet and paced to the other side of the room, then slammed both palms against the wall, making a framed picture of a palm tree overlooking a beach scene rattle against the plaster. Lottie jumped and Mary closed her eyes. She hated to see him upset and in pain, but there wasn't anything she could do about it. She'd done her best to protect Lottie—she had nothing left to give.

"So, you're on the run from the law for that, as well?" He faced her, eyes blazing.

"I don't think so. We left after the police officer told the Forrests he thought it was a drunken accident. But I can't help thinking they'll figure it out if they look into it."

He rubbed a hand over his mouth, then inhaled deeply. "They'll see the wound if they look closely."

"Yes," she admitted.

"Then we have to keep you out of sight until this all blows over."

"How?" asked Lottie. Her lower lip, still covered in chocolate crumbs, trembled.

Harry strode to the bed and pulled Mary to her feet. He kissed her hard on the lips. The love she felt for him was imperishable, as vast and deep as the ocean they'd crossed to reach the shores of this wild and distant land. A land they'd once anticipated with trepidation and hope that'd now become their home. A love that time could never be taken from them because time itself was woven through and about it. The world blurred around her in that single blazing moment. Heat surged through her body, hope filled her heart, as his lips explored hers.

"I love you, Mary," he whispered, his breath hot on her cheek.

Tears wet her face. She didn't know where they'd come from—they took her by surprise. And the words that erupted from her mouth issued from a place deep in her heart that'd been hidden for so long, she'd forgotten it was there. Beneath mounds of pain, anger, suffering, shame and fear, she tore them and set them free.

"I love you too."

She was vaguely aware of Lottie sniffling at the other end of the bed. But her gaze didn't stray from Harry's face. His brown eyes, so deep and full of love, held onto hers.

"So, let's get married."

"But what about...everything?"

He shrugged. "This is the best way to change your name. That way, you can hide in plain sight."

"But they know we're friends," she objected. "I'll put you in danger if I stay."

He cupped her cheeks with both hands. "You'll destroy me if you go. I can't be without you again. We'll face whatever comes."

"I don't want to get married just to hide," she objected.

He kissed her lightly, his lips brushing over hers. "We talked about this — I want to marry you because I can't bear to be away from you. I want to be with you always."

"I do too," she admitted. "All right, let's get married."

❦ 43 ❧

MAY 1960

MARY

Black wrought-iron streetlamps stood in military formation down the length of Adelaide Street. People bustled back and forth across the street. Mary waited for the tram to hurry past on its cable and tracks, then ducked across the street to the small boutique tucked between a pie shop and a jeweller.

Inside, she unpinned her hat and set it behind the counter, then straightened her hair in a mirror that hung on the wall.

"There you are," said Marion Underwood, the shop owner. "Just in time to open the doors."

"Good morning, Miss Marion," she said.

"And to you, darling. How delightful you look today. Is that one of my frocks you're wearing?"

Mary grinned. Marion knew full well it was. She'd given the dress to Mary a few days earlier after finding one of the seams had come undone. Mary fixed it up in no time, and Marion had said she could keep it. She couldn't have her employees looking as though they'd walked out of the poor house. She'd winked as she said it, and Mary could hardly believe her luck. The dress was white with a green rain-forest pattern over the full skirt, and a tight bodice that showed off her figure perfectly.

"Yes, Miss Marion. You're amazing — I love it. I can't believe you get to design dresses for a living. What a dream."

Marion laughed, throwing her head back so that her red curls danced down her back. "You're a sweet girl. Let's open up now, and hope for lots of very rich customers to come through the door and throw their money at us."

Mary hurried to open the door, enjoying the feel of her dress as it swished around her bare legs. She longed to buy nylons, the ones with the lines down the back, but she couldn't afford it yet. Marion laughed when she told her that, said that nylons were going out of style, and she was the height of fashion without them.

She'd never considered fashion much before in her life. It wasn't something that occupied her thoughts. Getting enough food into her clamouring stomach and surviving rated much higher on her list of priorities. A week after she and Lottie moved into an empty room at the boarding house with Harry, she'd struck out with a printed resume, courtesy of Harry's second-hand typewriter, in search of a job. It hadn't taken long for her to find one at Marion's dress shop. Marion had paid for her to get her hair cut at a real hairdresser's and had given her several outfits to get her started. She'd argued that it wasn't right for her to take so much from Marion, but the older woman had shushed her and countered that Mary would be selling her designs, so she had to look the part. Mary couldn't disagree with that, so went along with whatever Marion suggested. She felt pretty, fashionable, and confident when she stepped out of the house each morning to walk to work.

She told Marion her name was Virginia May. Soon, she'd be Virginia May Evans when she married Harry. She'd always liked the name Virginia, had imagined that anyone with such a posh name must be rich and glamorous and wouldn't ever go to bed with a grumbling tummy. Still, she often looked over her shoulder with a start whenever the bell rang over the shop door to announce a customer. And she couldn't help skirting around police officers whenever she saw them, careful to hide her face from view as best she could.

There was a television set in a shop window on Queen Street Mall and she'd stopped there one afternoon after work. The news was on, and she caught the end of a story about two girls on the run after having escaped the Fairbridge Farm School. They'd shown a photograph of her and Lottie in their shorts and shirts, with lopsided hairstyles and sullen expressions. They weren't those girls any longer. Lottie was Charlotte May and had already started attending a local school under that name. Soon, she'd be Virginia and Harry's adopted daughter, Charlotte Evans, and they'd leave Mary and Lottie behind them forever. No one had come looking for them in Brisbane. At least, not yet. They hadn't called Harry, and no police had knocked on their door. But she'd always live with the fear that they would someday.

The workday passed by swiftly, and excitement built in Mary's gut. They were headed to city hall directly after work. She'd be married before dusk. And she couldn't wait. It didn't seem possible she could be so happy after so many years of pain and loneliness.

When they closed up the shop, Marion wished her luck, kissed her cheek, and studied her a moment with tears glistening in her eyes. "I wish I could be there, but I know you want a private ceremony. Still, we're going to celebrate tomorrow when you come in to work. I wish you all the happiness in the world, my darling girl. I'm so glad you traipsed into my shop when you did."

Mary swallowed around a lump in her throat. "Thank you, Miss Marion. I can't tell you how much I appreciate you and everything you're doing for me and my family."

Marion patted her arm, then dabbed at her eyes. "Well now, enough of that. Off you go and have a wonderful wedding. Harry is a lucky man."

The Hobolts had asked her in private whether she really thought it a good idea to get married quite so young. She hugged them, told them she'd thought it through and thanked them for letting her and Lottie stay.

Their house was full to the brim with the two girls in the last empty room, but they didn't seem to mind. Said they hadn't seen so much excitement in twenty years. She'd told them she and her sister were recently orphaned and travelled from England on the ten-pound pom program the Australian government offered. Ten pounds to move to Australia. They had no reason not to believe her.

She pulled the shop door shut. Marion locked it and waved goodbye. Then Mary shucked off her high heels and ran with them in hand down the street to city hall. Harry and Lottie were already there waiting for her. She kissed Lottie's cheek, then threw herself into Harry's arms. He kissed her, took her hand, and said, "Ready?"

"Wait a moment. I want to say something."

He waited, poised and ready to climb the stairs. "Oh?"

She took both his hands in hers and faced him, her expression serious. "I want to thank you."

"For what?" He laughed.

"For rescuing me."

"I didn't rescue you really..."

"Yes, you did. On the ship so long ago. You were the one who helped me get past my fear. You saved me from the emptiness that threatened to consume me. You held my hand when I was so scared of what was to come that I could barely put one foot in front of the other."

He leaned forward to kiss the tip of her nose. "You never seemed afraid. Always so brave."

"I was scared, but I couldn't show it."

"You saved me as well, you know."

She smiled. "Did I?"

"I was a lonely, sad little boy with no one to love. And you came along and opened my heart up to the possibility."

She leaned into his chest, listened to his heartbeat, steady and strong. It calmed her nerves. "We saved each other, I guess."

Close by, Lottie sighed. "You two love birds ready to get married, or what?"

They laughed and tucked Lottie into the embrace between them. "We're in this together," said Mary.

Lottie rolled her eyes and wriggled free. "Only until I find my own adventure."

"Not till you're eighteen," admonished Mary, wagging a finger and releasing her sister, who burst free with a grunt.

Harry huffed. "You're one to talk."

She grinned up at him. He leaned in to kiss her softly, a smile tickling his lips. "Let's go then, my love."

With a nod she entwined her fingers with his, and they walked into the building to get married.

❧ 44 ❧

MIA

I don't know how to say goodbye. How do you tell your baby boy that he needs surgery? How do you tell your heart that you might not ever see it again? It's too much for a mother's soul to bear. But I do it because I have to. And because Ben is beside me, his arm around me, holding me up so that my legs don't collapse and leave me in a sodden pile of tears, snot and bruises on the hard linoleum floor.

The hospital is full of sounds that bother me in ways they never have before. A distant cry of someone in pain. Whispered conversations between doctors and nurses. The beep of equipment that's holding someone's life to this earth as they struggle not to let go. I don't like it. I want to take Brody in my arms and run away from this place, never to come back again. But I can't, because he needs this surgery, and I need him. So here we are.

We're sitting in the waiting room. We said our goodbyes and they rolled my heart away on a gurney. Ben is beside me, one leg jiggling as he scrolls on his phone with a blank stare. Gammy, Gramps and Auntie

Char sit across from us, whispering together over a crossword. Mum and Dad are back in Paris, but have begged us to video call them once we have news. If only the time between now and then would pass more quickly. If I didn't have to sit here imagining the worst for hours while everyone around me tries to distract me from my own thoughts.

Gammy's given up on the task for now and retreated after I failed to answer any of her questions. I couldn't bring myself to focus on her voice. It wasn't intentional. My heart is about to jitter out of my chest. I need to move, think about something else, do anything other than this.

Gammy sees my struggle and rises to her feet. "I didn't tell you the story about how Char and I escaped from the farm," she says, coming close and lowering herself into the chair beside me with a grunt. Gramps follows, complaining about a pain in his hip. Ben pays no attention. He's hunched over his phone, elbows resting on his thighs.

Auntie Char watches us for a moment, then with a sigh, she joins us as well, she wrests two chairs across the floor to sit opposite. The legs screech on the shiny hard surface. A nurse glances up from the paperwork on her desk beneath lowered brows, but doesn't say anything. Char takes one chair and Gammy shifts across into the other so that she's sitting in front of me, looking directly at me.

"That's better."

"I don't know if I can focus on your story right now, Gammy. And I want to give it all the attention it deserves," I say, looking at my watch and wondering how there are so many minutes in an hour and when they became so slow.

"That's okay, love. You listen or not—it's fine with me. I'm gonna talk anyway. Right, Char?"

Auntie Char cocks her head to one side. "No one's ever been able to stop you before. So..."

Gammy slaps Char's leg. Char chuckles. "Ouch. And she's violent too."

"Okay, Gammy." I don't have the strength to object further. If she wants to talk, that's fine with me. Maybe it'll distract me, if I can pull my attention away from the ticking hands of the clock on the wall opposite.

Gammy opens her purse and pulls out an envelope. Inside there are photos similar to the ones I've seen before. They feature the same children, with the crazy hairstyles and the uniforms that don't quite fit, with the skinny legs and the knobbly knees. They're smiling, or eating ice creams, or riding horses or working on the mechanics of a tractor. I assume they're Fairbridge children, now I know a lot more about them.

I've done some research in the past few weeks. I've learned about Principal Forrest and the children who lived under his care. I've read of cottage mothers, and Nuffield Hall, and the cold that seeped through the children's bones when snow fell over Molong, and they slept beneath a single blanket with the windows open. About the weevils that made the porridge inedible, and the physical abuse that some of the children endured. I've read enough to make my skin crawl, my heart ache, my throat tight, and I've wished with everything within me I could've been there to save Gammy and Gramps and Auntie Char from it all. But I couldn't because I wasn't alive. And there was no one else to save them either.

I hold the photographs carefully around the edges. I don't want to leave my fingerprints on these priceless possessions that shed light on a world that no longer exists. A time that will never be seen again. People who've long since grown, moved on and built different lives for themselves. But they're scattered throughout my community. They're all around me, hidden in plain sight. Broken and lonely, never able to fill the hole that was left in the centre of their souls when their mother or father left them behind, or pushed them away, or died, or abandoned them, or wanted them but were lied to and stolen from. The emptiness that became their constant companion when they were gifted this affectionless fate.

"Here's one of me and Gramps," says Gammy as she hands me a photograph. It's wrinkled and faded, but it's definitely them. They're standing side by side holding ice creams and smiling into each other's eyes. "We had a sports carnival, and then got the most delicious ice creams. Do you remember that, Harry?"

"Huh?" Gramps holds a hand curved around the outside of his ear.

"Never mind," replies Gammy with a wave.

"So, how did you get away?" I ask as I go through the images.

She leans back in her chair with a sigh. "It was after I killed Crew."

My breath hitches in my throat. "What? I thought you said it didn't happen."

Gammy's blue eyes find mine. They're full of sorrow and pain, but there's love in there too. And she grasps my hand. "I know what I said, love. But there you go."

"And?"

"He hurt me. He wanted to go after Char. I couldn't let him do that. So, I killed him. I didn't mean to. Or maybe I did. I don't know. But either way, he died. I tried to make it look like an accident, and I succeeded, I believe. We never did find out whether they were looking for me because I came to Brisbane, married your grandfather, and changed my name."

"You were Mary Roberts?" I exclaim. I know it's true even before she acknowledges it. It was lingering on the edges of my mind all the time. But I couldn't see how it would resolve, where it would be set right.

"I was Mary Roberts, and Char was Charlotte Roberts. Or Lottie, as we called her."

And then Gammy tells us the rest of the story. All of it. She doesn't hold anything back. And by the time she's finished, Ben is as absorbed in her tale as I am. I'm crying, Lottie's sobbing, Gammy has a handkerchief pressed to her eyes, and Gramps is pacing back and forth across the room in his awkward swaying shuffle.

"I wanted to tell you this a long time ago. You and your father. But I was afraid they'd find me. That it wouldn't be over. I've lived with that fear a long time. It's easy to fear when you have so much to lose. And I do — I have all of you, and I love you so much." Gammy sobs and wipes her eyes.

I'm close to wailing, but I hold some of it back because I don't want to alarm the other people in the hospital waiting room around us. Instead, I bury my face in one hand and squeeze Gammy's with the other.

"You've got to talk to Dad about this," I say.

"I did, last night," confesses Gammy. "Gramps and I called him and told him the whole thing. Well, it was mostly me. But Gramps was there."

"Wow, I can't believe you told him. But I'm so glad." I wipe my eyes and try to smile through the tears. "That's great."

"I think so too," admits Gammy.

"It's good for us all to finally have it out in the open," says Char, sniffling into a tissue.

"Gramps became a solicitor and had a wonderful practice. He never made a lot of money because his heart was too soft to charge anyone who couldn't afford it. And he didn't like to tell them no, either. But he was well known for it, and he did a lot of good."

"And you?" I ask.

"I worked in that dress shop until I had Patrick. Then Sonya came along, and I had my hands full. I spent the rest of my life as a mum and wife. Now I'm a grandmother and a great-grandmother. My heart is as full as my hands once were."

"Did you ever see your mother again? Did Gramps?"

Gammy's smile faltered. "Once."

I can tell she doesn't want to say more, and honestly, I don't think there's much more I can take right now. I'm overwhelmed by what she's told me, by Brody's surgery. My heart and emotions are pulled to the breaking point. All I need now is for my baby to be okay, and to sleep for a very long time. An old love song comes on over the radio. Its soft crooning fills the waiting room.

Gramps stops in front of Gammy. "Mary?"

She lumbers to her feet. "I'm here, Harry."

He takes her in his arms and waltzes her back and forth to the music. His eyes are fixed on hers and he's holding her close, their joined hands tucked up on one side, and his other hand on the small of her back. Gammy laughs up at him and rocks back and forth. They move as one in a steady, swaying rhythm.

"It's good to see you, my love," she says, pressing her cheek against his chest.

He nods and spins her gently. "You too, darling girl."

It's a beautiful sight. Gramps has clear-headed moments every now and then, but he seems to have travelled back in time and it's everything to me to see them like this.

"A hell of a life we've had, my dear," he says, kissing the top of her grey head.

She sighs. "More than I could've asked for."

"More than I ever dreamed," he replies, as if it's something they've repeated to one another over and over again.

She raises her head to meet his gaze, and he presses his lips to hers in a kiss that seems to last forever. Ben slides an arm around my shoulders and pulls me to him. I lean my head on his shoulder, watching my grandparents waltz around the room. I feel like I'm going to burst with the joy of it. Auntie Char watches a moment, then she lets her eyes drift shut and sways along to the music herself, humming a soft tune.

"Mr and Mrs Sato?" Doctor Harris strides into the room in blue scrubs. His surgical mask dangles from a string around his neck. He looks tired.

Ben launches to his feet. I'm slower off the mark, but I stand beside Ben, my heart in my throat. "Yes, we're here," he says.

"The surgery went well. We were able to repair the hole with no complications. Brody is in recovery, and you should be able to see him soon."

I collapse into Ben's arms as soon as the doctor leaves the room. Relief floods me in a wave of emotion, fatigue and joy. We kiss, then embrace and Ben spins me around until my head flies back and I laugh at the ceiling.

"He's okay," he whispers over me.

EPILOGUE

HARRY

The amount of noise in the house was no doubt more than his mother had ever had to endure. But she didn't seem bothered by it. She simply smiled at young Patrick and Sonya as they charged about the house, flying toy planes or chasing after the cat. Harry didn't want to admonish them, as they'd been so good for so long. The flight to the UK was long and tedious for an eight- and five-year-old child. But they coped admirably well, especially with Gina's help. It'd taken him a while, but he'd become accustomed to calling her Gina instead of Mary. He sometimes slipped up, but they'd used the name from the very first day, even with the Hobolts, so no one knew her as anything else.

He finished his studies while they lived together in that small room at the Hobolts. The couple allowed Charlotte, or Char as everyone now called her, to keep the room the girls had shared. So, the three of them were snug and content in their new accommodations. Harry continued to fix things around the house and work in the garden. Gina and Char did the cooking, cleaning, and laundry. The Hobolts gave them room and board without charging Harry any extra in return.

After he graduated, he took the money he'd saved, and they moved into a two-bedroom unit in Toowong. Since then, they'd purchased a small house in the suburbs, and a family car. It was often difficult to make ends meet, but they managed, and they were happy. The next priority was tickets to England to see his mother. He'd always intended on doing it after he received the letter that told him she was alive after all. And they'd finally made it. They'd stayed with her for three days so far, although it seemed as though they'd been with her much longer.

At first, he'd been stilted and uncomfortable. She had a clipped English accent, and his Aussie drawl made them seem like strangers. But she was kind, gentle and sweet, exactly the way he remembered her. He'd been afraid all this time that his rose-coloured memories of her couldn't possibly be true. But they were, and he was grateful. She'd fallen on hard times, she told him, when she was young. His father was a married man in the village of Newquay where she'd lived as a young girl. He hadn't wanted anything to do with her or the baby. She'd moved away to London to escape the shame of having a baby out of wedlock, and with no one to help her, she'd struggled to find work and pay their way.

The orphanage was intended as a temporary fix. A short-term respite for a single mother doing it tough that'd become long term when she could never quite seem to get on her feet. But then they'd sent him away without letting her know, and she'd grieved his loss ever since.

"I tried to get you back," she'd told him with tears glimmering in her eyes. "For years, I wrote letters. I looked for you. They wouldn't tell me where you were or help me send for you. I'm sorry, Harry. I didn't know what else to do. It broke my heart over and over every time I wrote and didn't hear back from you. Knowing that you were out there, somewhere, thinking I didn't want you." She'd sobbed then, and he'd held her in his arms, as though he was the parent and she the child. So many times he'd wished to be held the same way by her when he'd cried alone in his bunk at night, shivering in the frigid air. And there she was, alive in her hometown, thinking of him. Wanting him.

She remarried a year later and had two more children. But she was a widow now and the children had moved away. She lived alone, but had extended family throughout the village and had rebuilt a life there. His father, she told him, had died of cancer a decade earlier, and had never spoken to her about him or asked where he was. Harry wouldn't get the chance to meet him.

In spite of it all, she seemed happy. And he was glad for it. It would've broken his heart to find her in a sad and sorry state. But she was cheerful and had surrounded herself with friends and family. Her beautiful dark, glossy hair was now grey and short. But her deep brown eyes, so much like his own, still twinkled in the same way, and she walked as though she music played in her head, just the way he remembered. She'd taken up painting, and there were beach scenes on canvases hung on every wall in her flat and leaned against pieces of furniture.

"You don't mind watching them?" asked Gina, worry creasing her forehead.

"Not at all," replied his mother. "You two go on now. You'll miss your train."

Gina's mam had written to her over the past year or two. Always the same refrain — *I'm sick, please come and see me.* Gina hadn't wanted to, but Harry had convinced her. She only had one mother, as flawed as she might be, and she'd regret it if she missed the chance to see her while they were in England.

Harry kissed the kids goodbye — Patrick with his floppy brown hair and Sonya with her blonde. Sometimes they seemed like little mirror images of the children Harry and Mary could've been if they'd had parents who loved them and were capable of taking care of them. They looked so much alike, but they were happy, innocent and carefree in a world where the sharp corners had been shaved smooth for them. He loved them with an intensity that left his heart aching at times.

"Time to go," he said.

Gina slung her purse strap over her arm. She wore a short, brightly coloured dress with a high waistline, knee-length white boots and a hairband, with her short blonde hair curled and shining around her pretty face. She was the height of fashion and sophistication. It was hard to believe she was the same girl who'd spent years sporting ill-fitted khaki shorts, bare feet, and an off-kilter haircut. She was a woman now, and a beauty who drew the attention of people wherever they went. He was proud that she was his wife, and grateful they had each other to lean on.

They donned coats, scarves and knitted caps. Then they walked through the village to the local train station and climbed aboard with the few other people who were headed to London. Seagulls cruised overhead. He watched them through the window as they landed on a bench seat on the platform. The salt air filled his lungs, and he drew a deep breath of it to remember the village by when they were gone. All those years he'd longed to live by the beach, and yet all the time his mother was in Newquay with a view of the ocean from the living room window in her flat.

"If only I'd had the chance to live here with Mum, how different my life would've been," he mused, his breath leaving a fog on the glass in the warm carriage.

Gina's hand was in his. She rubbed a circle on his palm with her thumb. "There's no sense in what-ifs or should-haves, and you know it. We can't change the past, my love."

He agreed. "You're right. Only, sometimes I can't help thinking about it."

"Let's enjoy the time we have together now."

"I could say the same for you and your mother," he said, shooting her a knowing look.

She huffed. "Don't start."

"Well..."

"I'm going to see her, aren't I?"

"Under duress," he said.

She crossed her arms and leaned back in the seat, staring out the window as the train pulled away from the station with a buck and a grinding of wheels. "I *want* to go. I'd like to see her again. Only my stomach is swirling over it. I don't know why I'm so nervous. The last time I saw her...well, she took me and Char on the train. And here I am, on a train again headed to see her."

Harry kissed her on the cheek. "It's all going to be okay. You're a grown woman now —she can't hurt you any longer. She can't do anything to us. I won't allow it. Okay?"

She nodded, her face pale.

He only hoped he was right. He didn't know Gina's mother, from everything she'd told him about her, the woman didn't seem to have a heart. But she was ill, and if Gina didn't visit her now, she might never get a chance to see her.

◈

The Tower Hamlets council estate where Gina's mam, Sylvia, lived was a tall brick building with external corridors linking each of the flats. Lines of washing hung along the corridors. Harry and Gina ducked through the frozen clothing and knocked on the door with a skewed number eighteen on it. Harry shivered and blew a warm breath onto his gloved hands, stamping his feet while they waited. He'd forgotten what it was like to be cold to his core after living so long in humid Brisbane.

There was a thud inside the flat. Then a voice called out. "Yes?"

Gina knocked again, then turned the knob. It was locked. "Mam, it's Mary. Will you let us in?"

The door swung open, and a small, thin woman stared at them through pale blue eyes that were bloodshot and red-rimmed. She wore a bedraggled and stained house dress in browns and blues. There were slippers on her feet, and her hair was pulled into a straggly bun on top of her head. There were a few teeth missing from the front of her mouth when she pulled her lips into a smile.

"Mary? Is it really you? Sure you look like a movie star."

Gina stepped forward to embrace her mother. "It's me, Mam. And this is my husband, Harry."

The woman shook his hand, then stepped back to wave them in. She coughed, the effort wracking her body. "Come on in. Sorry it's such a mess. But the cleaner's off sick." She laughed at her own joke, then broke into another fit of coughing.

They hadn't been sure of what they'd find. After the letters complaining of an illness which she'd never identified, Harry was

373

concerned they'd discover Gina's mother lying in bed in her last few days of life. But the woman who greeted them shoved old magazines and newspapers from a worn couch and offered them a place to sit, then disappeared into a small kitchen to set the kettle to boil. She soon returned with a tray holding a teapot, three cups and a plate of sweet biscuits.

"Let's have a cuppa and catch up," she said, sitting in an armchair across from them to pour the tea.

"It's good to see you again, Mam," said Gina, tucking her hair behind her ears.

"You too, love. I can't quite believe it myself. You've turned into a right looker."

"Thanks, Mam. I hope you don't mind, but we left the kids with Harry's mother today. We thought we could try to bring them to see you tomorrow, if you're up for it."

"Well, I don't know if I'll be feeling well enough. Let me think on it."

Gina swallowed her disappointment. If Harry didn't know her so well, he wouldn't have noticed the flush in her cheeks or the glitter of her eyes. "I do wonder how you found me, Mam."

"You didn't make it easy," admitted Sylvia. "But it was your sister who let me in on the secret."

"Oh?" Gina's eyes narrowed. "What secret is that, exactly?"

"Where you lived. Why, do you have another?" Sylvia laughed again, the cackle soon devolving into a lurching cough. She plucked a packet of cigarettes from her dress pocket, along with a box of matches, and lit one. A long drag was soon followed by the exhale of a breath of smoke. She offered the packet to Harry and Gina. "Smoke?"

Harry took one, lit up and pulled in a lungful of smoke. It soothed his nerves and he leaned back on the couch to take another drag.

"No, nothing else to report," replied Gina. "So, Lottie contacted you?"

"Yep. Right out of the blue. She sent me a letter, said she wanted to get in touch and to see me again if she could. She came last year—not sure if she told you. Brought that boyfriend of hers from New Zealand. Can't recall his name."

Gina shot a furious look at Harry, who shook his head as if to let her know he hadn't been in on the secret. Gina and Char shared everything. There wasn't anything they kept from one another. Except this. Char had reached out to their mother without telling Gina about it. Had visited her, when she'd told them she was traveling through Indonesia on some kind of spiritual quest.

"I didn't realise she'd found you," said Gina, crossing one long tanned leg over the other.

"She wouldn't give it up. Said I should write to you, that you'd forgive me if I gave you the chance. And I wanted that, so I wrote. I mean, everything that happened back then — I'd change it if I could. I missed you girls as soon as you were gone. And that good-for-nothin' Stan tossed me out on my ear the first chance he got. So, I was all on my own, and couldn't think about anything much other than the way I'd given you two up. But of course, I knew it was for the best and that you'd get to live the kind of life I wouldn't. And here you are, all posh and la-di-da." Sylvia waved the hand holding her cigarette in Gina's direction. "So, I did the right thing for ya, even if it was so hard on me. But no need for you to pity me over it. I managed on my own. And here I am, still alone all these years later, and you with a lovely family to keep you company. I suppose some things are meant to be."

Harry marvelled at the way Sylvia managed to make herself the victim in the story. Gina had told him how she'd always been able to do that. That even when they were small, she'd blamed Gina for everything that'd gone wrong in their lives. And she was doing it still.

Gina's lips tightened, a muscle in her jaw clenched, then she sighed and reached for her mother's hand. "Thank you, Mam. You gave us a chance to have a better life. It was hard on us all, but now my kids can live in a nice house and go to a good school. They'll grow up with every opportunity to do what they want with their lives, and all because of you."

Sylvia's eyes glistened, and she offered them a wobbly smile. "I'm glad to hear it. Although, it has been rough on your old mam. Still, I always was a sucker for you girls."

When they left the flat, Sylvia was ready to lay down for a nap. She had cancer, she told them. Only a matter of months until it was all over. And so, they made plans to bring the children to see her the next day. They wouldn't get another chance.

They walked hand in hand through the East End of London. Their breath left a temporary trail of white clouds as they went. There was no snow on the ground, but the sting of it hung in the air around them. Gina pointed out the streets she recognised, and the things that'd changed since she left. They ate a plate of roast beef and chips at the local pub, then caught the train back to Newquay to find the children bursting with happy energy.

"How about a walk along the beach?" suggested Harry.

They bundled the children into warm clothes and headed out. As they strode along the sand, Harry ducked low to chase the children towards the water's edge. The waves were small, insipid. They didn't compare to the curling barrels of brilliant blue that arced to golden shores back home. Those waves that'd once carried them to a strange and distant land. Waves that'd threatened to crush them, body and spirit, to dust. But they'd lived through it and come out the other side, beyond the crushing waves, to a place of peace and hope. Beyond loneliness and despair, to embracing a lively family and a deep love — one he never imagined he would find while his head was bowed in prayer beside the small, hard bed at Barnardo's.

The ocean was dark and clouds hurried by overhead, projecting moving shadows onto the water. A boat chugged by with its bright red hull brazen against the dark waters. Seagulls cawed and hovered, chasing the family in hopes of finding scraps of food.

The children squealed with laughter as they ran from Harry's outstretched arms. He shoved his gloved hands deep into the pockets of his coat to watch as Patrick and Sonya got to work building a sandcastle. Above them, the grass-covered cliffs encircled the beach, with white-faced houses squatting on top as though to keep watch.

Gina walked to him, settled herself in his arms, her own sneaking around his neck. The wind blew her blonde hair into her face, and she smiled up at him.

"Are you happy?"

He arched an eyebrow. "Happy? Yes, deliriously. Why do you ask?"

She laughed. "I think I am too."

"Glad to hear it," he said, leaning forward to kiss her cold lips. "So, it was a good idea to visit your mother, then?"

"Yes. A good idea."

"And whose idea was it? Just so we're clear."

Her eyes narrowed. "You always have to be right. Don't you?" Then spun on her heel to walk away.

"I don't know if I *have* to be, but I often am. Still, you didn't answer the question — whose idea?"

She glanced back over her shoulder at him, contempt clearly written on her face.

With a laugh he chased after her, caught her up in his arms and held her against his chest as his lips searched for hers. She giggled and squirmed in his arms as if to break free. Then she relaxed against his chest and wound her arms around his neck. And as they kissed, he knew that everything he'd been through was for this precise moment. The loss, the pain, the sacrifice — all of it meant that he could hold Gina in his arms, his love, his Mary. That he could kiss her soft lips and know that every day for the rest of his life, she would be by his side. It'd all been worth the pain and the loneliness so that he could be loved and could truly love in return. No matter where he lived, with his girl in his arms, he was home.

THE END

ALSO BY LILLY MIRREN

FAR FROM HOME SERIES

Under a Sunburnt Sky

When one boy risks his life to save countless others, and a family says farewell to sons who must fight for the world's freedom, they will find themselves far from the homes they know and love in a battle of good versus evil.

A heartwarming World War II historical fiction novel.

Coming to your favourite retailer in 2022

THE WARATAH INN SERIES

The Waratah Inn

When Kate discovers her late grandmother's journals, she unearths information about a long-buried family mystery that leads her back to her grandmother's run-down inn, in Cabarita Beach. As she works to unravel the truth, can she find a path to healing along the way?

One Summer in Italy

Reeda leaves the Waratah Inn and returns to Sydney, her husband,

and her thriving interior design business, only to find her marriage in tatters. She's lost sight of what she wants in life and can't recognise the person she's become.

The Summer Sisters

Set against the golden sands and crystal clear waters of Cabarita Beach three sisters inherit an inn and discover a mystery about their grandmother's past that changes everything they thought they knew about their family...

Christmas at The Waratah Inn

Liz Cranwell is divorced and alone at Christmas. When her friends convince her to holiday at The Waratah Inn, she's dreading her first Christmas on her own. Instead she discovers that strangers can be the balm to heal the wounds of a lonely heart in this heartwarming Christmas story.

EMERALD COVE SERIES

Cottage on Oceanview Lane

When a renowned book editor returns to her roots, she rediscovers her strength & her passion in this heartwarming novel.

Seaside Manor Bed & Breakfast

The Seaside Manor Bed and Breakfast has been an institution in Emerald Cove for as long as anyone can remember. But things are changing and Diana is nervous about what the future might hold for her and her husband, not to mention the historic business.

Bungalow on Pelican Way

Moving to the Cove gave Rebecca De Vries a place to hide from her abusive ex. Now that he's in jail, she can get back to living her life as a police officer in her adopted hometown working alongside her intractable but very attractive boss, Franklin.

Chalet on Cliffside Drive

At forty-four years of age, Ben Silver thought he'd never find love. When he moves to Emerald Cove, he does it to support his birth mother, Diana, after her husband's sudden death. But then he meets Vicky.

Christmas in Emerald Cove

The Flannigan family has been through a lot together. They've grown and changed over the years and now have a blended and extended family that doesn't always see eye to eye. But this Christmas they'll learn that love can overcome all of the pain and differences of the past in this inspiring Christmas tale.

HOME SWEET HOME SERIES

Home Sweet Home

Trina is starting over after a painful separation from her husband of almost twenty years. Grief and loss force her to return to her hometown where she has to deal with all of the things she left behind to rebuild her life, piece by piece; a hometown she hasn't visited since high school graduation.

No Place Like Home

Lisa never thought she'd leave her high-profile finance job in the city to work in a small-town bakery. She also never expected to still be single in her forties.

AUTHOR'S NOTE

DEAR READER,

I'm so grateful you found this book and I hope you've enjoyed it. The characters and situations in this story are entirely fictional, however they were inspired by accounts of true events and the people who endured them. A special thanks to David Hill, whose autobiographical work, "The Forgotten Children," was instrumental in my research for this book. Also thank you to the *Child Migrant's Trust*, for providing vital resources that describe this period in history.

Many people are unaware of the occurrence of British forced child migration. Britain is the only country in the world with a history of child migration. Between 1922 and 1967 somewhere around 150,000 children with an average age of eight years and as young as three, were sent out from British shores to the colonies in Australia, Rhodesia, New Zealand and Canada. The Fairbridge Scheme was one of several that played a role in this mass deportation of poor and orphaned children. Approximately 5000 to 10,000 children made their way to Australia on ships as part of this widespread program.

The idea, coined by Kingsley Fairbridge, was to populate the far reaches of the British Empire with good white stock, to supply these colonies with farm labourers. While at the same time, dealing with the problem of the large numbers of impoverished and orphaned children in England who were believed to be headed for a life of criminality and hopelessness if left alone.

Some of these children, like Mary and Lottie, were sent by their parents in hopes they'd find a better life. Some of these parents travelled to the colonies a few years later to join the children and began new lives together there, under the *One Parent* or *Two Parents* Schemes. Others were orphans, or like Harry were told that their parents had died when in fact they had not. Still others were told they were going on a picnic, in the way Max described. Almost all were convinced they were headed to a luxury tropical paradise where they'd ride horses or kangaroos to school and pick oranges from trees along the way. And that they'd get educational and vocational opportunities that would set them up for life.

The child migrant scheme had mixed results. Many of the children who participated in the scheme came out of it wounded by the lack of love and affection, coupled with neglect and a poor education. Many were almost illiterate. Not to mention the pain endured by those who believed for decades that their parents were gone, only to find out in their golden years (when it was too late) this had never been true. The lies that robbed them of knowing their parents, some only discovering the truth after their parents had passed, caused intense emotional pain to a subset of child migrants. Yet some of the children credit the scheme with having saved them and given them a better chance at a good life. Still, it's generally widely accepted that all of the child migrants received levels of care well below what they would've had if they'd remained living in British institutions.

I chose to write about the Fairbridge Farm School program, because this particular program garnered mixed results. The people who were involved in developing and running the Fairbridge Farms, appear to have meant well for the children involved, although their plans didn't always work out the way they'd hoped. Budget shortfalls and the hiring of some staff who turned out to be abusive and corrupt, meant that the children never benefited from the entirety of the funds intended for their wellbeing, and were often mistreated. Regardless of the fact that it was one of the better programs, many of its graduates were neglected and/or abused and have born the brunt of that psychological trauma for the rest of their lives.

There were other schemes like the Bindoon Boys Town home, run by the Catholic Christian Brothers, in Western Australia, where boys were starved, abused, tortured and raped in such a systematic manner that it appears to have been designed with that intent by predatory men who infiltrated the charitable group. The incidence of suicide later in life among this group of boys is sobering, to say the least. And my heart goes out to the survivors, many of whom have spent their lives in utter emotional turmoil and pain because of how they were treated by evil men, who never saw justice for their horrific crimes.

The principal, Mr Forrest and his wife Mrs Forrest, are the only characters in this story who were inspired by real people. Mr and Mrs F.K.S. Woods who operated the Fairbridge Farm School at Molong from 1938 to 1966 were viewed, as were Mr and Mrs Forrest in this book, inconsistently by different children. Some children recall Mr Woods as a violent and abusive tyrant, while others describe him as a kind if rigid father figure who did everything he could to help them along in life and gave them the discipline and character they needed for success.

It should be noted, that the incident with the cricket bat is based on a true event recounted about the principal, the weapon used instead was a hockey stick.

As with everything else in this world, there are shades of grey in how successful or destructive the various people involved saw the Fairbridge Farm Schools scheme and the staff who ran it. I chose to highlight both perspectives in this story to give some balance, and to show that people are capable of both good and bad in life, even with the best of intentions.

Mr and Mrs Woods dedicated a large portion of their lives to serving at the Fairbridge Farm School, raising hundreds of children who were not their own and living a meagre and harsh existence. This shows a certain level of idealism and philanthropy on their part, balanced with clear cases of violence, abuse and neglect as told since by some of the children. Mr Woods was repeatedly accused of abuse by a number of different children, all reports of which were swept under the rug by the governing bodies.

It has only been in recent years that some of the stories of the child migrant scheme have come to light. The International Association of Former Child Migrants and their Families (IAFCM&F) came into existence to help former child migrants receive compensation for their treatment.

In 2001 the Australian Government held an inquiry into the child migrant scheme, and in 2002 they announced a package of measures to support former child migrants: a travel fund to allow migrants to visit Britain to see their families.

On 24 February 2010, the British Prime Minister Gordon Brown issued an apology to child migrants. The Prime Minister announced the Family Restoration Fund, to help reunite former child migrants with their families. The Fund is administered by the Child Migrants Trust and is open to any former child migrant sent before 1970 from England, Northern Ireland, Scotland or Wales as part of child migration schemes.

I wrote *Beyond the Crushing Waves* to highlight what is a generally forgotten, or brushed over, portion of history. Although the British and Australian governments have acknowledged and apologised for what happened, many people are still unaware of this terrible chapter in history. My hope is that by telling these stories, I can shine some light on their failings and help prevent anything like this from happening again.

If you'd like to read a short bonus scene involving Mary and Harry, please subscribe to my newsletter. I'll also tell you when I have a new book available for purchase. This scene doesn't continue the story, as the story is complete. It is an additional scene to give you a little bit more time with Mary and Harry, as I hope you've come to love them both by now the way I do.

Warmest regards,
Lilly Mirren

GLOSSARY OF TERMS

Dear reader,

Since this book is set in Australia there may be some terms you're not familiar with. I've included them below to help you out! I hope they didn't trip you up too much.

Cheers, Lilly xo

Terms

Bindi - prickle

Blasted - darned

Bottle-O - liquor store

Bub - baby

Bubbler - water fountain

Bum a ciggie - have a cigarette

Bitumen - tarmac

Codger - derogatory term for an elderly man

Coke - coal for fires

Cutlery - silverware

Dressing gown - house coat or robe

Esky - cooler

Flogging - beating

Fret - worry

Frock - dress

Get what for - to be told off or receive a hiding

Grub - food

Guttersnipe - street dwelling child

Gymkhana - an equestrian competition

Jumper - sweater

Knickers - underwear

Lady Muck - a haughty or socially pretentious woman.

Mam - mother

Muster - to gather or round up

Nappy - diaper

Nick - steal

No dice - used to refuse a request or indicate that there is no chance of success

Oat stook - a shock or stack

Off license - Alcoholic drinks could be bought from the off-licence, often part of the local pub; again you would return the bottles in exchange for a few pence.

Pony Club - A voluntary organisation designed to give children opportunities to ride horses and compete

Post - mail

Right as rain - to be perfectly fit and well

Shout - to shout someone a drink or meal is to pay for it.

Smarmy old tosser - a contemptible person

Snag - sausages

Sook - cry baby

Splodge - watery porridge

Street Arab - street urchin or gutter child

Sweets or sweeties - candy

Ta - Thank you

Tim Tams - chocolate cookies

Tea - Dinner or supper; Or a hot beverage made from tea leaves.

The pictures - the movies
The sack - fired from employment
Too right - "Thats for sure"
Tuck shop - cafeteria
Wallop - hiding, or spanking

DISCUSSION GUIDE

BOOK CLUB QUESTIONS

1. Can you identify some of the themes running through the book?

2. Did migration to Australia give any of the characters a better life? Who and how?

3. Discuss the family tensions and conflicts that are reflected in each of the generations depicted.

4. How did the food change throughout the book?

5. What was the worst thing Harry and Mary had to overcome in order to move beyond the crushing waves?

6. Can you identify any metaphors in the storyline?

7. How were Mary and Charlotte different from one another?

8. What did Harry want more than anything, and did he get it in the end?

9. What did Mary want more than anything, and did she get it in the end?

10. Which character did you most relate to?